THE ENIGMA AFFAIR

BOOKS BY CHARLIE LOVETT

The Engima Affair
Escaping Dreamland
The Lost Book of the Grail
The Further Adventures of Ebenezer Scrooge
First Impressions
The Bookman's Tale

THE ENIGMA AFFAIR

CHARLIE LOVETT

BLACK STONE PUBLISHING

Copyright © 2022 by Charlie Lovett
Published in 2022 by Blackstone Publishing
Cover design by Gunjan Ahlawat

Printed in the United States of America

First edition: 2022
ISBN 978-1-6650-4707-4
Fiction / Thrillers / General

Version 1

CIP data for this book is available
from the Library of Congress

Blackstone Publishing
31 Mistletoe Rd.
Ashland, OR 97520

www.BlackstonePublishing.com

To the memory of
Mavis Batey (née Lever)
&
Betty Stockwell (née Swan)

XJZSZ ELKQM NTTEZ KHPQJ BX

SECTION ONE:
ALTA VISTA

I

It wasn't just the bullet passing by Patton's left ear that concerned her. After all, she had sustained gunfire before, even been hit once—if you could call a graze on the forearm that barely left a scar a hit. No, what worried Patton was the sound this bullet made, or rather the sound this bullet didn't make. Every bullet that had ever traveled near her had brought with it the distinctive crack of an object in supersonic motion. But this bullet merely hissed quietly as it crossed the kitchen before embedding itself in her refrigerator. This bullet was subsonic. This bullet didn't come from a confused deer hunter or some nut whose idea of target practice was taking potshots at her fence posts. Such things did happen at the lonely end of Lone Pine Road just outside the town of Alta Vista. In her experience though, only one type of marksman went to the trouble of ensuring his rounds were subsonic and therefore nearly silent. This bullet had been fired by a professional assassin, and he was not likely to miss twice. Patton thought all this in the split second it took her to drop to the floor behind the kitchen island. The second round exploded the bag of flour on the counter, filling the air with white dust. The perfect cover, she thought.

Most women who suddenly came under fire in the middle of a Sunday morning bake would be terrified or panicked or at the very least shocked. A woman like Patton Harcourt, with her particular history, might also be laid low by anxiety or even kicked in the gut by a flash-back. But Patton felt none of these things. Patton felt pissed. She had been making chocolate ganache–filled profiteroles like the ones she had seen on *The Great British Baking Show* last week, and if they turned out, she planned to take a batch to Jasper. Now she lay on the floor listening to the mixer overbeating her choux pastry and thinking of the ruined profiteroles and of Jasper waiting for her visit while she spent her day dealing with a fucking sniper.

She flipped onto her back for a moment, looking at the way the midmorning sun flickered through the cloud of flour. Even though it reminded her of the sunlight filtering through the dust on that day ten years ago, she felt no panic, no anxiety, only cool under fire as another round hit the fridge, no doubt burying itself in the leftover meatloaf. That was no great loss, but she had just spent twelve hundred dollars on the fridge, and she doubted that the warranty covered gunshot wounds.

She counted to sixty without hearing another bullet. That meant one of three things. He might know he had missed and be waiting for her to reappear. He might think she was hit, in which case, given that no one was around to see him, he would probably come to check that it had been a kill shot. Or . . . She pushed the third possibility out of her mind. This was no time for wishful thinking. Wishful thinking led to laziness and laziness got people killed.

She rolled back onto her stomach and shimmied across the floor and into the corridor that led to her bedroom. Luckily, she had not opened the blinds that morning, but she still kept low. She didn't want to cast any shadows. She opened the closet door slowly, so the movement didn't register through the translucent blinds. She was glad she had opted for a floor safe instead of one mounted on a shelf. That meant she could stay prone while she twirled the dial. She lifted out her passport and her Beretta M9, slipping the former into her jeans pocket and clicking a magazine into the latter. She turned over, slid up against the closet wall to a sitting position, lifted the gun steadily in front of her, flipped off the safety, and pointed it out the open door. She regulated her breathing, taking exactly fifteen breaths in the time it took her to count to sixty again. She heard nothing but the whirring of the mixer and the song of a towhee chirping in the edge of the woods out back. She knew better than to allow herself to become impatient, but honestly, she wished the guy would just show up in her bedroom so she could get this over with.

The one-stoplight town of Alta Vista is tucked into the mountainous folds of the northwest corner of North Carolina. But for the rugged ridges that rise behind three sides of the town, one could stroll into Virginia or Tennessee. Because no roads cross those ridges, Alta Vista is on the way to precisely nowhere. Too deep in the hills to attract many tourists, the economy depends on Christmas trees and a small community of retirees of modest wealth. Main Street is a mixture of deserted storefronts and art galleries interspersed with a café, an outfitter, and an organic grocery, all of which are, to their owners, hobbies rather than profitable businesses. Practical shopping happens at the Walmart twenty miles away in Greenfield. Most of the population ended up here because they couldn't go any farther—the few old-timers left might call them hippies, but the truth is the majority of the people in Alta Vista are running from something, hiding from something, or trying to forget something. Patton was doing all three.

Like just about everyone in Alta Vista, Patton had a past she'd like to forget. But most people's pasts didn't show up on a Sunday morning and start shooting at their new refrigerator. From where she sat on the floor of the closet, she could see the clock radio on her bedside table. In an era of iPads and cell phones, Patton Harcourt still loved her clock radio. She liked to listen to classical music while falling asleep—or trying to fall asleep—and she preferred the tinny sound of the old radio tuned through the static to NPR to the crisp, clean sound of some streaming service. The clock radio also came in handy when you were holding a pistol in front of yourself and didn't want to reach into your pocket for a cell phone but did want to know how much time had passed since the last bullet hit your fridge.

She watched the numbers turn over three times and as 10:31 a.m. rolled into 10:32 a.m., she heard the creak of her front door opening.

She hadn't locked it when she got back from her morning run, but she hadn't sprayed any WD-40 on the hinge either, so the squeak served as an alarm. She decided to wait for a count of ten before yelling at the intruder.

Nemo's morning was not going the way he expected, he thought as he stepped through a kitchen dusted with flour and noted the bullet hole in the fridge. This whole job wasn't going the way he expected. It was supposed to be an easy job. Some jobs are complicated. They take months of planning and a deeply laid backstory. They involve extreme risk, great expense, and major resources. Afterward, Nemo can't work for a few months or even a year—that is, he can't take a new job. He's always working. Living in the shadows, leaving no trail, staying invisible—that takes work. It takes work to be Nemo, to be no one. So he likes it when a job like this comes along. A couple of weeks' surveillance, wide-open target, easy in, easy out. True, it only paid twenty-five grand, but that wasn't bad for two weeks' work.

The target's movements were like clockwork. Up at seven, a walk to the Alta Vista library at nine. Lunch at the café on the corner of Main and Mountain Streets, then back to the library until closing time. A quick stop at the market on the way home, dinner, in bed with the lights out by nine thirty. Little social life, certainly no love life. Occasional visits with an acquaintance from the library, but no close friends; mail limited to bills and catalogs; phone calls limited to insurance scams and pollsters. No contact with family. Nemo couldn't imagine why anyone would choose this target, but that didn't concern him. After all, one of his professional rules was "Never know the client's endgame." So he watched and waited and enjoyed the mountain air.

He had been lodging in an abandoned motel on the edge of town, a relic from the days when travelers still ventured this far back in the hills to marvel at the autumn colors. The windows and doors had been boarded up years ago, the parking lot was just patches of weeds, the roof sagged in some places and had ceased to exist in others. But in Room 6, Nemo found a spot with no leaks in the roof and something still recognizable as a mattress in one corner.

Nemo had no qualms about living rough. He felt equally at home squatting in an abandoned motor lodge and posing as a wealthy businessman in a five-star hotel. Neither situation would last long, and after each he would shed his identity and begin again. He kept no phone or computer. When he needed to look for a new job, he simply lifted an iPad or laptop from a Starbucks, pitching it into the storm sewer when he'd finished with it. He had no permanent address, though he did rent seven safety deposit boxes in different cities, all under different names. He traveled with no more than he could carry, acquiring the tools for each job as the need arose. This time, he had stashed everything he might need in the trunk of his car—a used gray Ford Taurus he bought for cash a few weeks ago. He had already ground off the VIN number, and when he finished this job he would abandon it somewhere no one would notice. There are a surprising number of such places. His black backpack contained three identities, $15,000 in cash, a change of clothes, and a few toiletries.

Nemo was forty-seven, though the few people with whom he came face-to-face might easily be forgiven for thinking him in his sixties. They had not been easy years. While he had a ragged scar on his left forearm, a reminder of a job that had almost gone wrong, he wore his worst scarring on the inside, where it ached more than the freshest wound. If asked to describe him, even a careful observer would be unsure about his race— was he a white man who had lived his life outdoors? Italian or Middle Eastern? Perhaps mixed race? People tended to see what they expected. For this job he sported unkempt hair, a ragged growth of beard, worn jeans, rugged work boots, and a black T-shirt covered with an unbuttoned plaid flannel. In Alta Vista, he may as well have been invisible, and that was the point. Wherever he went, Nemo always remained one thing to those he passed in the streets—forgettable. Certainly no one who glanced at him as he walked by, hands in his pockets and eyes on the sidewalk, would guess that his net worth was just over $5 million, most of it in a Swiss bank account.

Nemo had settled on early Sunday morning for what he expected to be the easiest job of his career. He had long ago mastered the art of sleeping when the situation required it, so he went to bed in the midafternoon and woke up deep in the night. He made instant coffee with water warmed on the engine block of the car and ate some Cheerios from the box. He sat in the car for two hours, listening to gospel music on a radio station from Boone through a cloud of static, eyes closed, rehearsing each move of the job. At 6:00 a.m. he threw the car into gear and headed toward Lone Pine Road. If there were no surprises, he thought, he would be out of Alta Vista in less than an hour. But there *had* been surprises and now he was going to end up leaving flour footprints all over this damn house.

"You come one step closer and I'll fucking waste you!" yelled Patton.

"If you're talking to the guy who just put three rounds in your house I don't blame you," said Nemo. "But that's not me."

Patton did not recognize this voice, that was the first piece of good news. She knew three people who might want to ruin her morning baking with a little gunfire and this gravelly baritone didn't belong to any of them. The sound of the mixer stopped, and the house fell silent for a second.

"Then who the hell are you?" said Patton.

"I'm the guy who neutralized your friend out there," said Nemo. "I'm coming back."

"Don't you come near me," said Patton in a calm but loud voice. "I've got a Beretta M9 with a full magazine and the safety is off. I know what I'm doing."

"I'm sure you do," said Nemo, taking a step into the hallway toward the open door the woman's voice was coming from. "I don't want to get into a shoot-out; I just want to talk to you."

Patton waited another beat. "Are you armed?"

"Yes," said Nemo, "but I have my safety on." He didn't.

"Judging from your sniper fire, I'd say you're ex-military."

"It wasn't my fire," said Nemo. "And I'm not ex-military. But I'm pretty sure your friend out there was."

"Stop calling him my friend," said Patton. "Whether it was you or someone else, it wasn't any fucking friend of mine."

"Just an expression," said Nemo. Flattened against the wall of the corridor, he peered through the open door into a small bedroom. Above the bed was a large framed photograph of rhododendron on the Blue Ridge Parkway. In the glass, Nemo could just make out the reflection of a woman sitting in a closet across the room, pointing a gun at the door he had been about to enter.

"That's a nice firing position you've got there," said Nemo. "Maybe I should ask if *you* are ex-military."

Patton looked at the picture above her bed and saw the man's reflection. "If you can see me, I can see you." The scruffy face Patton saw reflected in the glass did not belong to any of the three trained killers most likely to send shots into her kitchen on a Sunday morning. But if this guy wasn't the shooter from outside, one of those three men might be out there right now.

"So this sniper out there," said Patton. "This sniper who is not my friend. You just happened along and neutralized him?"

"Something like that. You want to put the gun down?"

"I don't see you putting yours down."

"Fine," said Nemo. "We'll talk like this. Do you know a man named Jasper Fleming?"

"You claim you just killed a man who was trying to kill me, and you want to know about Jasper Fleming?"

"I never said I killed him. You think I want Tommy Linton coming across an unidentified body and asking a bunch of questions?"

"How do you know Tommy Linton?" asked Patton.

"It's a small town, and he's the sheriff," said Nemo.

"But you don't live here," said Patton.

"Nevertheless."

"If you didn't kill the sniper, what did you . . ."

"Tranquilizer dart," said Nemo. "And then I locked him in your shed. Now about Jasper Fleming."

"Why the hell do you just happen to be wandering my property with a tranquilizer gun on a Sunday morning? And how do I know you're not the shooter?"

"You don't," said Nemo. "But right now, your choices are to trust me or to wait for the sniper fire to start again. The man who is not your friend had a partner watching the turnoff to your road—that's what, maybe a mile and a half? And I figure we have three or four minutes before he realizes that radio silence means his buddy is down and he starts humping it up here to send some more rounds through your living room window. Takes him maybe fifteen minutes to get here *if* he's smart enough not to risk driving. That gives us nineteen minutes at best and we've already used six of them. So do you want to ask me questions or do you want to give me answers? Do you know Jasper Fleming?"

"Throw your gun in here and I'll tell you," said Patton.

"Seriously?" said Nemo. "I don't have time for this shit."

"If you don't have time, then you'll throw your gun on the bed and you'll walk in here where I can see you."

"Where you can shoot me, you mean," said Nemo.

"Clock's ticking," said Patton.

"Fine," said Nemo. He clicked the safety on his own Beretta and tossed it through the door onto the bed.

"And keep your fucking hands where I can see them," said Patton.

"Jesus, you are a piece of work," said Nemo. "I guess no good deed goes unpunished." He raised his hands and walked through the door, directly into the woman's line of fire. She did not move. "Now can we talk?" he said.

"You want to know about Jasper Fleming?" said Patton. "Yeah, I know Jasper."

"Does he have any property other than his home at 173 Lone Pine Road?"

"Not that I know of."

"What about that you don't know of? How would you find out?"

"I'd ask him," said Patton.

"Let's assume that's not a possibility."

"Did you do something to Jasper?" said Patton. "Did those . . . those guys out there hurt Jasper?"

"Try to focus here," said Nemo. "We don't have time for emotion. How could we find out if Jasper Fleming owned a place other than his house?"

Just as Nemo said this a flash of light flickered across the blinds covering the window to his left. Nemo pulled the blind slightly to the side and looked out to see a man dressed in black with a rifle slung over his arm maybe fifty yards away and walking toward the house. The idiot was wearing mirrored sunglasses which reflected the morning light against Patton's window.

"Looks like our time's run out," said Nemo. "The backup man is walking up your driveway."

"You think I'm going to fall for that trick?" said Patton.

"Fall for it or don't fall for it," said Nemo, for the first time in the conversation sounding angry. "I don't give a shit. That guy is a lot more heavily armed than you are and at this point I don't really care why he wants to kill you. I just want to get out of here. You got a back door?"

Patton paused just a moment before jumping to her feet. She didn't trust this guy, but on the other hand, she didn't relish getting into a shooting match with somebody whose assets included a high-powered sniper rifle and a buddy locked in her shed. Plus the intruder had said one thing that resonated with Patton. "We don't have time for emotion." This was combat, Patton thought, and the man was right—combat was no place for emotion. She crossed the room in two steps and swept Nemo's gun off the bed, tucking it into her belt while keeping hers trained on him. "Back through the kitchen," she said. "And keep low."

———

On the day Nemo arrived in Alta Vista two weeks earlier, Ingrid Weiss sat in the back room of her modest house on Döbereinerstrasse in the Obermenzing district of Munich looking out at her compact garden. A tall evergreen hedge lined the high fence that surrounded the space, so her neighbors would have had to look out their attic windows to glimpse the delights of her garden. On this late spring morning she especially liked the roses, just past peak bloom—reds and pinks starting to drop their petals to form a carpet on the ground. Those who passed by the front of her house might have seen evidence of her green thumb in the window boxes upstairs— the front garden, too, was hidden by the thick hedge. But neighbors rarely came calling, and when they did, Ingrid rarely answered the bell.

Ingrid loved her solitude as she loved her garden. Most days she worked here in the sunny back room, papers and books spread out on a wide farm table, computer and phone close at hand. This morning, in between sips of rich coffee and sweet sticky bites of her daily *Pudding-brezel*, she was engaged in the work of Columbia House Enterprises, of which she was founder and chief officer. The three other associates of Columbia House lived in Germany, but sometimes worked abroad. Only at their quarterly meetings, or if some bit of unexpected business arose, did she see them all face-to-face. Those meetings took place in her unassuming home. She never wondered what the neighbors thought when, every three months, two men and a woman, dressed in business suits, passed through her usually tightly shut gate.

Draining her coffee and dusting the crumbs of the puddingbrezel off her hands, Ingrid opened the file folder that lay on her table next to a battered copy of the 1921 volume of *Mathematische Annalen*, the German mathematical journal that contained Emmy Noether's ground-breaking paper "Idealtheorie in Ringbereichen."

The file folder contained a single sheet of paper on Columbia House letterhead:

Report on Original Owner Mathematische Annalen:

Emil Hochberg, professor of mathematics, University of Freiburg, 1920–1933. Dismissed due to civil service laws. Wife Rosa. Both died in Dachau.

Daughter Sarah, born 1930. Immigrated USA 1934 with paternal aunt Marta who married Albert Katz. Sarah married Ralph Simpson 1956. One child, Jean, born 1982.

Jean Simpson married John Lilly 2004. Divorced 2010. Current address: 125 College Street, Ridgefield, North Carolina, USA.

Ingrid opened the cover of the book and examined the writing on the endpaper. "To Emil Hochberg, from his great admirer and colleague Hans Schüber, University of Freiburg, 1921." Hochberg had left the university after the civil service laws of 1933—the same laws that had removed the mathematician Emmy Noether and every other Jewish academic from their posts in Germany's universities. Ingrid took out a fresh sheet of her personal stationery and picked up her fountain pen. She liked to write these letters by hand.

Dear Ms. Simpson,

As the founder and president of Columbia House Enterprises, I work to return items looted by the government of Nazi Germany to their rightful owners. While other organizations deal in return-ing valuable items such as paintings and objets d'art, we recognize that almost no one is working to return more everyday items. As a book collector, I have a particular interest in returning books that fell into the hands of the Nazis.

As I'm sure you know, your grandfather Emil Hochberg was a distinguished Jewish professor of mathematics who lost his position due to the policies of the Nazi regime and, along with your grand-mother, ultimately died in Dachau concentration camp.

The enclosed copy of the mathematical journal Mathema-tische Annalen *belonged to your grandfather, and I am pleased on behalf of Columbia House to return it to you. While it does not hold a great monetary value, I hope you will treasure it as a reminder of your grandfather's work and of his courage.*

I remain at your service,

Ingrid Weiss

Ingrid had found this book several months ago—it took time to track down the recipient. She would like to see the reaction of Jean Simpson of North Carolina, USA, when she opened the pack-age containing this book. She might smile and brush away a tear at the thought of the grandfather she never knew. She might even tell someone at the local paper which, in a small town, might run a feature on the front page of a smiling Jean Simpson with the book Ingrid had sent. It warmed Ingrid's heart to imagine such a scene. She sealed the letter in a thick, cream envelope and placed it on top of the book. She would have another cup of coffee, in the garden this time, then carefully wrap Jean Simpson's package for shipment to America.

———

Patton and Nemo slipped out the back door and dashed across the yard into a stand of white pines. She kept her gun trained on him as they ran, then grabbed his arm and pulled him behind a thicket of brambles where anyone walking through the yard would be unlikely to see them.

"You got any great ideas how to get away from these guys?" she said.

"Do you know that first curve in Lone Pine Road after it turns off the main road?" said Nemo. "There's a little gravel pull-out there that leads behind some trees. Looks like people use it for a make-out spot."

"I'm not going to make out with you," said Patton.

"I've got a car there," said Nemo. "They might know to look out for yours."

"And you expect me to just go with you?"

"You're holding the gun," said Nemo. "I think you'll be safe."

"Good point," said Patton. "Yeah, I know the spot."

"Can you get us there without being seen?"

"You mean cut through the woods? Sure. I know this mountain like the back of my hand. It's rugged going, but we could make it in twenty minutes or so."

"Perfect," said Nemo.

As she started to motion to him to make his way downhill, they heard voices. Not menacing assassins, but jocular voices. Sheriff Tommy Linton and his volunteer deputy, Art Handy—the entire law enforcement community of Alta Vista—were walking across Patton's yard.

"It's OK," whispered Patton. "I know these guys. They're cops."

Nemo held up a finger and shook his head slowly. As much as she wanted to greet Tommy and Art, she saw the warning in Nemo's eyes. She had seen that look before, and her instinct told her to heed it.

"I don't see nothing," said Art, standing at Patton's back door where she could just glimpse his ball cap through the branches.

"Like I said," came Tommy's voice, "just somebody hunting out of season. Jane Harper had nothing better to do this morning than call and say she saw somebody with a rifle up here. Tell P.J. to keep an eye out and to call if she sees anything."

Patton leaned a few inches to her left so she could see Art peering through her kitchen window. "I don't think she's home," he said.

"Well, we'll stop in and chat with Jasper," said Tommy's voice.

Art turned away from the house and for an instant Patton thought he had seen her. And then his cap flew across the yard and the side of his head blew off and he dropped to the ground like a sack of potatoes.

It wasn't the first time Patton had seen a man die, but she had never seen someone murdered in cold blood on a peaceful sunny morning, and the sight knocked her backward and took her breath away. She struggled to stay standing, fully expecting to feel the weight of a flashback crashing onto her. But instead, she felt Nemo pulling on her arm, pulling her back to the present. Tommy shouted in a panicked voice but Patton's brain did not even register his words. Nemo pulled her farther from the chaos, and at last she turned to him and they plunged deeper into the woods.

Ten minutes later, at the bottom of a steep ravine, they stopped, neither speaking until their heavy breathing had slowed.

"Jesus," said Patton. "They killed Art Handy. Sweet, gentle, half-literate Art Handy. Why the hell would they kill *him*?"

"These guys mean business," said Nemo.

"Yeah, but what business?" said Patton.

"So, they call you P.J., do they?"

"What the fuck!" said Patton. "A guy just got killed in front of us and your reaction is *they call me P.J.*?"

"You know," said Nemo, "you didn't seem too surprised to come under fire back there. And that wasn't the first time you've seen somebody shot."

"Nobody who wants to kill *me* would take out somebody in uniform," said Patton.

"Nobody that you know of," said Nemo.

"God, poor Renée."

"Who's Renée?"

"Art's wife . . . his widow. Jesus, if they would do that to Art, you don't think that . . . Jasper."

"Yeah, speaking of Jasper, if you want to stay ahead of those guys we still need to find out if Jasper had any other property besides his house."

"What the hell does that have to do with anything?" said Patton.

"Listen, I appreciate that you just saw a friend get killed and that you don't trust me or know anything about me. But hopefully that shit show just now proved to you that I'm not the bad guy here. Now, take a breath and tell me if there is any way to find out if Jasper Fleming—"

"Real estate records in the courthouse," said Patton. "But it's not open on Sunday."

"I don't exactly want to talk to the county clerk," said Nemo. "We'll break in. I suppose there's an alarm . . ."

"We don't have to break in," said Patton. "I have a key."

"You have a key? Who the hell are *you*?"

"Patton Jackson Harcourt, director of the Alta Vista Public Library."

"You're a fucking librarian? I doubt that."

"Doubt all you want," said Patton. "It's true. You want to tell me who you are?"

"You can call me Nemo."

"Okay. The library's in the same building as the courthouse," said Patton, "and I have a passkey and the security code."

"I don't like to count on luck in my business," said Nemo, "but it's nice when it comes along."

"What is your business?" said Patton.

Nemo did not answer.

———

JANUARY 1937

"I am a strong believer in the doctrine that, in the end, only good blood can achieve the greatest, enduring things in the world."

Along with the masses around him, Storm Trooper Helmut Werner cheered the speaker, giddy with the thrill of being in his presence for the first time. Reichsführer Heinrich Himmler, chief of the SS, stood on the rostrum addressing a gathering of the organization Helmut was so proud to have joined. He had passed every test Himmler had devised to screen out those of weaker blood—his hair, eyes, skull measurements, and height all indicated pure Aryan blood, free of foreign or Jewish corruption.

"I shall not accept people," said Himmler, "whom I expect to quit, to complain, to become disloyal and traitors, to have bad soldierly manners and the like at the moment of political tests, because of the nature of the composition of their blood."

To the casual observer, Helmut may have seemed almost indistinguishable from those around him. They all wore the same black uniform, they all stood tall and broad-shouldered with gleaming blond hair and sparkling blue eyes. But even among his pure-blooded brothers, Helmut was determined to distinguish himself.

"We must clearly realize that Bolshevism is the organization of the subhumans, it is the absolute foundation of Jewish sovereignty."

Himmler was smaller than Helmut had imagined—slim and bespectacled with a receding hairline and a wisp of a mustache. If one passed him in the street, one might easily dismiss him as a failed middle-aged businessman. But as Helmut watched him standing on the rostrum speaking with passion to the crowd, he knew that in the presence of Reichsführer, he was in the presence of a greatness seen only once in a generation. Even from where he stood near the back of the crowd, Helmut could feel Himmler's power, and more than anything Helmut wanted to share that power. He wanted to fight for the pure blood of Germany, to rid his homeland of the scourge of Jews and Bolsheviks. But most of all, he wanted to stand side by side with Himmler himself, to serve not in the rank and file of the SS, but at the right hand of the Reichsführer.

"This general movement is also directed against the white race, but we are qualitatively more valuable than the others. We are more valuable because our blood enables us to invent more than others, to lead our people better than the others; because it enables us to have better soldiers, better statesmen, higher culture, better characters."

Yes, thought Helmut, they were more valuable than others, *he* was more valuable than others. And when the war came, as it surely would, he would prove that to Reichsführer Himmler. And when victory came, as it certainly would, he would be standing by Himmler's side, the true chosen one, pure of blood and ready to serve the great leader.

II

Just after midnight, ten hours before his friend P.J. Harcourt would come under fire, Jasper Fleming started awake in a cold sweat to which, though it felt as familiar as his own skin, he had never fully inured himself. He slouched on the sofa in the silent flickering light of the television. The dream never changed. Though in his sleep he only saw the images and heard the sounds, on waking he also knew the facts. The dream took place on April 29, 1945. The dream took place just outside Dachau concentration camp in Bavaria in southern Germany. The dreamer was a private first class in the Third Battalion, 157th Infantry Regiment, Forty-Fifth Infantry Division of the United States Army. Adolf Hitler would commit suicide less than twenty-four hours later. The war in Europe would officially end in nine days. Jasper knew all this because the dream, though truly a dream, was also a memory.

He recalled every sensory detail of that last moment before the dream became a nightmare in crystal clear high definition—the sunlight glistening in a drop of dew on a spider's web, the sound of the mud sucking at his boots, the sour taste of canned ham and eggs from a morning K ration lingering in his mouth, and the stone of well-justified dread sitting in his gut. And then his life changed. Jasper had relived the moments that followed a thousand times. Ten thousand times. Both waking and sleeping they had haunted him. In trying to escape them he had driven away everyone who had ever loved or cared for him, and despite his constant desire to find the courage to end the dream, he had outlived them all. That had been the cruelest fate—that his own cowardice should be accompanied by the misery of longevity. But if the man Jasper had seen following him the past few days was there for the reason Jasper suspected, tonight might finally be different. Tonight the dream might end at last.

He had woken a little after four that Sunday morning at the end of April 1945. He and the rest of his division had begun the day no more than a dozen miles from Munich, where they expected to encounter significant German resistance. After his unappetizing K-ration breakfast, Jasper, weary from a poor night's sleep, shouldered his rifle and fell in with the rear guard. He had been in Germany over a month and in France before that, since they had landed the previous August at Sainte-Maxime. He had come under heavy fire, sustained a minor gunshot wound, watched a friend die in agony, and killed at least four of the enemy. Like the rest of the soldiers around him, he felt hardened at this point. He just wanted to get the job done and get home. Munich, they all assumed, would be no different from Aschaffenburg or Nuremberg—easier perhaps, as with each encounter the Germans seemed less organized and more resigned to the ultimate outcome of the war. Yet despite all this, Jasper felt a tightness in his stomach that hadn't been there since his first few days in France. Then word trickled back that they would be making a slight detour. There would be another task before Munich.

The first indication of something wrong was the sound of crying. He had heard soldiers crying before, but only after gunshots or explosions, only as they lay dying thousands of miles from home on a patch of land they weren't even sure why they were defending. But there had been no gunshots and no explosions. They marched on a railway spur, and ahead Jasper saw about a dozen or so boxcars, doors open, with something cascading out of them and onto the ground. Not until he came almost abreast of the cars did he realize that the something was dead bodies—not the bodies of soldiers in uniform, but civilians in ragged clothes who looked as if they had starved to death. Jasper felt the knot in his stomach pull tighter. The K ration started to seem like a bad idea.

The sound and the smell struck him at the same time—shouting that seemed simultaneously the most joyful noise Jasper could imagine and the most mournful dirge uttered by man, mixed with a stench he could not venture to describe. It was the smell of more than death—it was the smell of despair, of cruelty, of unadulterated evil. Jasper followed the soldiers in front of him through an open gate and past a few blocks of apparently deserted brick buildings. Turning past the corner of the last building, he saw the fence, and he saw what stretched out behind the fence, and he knew at last what he had been fighting for, or at least what he had been fighting against, all these months.

The camp was called Dachau. Jasper would later learn that tens of thousands of people had died there during the war. Political prisoners, Jews, homosexuals, Jehovah's Witnesses, and foreign nationals had all been imprisoned there and treated in the most inhumane ways. They had been subject to forced labor, medical experimentation, and physical torture that left many dead. Others died of malnutrition and disease or were executed by the SS guards who ruled Dachau. But Jasper knew none of this as he rounded that brick building. He had never heard the term "concentration camp" or "final solution." Nothing in his past experience had prepared him for what he was about to see.

A tall fence topped with barbed wire stretched in front of him and on the other side, a foot or two away from the wire, seethed a mass of humanity that did not look human. These were the living dead, skeletons stretched with skin, crying in joy and sorrow, reeking of death and torture. At first Jasper did not even understand what he saw. The bulk of the survivors crowded around the area where the American soldiers had arrived. "The electricity is off," cried one soldier, and the prisoners surged closer to the fence.

That first sight of the prisoners, their bodies a barely living testament to the unimaginable cruelty of their captors, would, for the rest of his years, remain the single most shocking thing Jasper ever saw—if not the most disturbing. By the time he saw American soldiers lining up the few remaining SS officers and shooting them, by the time he saw a guard literally pulled apart by inmates as if they were a pack of wolves, by the time he saw heaps of bodies thrown away like so much rubbish, he had become numb. Those images and sounds and their accompanying stench, which only seemed to deepen as the day wore on, would stay with him, but neither they, nor that gut-punching first view of the camp, would dominate Jasper's memory and his dreams like the first two deaths he witnessed at Dachau.

Far off to his right, away from the bulk of the prisoners, Jasper saw a solitary man clinging to the fence. He seemed barely able to stand and he could not have weighed more than eighty pounds. Jasper stepped away from the rest of his division and walked over to the man, in part to escape the overwhelming incomprehensibility of the crowd before him. He looked into the man's eyes and felt as if he were falling into a bottomless well of blackness. Was there anything left behind those eyes that could be called human? Jasper tried to treat this meeting like any other, tried to smile as he pulled a half-eaten chocolate bar from his pocket and passed it through the fence to the man, tried to sound nonchalant as he said, "I'm Jasper. Everything is going to be OK," to a man who almost certainly spoke no English, if he could speak at all. And even as he said the words, Jasper knew that nothing would be OK ever again. The man's fingers barely clung to the fence and his body sagged below his outstretched arms, but he returned Jasper's gaze and for just a moment, Jasper saw a flicker of life behind those dull eyes.

"*Bitte*," said the man, the sound barely escaping his cracked lips. "*Bitte*."

"I'll come around and help you," said Jasper, but before the words had escaped his mouth the man fell sideways, his grip on the fence giving way. Jasper tried to reach through the fence, tried to catch the man by the wrist, but he could not. When he squatted to look into those eyes again, he could tell the man was dead.

For a moment, Jasper could not breathe. He had never felt so helpless or so angry. Anyone who could do this to another human being didn't just deserve to lose a war—he deserved the worst sort of pain, the most miserable sort of death that man could devise. Jasper seethed inside even as he wept for this man whose name he would never know. Later he would read that even after the liberation of Dachau, hundreds of former prisoners would die of typhus every day, but all that mattered to him today was that this one man had been stripped not just of his life but of his humanity.

When he could draw breath again, he felt the K ration coming up and he dashed back out the main gate of the compound and into the trees on the other side of the railroad track where he was violently sick in the weeds. And there, alone in those trees, his nightmare would evolve, for there his own anger would drag him down to the level of those who had contrived this place of horrors. After he stopped retching, he heard a soft sound coming from slightly deeper in the woods—the sound of more crying. Assuming it was another soldier who had been broken by what he saw in the camp, Jasper made his way through the bushes until he saw a young man in a German SS uniform leaning against a tree, weeping. He had the blond hair and blue eyes that Jasper had seen in many German soldiers, but this man did not seem a threat—he was practically a boy. Jasper had heard stories of children being recruited into the German armed forces in these late days of the war. This boy couldn't be more than fifteen.

But that made no difference—he was a German soldier, cowering outside a factory of atrocities, and Jasper felt no space in his soul for mercy. He pulled out his sidearm and pointed it at the soldier. The boy cowered against the tree, shaking with fear and raising his hands to his face.

"*Bitte,*" he said. "*Bitte. Ich wusste es nicht. Ich wusste es nicht!*"

But in his pathetic plea, Jasper could hear only the final word spoken by the man who had died by the fence—*Bitte*.

"I don't speak German," hissed Jasper. "And neither will you where you're going, you bastard." He raised his gun and fired two shots into the boy's head.

He watched the boy fall to the ground, then stood for a moment looking at the body, a child who looked even younger in death than in the last moments of life. Then Jasper holstered his weapon and walked back into Dachau to see if he could help. But even before he had made it back to the camp, the guilt began. Because Jasper *did* speak German, or at least enough German to understand what the boy had said.

"I didn't know."

That was Jasper's story, his nightmare, as he had confessed it to P.J. And he was glad he had confessed to her. It had not eased his mind or assuaged his guilt, but it had meant that the dream, and the lessons that went with it, would not die with him. And when P.J. told him *her* story, he realized how well he had chosen his confessor. She, of all those people he had ever loved and pushed away, could understand the dream and the guilt and the desire for escape. It was too bad, he thought, that he hadn't met P.J. fifty years ago. But, of course, she hadn't been born yet.

He had left out only one small detail in his confession to P.J., something that, in the great scheme of what had happened that day, might seem insignificant. Now, as he made the same preparations he had for the past several nights before trying to get a few more hours' sleep on the sofa, he began to wonder if he ought to have told her.

———

Jean Simpson taught art history at Ridgefield University. Although the university had grown in the sixteen years since her arrival, she liked the fact that Ridgefield still felt like a small town. Jean knew just about everyone there, and that included Patricia Jameson, who delivered the mail both on campus and in the neighborhood nearby inhabited mostly by faculty members. So when Patricia had a package to deliver to Jean, she usually dropped it by the office, even if it was addressed to the house on College Street.

"From Germany," said Patricia, setting the parcel on Jean's desk. "Have you been ordering books again?"

"I haven't," said Jean, staring at the box, thick with tape and stamps, and feeling nonplussed.

"Well, enjoy it, whatever it is," said Patricia.

Jean pulled a Swiss Army knife out of her desk drawer and sliced into the package, peeling away layers of tape, cardboard, and bubble wrap until a thick old book and an envelope bearing a return address in Munich lay on her desk. She read Ingrid Weiss's letter and then turned to the book. It was volume 83 of a German mathematical publication called *Mathematische Annalen*, and according to Weiss, it had belonged to her grandfather. She opened the book, shook her head in confusion, then crossed to a tall bookcase. Scanning the shelves, her eyes fell on five identical volumes—volumes her grandfather had sent to her great-aunt Marta after Marta had moved to America. Aside from a few photographs, those books were the only evidence Jean had that her grandfather had walked the earth before perishing in Dachau. Five volumes of *Mathematische Annalen*. Volumes 82–86. She pulled the second volume out just to be sure. Opening to the title page she saw the words in German: volume 83. It was thoughtful of Ingrid Weiss to send her her grandfather's copy of this old volume of mathematical papers, but Jean already had it.

She had a class starting in five minutes, and after that a committee meeting and then her regular thrice-weekly twenty laps at the university pool. Then one thing led to another and she forgot all about the book until she was cleaning off her desk a few days later in preparation for a student conference. After she had met with Chuck Campbell for an hour, she picked up the two books and headed across campus to the library. She hadn't seen Arthur Prescott, who, when he wasn't teaching English, could always be found in the rare books room, in a couple of weeks so she updated him on the latest additions to her collection of antique art books as they sat at the wide oak table in the center of the Devereaux Room, then pulled the two nearly identical books out of her bag.

"A duplicate to donate to the library?" said Arthur, examining the two volumes.

"Once I answer some questions," said Jean. "For instance, why did my grandfather have two copies of the same book?"

"Or *did* he have two copies of the same book?" said Arthur.

"Exactly," said Jean. "This Ingrid Weiss says she returns books stolen by Nazis to their rightful owners."

"But you don't think this one is rightfully yours?"

"It might be, but it's awfully odd. I have five volumes of my grandfather's books, and they all have his signature in the upper right corner of the front endpaper. This book," she said, opening the volume from Weiss, "doesn't have a signature, just a gift inscription. 'To Emil Hochberg, from his great admirer and colleague Hans Schüber, University of Freiburg, 1921.'"

"Your German is impressive," said Arthur.

"An odd volume of a mathematical journal seems a strange gift," said Jean.

"There are two possibilities, as I see it," said Arthur. "Either this book really *did* belong to your grandfather, or someone, for some reason, forged this inscription."

"But how do I figure out which?"

"You want to know if this is a forgery? I'd take it to Ridgefield's resident expert."

Twenty minutes later, Jean stood on the front porch of a 1920s bungalow a few blocks from campus waiting for someone to answer the doorbell. She loved May in Ridgefield—the dogwoods and azaleas blazed in full bloom and the smell of freshly cut grass had returned to the tree-lined streets near the college for the first time in months. Jean eyed a pair of rocking chairs on the porch and was considering taking a book out of her bag and sitting down to read while waiting, when the door opened.

"Jean, how nice to see you," said Liz Byerly, her English accent as delicious to Jean as the smell of the Ridgefield spring. "Sorry it took me so long to get to the door. Spring cleaning, you know."

"I was hoping to catch Peter at home," said Jean. "I have a question about forgery."

"Oh, he's down in the basement fiddling around with his old books," said Liz, dusting her hands off on her jeans. "Come on in and we'll see if we can roust him."

Ten minutes later, in a basement room lined with bookcases, Jean stood with Peter Byerly by a table cluttered with books and papers. Peter looked a little like Sherlock Holmes with his neatly trimmed gray beard, tweed jacket, and a magnifying glass gripped in one hand as he leaned over the book Jean had received in the mail, examining the inscription. He was something of a legend in Ridgefield—a widower and heir to the Ridgefield family fortune who had made a magnificent bibliographical discovery many years ago and who offered his services free to the university rare books department during the six months of the year he and his second wife spent in Ridgefield. Jean had been lucky enough to catch him before they had departed for their cottage in the English countryside.

"I could do a chemical test on the ink," said Peter, "but I feel pretty confident what the results would be. It's not just that this ink is glossier than one would expect for a nearly hundred-year-old inscription. Look here on the half title—see how the foxing is seeping through the printing? Now look at the inscription. This ink is sitting *on top* of the foxing. This inscription was made after this was already an old book. The question is, why?"

"I can't imagine why anyone would want to associate a book with my grandfather. He was a virtually unknown professor. It's not like this inscription would add anything to the value of the book."

"And Ingrid Weiss is right," said Peter after typing away on his laptop for a moment. "The book's not worth much to start out with, even with Emmy Noether's paper."

"Who was Emmy Noether?"

"Einstein called her the most important woman in the history of mathematics," said Peter. "I only know about her because I read that book you gave me about Jewish scholars who lost their positions in Nazi Germany."

"I skipped the part about math and science," said Jean sheepishly, "once I had checked the index for my grandfather."

"Apparently Noether developed something called the theory of rings. I've no idea what it is, but this volume contains the paper she published on the subject. But look . . ." Peter spun his laptop around. "There are six copies for sale right now, ranging from fifty to a hundred dollars."

"So it's not exactly a rare book."

"No," said Peter, taking up the book again. "Look, you're an art historian. I think you need to approach this as a historical investigation."

"I'm not sure what I'd investigate. I already know everything I can find out about my grandfather."

"I don't think it's your grandfather you need to investigate," said Peter, looking up from the book. "It's Ingrid Weiss."

———

The basement of the Lansing County courthouse was well lit by the late morning sun pouring through the small, rectangular windows set high in the walls. Thank God for that sunshine, thought Patton. On a dim, overcast day, this basement would be just the sort of place to trigger a flashback, and Nemo had refused to let her turn on the overhead fluorescents.

"No point in announcing we're down here," he said.

They descended the stairs into a maze of rough wooden bookcases crammed with ledgers.

"Don't they have all this stuff on computers?" said Nemo.

"Not in Alta Vista," said Patton. "Nothing here but good old-fashioned deed books. Luckily there is a set of volumes that just lists owners with cross-references to the deed numbers."

"How do you know all this?"

"I helped them arrange everything down here after a water pipe burst a couple of years ago."

"You arranged it all? That seems convenient."

"Well, I'm the closest thing to an archivist in Alta Vista."

"You know how to drop down out of the line of fire, you handle a Beretta M9 like you were born with it, you seem to expect people to shoot at you, and you expect me to believe you're an archivist?"

"I told you I ran the library," said Patton. "Here we go, volume two, D through F." She pulled a large, dusty, clothbound ledger off a shelf and carried it over to a utilitarian metal table at one end of the room. When opened, the book covered almost the whole tabletop and Patton began rapidly flipping the pages.

"It stinks," said Nemo as a sour smell permeated the room.

"Yeah, when it flooded down here everything got moldy and the county can't really afford to have these records archivally treated, so instead, it stinks. Here we go, section F. Under each letter the entries are chronological, but I know Jasper came up here sometime in the late seventies, so he shouldn't be too hard to find. It's not like we have thousands of real estate transactions a year. If I start in 1976 . . ." Patton ran her finger down the page, scanning for the name Fleming. Three pages later, she found it.

"Here it is—Fleming, Jasper, deed number 19456. June 24, 1977. You look that one up in those books over there and I'll see if there are any other entries."

Nemo squinted at the faint lettering on the spines of the volumes that Patton had pointed to until he found one labeled "17862–22983." He pulled it down and propped it on the edge of the table, leaning his head back as he turned the pages in an unsuccessful attempt to minimize the reek of mold. "OK," he said, "Here's 19456. Fleming, Jasper. 173 Lone Pine Road. And then there's a lot of other stuff I don't understand."

"That's his house," said Patton, glancing at the entry. "But look, in 1981 there's another Jasper Fleming entry. Deed 24752."

A minute later another ledger lay open on the table and Nemo and Patton read the description of deed 24752—the purchase by Jasper Fleming of an undeveloped piece of property at the end of Ebenezer Road.

"Do you know where this is?" said Nemo.

"About six miles outside town," said Patton. "But I don't think there's anything up there. It's pretty rough country."

"Let's go," said Nemo, turning for the steps.

"You go," said Patton. "I don't see why I should. I gave you what you asked for."

"You want to take on a couple of assassins by yourself?" said Nemo.

Patton considered the question. She wasn't scared to confront a pair of killers, but an ally could prove useful. "Why do you even want me to come with you?" she said.

"Call it insurance," said Nemo. "I don't want you telling those guys what we just found out."

"And I thought you cared about me."

"Don't flatter yourself. Now are you coming?"

"Hang on," said Patton, lifting up one of the ledgers. "We have to put these away."

"You don't seem to understand that we are possibly running for our lives."

"And you don't seem to understand that if we leave these lying open on the table, someone could figure out where we're going," said Patton calmly, lifting the volume back in place.

"Good point," said Nemo.

Once they had put away the ledgers, they slipped out the back of the courthouse. They could hear sirens in the distance as Nemo pulled out of the rear entrance of the parking lot.

"Turn left," said Patton, sliding down in her seat. Paranoia seemed reasonable given what had happened so far this morning.

"Nice weather today," said Nemo after a moment of silence.

"You should know," said Patton matter-of-factly, "that because I've been shot at this morning and watched an innocent man dropped by a sniper, I'm willing to go along with you for a while, but the time is coming, and it's coming soon, when you're going to have to tell me who the hell you are and what the fuck is going on."

"Noted," said Nemo.

Ebenezer Road eventually faded into a dirt track that would have been impassable in the old Ford if there had been any recent rain, but the dry spring meant Nemo could gun it up the hill and end up on a patch of matted grass outside a dilapidated barn tucked into the edge of the woods. It had probably been used to store hay in the days when this had been a county of dairy farms, but the side facing them had little left in the way of a roof and did not promise protection from the elements. However, when they crept in through a space where two rotted boards had fallen away, they discovered, built inside the shell of the barn, a pre-fabricated aluminum building secured with a Yale padlock.

"Nicely hidden," said Nemo.

"I can't believe he never mentioned this place to me," said Patton.

"We all have our secrets."

"Yes," said Patton in a low voice. "But Jasper *told* me his secrets. His secret." She couldn't imagine the old man had assembled this building by himself. But then again, Jasper had owned this property since 1981. The padlock looked new, but the rest of the structure could easily be thirty years old or older. It might have even been here when Jasper bought the place. Dents pocked the sides in spots, and moss grew on the lower third of the walls. Patton walked slowly around the building, trying to imagine Jasper in this lonely place. Why had he come here? What had he hidden inside? The barn smelled faintly of stale gasoline, and when she turned the corner, Patton saw a gas-powered generator, with cables running through a small piece of PVC in the aluminum wall. She paced across the back and down the far side from where they had entered and estimated the building measured about twenty by fifteen feet. Room for all sorts of things. By the time she got back to the door, Nemo stood there with a pair of bolt cutters.

"Where did you get those?" said Patton.

"Just had them in the trunk."

"You just happen to have bolt cutters and a tranquilizer gun in your trunk?"

"Tools of the trade."

"What the hell is your trade?" But as Patton asked this question, Nemo snipped through the padlock and it fell to the ground.

"After you," said Nemo, pulling the door open.

The room was dim, lit only by the light coming in through the door and a couple of skylight panels in the roof, but as Patton stepped in she caught a hint of Jasper's Bay Rum aftershave. He had been there recently.

A long wooden work counter stretched down one side of the space, and above this hung neat racks of tools and bins of screws and bolts. On the opposite wall stood several large power tools, the only one of which Patton recognized was a drill press. At one end of the room a small armchair sat next to a table holding an electric coffeepot. Patton wished for more light so she could see better, and just at that moment a bright beam swung across the wall. She turned to see Nemo standing in the door with a flashlight.

"Jesus, you scared the crap out of me," she scolded.

"You're cool under fire but a flashlight freaks you out?"

"What is this place?" said Patton.

"I was hoping you could tell me," said Nemo. "Looks like a nice workshop. He's got the tools for a little carpentry, some metalworking, some electrical stuff."

"But what was he working on?"

"Maybe that," said Nemo, shining his light on an old checked tablecloth that covered something at the far end of the counter. He stepped across the room and pulled away the cloth, revealing a wooden box that resembled a typewriter. It had a set of keys that looked like they might have been pilfered from an old Remington manual, but it also had wires spilling out of the front and the sides and another set of letters inset in a panel above the keyboard.

"Let me guess," said Nemo. "Jasper was trying to invent the electric typewriter?"

Patton stepped carefully toward the machine, turning her attention to a wooden rack next to it that held several notched metal disks. "Wow," she said reverently. "I've studied all about them, but I've never seen one." She ran her hands lightly across the keys, then picked up one of the metal disks and pressed it into a slot at the top of the machine.

"Never seen one what?" said Nemo.

"But this only has space for two rotors. He was still working on it. This is amazing. Did he build this whole thing from scratch? I wonder how . . ."

"Build what from scratch?" said Nemo more insistently. "What is that thing?"

"Something that has no business being in a barn outside Alta Vista, North Carolina," said Patton. "Jasper Fleming was building an Enigma machine."

"What the hell is an Enigma machine?" said Nemo, pressing one of the keys.

"It's an enciphering machine the Germans used to send coded messages during World War II," said Patton.

"The Germans?" Nemo picked up one of the metal rotors and held it in front of his flashlight, the beam glinting off the polished surface. "That guy I took down at your place—I'm pretty sure he was German."

"You said he was ex-military."

"Yes, but I didn't say ex–US military. Judging from his weaponry, I'd say German is the most likely. He wasn't carrying any ID."

"Why would a German ex-soldier take shots at me?" said Patton. She still assumed, in spite of all evidence to the contrary, that the sniper must be connected to the three people she knew actually wanted her dead, but that theory was getting harder and harder to support.

"Why would an old man try to build a German code machine from World War II?"

"Jasper fought in the war," said Patton, unwilling to offer Nemo any more of what she knew about Jasper's experiences. "But that doesn't explain why he wants an Enigma machine."

"Do you know how this thing works?" said Nemo.

"I know the basics," said Patton. "You set the rotors to a certain starting position and wire up the plugboard a certain way—they used different starting positions and wiring configurations every day. Then you type in your message, and with each letter the rotors move to a new position and a letter lights up on here." Patton pointed to the second set of letters above the typewriter keys. "You write down those letters, send them via Morse code, and then the person at the other end, with his machine set up the same way as yours, types it in and the original message lights up on the board, one letter at a time."

"So all you need to decode the message is one of these machines configured the right way?"

"Yeah, but even with a three-rotor Enigma there were something like one hundred and fifty trillion possible settings. And some machines had four rotors."

"Wouldn't they just run it through a supercomputer or something?"

"Not in early 1940s. There were no computers to speak of. The British basically invented modern computing to help break Enigma. You see, there was this guy named Alan Turing—"

"You say this machine doesn't work?" said Nemo, interrupting.

"It's not finished," said Patton. "Not enough rotors and the—"

"We'd better take it anyway. Don't want Fritz and Franz finding it."

"Fritz and Franz?"

"My nicknames for your Aryan buddies using your fridge for target practice."

"Aryan? You said—"

"I said German, yeah, but the one I dropped was as blond and blue-eyed as they come. Looked like a regular Gestapo poster boy." Nemo scooped up the Enigma machine, wires dangling from its back and underside. "Grab those rotors, will you," he said.

Patton took the rotors off the counter and followed Nemo back into the daylight. "Slow down," she said as he opened the trunk and tossed the machine in.

"It doesn't pay to hang around in my business," he said, opening the driver side door. "A lesson you'd think I'd have learned by now, but after this morning apparently not."

Patton slid into the passenger seat and pulled on her seat belt. "And I suppose if I ask you once again what your business is, you'll say . . ."

Nemo started the engine but did not put the car in gear. He turned to look Patton directly in the eye for the first time since they met. "Did Jasper ever give you anything?"

"No," said Patton. "Just advice and companionship. He loaned me a book once."

"He never gave you a key to something?"

"You mean like a key to this place?" said Patton.

"I thought so," said Nemo, "but it must be something else. What book did he loan you?"

"Just an old thriller. *The Key to Rebecca*. It's about . . . oh . . ."

"What?"

"It's about World War II codebreaking."

"Jesus. And it's called *The* Key *to Rebecca*? Where is it?"

"He told me to take care of it, but I'm afraid I didn't. I spilled a glass of water all over the back of it. That's not like me. I'm usually pretty careful with books. But it was a beat-up old book club edition, so I figured I'd go online and buy him a replacement. Maybe a first edition if I could find one."

"Charming story, but where did you put *his* copy?"

"I donated it to the library book swap a couple of days ago. There's a case outside the main entrance where you can leave a book and take a book."

"Let's hope it's still there," said Nemo.

"You think Jasper left something important in that book without telling me?" said Patton.

"Unless I'm mistaken, those gentlemen callers from this morning think you have something that belonged to Jasper—something they want. If we get it first, we might have a little leverage when it comes to things like staying alive." He threw the car into gear, spinning his tires on the grass for a second or two before gaining traction and shooting off down the gravel road.

Patton and Nemo could hear sirens as they drove back into town, but the parking lot of the courthouse was still empty. It took Patton only a minute to find the copy of *The Key to Rebecca* Jasper had given her wedged on top of a stack of paperback crime novels on the bottom shelf of the "Take a Book, Leave a Book" case that stood in the sheltered entryway to the library. She tugged the book off the shelf and ran back to the car, relieved she didn't hear the sound of bullets hitting the pavement, or the car, or herself.

"You think this is what they shot up my kitchen for? It doesn't seem like much of a treasure."

"It has to be," said Nemo. "And if it's not, we don't have time to stick around and find out." As he turned onto Main Street, a pair of state trooper cruisers sped by, sirens blaring.

"So I'm just supposed to go with you? A total stranger who broke into my house and seems . . . well, no offense, but who seems pretty dangerous."

"I *am* pretty dangerous," said Nemo.

"And you expect me to ride out of town with you?"

"You have options," said Nemo. "You could shoot me and face Fritz and Franz on your own. Or you could give me the book and I could let you go to face Fritz and Franz on your own. Only now that I think of it, you know a lot about Jasper and about this, this Enigma thing he was building, so I probably wouldn't let you go."

"So my option is to shoot you," said Patton.

"Yeah, I guess that's about it. Or you can stay with me and have a decent chance of not getting killed."

"A decent chance?" said Patton.

"At least fifty-fifty."

"Wow, I feel so much better," said Patton, pulling on her seat belt. "Let's go."

Main Street rapidly became State Highway 14 and, as Nemo sped up to sixty, Patton pulled the two guns out of her waistband.

"Decided to shoot me?" said Nemo.

"Not yet," said Patton. "They were digging into my back." She set the guns on her lap, then took out her phone.

"Are you fucking crazy?" said Nemo, raising his voice. "Don't you know they can track a cell phone?"

"Of course I know they can track a cell phone," said Patton. "That's exactly why I'm turning it on."

"Like hell you are," said Nemo, reaching for the phone. "You may think that I'm bad, but trust me Fritz and Franz are worse."

"Jesus, don't get your panties in a wad," said Patton, holding the phone away from Nemo. "I'm trying to help us out here. You got any duct tape?"

"In the glove compartment," said Nemo.

"Tool of the trade?" said Patton.

"Something like that."

"Pull into that gas station up there," said Patton.

Nemo steered the car into the roadside service station with two semitrucks parked out front, one pointing in each direction.

"Are we going to keep heading east?" said Patton.

"That's the plan," said Nemo.

Patton hopped out of the car. Checking to be sure no one was watching, she tore off a piece of tape and attached the phone to the underside of the running board on the truck pointed west. Ten seconds later she was back in the car.

"Let them chase that for a while," she said with a smile.

———

At 4:00 p.m. Munich time, Ingrid Weiss logged on to her private encrypted email server and sent a coded message to the other three chief associates of Columbia House Enterprises. An operative working to retrieve a stolen artifact had been scheduled to report in an hour earlier. The lack of communication meant there were likely complications. Complications that could prove embarrassing for Columbia House if not dealt with promptly. The operation, while dangerous, had promised results that could transform Columbia House from a small organization run out of a house in Munich into a significant player on the world stage. If problems had arisen, Weiss wanted her team together to deal with them and to oversee the next steps. Within ten minutes she had received replies from all three associates. The one who lived in the Munich area would be there within the hour. The one in Stuttgart wrote that she would be on the next train and should arrive by about seven. The one working in Amsterdam was on the way to the airport and would land in Munich at seven thirty and arrive at Ingrid's house as quickly as a taxi could get there. Weiss brewed a fresh pot of coffee, filled a platter with bread, cheese, and salami, and descended into her cellar, prepared for a long night.

———

Hours earlier, in the light of dawn, Jasper had caught sight of a moving shadow out of the corner of his eye. Feigned sleep seemed the best way to invite the visitor in, and after ten minutes of leaning back into the sofa cushions with his eyes closed, he heard the swish of the front door sweeping across the welcome mat. He opened his eyes and saw for an instant the face that had haunted him for seventy years. Then the boyish blue eyes and the tousled blond hair faded away, and Jasper knew this was not really the boy whose life he had taken in 1945, but he also knew that the memory and the dream were closing in on him at last, that his mind was playing merciful tricks. And he knew, somehow, that the man who had been following him for the past two weeks had been sent to deliver him sweet relief at last. Even though Jasper would not accept that relief at the hands of a stranger, he felt comforted by the man's presence—an insurance policy in case Jasper lost his nerve. When the face dissolved from that of a fifteen-year-old boy into that of a scruffy middle-aged man, Jasper spoke.

"You've come at last."

"I thought you were asleep," said the man.

"I've been waiting for you. You are death, aren't you?"

"Not exactly," said the man, stepping warily closer.

"But you came to kill me."

"Yes."

"So it amounts to the same thing."

"I suppose," said the man.

"Thank you," said Jasper.

"People in your situation don't usually thank me," said the man.

"Have you seen a lot of people in my situation?" said Jasper.

"A fair few."

"I only wish you had come sooner," said Jasper.

"I didn't really come here to chat," said the man.

"Right. You came to kill me," said Jasper. "Only I can't let you do that. It wouldn't be fair to you. You have no idea why I deserve to die."

"I don't care why you deserve it. I don't even care *if* you deserve it."

"Well I do," said Jasper, "but you shouldn't have to carry the guilt of killing me."

"Listen, I'd love to continue this conversation, but I'm on a schedule here, so if it's OK with you, I'm going to get on with my job."

"I don't think you are," said Jasper. And then he did something the man did not expect.

The part of the dream, the part of the memory, that Jasper had not confessed to P.J. was the last thing he thought of. In the seconds after he did what the man had not foreseen, Jasper relived the part of his history that had remained secret. The German boy lay dead in front of him, slumped against the trunk of a tree, the look of terror frozen onto his bloody face. Jasper stood there looking at him for a moment, searing the image into his memory, knowing it would haunt him for the rest of his life. In that instant, had someone offered him the chance to trade places with the German boy, he would have accepted without hesitation. But cowardice is a stealthy foe—it creeps upon you slowly and before you know it you are ninety-two and still haunted by the same dream, too afraid to end it.

Jasper heard shouts in English from a short distance away and knew he could not remain hidden for long. He reached down and grabbed the German by the lapels, at first thinking that he would lie him out on the forest floor, close his eyes, and maybe drag a couple of branches over him. But the weight of the boy popped the buttons on his jacket as his body slipped to the ground and Jasper saw some papers in the inside pocket. He had seen American soldiers take sidearms and helmets and belt buckles from dead German soldiers; what harm could there be in taking a few papers? One paper, as it turned out.

He didn't even look at it. He didn't think perhaps it might be something important, something that should be handed over to someone in authority. He didn't really care what it was, he just wanted to take something with him as a tangible reminder of this moment. Something that, whenever someone said that Jasper was a good person, he could look at and know they were wrong. Jasper might have started out as a good person, but war had turned him into a monster. That piece of paper would serve as a mirror he could look into if he ever felt the guilt slipping from his shoulders—a mirror that would remind him how he deserved to feel for the rest of his life.

He folded the paper and slipped it into his pocket. It would be years before he unfolded it and wondered what those enigmatic combinations of letters might mean. It would be decades before he read an article about the Enigma Code and began to understand what he had stolen. Then he bought a tract of land with an old barn on it, built a hidden workshop, and tried, without much success, to figure out how to build an Enigma machine. He gave up after a year or two, but then, seventy years after he marched out of Dachau headed for Munich and the next battle, he saw an advertisement for instructions to build your own Enigma machine and wondered if he should try again to decode the message on the paper, if that would somehow honor the memory of the boy he had killed. He went to his workshop often for a month or two and made real progress. But when he spotted a man following him, he stopped going. The Enigma message he pocketed outside Dachau that day would always be a reminder of his darkest secret—a secret he would keep to his grave.

But all that lay in the future. That day he holstered his sidearm and walked back toward the camp, the words of the murdered boy pounding in his head.

Ich wusste es nicht.
I didn't know.

III

"Are you sure there's nothing in that book?" said Nemo when they had started to drop out of the mountains toward the piedmont on a twisting two-lane road.

"I flipped through it twice," said Patton. "No bookmarks, no letters or receipts for safe deposit boxes, no circled words or underlined sentences. What makes you so sure it's even important? And for that matter you never did tell me how you know about Jasper or *what* you know about Jasper."

"I guess I don't know as much as I thought," said Nemo, "if there's nothing in that book."

"When I said back at the house that I wanted to talk to Jasper you said we should assume that's not a possibility," said Patton. "What did you mean by that?"

"Nothing. Don't worry about it."

"But I do worry about it. Is Jasper dead? Did you kill Jasper and then start taking shots at me and then pretend to rescue me?" Patton spoke evenly, but there was a tinge of anger and accusation in her voice.

"I didn't shoot at you and I didn't pretend to rescue you," said Nemo.

"And Jasper? Is he dead?"

"Yes," said Nemo flatly.

"Jesus," said Patton, turning to look at the passing landscape. She had suspected it since this morning. Hell, she had expected it every day since she had gotten to know Jasper. Anytime you have a friend in his nineties you think about death every time you see him. But Patton felt the blow with an unexpected weight. Jasper had been her only real friend in Alta Vista. Her only real friend anywhere, she thought.

She turned back to face Nemo, because now she wanted to know, she *needed* to know how he knew about Jasper. "Did you kill him?" she said.

"You don't want to go there, Patton," said Nemo, but she could see the white in his knuckles as he gripped the steering wheel more tightly.

"Did you kill him?"

"I was *hired* to kill him," said Nemo.

"Stop the car," said Patton.

"I'm not going to stop the car."

"I said stop the car."

"I'm not going to stop the car. We don't have time for me to stop the car."

"Stop the damn car or I swear to God I'll blow your fucking head off." Patton leveled her gun at Nemo's temple, but he didn't flinch.

"You do that and the car will crash and we'll both be dead."

"OK," Patton said, moving the gun. "Then I'll take out your left kneecap. You want to find out what that feels like, or do you want to stop the car?"

"Just give me ten more minutes," said Nemo, "then we'll be someplace safe and I'll tell you whatever you want to know. Now stop waving that damn gun at me."

But Patton did not lower her gun as Nemo turned onto a narrower road and then, a couple of miles later, onto an unpaved track. A few minutes later he pulled the car to a stop behind the remnants of a house that looked like it had first collapsed and then burned and both a long time ago. The area was thick with weeds and briars that stood taller than the car, and forest surrounded the house on three sides. He switched off the engine and turned to look at Patton.

"We should be good here for a few hours," he said.

"How would you know that?" said Patton.

"Because I've already staked the place out," said Nemo. "Always have a place to retreat."

"Smart strategy," said Patton, still pointing the gun at him. "Now who the hell are you? And *what* the hell are you."

"You don't want to know what I am," said Nemo.

"Maybe not, but I *need* to know."

"There are a lot of words for what I am," said Nemo. "Hit man, hired gun. The point is I make my living by killing people."

"But why . . ."

"Just let me tell you about Jasper. Let me tell you and then if you want to shoot me, fine."

Patton nodded. She could feel a tear trickling down her cheek. Tears really pissed her off. Emotional weakness, her father called them, and she did not want to show weakness in front of Nemo, but she wasn't about to move the gun to brush the tear away.

"Somebody hired me to kill Jasper. Seemed like a simple enough job, but when I got there, your friend was expecting me. At first I thought he wasn't completely in his right mind because he seemed to think I was the angel of death. But he knew exactly what he was doing. He told me he didn't want the guilt of his death to rest on me. And then he very calmly unwrapped a candy bar and started to eat it. I didn't understand what he was doing, and I was getting a little impatient, when his face turned red and his lips swelled up and he started to gasp for breath."

"Jasper was allergic to Brazil nuts," said Patton, the tears coming more regularly now.

"I figured it was something like that. Anyway, that's when he looked at me and said, 'Find Patton. She has the key.' And then he stopped breathing. So my job was done. I wasn't hired to find a key; I was hired to eliminate Jasper Fleming and he was eliminated."

"No thanks to you," said Patton, sniffing.

"Yeah. He was a real gentleman if you think about it. Anyway I'm leaving the house when what do I see parked about fifty yards up the hill but a black van. Subtle, right? Now I don't know if somebody's watching me, if these are cops, or if it's just some kids looking for privacy. So I go back to my car and I decide to watch for a couple of minutes. Nothing happens, so I drive down toward the main road and when I get around the curve I park my car in that pull-off and walk along the edge of the woods to where I can see the van and the house. Sure enough, these two guys get out and walk right into Jasper's house. I'm curious, which is stupid of me, but I watch. They're in there for a good three hours, then they go back to the van, and one of them stays there and the other takes a rifle and heads up toward what turns out to be your place."

"And you followed him," said Patton.

"You're welcome," said Nemo.

"But why? Why didn't you just leave?"

"Because somebody was using me, and that pisses me off. These guys are serious muscle but they need me to kill Jasper for them? No way. But they also don't trust me to find whatever they're looking for. Looks to me like somebody wants me to take the rap for a murder while they get whatever is in that house that's so important."

"Only they didn't find anything, did they?"

"Apparently not. And then they came after you."

"So for some reason they figured I had it."

"You were Jasper's only friend."

"Been watching him, have you?" said Patton.

"Little bit," said Nemo.

"So you're like a big-time professional assassin?"

"I wouldn't say that."

"Why would someone hire a person like you to kill a ninety-two-year-old man?" said Patton. "Why not just hire some local thug?" She had lowered the gun and finally dragged her sleeve across her damp face.

"I got hired for the same reason I always get hired. Because I have something lacking in Fritz and Franz. I have subtlety. I have discretion. Shooting up your house because they thought you had something important, murdering law enforcement—that's not just wrong, it's stupid. That's not how you conduct yourself in this business if you want more than one job. These guys are not subtle and they're probably not smart, but they are dangerous."

"What do you mean you have subtlety?"

"It's my second rule," said Nemo. "Never leave a crime scene."

"You have rules? You kill people for a living and you have rules?" There was a hint of accusation in her voice even as Patton thought about the rules under which she had killed people.

"Four," said Nemo.

"How can you never leave a crime scene if you're a professional murderer?"

"Because as far as law enforcement is concerned, everyone I've ever killed died of natural causes or in an accident. It takes a lot of hard work to commit a crime that nobody knows is a crime. That's why they pay me the big bucks."

"What are your other rules?" said Patton.

"Plan the escape before you plan the crime," said Nemo. "Never know the client's endgame, and always have a retreat—like this one. This is the first time I've ever intentionally broken a rule."

"But you said Jasper killed himself, so you didn't leave a crime scene."

"True. But whoever hired me didn't trust me to do the second part of the job—to find whatever he's looking for. So he sent those thugs after me to get the treasure and probably leave my body in a ditch somewhere or turn me over to the sheriff. That makes me angry. It's not a good idea to be angry in my business because anger makes you do stupid things. But I don't care. I'm angry so I'm doing a stupid thing. I'm going to find out the client's endgame."

"Why?" said Patton.

"Because it's a definite possibility that part of his endgame is to kill me, and maybe kill you, and I'd rather that didn't happen."

"Who is this client?"

"I wish I knew."

"An anonymous customer?"

"They all are," said Nemo. "The dark web is a mysterious place.

Anyway, when I saw Fritz trying to ruin your day, I figured I had to find whatever he was looking for before he did and get the hell out of Alta Vista. Since Jasper said you had the key, and they didn't find anything in his house, I guessed that meant another property someplace. But you said he never gave you a key. Just an old book."

"Wait a minute," said Patton, suddenly remembering something. "When I flipped through that book, *The Key to Rebecca*, the back pages were in perfect condition."

"So?"

"So, I spilled water all over the back of that book and it's a cheap book club edition. It should have soaked through the cover in no time."

"What's your point?"

Patton lowered her gun and placed it, with Nemo's, on the floor, well out of his reach. She pulled the book out from under her seat. The rear panel of the dust jacket was badly water damaged, but, as she had recalled, the inside of the cover wasn't affected at all. Patton carefully peeled back the dust jacket to discover, taped on its back side, a thin plastic bag containing a single sheet of yellowed paper with one of its corners chipped off. Printed at the top were what looked like two lightning bolts and the word "*H-Sonderkommando.*" Below that were two German words written in pencil and then a series of typed five letter words that weren't words, as far as Patton could tell. Not even German ones.

"You think this might be what they're looking for?" she said, holding up the dust jacket so Nemo could see the paper.

"Holy shit," said Nemo. "Is that . . ."

"If I'm guessing right," said Patton, "this is a message from the Nazi SS encoded with an Enigma machine."

"The SS? Like storm troopers and . . ."

"And concentration camps and Heinrich Himmler."

"Apparently it's a message worth killing for, even all these years later," said Nemo.

"Yeah," said Patton. "So what are you waiting for? Let's get the hell out of here before Fritz and Franz track us down."

"They're not going to track us down—at least not here. Can you break this code?"

"If you give me a computer and Internet access," said Patton.

"Absolutely not," said Nemo. "We need to stay off the grid."

"What about a computer at a library or something?" said Patton.

"What would you use it for, exactly?"

"There's a site that uses statistical techniques and the hill-climbing search algorithm to find the key for an Enigma message," said Patton.

"Just one site?" said Nemo.

"Just one."

"Then you can be absolutely sure that whoever hired me is watching that site. We use it to break the code and we hand them our only bargaining chip."

"That's inconvenient," said Patton.

"Isn't there another way? A way to break it without the Internet?"

"There is," said Patton, "but you'd need an Enigma machine, something called a Bombe, and an old friend of mine who happens to be an expert in the field. Lucky for us they're all in the same place."

"Where's that?" said Nemo.

"Bletchley Park, about fifty miles north of London. Not exactly convenient."

"The first thing I do whenever I finish a job is leave the country," said Nemo, "so it suits me. You have a passport?"

"Yeah," said Patton. "But given that Bletchley is the obvious place to go to break an Enigma message, don't you think they'll know that's where we're headed?"

"Probably," said Nemo, "which means stealth is more important than speed at this point. So, we stay here for a few hours, get some sleep, then head out." Nemo took a sleeping bag out of the trunk and led Patton a short way into the woods to a small clearing. "You can take the bag," he said. "I can sleep anywhere."

Patton shoved the two guns into the foot of the sleeping bag and crawled in. She thought the idea of sleeping in the middle of the afternoon foolish, but ten minutes later she was out like a light. When she awoke, Nemo and the car had both disappeared.

———

They were not named Fritz and Franz. They were named Karl Gruning and Erich Koepler and they were smart enough to know they had fucked up. Or at least Karl was. Erich was the one who had gotten trigger happy twice in one morning and ended up killing someone who worked for local law enforcement. Not a smart move. Karl had followed his companion up the road after Erich failed to answer a radio message. He had heard noises coming from the toolshed and had pried the lock and hasp off the rotting wood of the door with a knife to discover Erich groggy from the effects of a tranquilizer dart. They wanted to search P.J. Harcourt's house, but when they came out of the shed, they saw a sheriff's car pull into the side yard. Afraid their escape might be blocked, and still a little loopy from the tranquilizer, Erich had taken a shot at one of the men who got out of the car. Karl grabbed the gun and considered shooting the other man, but no one had seen them, and he didn't want to compound Erich's mistake. Their employer would be angry enough about one dead cop. Luckily, the ensuing confusion on the part of the survivor gave them plenty of cover to get the hell out of there. They knew that pretty soon cops would be crawling all over the place, so they ran back down the road to where they had left the van and drove away, turning right on the main road, away from town. They would take back roads down the mountain to avoid any police who might be coming in from town. It might take an hour longer, but there was no point in rushing. Nemo and the woman could be anywhere by now.

Lack of sleep had probably contributed to their poor judgment that morning, but their employer wouldn't care anything about that. They had been watching Nemo for the past week, and you never knew when he was going to sleep or wake up. When Nemo finally went in to kill

Jasper, they were ready to search the house as soon as he left, but after three hours they hadn't found anything, and they decided P.J. Harcourt must have the paper. She was the one person who had regular contact with Jasper. Even though Erich wasn't brilliant, he was observant, and he had seen P.J.'s name on one of the two mailboxes at the end of Lone Pine Road—the box that didn't say Fleming.

They figured they would take out this Harcourt character, find the paper, and be out of there as fast as possible. Erich would do the job; Karl would stay in the van, monitor the police radio, and watch the road for Nemo, in case he came back. But Nemo had stayed hidden as he followed Erich to P.J.'s house and the morning hadn't gone quite the way Karl and Erich had expected.

Thirty minutes after hightailing it away from the body of a dead sheriff's deputy and finally back on the main highway, Karl and Erich picked up a signal from Patton Jackson Harcourt's cell phone, which their employer had helped them hack into.

"They're headed west," said Karl, "toward Tennessee."

"Where in Tennessee?" said Erich.

"Who cares where," said Karl. "Just get on Interstate 40 and drive west. And don't get too close. We don't want them to know we're following."

They were well past Knoxville when the signal came to a stop in the parking lot of a BBQ joint.

"You stay here," said Karl, pulling the van around to the back of the building. "I'll check to see what they're up to." Karl slipped in through the back door and got a view of the entire dining area before someone asked what he was doing in the kitchen. He didn't see Nemo or the woman anywhere.

"Sorry," said Karl in English. "My mistake." Five minutes later he found Patton's phone taped to the running board of a semitruck in the parking lot.

"Bitch thinks she's smarter than us," said Karl, slamming the door as he slid back into the passenger seat of the van. "If she sent the phone west then she's going east, but she's got a hell of a lead on us now."

They pulled back onto the highway, heading east, and Erich gunned it to eighty.

"Slow down," said Karl. "The last thing we need is to get pulled over by the police."

"Do you think the assassin is with her?" said Erich.

"Well he's not locked in the toolshed," said Karl, "so for the time being I think we have to assume so."

When they had crossed back into North Carolina, Erich insisted on pulling into a rest area. Karl decided he could delay no longer and took out the burner phone to make an uncomfortable call. Even though they had broken protocol already that morning, not least by killing a member of law enforcement, this was one protocol Karl was not willing to suspend. In the event of failure, ring the home office.

Once Karl explained the situation, the voice on the other end of the line did not shout, but it nonetheless made Karl's blood run cold. He, of all people, knew just how ruthless his boss could be and he wanted nothing more than to make this right before he got called in from the field.

"They can't use computers or cell phones," said the voice. "He's smart enough to know we would track them. There's only one place in the world to do what they need to do without going online. If I can think of anyone else to send I will but you and your idiot companion represent the whole of our field operatives at the moment, which is exactly why this operation needs to succeed. I'll let you know the details as soon as we make a decision here."

The voice explained where Karl and Erich needed to go next. They would need to dump their weapons, of course, and the voice told Karl that, if things played out as it suspected they would, he might need to improvise. The voice signed off in the usual manner and Karl dropped the phone into a cupholder.

"Where do we go?" said Erich.

"Closest international airport," said Karl.

"Are they calling us home?"

"Sounds like we might be going to London," said Karl.

"Looks like from here the closest major airport is Atlanta," said Erich, looking at the map on his phone. "Plenty of flights from there."

———

Jean Simpson had just turned off the lights in her office when the phone rang. She considered ignoring it—anyone important would call on her cell phone. But Jean had been raised with manners, and that meant answering a ringing phone no matter how likely it was a student complaining about a grade or wanting to have a conference outside office hours.

"Jean, it's Peter Byerly. I've been looking a little closer at that book you left with me and I've found something . . . well, something a little disturbing to be honest."

"Funny you should say that," said Jean. "I've been digging into Ingrid Weiss and Columbia House and I've found several disturbing things. Would you like to meet for coffee at the Rathskeller?"

"I don't drink coffee," said Peter. "But I'll be there in ten minutes."

The Rathskeller was Ridgefield's rebellion against Starbucks—a throwback to the time when coffee shops near college campuses were more about poetry and folk music than lattes and cappuccinos. Located in the basement of a building on the strip across from the main entrance to campus, it had dark corners, cheap coffee, spotty cell service, and no Wi-Fi. It was the best place in Ridgefield to have a chance of spotting the socially anxious Peter Byerly in public, and Jean knew that. The two of them sat in a booth in a back corner where Jean sipped a coffee and Peter ignored a mug of tepid tea.

"I don't think this book belonged to your grandfather," said Peter, indicating the volume that sat on the table between them, "and I don't think anyone rescued it from a charity shop or bought it from a rare book dealer. I think somebody stole it from the National Library of the Czech Republic in Prague."

"That's a very specific suspicion," said Jean.

"Tell me what you found out about Weiss."

"Nothing concrete," said Jean. "Just a pastiche of oddities that may or may not add up to something."

"Oddities like what?"

"For starters, she lives on Döbereinerstrasse in a neighborhood of Munich called Obermenzing."

"And other than a chance for you to show off your German pronunciation, what's disturbing about that?"

"I went to a conference on art forgery once and the mantra was *never take anything at face value.* Always look below the surface. So, I looked below the surface of Ingrid Weiss's address and she lives in a district that was popular with Nazis back in the day. And Döbereinerstrasse wasn't always called that. During the war it was Hermann Göring Strasse. Göring lived in the neighborhood for a while, although I can't find his exact address."

"Surely there are plenty of neighborhoods in Germany once inhabited by Nazis," said Peter. "And plenty of streets that once had—shall we say, politically incorrect names."

"Of course, but that's just the beginning. She runs an organization called Columbia House, but other than giving away old books, I can't figure out what they do. The website says something vague about international business concerns but the only mentions I can find elsewhere are about their charitable work returning books stolen by the Nazis."

"Seems reasonable that those activities would get the press."

"True, and I did track down several dozen stories about books being returned. It looks like they've been doing it for a year or so."

"Then what's the problem?"

"I read about forty or fifty of these articles, and almost half of them include this same sentence, with the exact same wording—'Columbia House has returned over a thousand volumes of literature and academia usurped by Nazi Germany to their rightful owners.'"

"That's a strange sentence," said Peter.

"It's a *very* strange sentence," said Jean. "And it turns up again and again in these articles. I think every time Columbia House returns a book, they send a copy of a press release to the local papers. It's like they're more interested in getting publicity than in actually reuniting people with lost heirlooms. And if they have really returned a thousand books, how come I could only find a few dozen articles? I will say this, they seem to return books all over the world—Germany, the UK, a woman on the Upper East Side of New York City."

"Let me guess. You called the New Yorker."

"She said she received a book a couple of months ago that supposedly belonged to her great-uncle. She never thought to question the story, but she called me back an hour later to say she found some marginalia in the book that was definitely *not* in her great-uncle's handwriting."

"He might have loaned the book to someone or bought it second-hand."

"Maybe," said Jean, "but there seems to be a pattern here. And there's one more thing."

"What's that?"

"The name of the company. Columbia House."

"The same as that outfit that used to get you to buy records, right?"

"That's what everyone in our generation thinks of, but there's another antecedent. Columbia-Haus was one of the first Nazi concentration camps. It's not well known because it was only open for three years from 1933 to 1936, before they tore it down to make way for an expansion of the Berlin airport."

"So you think Ingrid Weiss is living on a Nazi street in a Nazi neighborhood and running a company with a Nazi name in order to send people books for free that they actually have no right to?"

"Sounds ridiculous, I know."

"There's a narrative that explains it all," said Peter. "You just haven't discovered it yet. But there's something else that's bothering me."

"Besides the fact that my book was stolen from the national library in Prague?"

"Oh right, that," said Peter, sliding the book across the table to Jean. "Look at page 157 and at the rear endpaper. In both cases you'll see someone has tried to sand off a library stamp, but the ink has gone too deep into the paper to be so easily erased. If you look at the verso of those pages you can just make out the stamp of the Public and University Library of Czechoslovakia—what's now the National Library of the Czech Republic."

"Maybe it ended up there after the Nazis stole it from my grandfather."

"The stamp has an acquisition date—1921," said Peter.

"So it's been there since it was published."

"Until someone walked off with it."

"I doubt that was my grandfather," said Jean.

"Seems unlikely," said Peter.

"What was the other thing bothering you?"

"It's just this," said Peter. "I know the Nazis stole a lot of books. But so far as I know, they didn't stock them away in salt mines like they did with artwork."

"I thought of that, too," said Jean. "There's only one thing the Nazis are famous for when it comes to books."

Peter smiled and finally took a sip of his tea, then nodded to Jean as he said, "Burning them."

"I don't know why I even care about this," said Jean Simpson, draining the rest of her coffee cup and pushing back her chair. "I should just mail the book back to the library in Prague and let them deal with Ingrid Weiss—if she really is a book thief."

"Yes," said Peter, "that's exactly what you ought to do. It's probably no more than petty theft and someone trying to inflate their charitable résumé. Just send the book back and let it lie."

"Is that what you would do?"

"Absolutely not."

"You'd be on the next plane to Prague."

"It's a lovely city."

"Well, not everyone has Peter Byerly's taste for bibliographic mysteries."

"Not everyone," said Peter with a smile, "but you do."

"Exams are over in a couple of days," said Jean.

"And you go to Europe every May."

"Vienna this year," said Jean. "Two weeks including a conference on the art of Prussia."

"Sounds delightful. And I assume you already know how far Vienna is from Prague?"

"Four hours by train," said Jean. "And the same distance to Munich."

———

Patton couldn't decide whether to be angry, frightened, or relieved. If Nemo had left for good, maybe she could put this whole crazy affair behind her. But if Fritz and Franz thought she had the Enigma sheet, her life might still be in danger. And how did she know this place was secure? How did she know Nemo wasn't working with Fritz and Franz? How did she know they wouldn't be back any minute to finish her off and bury her in the middle of nowhere where no one would ever find her?

She felt in the bottom of the sleeping bag and was relieved to discover the guns were still there. She shoved Nemo's in her belt and held the Beretta in front of her, the safety flicked off, as she made her way toward the ruined house. A half-moon gave just enough pale light for her to find her way to the remains of the front steps where she sat waiting and trying to decide if she would be pleased or concerned if she saw headlights coming up the track from the road. An hour later, when she saw just that, two white lights bobbing up and down and growing gradually larger, she pointed the Beretta toward the lights and waited.

A minute later the gray Taurus pulled to a stop in front of her, and Nemo leaned out the window.

"Miss me?" he said.

"You might have told me you were going," she said.

"Hadn't really thought it through before you fell asleep. Hop in."

"Where are we going?"

"Flight to London leaves from Atlanta at seven tomorrow morning," said Nemo. "I've got coffee, fried chicken, and two first-class tickets bought with cash from a very happy travel agent in Wilkesboro."

"I didn't know there was still such a thing as travel agents."

"In Wilkesboro there is," said Nemo. "I also found a nice lake to dump everything we're not taking on the plane."

"Even Jasper's Enigma machine?" said Patton wistfully.

"Sorry," said Nemo. "No loose ends." Patton hated to think of the result of all Jasper's work rusting away on the bottom of some muddy lake, but she understood.

"I'll bet a mysterious assassin like you who lives his whole life in the shadows has no idea where to get good fried chicken," said Patton, putting the safety back on her pistol and climbing into the car. But she was wrong. It was the best fried chicken she'd ever had.

HRULL JLDXA SVRCV DXVSW TKPUH WT

SECTION TWO:
BUCKINGHAMSHIRE

IV

Ingrid Weiss sat in front of a wall of computer screens in the basement of her home on Döbereinerstrasse. Some monitored websites, others roamed the Internet looking for specific words and phrases, others focused on the task at hand—fixing the debacle of Alta Vista. It should have been a simple operation—a hired hand takes care of the risky bit, a pair of Columbia House "security personnel" retrieve the document, and no one is the wiser. Now she and her associates had to deal with the brutal murder of a member of law enforcement, a pair of runaways, and no sign of the document. If this Patton Harcourt woman had the paper, if she knew what it was, and if Nemo had teamed up with her as Karl suspected, the two might go to Bletchley Park to try to decode the message and they could be intercepted there. But that was a lot of ifs. If Harcourt didn't have the paper, the entire operation might have been a waste of time and money. The important thing now was to get Karl and Erich safely out of the US. This would all be so much easier if they had more money. They could hire more personnel and dispatch them to the UK to wait for the runaways, they could purchase Jasper Fleming's house and tear it apart brick by brick looking for that damn paper. But therein lay the catch-22 of *Projekt Alchemie*—once they completed the project they would have almost endless money, but the project might fail due to lack of funds at the moment.

Gottfried Bergman had been tapping away on a keyboard since he had arrived at Döbereinerstrasse an hour earlier. But airlines were hard to hack into.

"If they are headed for Bletchley, there are five flights leaving North Carolina for the UK tonight," he said. "If we assume they are flying to Heathrow, that eliminates two, but those incoming flights are still spread over two terminals. And of course they could drive to Atlanta or Washington and have dozens of flights to choose from. Plus, he might have enough bankroll to fly privately. In any case, the earliest I can get our team out of the US is tomorrow morning after that detour into Tennessee."

"Do we have pictures of them?" said Ingrid.

"Only her," said Gottfried. "He has no name, no online presence, nothing. As you recall, that's the reason we hired him."

"What's the worry?" said Dietrich Mueller, who had arrived from Amsterdam just moments earlier but had kept abreast of the situation via encrypted text message on his way from the airport. "We know where they're going, so we go there and intercept them."

"We *think* we know where they *might* be going," spat Ingrid. "Just like we *think* they *might* have the paper. We've made mistakes by jumping to conclusions before. Besides, if they take an overnight flight, they'll be hours ahead of our boys." She kicked a trash can across the basement, the clattering echoing against the stone walls. "Fucking Erich! I swear to God if I lay eyes on him again I'll rip that idiot's lungs out." She picked up a pistol from the table and fired two rounds into the trash can.

"Ingrid, calm down," said Dietrich.

"Don't fucking tell me to calm down," said Ingrid, slapping Dietrich hard across the face with the back of her hand. "I'll calm down when I'm goddamn good and ready."

Dietrich took a deep breath and a step away from Ingrid. "Look," he said, "if we're wrong about Bletchley, we'll have lost them anyway. And if they do go there, who knows how long it will take them to crack the code. I say send Erich and Karl to England."

"Maybe we should go to Bletchley ourselves," said Gottfried.

"And fight it out with a professional assassin?" said Dietrich.

"What do you think, Eva?" said Ingrid, her anger suddenly evaporated.

Eva Klein was the quiet member of the group—always watching and taking notes in her large brown leather folio, but rarely speaking. Ingrid suspected Eva was smarter than the other two put together. Her ability to analyze a situation and come up with the best course of action had saved Columbia House on more than one occasion. She stepped up to Dietrich and examined the mark on his face where Ingrid had slapped him, running a finger gently along his jawline.

"First, we need to stay here and watch the boards. Our final destination is almost certainly in Germany; our safe space is in Germany—now is not the time to leave the country, especially on a hunch. And Dietrich is right—we don't want to get into a firefight with Nemo. We hired him because he knows how to kill people. But that doesn't mean we can't keep an eye on Bletchley."

"I can make some calls to . . . sympathetic friends in the UK who might help us," said Dietrich.

"As far as Erich and Karl are concerned," said Eva, "even if they can't be traced back to us, it's dangerous to leave them in the US with a murder investigation going on. If they have to fly back to Europe, they may as well fly to London and see if they can pick up the trail. Book the flight, Gottfried, but keep working your magic. And send them the picture of the woman. Don't worry, they have to use a credit card sometime."

But of course, they didn't have to use a credit card. At least not one Gottfried Bergman would recognize. Nemo still had a few thousand dollars in cash. True, Patton's ticket had her real name on it, but even if they did hack the flight manifest—which was no easy feat—it would be no surprise they were headed to England. Once they got there, Nemo could rent a car under any of six different identities for which he carried credit cards and passports. They would never trace him. He had practiced disappearing for the past thirty years.

———

"Are you sure first class was a good idea?" said Patton, after their elegant dinner had been cleared away. The last time she had flown had been in the back of an army transport from Frankfurt to Washington.

"Trust me," said Nemo, "it's easier to hide in first class. And you don't get hassled by immigration when you have a first-class ticket and you look like this." Nemo had bought a suit, shirt, and dress shoes when he had gone out for plane tickets and fried chicken, and after shaving and washing his hair in the showers at the first-class lounge in Atlanta, he looked like the world's blandest businessman. He had made Patton buy a similar outfit in the airport, with cash of course. The first-class seats were comfortable, her business suit—not so much.

"So how do you break this Enigma Code?" said Nemo, sliding the plastic sleeve containing the yellowing paper onto his tray table.

"You aren't worried they're going to find us?" said Patton. She knew that airline manifests and customs and immigration databases were difficult, though not impossible, to hack into, but she still worried about arriving at such a public place as Heathrow. Nemo had boarded the plane as Grigore Florinescu of Romania and would rent the car as Oliver Moores of Darlington, North Yorkshire. Patton had gotten a glimpse of the bundle of passports and other papers in the black knapsack Nemo had carried on to the plane. ("In my business you should have as many identities as possible," he had said before zipping the bag back up.) But none of their precautions—not getting rid of Patton's phone or using only cash or Nemo's constantly switching identities—really made any difference. If Fritz and Franz, and whomever they worked for, knew what Patton and Nemo had found, they knew where they were going.

"They *will* find us," said Nemo simply. "And if we decode this message before that happens, we'll have a distinct advantage in our next encounter."

"It sure would be easier to do this online," said Patton, "but if you think whoever is after us is watching the decrypt website, then I guess we'll have to do it the old-fashioned way."

"And what is the old-fashioned way?"

"First we need to come up with a crib. Not so easy to do seventy years after the message was sent."

"A crib?"

"It's a guess at a piece of decoded text. Lots of German messages began with the weather or ended with 'Heil Hitler'—others were a lot harder to guess a crib for."

"So how do we even start?"

"Let me have that paper," said Patton. Nemo passed it from his cubicle to hers. "OK, we know some things about this message. According to the letterhead, it was received by someone in the H-Sonderkommando division of the SS. I have no idea what that is, and you won't let me go online to find out, but it's something. We also know it was probably received at Dachau on the day the Americans liberated the camp. That's April 29, 1945. I learned that from Jasper. He was there."

"But couldn't Jasper have picked it up anytime?"

"He told me the only time he ever watched a German die up close was when he shot a boy in an SS uniform just outside the gates of Dachau. It haunted him—he was obsessed with everything to do with that day. I think that's why he wanted to crack this code."

"Why didn't he just go online and do it like you said?"

"Well, first of all, who knows when he started working on it. It could have been decades ago when there was no Internet. And secondly, I couldn't even get Jasper to use email or a cell phone. He was a major technophobe."

"So you have a probable date and location—does that help?"

"It might, but not as much as this." Patton pointed to the two words barely visible in faint pencil at the top of the page.

"Projekt Alchemie," read Nemo. "What does that mean?"

"If we're lucky, that's the beginning of our crib," said Patton. "Maybe before the Americans showed up, that teenage SS officer was decoding the message."

"Yes, but what does it *mean*? In English, I mean."

"I don't know a lot of German," said Patton, "but I'd say it means that the Nazis were working on alchemy. Or at least someone in the SS was."

"Alchemy?" said Nemo. "You mean some medieval nonsense about turning lead into gold?"

"Yeah, only I doubt the Nazis would call it nonsense. A lot of the higher-ups believed in all sorts of bizarre stuff—witchcraft, parapsychology, the Holy Grail, the lost city of Atlantis. Didn't you ever see *Raiders of the Lost Ark?*"

"I don't get out much," said Nemo.

"Well, it wouldn't surprise me if the Nazis fooled around with alchemy."

"And you think they discovered how to turn lead into gold?" said Nemo, a hint of sarcasm in his voice.

"I doubt that," said Patton, "but it would explain why someone is so eager to get their hands on this message."

"Look, I may have led a . . . different sort of life, but even I know that turning lead into gold is nonsense. It *is* nonsense, right?"

"Hey, I'm no scientist," said Patton.

"And what exactly are you?" said Nemo. "Because I know you're something more than a small-town librarian who isn't a scientist."

Patton smiled and turned her attention back to the Enigma message, but Nemo wasn't done asking questions.

"And how is it you know so much about decoding secret messages from seventy years ago?"

"I could tell you," said Patton, looking Nemo directly in the eye, "but then I'd have to kill you."

That sentiment had come close to being the truth, thought Patton, recalling the day toward the end of her graduate studies when she had been called into an empty office in the basement of the university library and met two men in dark suits. They sat behind a table and asked her to sit down. Out of curiosity more than fear or obligation or the intimidation they seemed to be trying to wield, she did.

"Patton Jackson Harcourt," said the man on the left. "A good military name."

"I come from a good military family," said Patton. "We're like that guy in *Forrest Gump*—you know, the one whose family has lost sons in every American war?"

"And you are a talented mathematician with a particular interest in . . . shall we call it the history of military codebreaking."

"A casual interest. I went to a conference last summer."

"And distinguished yourself according to . . ."

"Dr. Ruth Drinkwater," said the man on the right, entering the conversation for the first time.

"Ruthie? She was great. What she knows about Enigma is remarkable."

"Yes, Enigma," said the first man. "You subsequently wrote a thesis on the postwar work of Alan Turing, one of the key figures in breaking Enigma."

"That's right," said Patton. The Englishman who helped break Enigma and basically invented the field of modern computer science had become a source of fascination for Patton ever since she'd first heard about him in an undergraduate history course. Two years later she decided to write her master's thesis in mathematics on aspects of Turing's work. While hardly an expert on either Turing or cracking Enigma, she certainly knew a lot more about both than the average graduate student.

"We were particularly intrigued by the idea you suggested that Turing's approach to both computer science and codebreaking could be applied to cracking modern computer-encrypted messages."

"You read my thesis," said Patton. "How thoughtful. If you count my adviser, that makes three of us."

"You also," said the man on the left, "checked out the first two volumes of *Military Cryptanalytics* from the university library."

"They made for great bedtime reading," said Patton. "Too bad the third volume was so heavily redacted it wasn't worth publishing. I guess you guys had something to do with that."

"I'll be frank with you, Miss Harcourt. We've been watching you for a long time and we like what we see. You're bright, tenacious, inventive, and growing up in a family like yours, you must understand what it means to serve your country."

"Who are you guys?" said Patton, leaning back in her chair and crossing her legs.

"We could tell you," said the man on the left with a smile, "but then we'd have to kill you."

"CIA, right?" said Patton. "I've heard about these little recruiting sessions."

"Are you ready to serve your country, Miss Harcourt?"

"In the CIA?" said Patton. "You haven't researched my family very well if you think they're going to let their precious little girl go into civilian work, no matter how important to national security. I'm sure whatever you have in mind for me would be fascinating, but I'm afraid it was always going to be military intelligence for me. Thanks for asking, though."

"If you change your mind . . ." said the man on the right, sliding a business card across the table. And the interview was over. Back in her apartment Patton looked at the business card. It bore a ten-digit phone number and nothing else. She memorized the number and burned the card in a saucer, washing the ashes down the kitchen sink.

"OK," said Nemo. "You won't tell me who you are, then let me guess. You're probably ex-military judging by how you kept your cool under fire, but you're smart and you know something about cryptanalysis, so I'm guessing either military intelligence or CIA or NSA. If you were former CIA or NSA, given what's happened in the last few hours, more than Fritz and Franz would be following us, so I'd go with military, and given that you're named after two famous generals, you probably come from an army family, so that would mean army intelligence, most likely a signals intelligence analyst. But since you're below retirement age and you took a job as a fucking librarian in the middle of nowhere, something must have gone wrong out there in the big bad world of warfare."

Patton could feel a cold sweat breaking out on her forehead. She'd spent the last ten years hiding everything Nemo had just said from everyone she met. He had known her less than twenty-four hours and had deduced everything. She tried to hold his stare but couldn't. As she dropped her eyes to the paper, Nemo smiled in a way that revealed a softness under the rough, loner exterior.

"You're not the only person who's good at figuring things out," he said. "I would have made a good intelligence officer."

"I didn't," said Patton.

"Want to tell me why?" said Nemo.

"Not particularly," said Patton.

"Then tell me about your army family. It's a long flight."

"I want to work on this crib," said Patton.

"Suit yourself," said Nemo.

Patton sat in silence for a moment watching as the letters on the page in front of her swam around, refusing to coalesce into anything that made sense.

"My dad called us a friendly fire family," she said in a low voice. "Boy, was that ever a stupid expression. Friendly fire. Trust me, there was nothing friendly about the misguided 105-millimeter Howitzer shell that killed my uncle in the Iron Triangle northwest of Saigon. Some poor bastard who hadn't slept in three days transposed two digits in the firing coordinates. And friendship certainly doesn't describe the relationship between my grandfather and the .50 caliber machine-gun fire that a P-47 Thunderbolt sprayed all over the unmarked train the Germans were using to evacuate Allied prisoners from their interrogation center in Diez after the Allies crossed the Rhine. The fire was a little more friendly to my great-grandfather. He just lost his leg in the Argonne in 1918 when friendly shells rained down on his battalion for a few hours before they managed to send a carrier pigeon telling the artillery to cease fire. Dad never told any stories about the Civil War, but I found a relative who died at Antietam—knowing our luck he was probably hit by some fellow Union soldier who didn't know how to fire his musket."

"So after all that you decided to join the army."

"That's right," said Patton. "And even though I had a master's degree, I didn't opt for officer training. In my family nothing but standard enlistment would suffice."

"But you're not in the army anymore," said Nemo. "You're not even working in the private sector where you could probably make six figures.

You're hiding out in the hills of North Carolina and you weren't that surprised someone with a sniper's rifle found you. You want to tell me what happened?"

"I do not."

"Friendly fire, perhaps?"

"Why should I tell you anything?" said Patton. "All I know about you is that you're a professional assassin hired to kill a friend of mine. That hardly qualifies you to know things I haven't told my own family."

"'Assassin' is a harsh word," said Nemo. "I've never taken out a public figure."

"So you're just an ordinary murderer," said Patton.

"I'm a businessman," said Nemo.

"You're an emotionless robot from what I can tell," said Patton. "Now leave me alone so I can work on this crib."

But Nemo wasn't emotionless. Emotion, after all, had launched his career; emotion had revealed his peculiar talent. True, he did not dwell on the past, did not dredge up those emotions. He didn't see the point. But being called an emotionless robot made him want to protest that he had felt emotions more deeply and more horribly than most. At first, watching Patton hunched over, scribbling, he couldn't understand why he felt this way. Why should he care what she thought? But then he considered how insulated he had been from real human contact for so many years. He had run a lot, and hidden a lot, but he had never done either with a companion, always alone. Patton seemed to waken some latent humanity in him, and he wasn't sure he liked that. He reclined his seat, leaned back, closed his eyes, and allowed himself, carefully, to return to that night it had all begun—the last time he had cared about anyone other than himself. He indulged in this exercise occasionally—the controlled reliving of those events. He reasoned that if he remembered them on purpose, with his emotional guard up, it might prevent their rearing up unbidden at some inconvenient moment, might prevent flashbacks and nightmares and cold sweat at three in the morning. Sometimes it worked. Usually it didn't.

Foster care had both ruined and given him his life. No one ever bothered to tell him what happened to his parents and he never asked. He could not remember a time before a new family every six months, a new school, a new set of problems. When the Gerrard family began to use the word "adoption," he dared to allow himself to love Jack. Jack who might one day be his brother. Jack who had been through as many foster homes as he had, maybe more. Nemo had a name in those days. He didn't know if it had been his original name or if one of his foster families had bestowed it on him, but he had loved hearing Jack call that name out, laughing as they played hide-and-seek or simply chased each other around the thin patch of dirt that passed for a yard.

"Dexter!"

He could still hear the joy in Jack's voice over the thrum of the airplane. "Dexter!" And then had come the night when Jack called to him in a different voice. Not a voice of joy and wonder and delight. A voice a ten-year-old should never need to use. The voice of fear and confusion and pain.

Patton stared at the paper in front of her and did her best to ignore the man beside her. She had just wanted to make some nice pastries to take to Jasper and now here she was sitting in a first-class airline seat next to a cold-blooded killer trying to decrypt an Enigma message. She couldn't believe her life had come to this. And she certainly couldn't believe that the Nazis ever mastered alchemy.

———

APRIL 1938

"I have served my time," said the man as Helmut gripped his arm and dragged him into the street. "I served in the Columbia-Haus concentration camp for two years."

"Perhaps the Reichsführer feels that two years is not enough," said Helmut.

He threw the man into the back of the Kübelwagen, climbed in after him, and instructed the driver to proceed. As the man shrank from him,

Helmut relaxed. It had been barely more than a year since he stood in the crowd listening to Himmler speak and already he had achieved his goal. He had not only met the Reichsführer but Himmler had accepted his offer of personal services. Helmut now had the honor to arrest this weasel in the name of the great Heinrich Himmler, his first mission for which his orders came directly from the Reichsführer himself.

Heinz Kurschildgen should have known better, thought Helmut. Even before he met Heinrich Himmler he had already languished in prison for defrauding investors who believed his claims to be able to turn sand into gold. He would pay the entire German war reparations with this manufactured gold, he had claimed, the filthy liar. But he had only succeeded in turning a quarter of a million marks of influential people's money into an eighteen-month stay in a Berlin prison. And then he decided to try convincing Heinrich Himmler, the head of the SS, that he could manufacture petrol from water. Imagine, Heinz had said, the power of a fighting force with an endless supply of inexpensive fuel. The mere gall of it turned Helmut's stomach. If he had been there, he thought, he would have put a stop to the whole thing.

But Himmler, in his great open-mindedness, had believed the huckster, had been among those who set him up in a laboratory in Berlin. Helmut had not yet worked his way into Himmler's inner circle when the great man naturally detected the fraud and sentenced Heinz to three well-deserved years in the Columbia-Haus concentration camp. Heinz had been released after only two. *What mercy the Reich shows*, thought Helmut.

"What does he have against me?" said Heinz. "So I am a failure as an alchemist. You can't blame me for trying. I only wanted to help the Reich."

"You only wanted to help yourself," said Helmut, jabbing Heinz in the gut with the butt of his rifle. "And now you'll be helping yourself back in the concentration camp. It's better than you deserve if you ask me."

Heinz could not speak for a moment after the blow from the rifle, but as the car raced through the streets of Berlin, he eventually recovered his breath. "I don't understand," he said, "what Herr Himmler has against failed alchemists." This time Helmut aimed the rifle stock at

Heinz's head and put an end to the conversation. Twenty minutes later, he delivered the unconscious vermin to the gate of Columbia-Haus. Riding back to Himmler's office he thought that he knew the answer to Heinz's question. Himmler hated failed alchemists because he dreamed of finding a successful one. Failure was a sign of impure blood, thought Helmut. But if ever the Reichsführer could find a pure-blooded alchemist, he might hope for success.

Of course, as he thought this, Helmut had not yet heard of a man named Karl Malchus.

―――――

Patton racked her brain trying to remember everything she had learned about cracking Enigma at that summer course at Harvard years ago. Mostly she remembered the cute English girl who sat at the desk next to hers. Ruthie's accent had almost made Patton swoon the first time she heard it. And Ruthie had the same enthusiasm for Alan Turing's work that Patton did. Ruthie told Patton the end of Turing's story—that he had been prosecuted for homosexuality, sentenced to chemical sterilization, and subsequently committed suicide. Patton had been horrified that such a brilliant man, who had been so essential in the defeat of Nazism, had been treated so inhumanely. But for that month at Harvard, she didn't dwell on Turing's fate. She dwelled mostly on Ruthie, whose lips had been soft and who had been innocent, at least at the start of the course. It had been a lovely summer—nothing serious but lots of fun. But soft lips and an English accent and lost innocence had also distracted Patton from paying attention to the coursework. Luckily, Ruthie had known more about Enigma than the professor did, and Patton could recall lying together on a narrow dormitory bed, the warm summer air wafting in the open window and carrying a hint of the sea, while Ruthie told her about cribs and loops and menus, about programming the Bombe and using the checking machine. Such pillow talk. But Patton had learned more on those nights with Ruthie's soft body pressed against hers than she did in the classroom during the day.

She copied out the encrypted text from the aging sheet of SS stationery onto the first page of a Moleskine notebook. Nemo had given her some cash to shop for necessities at the airport—the notebook, pencils, and a German phrase book from the bookstore in the international terminal. She examined Jasper's paper closely, in case it held any other hints, but all she could see in the dim light of the plane was the printed heading "SS H-Sonderkommando" and the barely visible words "Projekt Alchemie." That, surely, was the place to start. If that phrase appeared near the start of the message and she could guess another word or two, she might come up with a workable crib.

The Allies trying to crack Enigma took advantage of the one weakness in the machine the Nazis used to encode their messages—Enigma never encoded a letter as itself. So, if she compared a possible crib to the cipher text and any of the letters matched, the crib was wrong. What else had Ruthie told her?

"The Nazis used the letter 'X' to indicate a space between words," she had said as she lazily traced circles around Patton's breast with her index finger. "The Enigma machine didn't have numbers, so they had to spell them out," as she twined her legs with Patton's. "The messages were terse—like telegrams. No unnecessary words." And then they had proceeded to activities that also required no unnecessary words. Patton flushed slightly with the memory, but Nemo didn't notice. His eyes were closed, though she doubted he was asleep.

Nemo had been fifteen the first time Jack cried out in the night. He had assumed it was a bad dream—foster kids, in Nemo's experience, had a lot of bad dreams. But then he realized Jack was not in the room. Nemo had loved that room before that night. It reminded him of a room he had seen on an old TV show two or three homes ago—*Leave It to Beaver*. Two twin beds with a bedside table in between holding a lamp shaped like the *Millennium Falcon* from *Star Wars*—a detail that *did* differ from Wally and Beaver's room. A desk under the window, bookshelves on one wall, an actual chest full of toys at the foot of the bed. Even a view out the window of that tiny, dusty backyard that seemed so luxurious. That room, as much as the presence of Jack and the bedtime stories of Mrs. Gerrard, made him feel that this home might be different.

He still had the scars, and could still remember the bruises, that marked his passage through his previous foster homes. He had been whipped with a belt on the backs of his legs. He had been thrown down a flight of uncarpeted stairs. He had been slapped across the face so hard that his vision was blurred for two days. Adults, in Nemo's experience, existed to wage war on children. Lucky for them, every time Nemo had neared his breaking point and vowed to fight back, he had been removed from one home and placed in another, to begin the cycle of hope and disappointment all over. But now, in this room from a television show where the worst thing that ever happened was a slight misunderstanding, what could possibly go wrong?

That night, when Nemo woke to the sound of cries, Jack's bed stood empty. Perfectly made. "Dexter" had fallen asleep early, while Jack was still watching TV, and apparently Jack had never come to bed. And then the cries quieted without fading away altogether, and Dexter lay shivering under the covers despite the warmth of the summer night. A few minutes later, Jack crept into the room, tears streaking his face and a bruise blooming on his cheek. He wore no shirt and clutched a pair of torn pajama pants around his waist. Afraid, Dexter pretended to sleep as the boy he wanted for a brother sobbed quietly in the bed three feet away.

Two nights later Dexter awoke when only the moon lit the room and saw Jack's bed empty again. This time, he would not be a coward, he told himself, but he made it no farther than the door of Mr. Gerrard's bedroom—after that night he would never call him "Dad" again. The door stood slightly ajar and Dexter could see exactly what was happening on the bed, what Mr. Gerrard was doing to Jack. Though he did not have the words to describe or explain what he saw, the look on Jack's face told him all he needed to know. And then Jack saw him and flashed a warning with his eyes. Jack, the ten-year-old, was trying to protect fifteen-year-old Dexter. And Dexter knew that was wrong, but he crept back to his room and lay awake the rest of the night. Jack did not return.

Mrs. Gerrard was visiting her sister in Ohio and when Mr. Gerrard announced she would be staying another week, Dexter made up his mind. Jack would never have to warn him again. He spent the day preparing. While Mr. Gerrard mowed the lawn and Jack watched TV, he gathered what he needed, stowing much of it in a backpack under his bed. He rehearsed every move in his mind over and over, making Gerrard react differently each time and adjusting his plans accordingly. It became a puzzle, almost a game, and Dexter relished the challenge. The motive, strong as it was, began to take a back seat to the planning.

In the end, it was simple. Mr. Gerrard was like any other bully. He didn't expect anyone to fight back. And he certainly didn't expect to feel the sharpened blade of a carving knife slicing across his throat as he sat at the dinner table. Dexter had gotten up to clear the dishes, as he always did. He pulled on a pair of rubber gloves, slipped the knife out from under the dish towel where he had left it that afternoon, and looked right into Jack's eyes as he stepped up behind Mr. Gerrard. *This is for you,* his look said. *Because I love you and because this man is never going to hurt you again.* He gave Jack a nod that said, *Look away* just before he cut Gerrard's throat. Jack understood.

Dexter cut deeply and stepped back quickly. Gerrard hardly made a sound. He tried to turn in his chair but slid to the floor. Not until his head hit the tile with a thud did his eyes catch sight of Dexter. "That was for Jack," Dexter said as the ten-year-old left the room. And maybe Patton was right. Maybe he was an emotionless robot. Because, as Mr. Gerrard breathed his last, a look of surprise and incomprehension still on his face, Dexter felt nothing.

Patton started awake as the plane banked toward its final approach to Heathrow. She had not meant to fall asleep. In the next cubicle, Nemo was just finishing his tea. She flashed back over what had happened since yesterday morning and any hint of an appetite left her.

"Any luck?" said Nemo cheerfully, nodding to the notebook on Patton's lap.

"Maybe," said Patton. She had relied on vague memories of a

smattering of German picked up when she had been stationed in Stuttgart and the tourist phrase book they had bought at the airport. "I found a lot of phrases that didn't work because they encoded individual letters as themselves." She hadn't explained this aspect of Enigma to Nemo before, but she plowed on. "'Project Alchemy Completed,' 'Project Alchemy Abandoned,' 'Project Alchemy Failed,' none of those worked."

"So what did work?"

"It seems pretty unlikely that this is a good crib, but the only guess I had that passes the test is 'Project Alchemy Successful.'"

"If that's right, it would explain why people are willing to hire me and shoot you in order to get that paper."

"Yeah, but it's ridiculous," said Patton. "You can't turn lead into gold, everyone knows that."

"Two hundred years ago everyone knew you couldn't fly, yet here we are."

"You told me you thought it was nonsense—the idea that the Nazis mastered alchemy."

"I do think it's nonsense. But it doesn't matter what I think. What matters is what Fritz and Franz and the people who hired them think."

A flight attendant leaned over to remove the detritus of Nemo's tea and told them both to put away their tray tables and raise their seats to the upright position.

"Of course," said Nemo with a smile. "We certainly want to be uncomfortable in case of a crash."

"Should you call attention to yourself like that?" whispered Patton after the attendant had moved on.

"I promise you people use that line on him all the time. He'll forget me by the time he's at the back of the cabin. But I did distract him from looking at the notebook that has the words 'Project Alchemy Successful' underlined about six times."

"I guess you're pretty good at manipulating people," said Patton, wondering to what extent Nemo had successfully manipulated her over the past day and a half.

"It's not exactly manipulation," said Nemo. "It's just directing their attention where you want it to go—like a magician. And considering what else you wrote down, I thought some misdirection would be wise."

Nemo nodded to the notebook in Patton's lap and pointed to the two words written at the bottom of the page. Two words she had guessed might end the message.

"Heil Hitler."

———

Erich and Karl couldn't believe their luck. Because of their foray into Tennessee, they were too late to catch any overnight flights to London, but Gottfried had booked them on a morning flight out of Atlanta. When they had arrived at the gate, the woman whose picture Gottfried had sent them had been standing in the boarding line beside a man who, they decided, must be the assassin.

"I'm still sore where that bastard hit me with the tranquilizer dart," hissed Erich. "He's gonna pay for that."

"Shut up," said Karl. "We can't let them see us." He made a quick call to headquarters to relay the good news as he and Erich lurked at the far end of the boarding gate, their backs to Patton and Nemo. Remaining hidden from their quarry had proved easy. Nemo and Patton disappeared into the first-class cabin; Karl and Erich were flying economy. "The class system will do all the work for us," said Karl.

They had gotten off the flight when the first-class passengers were already in the immigration lines, and still managed to spot Nemo and Patton disappearing into the restrooms in the terminal. They hid behind newspapers and Erich didn't realize what had happened until Karl nudged him and nodded toward the door. A dark-haired man in a Versace suit and Gucci sunglasses strode toward the exit carrying only a shiny new leather weekend bag. Behind him a short-haired blond in jeans and a ball cap dragged a battered suitcase.

"What about them?" said Erich.

"That's them," said Karl, tossing down his newspaper and getting up.

"They don't look anything like them," said Erich.

"Yes, and they also don't look anything like anyone else who's gone in there in the past half hour," said Karl. "It's called a disguise. Now come on."

———

If someone looked hard enough online, they might come across an old picture of Patton in her uniform, but they would not recognize the woman who walked out of Heathrow into the cool night air. Nemo's shopping spree in Atlanta had netted a second set of new clothes for each of them—his distinctly more fashionable than hers. He had stolen a torn and empty suitcase, abandoned on the side of the baggage claim carousel and transferred Patton's new clothes and everything else she needed into it.

"No one notices when you steal a bag like this," he said, striding confidently through the customs area. He had explained how she should execute her transformation and told her to come out of the restroom exactly thirty minutes after going in. She had left Alta Vista a brunette with wavy hair that fell below her shoulders, a perfect complexion, and brown eyes. She stepped into their rental car a blue-eyed blond with short-cropped hair, a pockmarked forehead and florid cheeks, no longer wearing a business suit, but rather a baggy sweatshirt that read, "Atlanta United," a pair of jeans, and what a woman in the restroom had called "trainers," as in "Oh, I love your trainers." To Patton they were Nike running shoes. Add to that a pair of dark-rimmed glasses and a Braves cap to keep her face off CCTV and its pesky facial recognition software, and Patton Harcourt had completely disappeared.

In an Armani suit and designer sunglasses, Nemo looked like an aging Italian playboy, she thought—too old to be dressing in a style that he probably could have pulled off a decade earlier.

"I hope your friend is ready for us," said Nemo as he pulled the rental car onto the M25. Patton slid down in her seat, and so did not notice the black sedan two cars behind them. Not then, and not when it exited behind them from the M1 onto the A5 an hour later.

"How did you get so good at all this?" said Patton as the car raced through the darkness. "The disguises, the staying off the grid, the fake passports."

"Oh, the passports aren't fake," said Nemo. "Only the identities are fake. And I got good at it the same way anyone gets good at anything. I practiced. And I started young."

Once he was sure Mr. Gerrard was dead, Dexter stepped away from the body and went to find Jack. The boy was huddled under the covers in his bed, shivering.

"He's never going to hurt you again, Jack," said Dexter. "Do you understand?" Jack nodded but pulled away when Dexter stepped toward him. "It's OK, I won't hurt you, either. But you need to listen to me. Can you do that, Jack? Can you listen to me?"

"Yes," whispered Jack, clinging to his stuffed rabbit.

"You saw me after school with a tall white man. You went to bed early and when you woke up I was gone and you found . . . you found him. Tomorrow morning just run outside screaming and everything will be fine. Can you do that for me?"

Jack nodded.

"Now, where did I go?"

"I don't know," said Jack quietly. "I saw you after school with a tall white man."

"Right."

"And I went to bed early."

"Good, Jack. Good. Now you stay here, and I'll be right back." Dexter went into Gerrard's bedroom and felt his body tensing with the thought of what that monster had done to Jack. But he had no time for feelings. He ripped drawers out of the bureau, threw everything out of the boxes in the closet, and took Gerrard's secret stash of money, which was not as secret as Gerrard thought. The police would think there had been a burglary, plus Dexter had $450. That would get him a long way from here. He crept back into Jack's room, to see that the boy had calmed down a bit. He was lying down, still gripping the rabbit, but no longer shivering.

"I have to go now, Jack," said Dexter. "You take care of yourself."

"When will I see you again?"

"You won't," said Dexter. He took a step toward the bed, and this time Jack got up on his knees and leaned into Dexter, hugging him so tightly Dexter thought he might break a rib. And if Nemo was an emotionless robot now, as Patton had accused him, he hadn't been one then. He walked out of the house bawling from the pain of losing the closest thing to a brother he had ever known.

But he had discovered his talents, and he spent a lifetime honing them.

Bletchley Park on a cloudy night did not look like the sort of place where one might save the world. A few lights reflected in the lake and gave a slight glow to the facade of the Victorian pile that constituted the main house, but the rest of the place looked shabby and uninspiring. Long, low buildings with all the architectural distinctiveness of a garden shed sprawled out in every direction, reminding Patton of the temporary classrooms at Alta Vista High School. Some had been restored—but the structures were so unadorned and utilitarian, it was hard to tell the renovated ones from the derelict ones. In the eerie illumination of the occasional security light, it was hardly the sort of place to make the heart soar with pride and amazement at the achievements of a great generation.

But Patton's heart did soar. For a few minutes, as they wandered the grounds, careful to keep an eye out for any night watchmen, she forgot all about Fritz and Franz and sniper bullets and her assassin cum traveling companion and listened to the voices of the past. Here Dilly Knox developed the "rodding" technique to help break Enigma messages. Here Mavis Batey broke the Italian Enigma and decrypted messages that helped the Allies succeed in the D-Day landings. Here Alan Turing and Gordon Welchman created the Bombe—the machine that became a bridge between human intelligence and the computer age, a machine whose only purpose was to break Enigma. It had succeeded spectacularly. Perhaps most amazingly, all this work had remained secret. Despite thousands of people working at Bletchley at the height of the war, no one outside the gates had the slightest idea what went on there. The Germans believed until the very end that Enigma remained unbroken, and with the Official Secrets Act demanding silence on the part of all who had worked there, Bletchley's invaluable contribution to the war had remained a secret until the mid-1970s.

"I can't believe I'm walking in the footsteps of Alan Turing," said Patton as they made their way past one low building after another. "It's all a museum now, you know. I wish we could go in and—"

"Listen," said Nemo, "I appreciate that this is some sort of pilgrimage for you, but in case you didn't notice, another car pulled up to the gate just after we did. A car with its headlights off."

"We're being followed?" said Patton.

"Yes," said Nemo, "and I don't think it's by some fellow Alan Turing enthusiast. Now let's get on with the job at hand before we come face-to-face with good old Fritz and Franz."

"You think it's them?"

"Them or somebody just as dangerous," said Nemo. "Where is this friend of yours?"

"This way," said Patton, pointing to a sign reading "National Museum of Computing."

"Sounds like a great day out for the whole family," said Nemo, as they slunk up the hill toward another low, sad-looking building.

———

On Sunday night, Ruthie Drinkwater had stayed in the museum after closing time to make sure her favorite machine was shut down properly. She volunteered there often enough that she had her own set of keys and the complete trust of the small number of paid staff members, who were happy for Ruthie to take care of the shutdown so they could get home to their families. Ruthie had no family to get home to; her work with the machine that she cared for almost daily was the closest thing she had to an intimate relationship. The museum's director had offered her a paid position on several occasions, but Ruthie had a small inheritance that provided her modest living expenses, and she preferred to work as a volunteer, free to come and go as she pleased and not accountable to any supervisor.

So she happily stayed late and returned all the settings to their default positions, carefully covering the machine with its protective sheeting before turning out the lights and hopping on her bicycle to pedal the three miles home. In her tiny detached cottage at the end of a narrow country lane just outside Newton Longville, she ate a simple supper of roast chicken and potatoes, watched an old episode of *Inspector Morse*, and retired early with a book. She was just drifting off when her cell phone pinged with a text message that gave her, for the first time in years, a case of insomnia.

After hours of thinking over the ramifications of those words, she finally fell into a restless sleep, but she woke before five as the predawn light seeped through her curtains. She reached for her cell phone, re-reading the message. "Ruthie, it's Patton Harcourt, your summer fling from Harvard. I hope you still remember me, because I certainly remember you—especially those nights in the dorm with the window open. Good times. Now, I need your help. Can you meet me at the museum tomorrow night around midnight? I need to use the Bombe. This is a burner, so don't text back. And don't tell anyone." It had been fifteen years since Ruthie attended that summer course at Harvard on the early history of computer codebreaking, but she remembered Patton Harcourt like it was yesterday—the pixie haircut, the not-so-innocent smile, and the eyes that stayed laser focused on Ruthie's own even after three pints. And Patton had remembered Ruthie's phone number—but then Patton had a way with numbers, among other things. Ruthie recalled Patton's surprising talent at darts and her even more surprising talent at kissing—and more. A pretty girl had never flirted with Ruthie, and so of course, though she hadn't told Patton, Ruthie took it all much too seriously. She didn't understand it was a flirtation, a summer fling, a bit of fun and not a lifelong romance. So, when the course ended, Patton had flounced away and Ruthie had returned to England with a broken heart.

Now a tiny corner of Ruthie's heart leaped when she read those first words—"Ruthie, it's Patton Harcourt." Patton didn't just remember her, she remembered her fondly. She might have called their affair a summer fling, but she also used the phrase "Good times." Yes, they had been, thought Ruthie. But Patton's text was more than just a flirtatious reminder of a long-lost love. Patton Harcourt needed to use the Bombe, the machine that had been created to crack the Enigma Code. Why? Did she want to show it off to some other girlfriend, trading on an old acquaintance to impress a new one? And if so, why all the secrecy? Why a burner phone? Did Patton actually need to use the Bombe for its true purpose? Surely she knew there were easier ways to do that in this day and age.

But Ruthie didn't care about the questions. In a few hours she would see Patton. Even if it meant nothing, even if Patton never stopped to think that Ruthie might still have feelings, might have ever had feelings, she would see her. And if Patton needed the Bombe, no one could do a better job with that than Ruthie. She rolled out of bed, ate breakfast, showered, and, for the first time since her cousin's wedding last autumn, decided she would wear some makeup.

Ruthie hated to drive, but she had no light on her bicycle and there was too much traffic on the road to risk riding at night. She could have ridden in earlier, she supposed; after all, the museum was closed on Mondays, but then she would have been stuck there in the middle of the night with no way home. So she cranked up her ten-year-old Mini Cooper for the first time in a week and eased away from the curb in front of her cottage and into the road. She still had not decided how she felt about seeing Patton after all this time—and under such bizarre circumstances. But as she approached the museum gates, she felt excitement rising up unbidden. Ruthie was typically a calm person—unusually calm, the staff at the museum would have said. Even with the most rambunctious school group threatening to overrun her and lay hands on her precious machine, Ruthie remained cool and level-headed. But now she found herself actually trembling with anticipation of the night ahead. As much as she tried to squelch it, as hard as she tried to tell herself it was wrong, misguided, and foolish, Ruthie's heart insisted on being heard, and what it said, in the loudest and most enthusiastic terms, was: "You have a second chance."

V

Karl had watched from the shadows as the woman and the hired gun climbed over the wall and disappeared.

"They have to come back this way, right?" said Erich.

"They won't get far without their car," said Karl.

"Should I disable it?"

But instead of answering, Karl took out the phone and called Weiss to discuss their next move.

"Excellent," said Ingrid, when she heard that the two fugitives had arrived at Bletchley. "They wouldn't be there if they didn't have the message. Let them do the work of decrypting, then take care of them when they come back out."

Karl smiled. Finally something had gone right in this debacle of a job. Once they had the decrypted message, there would be no stopping Columbia House. Projekt Alchemie would make everything possible. He switched off the phone, turned to Erich, and said, "Fix the car."

As Ingrid hung up, the landline rang. Jean Simpson had miscalculated the time change when she called Columbia House. She forgot that Germany was six hours ahead not six hours behind.

"That's the business number," said Gottfried, looking at a readout on his screen. "It's coming from America."

"Answer it," said Dietrich.

"Don't answer it," said Weiss firmly. "Can you get a better trace on it?"

"North Carolina," said Gottfried. "Eastern part of the state."

"Didn't we send a book there recently?" said Eva Klein. "Jean Simpson, Ridgefield, North Carolina." Eva had a near eidetic memory, which meant she could often access pertinent information faster than Gottfried and all his computers. A second later the recorded message played and then a voice proved Eva correct.

"This is Columbia House. Our offices are closed at the moment. You may dial your party's extension or stay on the line to leave a general voice mail." There were no extensions, but also no way for an outside caller to know that.

"This is Jean Simpson. I'm calling in reference to a book I received from your organization. If you could call back I'd be grateful." The voice left a number and then the line went dead.

The four associates of Columbia House, by now operating on coffee and adrenaline as they attempted to manage an international operation from this modest but well-wired house in the suburbs of Munich, sat staring at one another.

"It's nothing to worry about," said Dietrich.

"She didn't even bother to calculate the time change," said Gottfried.

"She probably just wants to say thank you," said Dietrich.

"We mailed the book about two weeks ago," said Eva. "Wouldn't she have said thank you before now?"

"Can you put a trace on that phone?" said Weiss to Gottfried. "So we can keep an eye on where she goes."

"I can only do that," said Gottfried with a smile, "if Miss Jean Simpson was foolish enough to give me her phone number."

"Now," said Ingrid. "What do we tell our boys to do with these American swine at Bletchley?"

"We send them in now," said Dietrich, slipping an arm around Eva's waist. "We let them get away before, let's not do it again.

Our boys can eliminate Nemo and I'm sure they'll have some creative thoughts on how to convince the woman to finish the decryption."

Eva leaned into Dietrich's embrace but did not look at him, instead addressing Ingrid directly. "I'm not sure that's the best idea," she said. "Nemo already took Erich out once. He's a professional killer, that's why we hired him."

"But he's unarmed," said Dietrich. "They went straight from the airport to Bletchley and they didn't check any bags. He can't possibly have a gun."

"Yes," said Eva, "and Erich and Karl are unarmed, too—for the same reason."

"If they leave Bletchley with the decrypt, I'll have no way of tracking them," said Gottfried, turning from his computer screens to join the conversation.

"True," said Ingrid, "but Karl is disabling their car. So they can't go far."

"Still," said Dietrich, "we have eyes on them now. On foot in the middle of the night, they could disappear."

"They don't know the car has been disabled," said Ingrid. "Let them finish the decrypt and have Karl and Erich eliminate them when they come back to the vehicle."

"All I'm saying," said Dietrich, "is we haven't done too well predicting their movements so far."

"Nonsense," said Ingrid, her sudden anger immediately commanding the attention of the room. "We predicted they would go to Bletchley; they went to Bletchley. Until they have the decrypt, we watch and we wait. And you stop trying to undermine my authority."

"I'm not . . ." protested Dietrich.

"Stop. Or I'll put a fucking bullet in your head. Three can do this job as well as four." Dietrich took a step back and Eva moved in front of him, between Ingrid and the immediate cause of her anger.

There was silence for several seconds and then Gottfried spoke. "What about our insurance policy?"

"We won't make that claim unless we need to," said Ingrid, still glaring at Dietrich. "The premium is too high."

"You realize that even if we get this right," said Eva cautiously, "there are a lot of other steps between obtaining the decrypt and completing Projekt Alchemie. Steps that will cost money. Money we don't have."

"That's not entirely true," said Gottfried.

"It is true," said Eva. "We need to arrange for transportation and storage, there will be fees for . . ."

"No," said Gottfried, "I meant it's not entirely true that we don't have money."

———

The National Museum of Computing sits at the top of a hill in the Bletchley Park complex. Ruthie had used her pass code to enter the main gate and parked her Mini Cooper behind the building, where it was less likely to draw the attention of the night watchman. She knew his routine well enough that she could avoid him fairly easily.

Midnight had come and gone, and Ruthie's pulse had finally slowed as the possibility that Patton would not show, that Ruthie would simply sit alone all night, began to set in. The museum, so full of clicks and whirs and hums during the day, was quiet as the night outside—quieter. So when a knock came at the rear door, it sounded to Ruthie like a thunderbolt. She eased the door open, and there, haloed in the security light above, stood Patton Harcourt, her hair a different color, her clothes a bit shabby, but still as beautiful as she had been fifteen years ago. For a moment Ruthie could not speak. She wanted to pull Patton to her, to crush her lips to hers, to lead her to the dark corners of the museum where they could linger. And then a man stepped into the light.

"Let's get inside," he said, and before Ruthie could react, or even say hello, he and Patton pushed past her and into the dimness of the back corridor.

"It's lovely to see you, Ruthie," said Patton. "Though in this light it's hard to see much of anything. Anyway, you look well."

You look well? Could there be any more dismissive sentence in the English language to hear from a former lover?

"You look, you look . . ." Ruthie struggled to find the right word and settled on, "wonderful."

"Listen, I appreciate the little reunion here," said Nemo sharply, "but we have work to do, and from what Patton tells me it could take a while, so can we get going before those goons at the gate get bored of waiting for us?"

Ruthie was about to ask what he meant by "goons at the gate," when Patton spoke up.

"OK, listen, Nemo. Up to this point I've let you run this operation because we required your particular expertise. But now it's my show for a while, and we require Ruthie's expertise. So stop being such a man and let me talk to my old friend for a minute. Because right now, she's the only hope we've got of convincing those goons you're talking about to back the hell off."

Ruthie felt her breath go shallow once again. Patton wasn't just standing up for her in front of this nattily dressed man, whoever he was. She *wanted* to talk to her. She was, apparently, in trouble and in a hurry, but still wanted to take a moment to . . .

"How the hell are you?" said Patton, pulling Ruthie into a tight embrace. Ruthie felt a warmth spreading through her body that she had almost forgotten existed. Patton didn't just remember, she harbored, well, at least nostalgia if not something more.

"It's really good to see you," whispered Patton before giving Ruthie a light kiss on the cheek.

Nemo saw immediately what Patton was up to. He knew that different people needed to be handled in different ways and obviously Patton knew exactly how to handle this woman, this invaluable resource. Rather than lose his cool, he backed off, stayed quiet, and let Patton work her magic on Ruthie. For some reason he had expected a wrinkled old woman, but Ruthie Drinkwater looked about Patton's age. Nemo had not asked that age, but he guessed it was around forty. Even in the dim light of the "Way Out" sign, he could see that Ruthie had tried to impress. Her shoulder-length auburn hair glistened in its perfection, she wore just a hint of eyeliner and lipstick, and her outfit was not the careless jumble Nemo expected from a math nerd who volunteered at a computer museum, but a crisp linen dress. A summer dress, thought Nemo. Not the sort of outfit one generally wore on a cool night in May.

Patton understood that the way to get Ruthie on their side immediately was not to explain that Nemo was a professional assassin or that they were being chased by German killers who might possibly believe in alchemy. They could have spent an hour trying to accomplish with explanations and entreaties what Patton accomplished with a single embrace and a peck on the cheek. She knew Ruthie had been in love with her. She had felt guilty about that, but not so guilty that she said anything other than a breezy goodbye at the end of that summer. If she tried to win Ruthie over by explaining their situation they could easily be delayed by tears and accusations as the memory of that goodbye came back to Ruthie. The sort of greeting that suggested that Patton was sorry, that she had grown and matured and might even have latent feelings for Ruthie would bypass all that drama and get them straight to the Bombe.

"We have an Enigma message we need to decrypt," said Patton after she had held the embrace for a count of twenty. "And we'd like to do it the old-fashioned way."

"And," added Nemo from the shadows, "we're in a bit . . ." but Patton shot him a look that told him to shut up and let her handle this. "A bit of awe at your abilities," improvised Nemo before pressing himself into a corner.

Using the flashlight on her cell phone, Ruthie led them into a room with glass cases around the sides displaying a variety of bizarre-looking cogs and wheels. On one side of the room, in a locked glass case, sat what Nemo recognized from Jasper Fleming's workshop as an Enigma machine.

"So this is it," he said, almost to himself, leaning over the case to take a closer look in the dimness. "It's beautiful."

"It is," said Ruthie, with a touch of pride in her voice. "When I first heard about Enigma, I didn't expect to have that reaction, but I did." Unlike Jasper's machine that sprouted wires and had sides of unfinished splintered pine, this had all the markings of a fine antique—a stained wooden box with polished metal hinges, that classic set of keys (not quite in the QWERTY arrangement, Nemo noticed) and the gleaming rotors and meticulously labeled plugboard. The whole thing was the size of a typewriter—heavy, but portable enough to be carried on a ship or in the battlefield.

"It's compact, elegant, and almost perfect," said Ruthie.

"Almost?" said Nemo.

"Well, we broke it, didn't we," said Ruthie. "Now, what have you got for me?"

Patton pulled the original Enigma message out of her notebook and set the plastic-covered paper on top of the glass case holding the Enigma machine. Ruthie bent over the message and gave a low whistle.

"This is from the H-Sonderkommando," she said. "Or at least they received it."

"What is that," said Patton, "some sort of special forces unit?"

"H-Sonderkommando was a unit of the SS supposedly investigating witches. The 'H' stood for 'hexen,' which is the German word for witch. It's all very fuzzy, but it's likely Himmler had something to do with it— he was head of the SS and fascinated by witches and anything related to the occult. He assembled a huge library of books on the subject."

"You mean Heinrich Himmler," said Patton, "the chief architect of the Holocaust?"

"That's the one."

"Any chance he was interested in alchemy?" said Nemo.

"Oh, he was very interested in alchemy," said Ruthie.

———

JULY 1938

As he ushered Karl Malchus down the corridor, Helmut glanced out the window toward the five-acre prisoner enclosure at Dachau. He admired

Himmler's design of the concentration camp. While it had principally been used for political prisoners and enemies of the Reich for the past five years, soon the real work of this, and other camps, would begin. The return of the Aryan race to their proper place of domination could only be accomplished by cleansing Germany of the inferior races, especially the Jews. Helmut could already imagine the fences of Dachau containing tens of thousands of Jews removed from society so that a pure-blooded Aryan Germany could flourish.

Karl Malchus hardly looked like a pure-blooded Aryan, thought Helmut. Malchus wore neither a uniform nor a business suit, unlike most of the people Himmler dealt with. He wore, instead, a shabby outfit of brown corduroy pants and a plaid shirt frayed at the collar which a white laboratory coat did little to hide. His mop of hair nearly fell in front of his gold-rimmed eyeglasses. But if Malchus did not have the perfect pure-blooded appearance of Helmut, that apparently didn't matter to Himmler, so long as he could deliver.

And Malchus had delivered. He had come to Himmler a few months earlier claiming to be able to manufacture gold and Himmler had brought him here, to the Dachau concentration camp—not as a prisoner, but as a scientist. Here, in the fine brick buildings outside the main camp enclosure, Malchus worked in secret, his well-equipped laboratory protected from the prying eyes of other high-ranking Nazis.

Helmut remembered well the day Malchus dropped a nugget of pure gold on Himmler's desk, proof of his success.

"What materials do you require?" Himmler had said with a gleam in his eye.

"Paraffin," said Malchus, "ordinary stones, and most importantly sand from the bed of the river Isar."

"Easily done," said Himmler. He picked up the gold nugget and rubbed it between his fingers. "You cannot fool me, you know," he said.

"Of course not, Herr Himmler. Your guard here searches me every morning to be sure I bring no gold into the laboratory, and he stands watch at the door all day while I work so no one can slip me a nugget. If it is a bit like being in prison, I am willing to accept the inconvenience, so long as it brings you peace of mind."

"If you were to fool me," said Himmler, "you would quickly discover that prison is a great deal more than an inconvenience."

"I'm sure anyone foolish enough to trick you would deserve whatever punishment you thought fit," said Malchus. Helmut had made sure that Malchus knew about the fraudulent alchemist Heinz Kurschildgen and his recent reincarceration.

"Gold from the sand of the Isar. A near-infinite resource," said Himmler, dropping the nugget back into a silver bowl.

Helmut thought he could still hear the clink of the gold hitting the bowl echoing in his ears, and he recalled all too well what Himmler said next.

"Is there anything you need to be more . . . comfortable?" said Himmler, turning toward the door. "Perhaps some brandy or some cigarettes?"

"Kind of you to ask," said Malchus, "but I roll my own."

That conversation had taken place a month ago. Now Helmut ushered Malchus into Himmler's office, gripping him by the arm, not tightly, but firmly enough to let the old man know who was in charge.

"You sent for me, Herr Himmler?" said Malchus, as Helmut pushed him forward toward the desk and then took a step back to stand by the door.

"Please have a seat, Herr Malchus," said Himmler, indicating a chair in front of the broad desk behind which he now sat. Malchus shuffled forward and lowered himself into the uncomfortable wooden chair.

"The work is proceeding very well," said Malchus with a nervous nod of his head.

"I'm pleased to hear it," said Himmler. "But not all our discussions need to be about work. We are allowed to socialize on occasion. May I offer you a cigarette?" He held out an engraved silver cigarette case, filled with Rothmans Blue, imported from England. Just because the Nazi

Party believed smoking caused ill health and tried to curb cigarettes in Germany didn't mean Himmler couldn't get the best.

"No, thank you," said Malchus.

"Ah yes, I remember, you roll your own," said Himmler, taking out a cigarette and snapping the case shut.

"Yes."

"Perhaps you would like to smoke one of yours."

"No, thank you," said Malchus.

Himmler tapped the cigarette against the desk and put it to his lips, leaning over to light it from a large crystal lighter that sat next to the telephone. "This lighter was a gift from the führer himself," said Himmler, inhaling deeply and blowing the smoke directly toward Malchus.

"How generous of him," said Malchus.

"You really should join me in a smoke," said Himmler, leaning forward.

"As I said, I'd rather not."

"Please," said Himmler, "I insist." He nodded ever so slightly at Helmut who took a step forward. Malchus slid down further into the chair, as if trying to disappear.

"Well, perhaps I will have one of yours," he said.

"Oh, I couldn't possibly foist one of these on you when you roll your own," said Himmler. "Surely an alchemist such as yourself must roll a perfect cigarette." He slid the lighter to the far edge of the desk, just in front of Malchus, and pressed down on the brass handle. A flame popped up and flickered in Malchus's face.

"I'm not sure I have one with me," said Malchus.

"I have no doubt Helmut here can help you find one, if you're unable to do so yourself."

With a look of abject misery, Malchus reached into his jacket pocket and pulled out a cigarette that looked almost as crumpled as he did. With shaking fingers he brought it to his lips and leaned forward to accept the light.

"Now, isn't this lovely," said Himmler. "Two friends enjoying a smoke together. Friends who are always completely honest with one another, isn't that right?"

"Yes, I suppose," said Malchus quietly.

Himmler leaned back in his chair and blew a cloud of smoke into the air above his head. A moment later there was a loud click as something fell from the tip of Malchus's cigarette onto the floor.

"Why, whatever can that be?" said Himmler. "It seems something was hidden inside your cigarette." He nodded to Helmut who stepped forward and leaned over to retrieve a nugget of pure gold, still soft from the heat of the cigarette in which it had been hidden.

"Gold," said Helmut with a smile, setting the nugget on the desk in front of Malchus.

"Now how in the world do you suppose this piece of gold could have gotten into your cigarette?" said Himmler, picking up the nugget and holding it under Malchus's nose. "Ah yes, as you said—you roll your own."

On Himmler's orders, Helmut oversaw the transfer of Karl Malchus from his comfortable quarters next to the laboratory at Dachau to the prisoner enclosure. Again Himmler had been taken in by a phony alchemist, again other Nazi leaders would ridicule him. It infuriated Helmut. Yet, a few days later, when he stepped into Himmler's office, the Reichsführer's mood was as jolly as Helmut had seen it in a long time.

"You won't be having any more trouble from Karl Malchus," said Helmut.

"Karl Malchus is of no concern to me," said Himmler.

"I never did trust the man."

"He served his purpose," said Himmler. "He reminded me of the true nature of alchemy. The transformation of that which is base and worthless into that which is priceless—bit by bit, nugget by nugget. Malchus taught me that it will be a slow process, yet it can, in the end, assure the future of the Reich."

Himmler took out a sheet of paper and began to write a series of numbers and letters on it. "These are my private Enigma settings," he said. "You will memorize them and then destroy this sheet. I want you to go to the Enigma room and send this message. Only six officers of the SS have my private settings, so only they will be able to read this, though the time is coming when we will send it to more."

Himmler wrote hastily on the paper, then handed it to Helmut. Below the Enigma settings the heading of the message read "Projekt Alchemie."

"Projekt Alchemie?" said Helmut, nonplussed. "But surely you do not still hope to solve the problem of alchemical transformation?"

"My boy, you misunderstand," said Himmler, turning to Helmut and laying a hand on his shoulder. "I have already solved it."

———

"I've got a possible crib," said Patton, "but I don't remember how to turn it into a menu."

"Because you didn't pay attention in class," said Ruthie.

"I paid attention," said Patton, laying a hand on Ruthie's bare forearm. "I just didn't pay attention to the professor."

"*Projekt Alchemie Erfolgreich*," said Ruthie, reading out of the notebook. "Project Alchemy Successful. That's a good crib, if it's correct. So we line up the crib with the cipher text . . ."

"I have that," said Patton, turning the page in her notebook. There she had arranged the crib under the cipher text, inserting an *X* for each space between words.

"So we just need to number the letter positions and then we can create a loop that will give us the menu to program the Bombe," said Ruthie. "Pencil?"

Patton pulled a pencil out of her purse and handed it to Ruthie who numbered the letters on the page before them from one to twenty-eight.

```
1  2  3  4  5  6  7  8  9  10 11 12 13 14 15 16 17 18 19 20 21 22 23 24 25 26 27 28
P  R  O  J  E  K  T  X  A  L  C  H  E  M  I  E  X  E  R  F  O  L  G  R  E  I  C  H
Q  W  A  R  S  G  E  K  L  Y  M  Q  Y  S  P  Y  H  Y  K  X  Q  O  M  E  Z  A  N  V
```

"Now we look for a loop," said Ruthie, scanning the letters.

The room fell silent and Patton was suddenly aware of the sound of her own pulse and of Nemo's breathing. For the first time since their arrival, Ruthie had turned her attention away from her old lover and Patton felt she could hazard a quick glance at Nemo. She nodded at him and gave him a thumbs-up, which she hoped he would interpret as *Don't worry, this is all going well.* Still lurking in the shadows, Nemo nodded back. *Message received.*

"Got one," said Ruthie a minute later.

"That was fast," said Patton.

"I may be the only person in the world who breaks Enigma messages for fun in my spare time," said Ruthie. "Look—at position 15 the letter 'P' lines up with 'I,' then at position 26 the letter 'I' enciphers as 'A.' At position 3 'A' aligns with 'O,' at position 21 'O' enciphers as 'Q,' and at position 1, 'Q' lines up with 'P' and we're back to the original letter and the loop is closed. Now I can program the Bombe."

"What is this bomb you keep talking about?" said Nemo. "I don't see how an explosion is going to improve our situation."

Ruthie glanced at the time on her phone: 1:14 a.m. The night watchman would be in the main house and walking the huts behind it for the next thirty minutes. She could risk turning on the lights. She flipped a switch and the room filled with a cool fluorescent glow. In the center of the space, where Ruthie had already uncovered it, stood a black machine about the size of two large refrigerators. The side facing them was covered with different colored wheels about five inches in diameter each with the letters of the alphabet printed around the front edge. The colored wheels gleamed in the light and the whole contraption seemed, to Nemo, to pulse with mystery and potential.

"This," said Ruthie, "is the Bombe."

"Alan Turing designed the Bombe starting with work done by the Poles," said Patton as Ruthie began fiddling with wires at the back of the machine.

"And then," said Ruthie, "Gordon Welchman came up with the

idea of the diagonal board and that meant . . . You have no idea what I'm talking about, do you?"

"Can this thing break the code?" said Nemo.

"This machine won the war," said Ruthie.

"But can it decode our message?" said Nemo.

"Not entirely," said Ruthie. "But if I set it up correctly, using Patton's crib and the loop we found, it can reduce the number of possible settings for the Enigma machine that encoded this message from one hundred and fifty trillion to about six hundred or so. The rest is fairly easy to do by hand."

"I told you we came to the right person," said Patton. Ruthie felt herself blush as she finished setting up the wiring and began flicking a series of switches on the side of the machine. Usually she programmed the machine for groups of tourists and schoolchildren, always deciphering the same sample message. But after closing time, she often worked on actual Enigma messages in the Bletchley archives, thousands of which had never been decrypted. She loved the challenge of decrypting a seventy-five-year-old message, even though it was of no importance whatsoever and could be decrypted by modern computers in a matter of seconds. But this message, apparently, *was* important. And not only was she decrypting an important message that had never been deciphered, she was doing it for Patton Harcourt. Patton who stood next to her and whose presence raised the same goosebumps on her arms that it had fifteen years ago—even with the metallic, oily odor of the Bombe filling the room.

"Now, we set the drums to the relative position of the first three letters of our crib," said Ruthie. She began to spin around the red, green, and yellow drums on the front of the machine, relishing Nemo's complete bewilderment. Patton's expression was one Ruthie remembered from class—that contracted face Patton made when trying hard to solve a problem. Ruthie knew Patton's confusion meant that she hadn't paid attention to the professor all those years ago, had instead focused her attention on the British girl at the next desk.

"There," said Ruthie, when she had finished setting up the machine.

"Now we power up and begin the run. The three rotors in the Enigma machine each have twenty-six possible settings, one for each letter. That means a total of seventeen thousand five hundred seventy-six possible rotor configurations. The Bombe can get through all of those configurations in less than fifteen minutes. Any time a setting seems to match our menu it stops, and we record the setting and test it against our crib. Usually you get four or five stops in a run, but only one of them will be right. Once we find the right one, we'll have the rotor configuration and one of the connections on the plugboard. The rest is easy."

"Easy for you," said Patton, laying a hand on Ruthie's shoulder.

"Are you ready?" said Ruthie.

Patton did not answer but squeezed Ruthie's shoulder. She felt a shiver run through Ruthie's body, and then the room filled with noise as Ruthie turned the machine on and the Bombe began its work.

———

Jean's phone call to Columbia House, and the questions she had for Ingrid Weiss, had gone unanswered, but as she began to hear back from the other people for whom she had left messages earlier in the day, she decided it was just as well Ingrid Weiss didn't know what she was doing. Even though Jean didn't exactly know herself, she suspected her investigation might not end well for Miss Weiss. After talking to Peter she had returned to her office and called back Suzie Stein, the woman in New York who had received a book from Columbia House. Suzie had promised to examine the book for signs it had been stolen from a library. Jean explained to Suzie and to Manfred Hopkins, just outside Birmingham, England, how to look for rough spots on the pages where someone might have sanded off a library marking. Hopkins was another "heir" mentioned in the articles about Columbia House as having received a book stolen from a family member by Nazis. In her search of newspaper archives, Jean had uncovered the names of several Americans who had received books from Columbia House. She had sent messages to eight of them through their social media accounts asking them to phone her. The first call came from Stanley Marx, of Oyster Bay, Long Island.

"I looked through the book," said Stanley, "and there are four pages with spots that look like they've been sanded, just like you said."

"Could you tell what had been printed there?" asked Jean.

"Not at first," said Stanley. "But I photographed the pages and zoomed in on my computer and on one page I definitely saw the words . . . my German pronunciation isn't very good, but it said, '*Bayerische Staatsbibliothek.*'"

"The Bavarian State Library," said Jean. "One of the largest research libraries in Europe. It's in Munich."

"You think this book was stolen?" said Stanley.

"I'm afraid it might have been," said Jean.

"I was rather pleased when it arrived. My grandfather was an art dealer in Berlin. It seemed perfectly reasonable that he would have owned a book on the old masters."

Twenty minutes later, after two similar phone calls, a pattern had begun to emerge. Jean had spoken to three owners of "returned" books and all of the volumes showed signs of having been stolen from libraries—two from the National Library of the Czech Republic in Prague and one from the Bavarian State Library in Munich. Ingrid Weiss had done her homework, though. In every case there was a reasonable link between the book and the person who had once allegedly owned it. She had spoken to the recipients of the stolen books while waiting to board her flight to Vienna. The next morning, she would be in Europe.

Sitting on the plane, Jean compared the images of stolen books given away by Columbia House that she had received via email over the past few hours. Four books, including the one she had received. What she saw might have surprised her a few days ago, but now seemed perfectly in keeping with what she knew about Ingrid Weiss. Each of the books bore some sort of inscription that identified it as belonging to a relative of the person to whom Weiss had sent it. But each of those inscriptions was in the same handwriting. Jean had no doubt that the books were stolen and the inscriptions forged. And Peter Byerly was right—she should probably just phone the police in Munich and let them confront Ingrid Weiss.

But Jean tended to take things personally. It happened whenever a student gave her a bad review on one of those "rate your professor" websites or when a man failed to call her for a second date. She often couldn't shake those sorts of rejections for several days and now she couldn't shake this. Ingrid Weiss had tried to dupe her. For what reason, Jean could not imagine, but some stranger in another country had picked out Jean as a sucker and tried to make her grateful for possessing stolen merchandise. She didn't want the Munich police to arrest Ingrid Weiss for fraud and theft quite yet. Just as she always wanted to confront that anonymous student or that man who didn't share his phone number, Jean wanted to confront Ingrid Weiss. She had the ammunition, in the form of incontrovertible evidence, and this time she had something she didn't have when a student reviewed her or a man didn't call. She had an address.

———

The drums on the front of the Bombe clicked as they rotated and the motor that drove the mechanism throbbed. "Imagine a room full of these things," said Ruthie, "all running at the same time. At the height of the codebreaking operation, the noise in the Bombe huts was deafening."

Patton stared in awe. She had seen a video of this Bombe working, but to be in the room, to feel the noise of the machine and smell the lubricating oil, to be able to reach out and touch those drums and feel them rotating under her fingertips as they searched for some combination that would decipher the message—it gave her chills. This beautiful combination of wires and screws, of brilliant concept and superb engineering, had probably saved hundreds of thousands of lives. By some estimates the work at Bletchley shortened the war in Europe by two years and allowed for the success of the D-Day invasions. Over two hundred Bombes had been manufactured, but after the war, they had all been dismantled. The British didn't want the Soviets to know they had broken Enigma. Patton had read all this in a book about Alan Turing and had assumed that had been the end of the story—until she met Ruthie.

As they lay in bed one night talking about Bletchley, Ruthie said, "You know the Bletchley Park Trust has assembled a team that's reconstructing a Bombe."

"You're kidding," said Patton.

"It's been going on for about a decade and they think they'll be done in another couple of years. They're engineers and machinists and amateur tinkerers. They went back to the original designs and they've had to custom make just about every part—even a bunch of things you could buy at your corner hardware store in the 1940s."

"Do they think it will work?" said Patton

"Oh, it'll work. They're going to install it at Bletchley." Ruthie rolled onto her side and lay her head on Patton's chest. "And I'm going to learn how to run it."

And she had. Patton had read an article a few years ago about the reconstructed Bombe and about how a volunteer at the museum named Ruthie Drinkwater had used it to decode old Enigma messages. She had guessed Ruthie would still have access to the Bombe. She had been right.

They had named the machine Phoenix and, as Ruthie, Patton, and Nemo watched, it clicked and rumbled its way through the task for which Alan Turing intended it.

Patton stepped closer to Phoenix and slipped her arm around Ruthie's waist, no longer trying to arouse some dormant passion in order to manipulate Ruthie. Now her genuine excitement at watching this hero of the war brought back to life made her want to reach out to Ruthie, to say, with her touch, not only that she was happy to share this moment with someone who truly appreciated its importance but how proud she was that Ruthie knew exactly how to ride this old warhorse. Ruthie leaned into Patton's embrace but did not take her eyes off Phoenix.

"How long did you say this is going to take?" said Nemo.

"That depends on whether we get a good stop," said Ruthie, not turning to look at him. "And whether it's the first stop or the second or . . ."

Just then the clicking abruptly ceased and the drums stopped rotating. Ruthie extricated herself from Patton's arm and picked up a pencil and Patton's notebook from the table in front of the machine.

"OK, we have our first stop," said Ruthie, copying down the positions of the drums in the notebook.

"Is that it?" said Nemo. "Have you cracked it?"

"Patience isn't his strong suit," said Patton.

But Nemo knew otherwise of course. His career required endless patience. After he had disappeared from the Gerrards' house he had spent years preparing for his first real hit. He had hidden in the wilderness of Pennsylvania, emerging every year or so to steal a birth certificate and apply for a driver's license or a passport. He had created a half-dozen identities and allowed the world to believe that the teenager who disappeared just before the grisly death of Mr. Gerrard had died long ago. In the end he had been overly patient and overly cautious—after all, no one had been looking for him.

When he did begin work, patience was the key to his success. He heard stories of others in the business who rushed their jobs and paid the price. Nemo took his time, happy to spend weeks holed up in a grubby room or even living on the streets as he watched and waited and planned. Even a little job like Jasper Fleming had required patience.

But there were times for patience and times to get moving. When you had broken into a museum in the middle of the night, and a security guard was on the prowl, and someone, most likely another trained killer, was stalking you—that was not a time for patience. But Phoenix didn't seem to understand that.

Ruthie set the machine going again, then stepped across the room to a device not much larger than Enigma itself. The black metal box had a row of twenty-six keys across the front and a corresponding row of letters just above the keys. An angled section held four drums that looked exactly like the ones on the Bombe.

"This is the checking machine," said Ruthie. "We use it to see if that stop was good." She fiddled with the drums for a minute, referring to the letters she had written down in Patton's notebook. "I'll type, and you write down the letters that light up," she said, handing the note-book to Patton. Ruthie began to type the cipher text into the machine. With each key she depressed, a letter lit up on the front of the checking machine. After she had keyed in twenty or so letters she took the note-book from Patton and glanced over the transcription.

"Gobbledygook," she proclaimed. "We'll just have to wait for the next stop."

Nemo paced as the machine clicked and then stopped and Ruthie dismissed another stop and then another as no good. More than ten minutes had passed when Phoenix, nearing the end of its run through the 17,576 rotor configurations, finally made a good stop. This time Ruthie sat down in front of the checking machine and began whirling drums and making notes.

"What is she doing?" whispered Nemo to Patton, the machine behind them finally silent.

"She has to figure out the plugboard settings," said Patton. "And even then we won't have the complete setup. We'll need to know the ring settings, but a decent codebreaker can work those out by hand pretty quickly."

Nemo had no idea what Patton was talking about. He was used to being in full control of every situation and ceding authority to a stranger made him nervous. He gazed out the window, down the hill over the sea of "huts," and began to wonder if he should leave. Maybe if he didn't have the message or its decryption, whoever had hired him would stop following him and chase Patton and Ruthie instead. And even if they wanted to follow him, alone he could evade detection easily. He'd done it for the past three decades. He had no loyalty to Patton. He had no loyalty to anyone but himself. But as soon as the thought formed in his mind he discarded it. He did have a loyalty to Patton, he thought. If not in so many words, he had prom-ised to see her through this ordeal and to protect her from Fritz and Franz and anyone else who might come after that seventy-year-old message. He was in too deep to back out now, and frankly, he didn't want to. Though a part of him couldn't believe it, at the moment he was more interested in knowing the contents of that message than in saving his own skin.

"What time did you say the security guard comes by here?" said Nemo, eyeing a bouncing light disappearing between two rows of huts in the distance.

"I didn't," said Ruthie. "But we should shut off that light and get out of here."

"Don't you need the Enigma machine?" said Patton. "I mean, once you have all the settings, you can set up the machine and then crack the whole message, right?"

"Two problems there," said Ruthie, sweeping up her notes and switching off the light. "First, it'll take me another hour or so to crack the ring settings. I can do that by hand, but we can't stay here any longer because of the guard."

"And second?" said Patton.

"I don't have the key for that case," she said, pointing to the display cabinet that held the Enigma machine.

"You mean we're going to have the solution but no way to decipher the code?" said Nemo. "Then this has all been a waste of time."

"Take it easy," said Ruthie. "All we need is an Enigma machine, and I know just where we can find one."

VI

Alex Lansdowne had spent the morning sandblasting a red swastika off the back garden wall at his home in Buckinghamshire. Considering the contents of his garden and of the warehouse-sized building that occupied nearly half of the three acres behind his house, he was, frankly, surprised he didn't have to do this more often. He never knew, on those days when he woke to a swastika on the garden wall or a crude portrait of Hitler in the post, whether he was being attacked by people repulsed by what he kept in that garden or encouraged by those who thought they understood his motivations. Somewhere between the progressives and the skinheads lay the garden, and the world, of Alex Lansdowne.

Alex felt only apathy for those who decorated his garden wall, regardless of their motivation. A man who amasses the world's largest collection of Nazi artifacts and memorabilia is bound to make some enemies along the way and that fact didn't much bother him. He had sandblasted his garden wall before and he would do it again. What the hell, he thought, it gave him a little exercise.

Despite what the neo-Nazis and the town council thought, Alex had no interest in glorifying the Third Reich. His interest in Nazi Germany was historical and intellectual, not political. History fascinated Alex, particularly the Second World War, and he believed if one did not study and understand that war in all its minutiae the world would repeat that unhappy chapter, this time with nuclear weapons at the ready from day one. So to the chagrin of his neighbors, Alex kept four restored Panzer tanks at the bottom of the garden and a machine gun cannon mounted on top of his shed.

Most of his collection, however, remained invisible to those who objected to it—stashed away in his prefabricated aluminum warehouse and crammed into every nook and cranny of his crumbling home. After nearly forty years of collecting, Nazi uniforms, posters, books, sculptures, documents, vehicles, weaponry, and even office equipment crowded in on Lansdowne from every side. His collection had subsumed his house, leaving him only a bit of kitchen and a corner of a bedroom; it had annexed his garden; it had depleted his inheritance; it had driven away his wife; but it had never dampened his enthusiasm or sapped his strength. He believed one day the world would understand the importance of his passion, and until that day arrived he happily sacrificed his home, his money, his family, and his time to preserve and protect this collection that told a story no mere history book could re-create.

So he had sandblasted his wall and retreated to clean and polish his latest acquisition—a four-rotor Naval Enigma machine.

That night Alex couldn't sleep. He had been sucked into a conversation online with an American who believed Hitler had not killed himself on April 30, 1945, but had escaped Germany in the closing days of the war, fled to South America, and lived out his days in hiding. Alex found such theories, and the tenacity with which some people clung to them, fascinating. He was neither quick to believe nor quick to dismiss and he never used terms like "conspiracy theory" or "alternative history," which people like the enthusiastic American would find pejorative. His open-mindedness and willingness to listen meant that people who held such ideas felt comfortable pouring out every detail of their theories to him. He had heard the "Hitler Flees to South America" story many times before, but with each telling he gleaned new details, which he recorded in one of the notebooks on a shelf labeled simply *Possibilities*.

Following his latest conversation, he had found his "Hitler in South

America" notebook and recorded the name of a village in Argentina that was completely new to him. Some theories about the Nazis had been scientifically disproved—like the story that the man who landed in Scotland in 1941 wasn't Rudolf Hess, but a doppelgänger. DNA testing had finally put that to rest, and Alex had moved his "Hess Was Not Hess" notebook off the *Possibilities* shelf and onto the *Debunked* shelf. But for many of these theories, Alex maintained the philosophy reflected in the words he had once read in an article about secret Nazi bases in Antarctica—"The absence of evidence is not the evidence of absence."

Alex reshelved his "Hitler in South America" notebook in between "Nazis Got Technology from Space Aliens" and one of his favorites, "Himmler Mastered Alchemy." They might be far-fetched notions, thought Alex, but so was the idea that a high school dropout would become Führer of Germany in 1934 and an ironfisted dictator who ruled over much of Europe.

———

"Do you have a car?" said Ruthie as they slipped out the back of the museum.

"No," said Nemo.

"Yes, we do," said Patton, confused.

"Put yourself in the shoes of those gentlemen waiting for us at the gate," said Nemo. "You are parked right next to our rental car. What would you do?"

"I'd be sure the car wouldn't start," said Ruthie.

"This one is all kinds of smart," said Nemo.

"I drive a Mini Cooper," said Ruthie, "but if one of you can fold up in what passes for the back seat we can take it."

"I'll drive," said Nemo.

"Why should I let you drive?" said Ruthie.

"Trust me, you want me to drive."

"I'd let him," said Patton.

"How does the gate open?" asked Nemo.

"If you're driving out, it opens outward when you approach it," said Ruthie.

"And there's no other way?"

"There's a keypad next to it."

"And you know the code?"

"I do."

"OK, give me the keys and here's what we're going to do." Nemo explained his plan, and despite objections from Ruthie, he and Patton eventually convinced her it was the best way to escape the men at the gate, at least for the time being. Patton crept around the perimeter fence until she reached the keypad next to the gate. She could see the two men waiting in their car, illuminated by the red glow of a cigarette held by the driver, but they did not see her.

Meanwhile, Nemo and Ruthie, after waiting for the security guard to go inside the museum, pushed the Mini Cooper around the side of the building and pointed it toward the gate. The road led straight down-hill from the museum car park, then made two quick turns around the Bletchley Park visitor center before reaching the gate. This meant Nemo and Ruthie could coast almost all the way to the gate without being seen. Twenty seconds before the moment Patton would key in the gate code, with Ruthie folded up in the back seat, Nemo shoved off, the car gaining speed as it coasted down the hill.

When the gate began to open toward them, the men in the car climbed out and walked to the center of the drive. They carried no weapons, but merely stood in front of the gate. As Nemo had guessed, they expected to meet two unarmed people on foot. But a second later the Mini came coasting around the corner, almost silently. It had no headlights on and in the time it took for the men to realize that a car was heading straight at them, Patton was able to run from the bushes and dive into the open passenger door. As soon as she was inside the car, Nemo cranked the engine and flicked on the high beams. Surprised and blinded, the two men barely had time to leap out of the way before the car roared past and turned right into the main road.

"I only got a quick look," said Nemo as they sped down the empty road, "but those were definitely our old friends Fritz and Franz."

"Who are Fritz and Franz?" said Ruthie.

"Just a couple of Germans who tried to kill me Sunday morning," said Patton.

"Look," said Ruthie, "it's lovely to see you, Patton, it really is, and I'm happy to help you with a bit of codebreaking, but I didn't sign up for being chased by German assassins."

"They're not assassins," said Nemo, hugging the side of the road as they rounded a sharp curve and thereby throwing Ruthie across the back seat. "Or at least not very good ones."

"Yeah," said Patton, buckling herself in. "Don't worry about them. If they were any good, I wouldn't be here."

"Now, where is this Enigma machine you told us about?"

"Straight through the next three roundabouts will take us to the M1," said Ruthie, her voice calming somewhat. "Then we can get up some speed and get away from those . . . Germans."

"I think they'll be able to go a little faster than this old thing," said Patton. "No offense, Ruthie dear, but it's not exactly a race car."

"Besides," said Nemo, easing off the accelerator, "outrunning them wouldn't be very sporting."

"What do you mean?" said Ruthie. "You want a couple of killers to catch us? If you want them to shoot us, what was all that cloak-and-dagger show back at Bletchley?"

"I don't want them to catch *us*," said Nemo. "I want us to catch *them*."

"Are you sure you know what you're doing?" said Patton.

"Have I steered you wrong so far?" said Nemo. "Look, that was definitely Fritz and Franz, and they came through the same airport we did. I don't imagine they wanted to check in to a flight with a murder weapon in their bag."

"A murder weapon?" said Ruthie. "You said they weren't very good."

"Fucking bastards," said Patton. "They shot Art Handy—he's a sheriff's deputy and—"

"The point is," said Nemo, "they're almost certainly unarmed at the moment. If they had any weapons, they would have drawn them when they saw the gate opening. And we have two deadly weapons."

"We do?" said Ruthie.

"Yes," said Nemo. "A Mini Cooper and chutzpah." He shot Patton a look that said, *Take care of the girl in the back seat*, and she nodded ever so slightly as a pair of headlights appeared behind them.

"It'll be OK, Ruthie," said Patton, reaching a hand behind her seat and finding Ruthie's knee. "He knows what he's doing." Ruthie grabbed Patton's hand and held it so tightly she winced, but Patton went on. "Their job is not to hurt anybody else—it's to find the Enigma message. So we let them follow us, and once we've gotten to wherever this machine is and finished the decrypt, we give them the message, they'll be on their way, and nobody gets hurt."

"OK," said Ruthie, a hint of panic still in her voice.

"That is the plan, right?" said Patton to Nemo.

"Yeah," he said, "something like that."

Nemo drove right past the M1 and into the countryside on narrower and narrower roads, always making sure he kept the headlights visible in the rearview mirror.

"We're not driving toward the Enigma," said Ruthie, when they had veered onto a wooded lane so narrow it had pull-offs every hundred yards or so for passing vehicles.

"What are you doing?" said Patton in a low voice. Ruthie was still squeezing her hand and her fingers had gone numb.

"Trust me," said Nemo as the car behind pulled closer. "Is everyone buckled up?"

Ruthie released Patton's hand in order to fasten her seat belt and Patton did not offer it back. She couldn't guess Nemo's plan, but at this point she had no choice but to hold on as he suddenly gunned the car down the lane, shooting past the trees at fifty, sixty, then nearly seventy miles an hour.

"If we meet anyone . . ." shouted Ruthie from the back seat over the roaring of the Mini's engine.

"Not likely at this time of night," said Nemo. The headlights behind began to recede slightly and then disappeared around a curve. Patton assumed Nemo had chosen this narrow lane as the perfect spot to assert his superior driving skills and leave Fritz and Franz behind, but after another minute or two he slowed slightly, swung wide into a pull-off, threw on the handbrake, and the next thing Patton knew, they were skidding backward as Nemo spun the wheels searching for traction and Ruthie screamed from the back seat. In another couple of seconds they were speeding down the road in the direction they had come, the headlights of the other car rapidly growing ahead of them.

"Are you crazy?" cried Ruthie. "Their car is twice our size. It'll destroy us!"

"And they know that," said Nemo calmly, nudging their speed a little higher.

For a split second the other car disappeared behind a bend in the road, then it loomed directly in front of them, no more than a hundred yards away. Facing death that closely, Patton might easily have fallen into a flashback or a searing attack of panic and anxiety, but instead she experienced a moment of the sort of calm she had only ever felt in combat. The roar of the engine, Ruthie's hysterical screaming from the back seat, the blinding lights ahead, all disappeared. They were at war and she had no choice but to trust her fellow soldier—in this case, Nemo. Her life was now in his hands, which felt liberating. For a split second, she was completely free. She recalled a time a fellow soldier had tackled her to get her out of a line of sniper fire. In the moment she felt his hand on her shoulders and heard a bullet passing by her ear she knew there was nothing she could do but fall. Now she watched as the car in front seemed to close the gap in slow motion. It was like a ballet—peaceful, beautiful, she could almost hear music. Ruthie, she knew, would close her eyes and pray, but Patton watched. Afterward she might be furious at Nemo, she might be annoyed at Ruthie, she might even be dead, but in that instant, she felt peace.

Then the screech and crunch of crumpling metal, the explosion of bursting glass, the compression of her chest by the seat belt as the car came to a stop, the crying of Ruthie from the back seat—all invaded that peace, and reality crashed back in.

"That worked well," said Nemo, sounding completely unfazed.

The pursuing black car had veered off the road at the last moment, crashing into a tree at about fifty miles an hour. Nemo had steered the Mini right past Fritz and Franz and stopped a short way up the lane. Now he backed up until they were even with the remains of the other car. The front right side was crumpled against a tree and the driver slumped through the side window. He wore no seat belt and so had been bludgeoned badly by the airbag. Patton wasn't sure if he was alive or not. The passenger, who had been smart enough to wear his seat belt, lay against the deflated airbag, moaning softly.

"You stay here," said Nemo toward the back seat, not that Ruthie seemed to need any convincing. "Patton, you come with me."

Nemo grabbed his backpack out of the trunk and strode quickly toward the wrecked car.

"You want to tell me why you did that?" said Patton. "You could have gotten us all killed."

"Not a chance," said Nemo. "These guys had orders to protect the Enigma message at all costs. They knew if they collided head-on at high speed with a Mini Cooper, everything in our car would be toast. Sure, we would be collateral damage, but the message would have gone up in flames. So I picked a narrow road with trees on the side so they would have to veer into something nice and solid. Looks like it did the trick on this one." He held his fingers against the neck of the driver feeling for a pulse.

"Jesus, is this what you always do? Somebody causes you trouble so you kill them? You don't think maybe there's a more subtle solution to the problem?"

"Look, I never lied to you. You knew I was a killer when you got on that plane with me. And I guarantee you, if we hadn't killed him, eventually he would have killed us."

"Is that the guy who shot at me?" said Patton.

"No, that would be Fritz over there in the passenger seat. Here, secure him, will you?" Nemo pulled out a handful of thick plastic zip ties from his bag and tossed them to Patton. The edges of the plastic digging into her hand took her right back to Kandahar and this time she did feel an attack of anxiety coming on—her stomach knotted, her vision blurred, and she felt dizzy as she gripped the strips of plastic.

The mission had been to plant surveillance devices, but her unit had come under fire and taken shelter in what they thought was an abandoned house. The next thing she knew, she was zip-tying two "enemy combatants" to secure them for interrogation. She could smell the dust and hear the gunfire and see the beams of the flashlight sweeping around the windowless room. She did her best to shake off the vision, swallowing the sour bile that rose in her throat, and letting the sense memory of how to secure a prisoner with zip ties take over.

Before Fritz could rouse himself from his stupor, she had bound his hands and feet and Nemo had searched the car, retrieving two small black bags which he tossed into the trunk of the Ruthie's car before dragging Fritz toward the Mini.

"What do we do with him?" said Patton, afraid of the answer.

"Judging from the way you handled those zip ties, I'd say you know exactly what we do with him."

"We interrogate him."

"Precisely."

"Using enhanced techniques?"

"Is that what they call it now?"

"You're going to torture this guy?"

"I'm going to persuade him to tell us a few things and then prevent him from causing us any further trouble."

"I don't like the sound of that, coming from you," said Patton.

"Looks like you get a friend in the back," said Nemo to Ruthie, who was still shaking in the back seat, tears drying on her cheeks.

"There's hardly room for one back here," she managed to say. "You can't put him . . ."

"Not him, silly," said Patton. "Me. I know it's cozy, but we've been cozy before." She crawled into the back seat, practically sitting on Ruthie's lap in order to wedge herself into the tiny space. Seeing the look of terror on Ruthie's face, and understanding that the last thing they needed at this point was a hysterical traveling companion, she slipped her arms around Ruthie and pulled her close. "It'll be OK," she said. "I'm here." She felt Ruthie melt into her and knew that dormant passion would win out over terror. Ruthie always had been easy to manipulate.

Nemo tossed Fritz, now mumbling incoherently in German, into the passenger seat, not bothering to fasten his seat belt, and threw the car into gear, heading down the road back toward Bletchley—this time proceeding at a more reasonable pace, though still fast enough to bang Fritz around a bit.

"What are the police going to think?" said Patton.

"If we're lucky, they're going to think it was a single-car accident, driver dead because he wasn't wearing a seat belt, and no passenger. Fritz here was kind enough not to bleed on anything."

"He was dead?" said Ruthie with a tinge of panic in her voice. "That other man was dead? Who are they?"

"The guy in the front seat tried to kill me," said Patton. "And I'm sure his buddy back there would have been happy to do the same. I wouldn't shed too many tears."

"But if he's dead then . . ." Ruthie's voice trailed off.

"Then what?" said Nemo.

"Then . . . then we're responsible. We should do something."

"We are doing something," said Nemo, swinging the car into a farm track. "And I think I've spotted a good place to do it." About a quarter mile ahead, on the other side of a wide field, the headlights illuminated a weathered wooden barn with several pieces of farm equipment parked nearby. Nemo pulled into the rutted track that led to the barn.

"This car isn't really made for roads like this," said Ruthie, as she and Patton bounced wildly around in the back seat, but Nemo paid them no mind, nor did he react in any way to the mumbled protests of their involuntary passenger. A minute later, he pulled the car behind the barn and shut off the engine.

"Keep an eye on Fritz for a minute," he said, stepping out of the car.

"Erich," the man in the front said as Nemo disappeared into the darkness. For a moment neither Patton nor Ruthie responded but then the man said again, in a slightly stronger voice. "*Ich heiße Erich.* My name is Erich."

"Well, I wouldn't get too comfortable, Erich my boy," said Patton in a jocular tone.

"He's German," whispered Ruthie, "like you said."

"You don't have to whisper," said Patton. "I think he knows he's German."

"But why? Why is some German man chasing after you?"

"You want to answer that one, Erich?" said Patton. But the prisoner remained silent. "I don't think he wants to answer.

"I'll be honest, Erich," Patton continued, "when I came under fire Sunday morning, I never expected it would be some random German guy."

"Who did you expect?" said Ruthie, pressing herself against the side of the car, for the first time that night actually pulling away from Patton.

"How are you, Ruthie?" said Patton. "How has life been treating you since last we met?" She had decided to take a page from Nemo's book—when questions got uncomfortable, change the subject.

"Why am I here?" said Ruthie. "Why did you even come to me? I know you didn't really want to see me."

"Of course I wanted to see you, Ruthie," said Patton, taking Ruthie's hand and gently stroking it. "I mean, yes, we need to decrypt that message, but how lucky for me that it brings us back together. I know I was a shit back then, but I've missed you, Ruthie, I really have." Patton was surprised to find that this was the truth, that she even began to tear up as she said it. In spite of the circumstances, in spite of the fact that she had fully intended to feign affection for Ruthie in order to get her to cooperate, it actually was lovely to see her old flame.

"If you needed a decrypt, why didn't you just do it online?" said Ruthie. "You know there's a website set up for that."

"I think that's another question for our guest. You want to field that one, Erich?"

The screech of the wide barn door being slid sideways on rusty rollers distracted them from Erich's lack of interest in answering questions. In another moment, Nemo returned to the driver's seat and cranked the engine.

"This place is perfect," he said.

"Perfect for what?" said Ruthie.

Nemo did not answer but backed the Mini into the barn where the taillights illuminated a space filled with the detritus of a century or two of farming—old tools, a decrepit-looking tractor, piles of burlap sacks, coils of rope, a few rotting hay bales, and other junk too dust-covered to identify. Nemo hopped out of the car and invited the two women to do likewise. By the time they had extricated themselves from the back seat, he had already pulled Erich out of the passenger side and sat him on the floor, leaning against an old wooden crate.

"Careful you don't get any splinters from that," said Nemo. Erich's only response was to spit in Nemo's direction. "Oh, a polite one," said Nemo. "Who are you?"

Silence.

"His name is Erich," volunteered Ruthie from where she stood in the shadows. Nemo had turned off the Mini's engine but had left the running lights on to provide some illumination.

"He did tell us that much," said Patton.

"Erich. A nice German name for a not so nice German man," said Nemo. "And would you like to tell me why you were shooting at my friend here back in America?"

Silence.

"No? And would you like to tell me who you work for?"

Again, Erich merely stared ahead, expressionless.

"Well then," said Nemo, "I suppose we need to give you a little motivation to talk to us."

Patton and Ruthie watched as Nemo took a coil of rope and tossed one end over a rafter about fifteen feet overhead. He took the other end and slid under the rear of the Mini. Thirty seconds later he was back on his feet and working with the other end of the rope. Patton realized what he was doing before Ruthie did, and felt her stomach once more trying to revolt. Luckily, she hadn't eaten anything in nearly twelve hours. Forcing a car off the road in the heat of a pursuit in order to save one's own skin was one thing, but this was different. They could have left Erich to be discovered by the authorities, but this was cold-blooded and calculated. In the excitement of trying to break the Enigma Code, she had forgotten, at a gut level at least, exactly what Nemo was.

When she saw Nemo slip a noose over Erich's head, the penny dropped for Ruthie. "Oh, my God," she said. "Are you going to . . ."

"I'm going to motivate him," said Nemo. "Nothing more, nothing less." He slipped into the driver's seat and turned on the engine, pulling the Mini just far enough outside the barn to take most of the slack out of the rope. Erich did not react to any of Nemo's actions, and Patton wondered if he was still in shock from the accident and didn't understand what was happening.

Nemo put the car in neutral and pulled up the emergency brake, but left the engine running. He stepped back into the barn, but instead of approaching Erich he walked deliberately up to Ruthie, standing almost nose to nose with her as she cowered next to Patton.

"Get in the driver's seat," he said quietly.

"I can't," said Ruthie. "I couldn't."

"It's your car," said Nemo. "Get in the driver's seat." There was a slight menace in his voice and Patton stepped in front of him, taking Ruthie's hand.

"Leave her alone," said Patton firmly, pulling Ruthie toward her.

"You are thinking with some part of your anatomy other than your head," said Nemo. "I need to chat with Erich; she needs to get in the car."

"I'll do it," said Patton. "I owe Erich. But just leave Ruthie out of this." She squeezed Ruthie's hand gently and felt a squeeze back.

"You want to do it?" said Nemo.

"I don't *want* to," said Patton, "but if I have to I will. She won't and she doesn't have to."

"Which is exactly why it should be her. As far as I'm concerned, she's a total stranger. She has no loyalty to us, or at least not to me. It's safer for us if she's involved."

"A loyalty test?" said Patton. "Isn't that a little cliché?"

"If you want to call it that," said Nemo. He grabbed Patton by the wrist and yanked her away from Ruthie so hard that she fell backward onto the ground.

"Now get in the driver's seat," said Nemo, taking a step toward Ruthie, "and if I say go, you slam that thing in gear and drive . . . ten or twelve feet should do it."

"But I couldn't . . ." said Ruthie.

"Listen," said Nemo, "I'm not going to ask again. Patton here knows what I'm capable of, and I'm sure you're not the only person in the world who knows where to find an Enigma machine. Now get . . . in . . . the . . . car."

"You'd better do what he says," said Patton. "I'm so sorry, Ruthie."

Ruthie staggered forward, breaking into sobs as she crossed the barn and slid into the driver's seat.

"Now," said Nemo, turning to Erich. "Let's have a little chat and see if we can keep our codebreaker over there from going for a drive."

———

"What do you mean 'it's not entirely true that we don't have the money'?" said Eva Klein.

"I mean that Ingrid's plan to raise money by sending books to people is actually working," said Gottfried.

"I never understood how that would work," said Dietrich. "Those books never really belonged to—what did Ingrid call them?"

"Displaced persons," said Ingrid.

"Right. So how do we make money stealing old books out of libraries and mailing them to random people?"

"The people are not random," said Ingrid. "I always find someone with a family member who has . . . spent time as a guest of the Reich and I always match the book to the career of that family member."

"But still," said Dietrich. "That doesn't generate income."

"It's beginning to generate publicity and good will," said Gottfried, "and it generates letters of thanks and, with the help of our press releases, it generates stories in newspapers and magazines."

"None of which will pay for security personnel, transportation, or storage," said Eva.

"Yes," said Gottfried, "but once we had all that I set up a FundThis page. It's a website that allows people to make donations to nonprofit ventures. You enter the information about your organization and what it does, provide links to press coverage to prove you're legitimate, and then set a fundraising goal and length for your campaign. Because they want every project to work on equal footing, and because they want to invest the money during the length of your campaign, you can't monitor your results in real time. You have to wait until the campaign is over and then you find out how much you raised and who your donors were. I set a goal of a hundred thousand euros and a schedule of thirty days. The campaign ended ten minutes ago."

"And how much did we make?" said Eva.

"Two hundred and thirty-seven thousand euros," said Gottfried.

"We're in business!" said Dietrich, jumping up from his chair.

Ingrid Weiss gave a sly smile. "Yes, we certainly are," she said. "I told you it would work. And all it cost us was the price of mailing a few books."

"Not only that," said Gottfried, "but listen to the names of some of the donors. David Goldstein of Brooklyn, New York. Josh Schwartz of Tel Aviv, Israel. The Women of Temple Beth Torah, Miami, Florida."

"That's rather delightful," said Eva. "Projekt Alchemie is being funded by Jews."

But Gottfried did not answer. He had turned his attention to a blinking box on one of his computer screens. "It's a message from Karl," he said. "They're on the move."

"Is that it?" said Ingrid. "They're on the move? That's all they said?"

"That's all," said Gottfried.

"Get them on the phone for me," said Ingrid.

"Can't," said Gottfried. "They turned off the phone again."

"Stupid fools," said Ingrid, throwing a coffee mug across the room where it shattered against the stone wall.

The four conspirators stood in silence for a moment and then Gottfried said, "Do you realize what we can do with two hundred and thirty-seven thousand euros?"

"We will complete Projekt Alchemie," said Ingrid calmly. She had regained her composure in a matter of seconds.

"If there even is such a thing," said Dietrich. "I've always wondered, myself. I mean, Himmler believed in a lot of strange things."

"Trust me," said Ingrid, "it's real."

"If it were real," said Eva, "don't you think someone else would have discovered it by now?"

"Not necessarily," said Gottfried.

"You're right that we can do a lot with two hundred and thirty-seven thousand euros," said Eva. "I say we use that money to advance our cause and stop chasing shadows."

"They are not shadows," said Ingrid, rising up from her seat.

"It was the deathbed confession of a deluded old man," said Eva.

Eva did not even see the punch coming. Ingrid landed a fist in Eva's gut with such force Eva couldn't breathe for several seconds. As Eva doubled up, Ingrid once again drew her pistol and pointed it at the young woman.

"My grandfather was a lot of things," said Ingrid, "but he was not deluded. If he says Himmler succeeded with Projekt Alchemie, he was telling the truth. Now, if you choose to continue doubting him, I am happy to eliminate you from this task force right now. You are hardly essential to the operation."

"If she goes, I go," said Dietrich, stepping in front of Ingrid's gun.

"How gallant," said Ingrid, her voice dripping with disdain. "Coming to his lover's rescue."

"If nothing else," said Dietrich, ignoring the jibe, "we need Eva for her healthy skepticism." He turned to Eva and laid a hand on her shoulder.

"You need her because you fancy her," said Gottfried.

"I don't doubt your grandfather," said Eva, regaining her breath. "I want Projekt Alchemie to be real as much as anyone else."

"She's just saying," said Dietrich, "if we've turned a few old library books into two hundred and thirty-seven thousand euros, maybe we've got our own Projekt Alchemie. And maybe we shouldn't spend every penny of that money on tracking down a seventy-year-old piece of paper."

"Maybe it won't take every penny," said Gottfried. "The point is, now we at least have the means to take action if the message leads somewhere promising."

"Which brings us back to Karl and Erich," said Ingrid, lowering her weapon. "Should we use some of this money to send in reinforcements, or should we trust them to get the job done?"

"If they could be trusted to get the job done," said Eva, "we'd be reading the message by now. We should send them help."

"Eva's right," said Dietrich. "If we don't get the message then Projekt Alchemie is dead."

"But we don't know where they are at the moment," said Gottfried.

"Let me know as soon as they come back online," said Ingrid. "Until we know more, we can't decide anything. I swear to God when I see them again I'm going to give them a lot more than just a punch in the gut."

———

"Who do you work for?" said Nemo calmly, as if he and the German with the noose around his neck were having a casual conversation at a cocktail party.

The German remained silent.

"Don't you understand English? It'd be pretty stupid to send you to America to frame me for the murder of Jasper Fleming and then steal his paper if you don't speak English."

"I didn't need to frame you for his murder," said Erich. "You killed him."

"Ah, you do speak English. But you are mistaken, my friend. I did not kill Jasper Fleming. But I will ask you again, who do you work for?" Again, Erich did not speak.

"Maybe you don't know," said Nemo. "Maybe your associate in the driver's seat—the one who wasn't smart enough to put on his seat belt—was the brains of the outfit. Maybe you're not important enough to know who the boss is. After all, you were stupid enough to shoot at my friend here and careless enough to miss." Erich, who had been staring at Nemo, now dropped his gaze to the ground. "And now you're not even smart enough to save your own skin," said Nemo.

"It doesn't matter what you do to me," said Erich, looking up again. "Whether I live or die is of no consequence. The project will be completed, the Fourteen Words will be fulfilled, and the world transformed."

"What the hell is he talking about?" said Patton.

"Would you care to elaborate on that?" said Nemo, leaning forward but Erich responded by spitting in the face of his interrogator.

"I thought you might require a little prodding," said Nemo. He disappeared into the darkness for a moment and Patton looked at the defiant face of Erich, glowing in the red of the Mini's taillights. In such demonic light, this whole place seemed like a dungeon, some chamber of terror from a horror movie, not the sort of place she should find herself thirty-six hours after starting work on her choux pastry in rural North Carolina.

"You should talk," said Patton, almost to herself. "It makes it easier for everybody." She had seen what happened when people didn't talk, seen the horror and inhumanity of it, seen the uselessness of it for all concerned. Whether he ultimately talked or not, if he did not talk *now*, all of their humanity would be diminished. Patton thought she knew what Nemo was capable of, and she definitely knew that she wouldn't stand in his way. She hadn't in Kandahar and she wouldn't here.

As Nemo reemerged from the shadows, Patton shook her head and stepped back. Erich remained still and silent. Nemo carried a rusty pitchfork and, in the red light, looked more like the cartoon image of Satan than Patton cared for. He stepped forward and pressed one of the tines into Erich's right cheek, in among two days' stubble. For a moment the only sound was the idling car outside and the barely audible weeping of Ruthie at the wheel.

"Now," said Nemo, "this will really hurt. I'm not just going to stab you in the cheek. I'm going to rip all the way through to your lips. And I can do that on both sides. The best facial reconstruction surgery in the world won't keep the rest of your life from being a misery—and when the authorities find out all the nasty things you've done, you won't get the best in the world. But that's all in the future. Right now, what you need to worry about is that it will hurt more than you can imagine. Think about the worst pain you've ever known and then double it and you're still way off. So before I rip your face apart, I'm going to ask you one more time. Who do you work for?"

Patton could see the deepening dimple where the tine pressed into Erich's cheek. Erich tried to turn his head away but there was nowhere for him to go.

"It's going to be a lot harder to answer my questions with a mouth full of blood and a torn-off cheek," said Nemo.

"The project will be completed, the Fourteen Words will be fulfilled, and the world transformed," repeated Erich through gritted teeth.

"I don't give a damn about your Fourteen Words, whatever the hell they are," said Nemo, pressing the rusty point of the pitchfork hard enough that a spot of blood bloomed on Erich's face.

"That's all I have to say," said Erich.

"You're sure about that?" said Nemo.

"Yes," said Erich. And Patton had heard that voice before. It had spoken Arabic instead of English, but it meant the same thing. Erich was telling the truth. No matter what Nemo did, no matter how much pain he inflicted, Erich would not say anything other than the mantra he had already repeated. Some people could not be broken. You could hear it in their voices—the unmistakable sound of devotion to a cause so intense that nothing, not the greatest pain and certainly not the threat of death, would break it.

"Very well," said Nemo. For an instant Patton breathed a sigh of relief. They would leave this man bound and gagged in a remote barn to be discovered barely alive in a few days. But that vision disappeared a second later when Nemo, an expression of rage suddenly exploding across his face, plunged the tine into Erich's cheek. A garbled scream issued from Erich as the blood filled his mouth. Nemo leaned close, looked directly into Erich's eyes, then yanked the pitchfork down, ripping a wide gash through Erich's cheek. The scream grew more choked as blood poured into Erich's throat.

"That was for Art Handy," said Nemo. He stood for a moment, watching his victim writhing in pain, then turned toward Ruthie. "Drive," he shouted, his eyes now looking positively possessed.

Ruthie sat in the driver's seat, her face buried in her hands. Nemo walked up to the car, tapped the bloody pitchfork on the window and shouted again, "Drive."

"Don't make her," cried Patton. "Don't drag her down to our level." She rushed toward Nemo, who whirled on her, pitchfork at the ready, and drove her back into the shadows. Then he turned back to Ruthie and screamed, "If you don't want your cheeks to look like his, then fucking drive!"

Trembling all over, Ruthie threw the car into gear and eased forward, the weight of Erich pulling on the Mini. When she had gone about ten feet she stopped, put on the emergency brake, and shut off the engine. In the sudden quiet the sound of life being slowly choked out of Erich seemed to echo with the volume of a cannon. Ruthie had not driven fast enough to break Erich's neck; only Nemo watched as the German twitched at the end of the rope. Patton rushed to Ruthie and helped her out of the car, throwing her arms around her as they both quietly wept.

"You really are a sick bastard," she said to Nemo over Ruthie's shoulder.

"Sometimes somebody has to be," said Nemo, a tone of reconciliation in his voice.

Erich's body finally stopped turning slowly back and forth as the rope twisted and untwisted, dispersing the energy of his final spasms. The blood from the wound on his cheek, which had soaked the front of his shirt, slowed to a drip and the only sounds were the slight creak of the rope and the occasional plop of a drop of blood on the dirt floor of the barn. Patton released her hold on Ruthie, took a deep breath, and stepped back into the barn.

"I thought you said never leave a crime scene," she said, surveying the damage. "This looks like a crime scene."

"Does it?" said Nemo. "I'd say this man was racked with guilt about the murder he committed back in the US, he tried to hang himself but the first time the knot didn't hold and he hit the pitchfork leaning against these hay bales—you know, the ones he jumped off of." As he said this, Nemo wiped off the handle of the pitchfork with his shirttail, then leaned it, tines upward, just underneath Erich's body.

"How in the world are the cops here going to discover he's the one who killed Art Handy?" said Patton.

"Well, he has your name and address on a piece of paper in his pocket to begin with."

"How do you know that?" said Patton.

"Because I'm going to put it there," said Nemo. "Throw in a little suicide note and the fact that he probably still has powder residue on his fingers, and they'll pin the murder on him. And after all, he probably did kill Art and he certainly tried to kill you. The cops will know from the start that he's a bad guy and trust me, they don't dig too deeply when investigating the deaths of bad guys."

Nemo backed the car into the barn, but it took all three of them to hoist the body back up and tie the end of the rope that Nemo had affixed to the axle of the Mini to an old tractor parked behind the stack of hay bales. Ruthie no longer objected to anything. She looked pale and numb but she did what Nemo asked.

"Looks like a suicide to me," said Nemo. He had placed two pieces of paper in Erich's pockets as Patton helped Ruthie back to the car.

"I can't believe you did that," Ruthie said softly when they were all back in the car.

"I didn't do it," said Nemo. "You drove the car. You killed him."

"Only because you threatened me," protested Ruthie.

"And who's going to believe that? By the time there's a trial I'll be long gone. Your car will match the tracks at the barn. You might not be convicted, but it won't be pleasant."

"But . . ." Ruthie looked horrified and leaned her head between the front seats as Nemo pulled across the gravel forecourt and toward the track that led back to the main road.

"You've made your point," said Patton. "Now leave her alone." She understood exactly what Nemo was doing. He wanted Ruthie to be as deeply involved as they were, to be at equal risk of exposure if anything went wrong.

"It's OK," said Nemo. "As far as I'm concerned it was suicide. I'm not going to tell anyone otherwise. Unless you give me a reason to."

"What do you mean 'a reason'?" said Ruthie in a shaky voice.

"Calm down," said Patton, reaching back for Ruthie's hand. "He's just kidding. No one's telling anyone anything." But Patton knew Nemo spoke the words for good reason.

"Where are we going?" said Nemo as he turned back onto the road.

Ruthie did not seem to realize he had directed the question at her.

"Your friend with the Enigma machine," said Patton. "Where does he live?"

"Outside a village called Hambleden," said Ruthie. "It's near Henley. Since you made me leave my phone back at Bletchley, you'll have to use the atlas under Patton's seat." The sky was beginning to lighten ever so slightly, though it would be hours until sunrise. Still, Patton managed to find Hambleden on the map.

"Keep us off the main roads," said Nemo. "Motorways have CCTV cameras, and you never know who might be watching."

Patton could tell from the way Ruthie gripped her hand that she was still in shock from what Nemo had done at the barn. Ruthie had probably never seen that sort of violence up close, never seen a man die, certainly never participated in the taking of another human life. Yes, Patton had been shocked by the pleasure Nemo seemed to take in practically ripping Erich's face off, but when she thought of Art Handy, she couldn't honestly say she had any regrets about the demise of "Fritz and Franz." And what happened in the barn was not so different from what happened in that house in Kandahar. But to Ruthie it was all new. Once she had directed Nemo onto a road leading more or less south, Patton turned to Ruthie and gave her hand a little squeeze.

"Do you still like Pinot Grigio?" she said. "Remember that little bar right off Harvard Square where we used to make it through a couple of bottles on half price night?"

She managed to distract Ruthie with recollections of their summer together, and under the influence of nostalgia she had almost forgotten that they had just killed two men, when Nemo turned to her and said, "I just have one question."

"What's that?" said Patton.

"What the hell are the Fourteen Words?"

———

APRIL 1942

Helmut Werner bounced in the seat as he drove the Kübelwagen up the steep gravel track. He had left Innsbruck nearly an hour ago, but some of these Alpine roads still had snow and ice covering them and it had been slow going. But Helmut was used to slow, solitary work. He had spent the last four years crisscrossing the Reich in the service of Projekt Alchemie, the full scope of his work known only to himself and Reichsführer Himmler. Even Helmut did not understand every mission. How today's assignment fit into the overall scheme of Projekt Alchemie he could not venture to guess, but he trusted the Reichsführer and would not dare question his instructions. And if, in the course of the day, Helmut had an opportunity to contribute to the grand work of ridding his fatherland of the Jewish pestilence, so much the better. Such opportunities did arise on occasion. He glanced over his shoulder at his MP40 submachine gun sitting in the back seat. He hadn't used it in nearly three weeks, but one could always hope. He slammed the car into low gear and ground up the last quarter mile to the house perched on the mountainside.

The man who answered Helmut's knock did not look like a threat to the Reich. Stooped with age, bespectacled, and dressed in shabby clothing, he possessed the merest wisp of white hair around the crown of his head.

"May I help you?" he said.

"Who is it?" said a frail woman's voice from within the house.

"I don't know yet," shouted the man over his shoulder. "I'll tell you when I know."

"I am Section Leader Helmut Werner of the SS," said Helmut. He spoke calmly and with deference, as if addressing his own grandfather. "May I come in?"

"Certainly, certainly," said the man. "It's someone from the SS," he shouted to his wife.

"Did you ask him in?" came the voice from within.

"Of course I asked him in," shouted the man. "Don't you think I would ask him in?"

Helmut walked past the old man, down a short corridor, and into a tiny sitting room. The window looked out into the valley from which he had just ascended and in front of that window, at a small table, sat a woman who looked even older and more decrepit than the man.

"You are Herman and Helga Schneider," said Helmut. It was not a question.

"Yes, yes," said the man. "What is it you want?"

"What does he want?" said the woman.

"I just asked him that," shouted the man. "So tell me," he said, turning back to Helmut. "I haven't got all day."

"And what are you so busy with that you can't take the time to talk to me?" said Helmut, allowing the merest hint of a threat into his voice.

"Nothing, nothing," said the old man. "I am at your service."

"You are a collector of books, I believe," said Helmut.

"Yes," said the man, for the first time sounding wary.

"Reichsführer Himmler was reviewing the auction records from a few years back and he came across an item he would like to add to his library. A certain scroll which I believe is in your possession."

"Surely the Reichsführer has other sources for books than an old man with a tiny collection."

"This scroll is, how would you put it, unique."

"Perhaps I could copy it out for him," said the man in a pleading voice.

And now Helmut released the fury in his voice which invariably cowed those before him. "Reichsführer Himmler does not keep a library of copies!" he shouted. "Now show it to me."

"I beg you," said the man. "I have always supported the Reich. I have my *Ahnenpass*—I can prove my Aryan blood. I am an old man. Can you not leave me in peace?"

"We are at war," snarled Helmut. "There is no such thing as peace." He was beginning to enjoy watching the man, who had begun visibly shaking.

"I can help you," said the man. "You want Jews, don't you? There is a family hiding near here. At the next house down the hill. I can take you to them."

"I am not a patient man," said Helmut. "Give me the scroll now, and perhaps I won't burn the rest of your collection."

Helmut could now see tears sliding down the man's face. His wife still sat in her chair, stoic, apparently, or perhaps too deaf to understand what was happening. The man shuffled across the room and leaned over to open a low cupboard. The shelves within were crammed with books, but he did not need to search. He knew exactly what Helmut wanted and exactly where it was. He lifted out a polished wooden box, and now openly weeping, he passed it to Helmut. "My greatest treasure," he said. "Please take care of it."

A smile crept across Helmut's face as he stroked the smooth surface of the box, then set it down on the table.

"Is there something else?" said the old man, stepping back from Helmut.

"Just one thing," said Helmut, feeling his pulse speed up with the anticipation of the pleasure to come. "Do you know the penalty for failing to report a family of Jews?" he said quietly.

Before the old man could respond, Helmut swung his weapon off his shoulder and began firing, watching as the bullets threw the old man and his wife against the window. The glass shattered and when he stopped firing, Helmut could hear birds singing outside.

"Now," he said aloud as he scooped up the box. "Time to go find those filthy Jews."

―――――

Alex Lansdowne was still awake at 4:00 a.m. when he heard the buzzer for his front gate. He had installed a security fence and gate with a key code years ago, after he tired of trespassers trying to steal or deface items in his collection. Now, someone pressed the buzzer in the middle of the night about once a week. Some local residents wanted to make his life unpleasant so he would move; some curiosity seekers wanted to wander around his grounds to glimpse the row of Panzer tanks they had spotted on Google Earth; and some skinheads and neo-Nazis came to pay homage. Alex ignored all such visitors, and every time the buzzer woke him from his sleep or disturbed his thoughts as he lay awake, he considered disconnecting it. But for some reason he never did. Later, he would think perhaps tonight was that reason.

He went downstairs to look at the grainy black-and-white video screen connected to his security camera by the gate and saw not a hooded teenager running into the night or a tattooed skinhead contemplating climbing the fence, but Ruthie Drinkwater standing by the driver's side of her Mini Cooper, staring straight into the camera. He didn't wait to see what she wanted but immediately pressed the button that opened the gate.

Alex had met Ruthie several years ago on one of his many trips to Bletchley. He constantly compared their collection of Enigma machines and related devices to his own and had worked with their restoration team to share some of his knowledge and even provided them with some parts cannibalized from one of his machines that was so far beyond repair it was only useful as a source for rotors and keys. While Alex only collected German machines (he had three fully restored Enigmas) the Allied machines on display at Bletchley fascinated him, particularly the re-created Bombe. Ruthie had been the volunteer operating the Bombe on the day Alex first saw Phoenix, and the two had struck up a friendship, occasionally meeting for tea in the Bletchley Park café. He had often invited her to view his collection, but she had always demurred. Now she stood in his kitchen, sipping tea from a cup that had once been used at the Eagle's Nest, Hitler's private retreat near Berchtesgaden.

Ruthie had calmed down on the drive to Hambleden, largely due to Patton's attentions. Though still a bit pale, she seemed to have forgotten about the horrors of earlier in the night and stood chatting amiably with Alex. She had introduced Nemo and Patton simply as old friends interested in his collection. She had made no mention of Enigma.

Nemo once again felt sidelined by Ruthie. He needed her, he knew, but all this chitchat frustrated him. Yes, he had disposed of Fritz and Franz, but that didn't mean they should dawdle. It was only a matter of time before whomever had hired him and Fritz and Franz figured out where they were and sent a new, probably more competent, team after them. When Ruthie asked for a second cup of tea, he finally spoke up.

"We didn't just come to chat and have a tour," he said.

"I thought not," said Alex. "But this is England, and a cup of tea before business is always in order."

"We've had a cup of tea," said Nemo.

"You'll have to forgive him," said Ruthie. "His social skills are somewhat lacking. But we do have a favor to ask."

"Name it," said Alex.

"I'd like to borrow one of your Enigma machines."

"For Bletchley?" said Alex. He was not in the habit of loaning out items from his collection, but he supposed he might make an exception for the museum.

"No, I mean I need to use it," said Ruthie. "I can do that here. It shouldn't take more than a couple of hours."

"What are you doing," said Alex with a laugh, "decoding a secret message?"

"None of your—" said Nemo, but this time Patton interrupted him.

"That's exactly what we're doing."

"Then follow me," said Alex. He led them down a long hallway and into a huge high room with a circular staircase in one corner and a balcony all the way around. Every wall was lined with glass cases displaying everything from uniforms and weapons to maps, books, china, typewriters, radios, medals, paintings, and more. "These are just a few of my nicer items," said Alex.

Patton gave a whistle. "How big is this collection?"

"Too big if you ask most people, including the neighbors," said Alex. "Just big enough, if you ask me at my more cogent moments. But I've lived long enough to know that the real answer is: not as big as it will be tomorrow."

He led them to a case against the far wall that held his trio of Enigma machines. He had two three-rotor machines, like the ones used by the army, and one four-rotor Naval Enigma, each restored to shiny perfection.

"Those are beautiful," said Ruthie.

"Few people would appreciate them as much as you," said Alex. "I'm pleased you came to see them."

"It's an SS message," said Ruthie, "so if I could use one of the three-rotor machines."

"Absolutely," said Alex. He took a key out of his pocket and unlocked the case, carefully lifting one of the machines onto the long table that stretched down the center of the room.

"We got a good start with the Bombe," said Ruthie. "So it shouldn't take me too long to finish the decrypt." She settled in a chair in front of the Enigma machine and Patton handed her the notebook with the transcription of the message and the work Ruthie had done at Bletchley. For a moment, Ruthie did nothing, just sat and stared.

"Is something wrong?" said Nemo.

"No," said Ruthie. "It's just—I get chills every time I do this. Actually decrypt a real message on a real Enigma machine. These things are worth hundreds of thousands of pounds and it's hard to . . ."

"Don't worry about it," said Alex, leaning over her shoulder and pressing a few keys, the others watching as letters lit up and rotors moved in their slots. "You won't hurt it. Besides, what's the point in having things like this if you don't get to use them?"

"If you're sure," said Ruthie.

"Of course," said Alex. "We'll leave you alone so you can concentrate. Maybe you two would like a tour?"

Patton felt more repulsed than fascinated by the artifacts surrounding her and a quick glance at Nemo told her he had no interest in listening to Alex boast about his collection. Besides, if Alex Lansdowne was an expert on Nazi Germany, maybe he could answer a few questions.

"Is there someplace we could just talk?" she asked.

"We'll go to my study," said Alex. "Ruthie, it's right off the kitchen. If you need anything else let me know."

Alex clearly never intended for his study to accommodate visitors, but as he explained, few people ever came to visit, and his collection had crowded out such things as sitting rooms and dining tables, where they might more comfortably have conversed. So Alex sat behind his desk (it belonged to one of Himmler's assistants, he bragged) and Patton and Nemo settled for two folding chairs set up in the tiny bit of floor space not given over to piles of books and papers, unopened packages, rusted weapons and helmets, and other unidentifiable detritus. Here, Patton thought, one could not tell trash from treasure.

"What's the topic for tonight?" said Alex. "Or should I say, this morning." It was after five and the thick curtains in the window did not keep out the light.

"Projekt Alchemie," said Patton before Nemo could speak.

"Projekt Alchemie," repeated Alex with a smile. "That's a term I haven't heard in a long time."

"But you have heard it?" said Nemo.

"Oh, yes," said Alex, reaching up and removing a notebook from his *Possibilities* shelf. "You know Himmler was interested in all sorts of occultism—witchcraft, the Holy Grail, ancient legends and mythology, and, of course, alchemy."

"But he didn't really turn lead into gold," said Nemo.

"Maybe he did and maybe he didn't," said Alex. "I've learned that the life of the open mind is much more interesting than that of the skeptic. Here are my notes on Himmler and alchemy, for what they're worth."

Alex tossed the notebook to Patton. "Some of that is pretty well documented—like Himmler's being bamboozled by Heinz Kurschildgen and Karl Malchus, but most of it is rumor and speculation and guesswork and theories."

"This is incredible," said Patton, paging through the notebook.

"Not the sort of thing you find in a typical history book," said Alex.

"Because rumor and speculation are not the same as fact," said Nemo.

"True," said Alex, "and most of it is probably utter bullshit, but I have known facts to turn out to be lies and rumors to turn out to be secrets."

"So what is the rumor and speculation about Projekt Alchemie?" said Patton.

"It varies," said Alex, "but the basics are that Himmler used H-Sonderkommando not just to try to scientifically prove the superiority of the Aryan race but for occult research as well."

"Research like how to turn lead into gold?" said Patton.

"I've never come across the word 'lead,'" said Alex. "All the stories I've heard are a little more veiled than that. The word I hear most often is '*Ausgangsmaterialien*.'"

"What's that mean?" said Patton.

"Base materials," said Alex.

"And did he succeed?" said Patton. "In turning base materials into gold?"

"That's the question, isn't it?" said Alex. "I've met people who say that he did, but I've met people who say a lot of things."

"Have you ever met anyone who mentioned something called the Fourteen Words?" said Patton.

"You're kidding, right?" said Alex.

"No," said Patton. "Why do you ask?"

"Because the Fourteen Words are among the things I've had to sandblast off my garden wall. A lot of people don't appreciate what I do and some people perhaps appreciate it too much—either way, whether they are put there out of disapproval or support, I've certainly seen the Fourteen Words more than once."

"You sound like you're just the person we need to talk to," said Nemo, leaning forward in his seat and showing a real interest in the conversation for the first time. "What are these Fourteen Words?"

"What makes you ask?" said Alex.

"A friend of ours mentioned them," said Patton.

"Interesting friends you have."

"Look," said Nemo, standing, "are you going to tell us what they are or not?"

"Take it easy there, buddy," said Patton, grabbing Nemo by the arm and pulling him back to his chair.

"It's no secret," said Alex. "The Fourteen Words are a sort of motto for the neo-Nazi, white supremacist movement. There are a few different versions, but the most common is 'We must secure the existence of our people and a future for white children.'"

"So, Fritz and Franz were neo-Nazis," said Patton.

"Doesn't surprise me," said Nemo.

"Fritz and Franz?" said Alex.

"Couple of German friends of ours," said Patton.

"About as Aryan a pair as you've ever seen," said Nemo.

"There is another version of the Fourteen Words," said Alex. "'Because the beauty of the white Aryan woman must not perish from the Earth.'"

"That's a sentence fragment," said Patton.

"I don't think grammar is a top priority for these people," said Alex.

"What about you?" said Nemo.

"What do you mean?" said Alex.

"You live in a house full of swastikas and SS uniforms and Nazi shit, where do you stand on the Fourteen Words? Where do you stand on all of this?" Nemo waved his hand around to indicate the museum Alex Lansdowne inhabited.

"I don't stand," said Alex. "I'm not political. I'm not here to pick sides. I'm just a preserver of artifacts. Someday it will be up to others to decide what those artifacts mean or what relevance they have."

"But you sandblast the Fourteen Words off your garden wall," said Patton.

"Not because I agree or disagree with them," said Alex, "because I don't want graffiti on my wall. I'd do the same thing if they painted 'Alex is a hero.'"

"I wouldn't hold your breath on that," said Patton with thinly veiled contempt.

"So Fritz and Franz were Nazis and this guy isn't much better," said Nemo. "None of that helps us find out who's behind all this and what that damn message says."

"You're wrong about one of those things," said a voice from the doorway. Ruthie stood there, silhouetted against the morning light that came in through the kitchen window, holding a sheet of paper. "I cracked the code."

————

Under ordinary circumstances, the funeral for Jasper Fleming would have drawn few mourners. In fact, if anyone had thought to consider Jasper's own wishes, there would not have been a funeral at all. But the only person who knew Jasper's wishes was P.J. Harcourt, and she had been missing for two days. Sheriff Tommy Linton would have thought nothing about P.J.'s being gone if it hadn't been for the murder that took place in her backyard—and that murder was the reason nearly a hundred people now crowded the chapel of Sheets Funeral Home paying their respects to Jasper Fleming. Gordon Sheets, the funeral director, had scheduled Jasper's service immediately after the one for Art Handy, the late deputy sheriff of Alta Vista. Most of Art's mourners had stuck around for Jasper. The two bodies were driven out to the cemetery behind the Methodist church on Highway 14 in the same caravan of cars.

At the cemetery, when both men had been buried and a few of the mourners still lingered, Art's widow, Renée, asked Sheriff Tommy about P.J.'s disappearance.

"We don't even know if it is a disappearance," said Tommy. "According to Susan at the library, she's been known to skip town for a few days every now and then. Says it helps her recharge. But it's an awfully big coincidence that she did it this time with bullet holes in her windows and a dead body in her backyard."

"Have you filed a missing persons report?" said Renée.

"We haven't listed her as a missing person," said Tommy. "Not yet. But she is a person of interest in the investigation, and that does give us the ability to put some feelers out."

"Any leads?"

"Two, actually. We searched the house and found the floor safe in her closet was open and empty. We don't know what she kept in there, but she doesn't have a safe deposit box at the bank and there was one thing we didn't find anywhere else in her house."

"What's that?"

"Her passport. I checked with the Passport Agency and she had a new one issued just last year."

"You think she left the country?"

"At first I didn't," said Tommy, "because of the second thing we found. Her phone turned up in the parking lot of a truck stop in Tennessee."

"You don't need a passport to go to Tennessee," said Renée.

"No, but you need one to go to London. Just to cover my bases I ran a check on her passport with Customs and Border Protection, and she boarded a flight for London in Atlanta the day after Art was killed."

"You don't think P.J. had anything to do with Art's murder?" said Renée. "I mean, she couldn't possibly."

"Not a chance," said Tommy. "But I sure would like to talk to her. And I sure would like to know why her passport is in England and her phone is in Gatlinburg."

The mourners had mostly returned to their cars and Tommy took Renée's arm and led her slowly back to the cruiser in which they had driven to the cemetery. She was holding up pretty well, he thought, but he had seen this before with the spouses of murder victims or people who died in accidents. They remained stoic through the funeral, but after a few nights home alone, after the casseroles stopped arriving and the visitors slowed to a trickle, the darkness set in. Tommy vowed he would be there for Renée in the days and weeks and months ahead. It was the least he could do for Art.

If Tommy had been focused more on police work and less on Renée that day, he might have noticed three men lurking in the cemetery, only one anywhere near the mourners. The two who sat smoking at the foot of the hill might easily have been mistaken for groundskeepers, loafing around waiting to fill the graves with dirt. The one who stood by a tree just close enough to hear the proceedings made notes in a small black book. Tommy only glanced at him, assuming he was one of the out-of-town reporters who had turned up for the funerals. The mysterious murder of Art Handy had made the papers all across the state, and when combined with the attempted murder of a former army sergeant and the apparent suicide by allergy of her elderly neighbor, the story was just bizarre enough to make it onto the wires and show up in a few national outlets.

The man with the notebook stood just within earshot of Tommy and Renée. Once the cruiser had pulled away, he met his companions back at their rental car. "It's definitely her," he said. "And she's gone to London."

———

"The punctuation and the capitalization are mine," said Ruthie, "and of course the translation, but the message seems clear enough." She held up the paper and read:

"Projekt Alchemie successful. Location of results indicated in Reichsführer Himmler's library catalog number AL1533. The project to remain secure despite temporary suspension of the Reich due to Allied action. Because of Projekt Alchemie, the Reich will rise again. Heil Hitler."

Nemo sat down in his chair and Alex leaned back in his. For a moment the room fell quiet, and they could hear the cooing of the doves outside.

"What does it mean?" said Ruthie.

"It's pretty obvious what it means," said Nemo. "It means they figured it out."

"You think the Nazis actually figured out how to turn . . . what was it you called them?" asked Patton, turning to Alex.

"Base materials," said Alex.

"You think the Nazis figured out how to turn base materials into gold?"

"If that's true," said Alex, "why didn't they do it? It could have made a big difference in the progress of the war."

"We think this message came from the very end of the war," said Patton. "Just days before Germany surrendered. But I still don't believe it."

"It would explain why my erstwhile employer has been hunting us down," said Nemo. "Anybody with that secret could . . ."

"Could rule the world," said Alex.

"So you think it's true?" said Patton.

"I've learned to keep an open mind," said Alex.

"You said . . . What did you just say? That anyone with the secret to alchemy could rule the world?" said Patton.

"Money and power are indistinguishable these days," said Alex.

"God," said Patton, standing up and taking the paper from Ruthie. "Oh, God."

"What's the matter?" said Nemo.

"That's what they want. They want to use money to rule the world—rule it in a way Hitler could only dream of . . . but true to his vision."

"The Fourteen Words," said Nemo.

"Exactly," said Patton. "Can you imagine what a gang of white supremacist neo-Nazis could do with limitless wealth and the Fourteen Words as their manifesto?"

"Like it says in the message," said Alex, "the Reich could rise again."

Nemo had never known his own ethnic heritage; he only knew his skin was far from white. Far enough that he could remember being called *half-breed* and *mongrel* as a child. He had lived mostly in the shadows as an adult, but he still heard it sometimes when he ventured into a bar or restaurant, or even when just walking down the street. He heard that snort of contempt or caught a glance of dismissive derision and the unspoken, and lately sometimes spoken, sentiment that he was somehow less. These were not organized bands of racists, just random people in the street. He could only imagine what an infinitely funded group of neo-Nazis would do with the likes of him. And then he remembered Jack—the face of the one person he had ever really loved, his deep chocolate skin glistening with a sheen of summer sweat after they had run the six blocks from the park to the house. What chance did Jack stand against alchemical racists?

"Heil fucking Hitler," said Nemo with contempt.

"Let me get this straight," said Ruthie. "You think that Heinrich Himmler discovered the secret to alchemy, that he kept it a secret, and that those people who were chasing us are planning to use that secret to bring about the return of the Third Reich or some sort of worldwide racist agenda?"

"We're entertaining the possibility," said Patton.

"There's one way to find out," said Nemo.

"What's that?" said Ruthie.

"We need to find that book in Himmler's library, the one in the message."

"Reichsführer Himmler's library catalog number AL1533," said Ruthie. "How exactly do you propose we figure out what that is, or where it is?"

"The Nazis were obsessive about keeping records," said Patton. "Surely Himmler kept a catalog of his library."

"Of course he did," said Alex.

"I don't suppose you have it tucked away on your shelves someplace?" said Nemo.

"No," said Alex, "but I know who does."

VII

Helmut Werner stood in an anteroom in Wewelsburg Castle. When he had returned with the scroll to Innsbruck, Himmler had sent word to deliver it personally to Wewelsburg and after nearly two days of traveling across Germany Helmut had arrived an hour ago and been shown by an SS oberführer down a long series of dimly lit stone corridors into the nearly empty room in which he now waited. He hadn't seen Himmler in person for several weeks and looked forward to a reunion with the man whom he saw as both idol and friend. Wewelsburg was ostensibly Himmler's base for training SS leadership, but Kurt knew that the primary work at the castle was scientific, including research on the prehistory of the German and Aryan people that would prove the superiority of the Aryan race. Helmut held the mahogany box he had recovered from the Schneiders and the wood seemed to glow in the dim light of the sconces that framed the massive wooden door through which he had come. An equally large door opposite now eased open and Helmut stepped in.

The room was slightly brighter than the one he had just left. Only two small windows admitted light from outside and every wall was lined with bookcases that teemed with ancient-looking volumes of leather and vellum. A ladder leaned against one case—even a man as tall as Helmut Werner could not reach the upper shelves. In front of a large stone fireplace stood a massive library table, with stacks of books at one end. Behind a wide wooden desk, as solid and permanent as the Reich itself, stood Helmut's old friend.

"Heil Hitler," said Himmler with a slight smile.

"Heil Hitler, Herr Himmler," said Helmut.

"It is good to see you again," said Himmler. "And I see you have brought me a gift."

"Herr Schneider was most happy to contribute to the good of the Reich," said Helmut.

"I'm sure," said Himmler, his smile now more pronounced. "Shall we have a look?" He took the box and walked over to the library table and Helmut followed. Himmler opened the box and carefully lifted out the scroll. When he had taken it from Schneider, Helmet had wondered what could be so important about an old scroll, and his curiosity only grew as Himmler unrolled it on the table. It reached from end to end, at least twelve feet. Himmler leaned over the long strip of vellum and his smile became a grin.

"Beautiful," he said.

The scroll was covered with bizarre images, illuminated in blues, reds, greens, and golds. A green dragon stood upon a winged globe; a scowling sun shed tears on a dove with the head of a king; a red-bearded man held a two-handled glass bottle inside of which was something akin to a graphic novel—scenes showing a group of people standing around a flask holding a woman who seemed to undergo some sort of transformation. In the center the same bearded man held aloft a crown of glittering gold which shone more brightly than anything else in the scroll. Helmut thought it must be decorated with actual gold leaf.

"What is it?" said Helmut.

"An alchemical scroll of the fifteenth century," said the Reichsführer, his eyes sparkling with delight.

"Certainly it is beautiful," said Helmut. "But I do not understand how it will assist with Projekt Alchemie."

"You are a good and faithful servant," said Himmler, laying

a hand on Helmut's shoulder. "But not everything is for you to understand."

———

"You know who owns the catalog of Heinrich Himmler's library?" said Patton.

"The world of Nazi collecting is small, and when something like that turns up, people know about it," said Alex. "It's like when the French Ministry of Foreign Affairs announced that they had Hermann Göring's catalog of his art collection. We all knew. I first heard about the Himmler catalog four or five years ago. Rumor was it had been stolen out of a library where it had been sitting in a crate that hadn't been unpacked in forty years or something. You hear this kind of thing all the time—collections that were packed up after the war and never got unpacked. Anyway, apparently some library employee recognized it and, since it wasn't in the library cataloging system, just walked off with it."

"You can't trust librarians," said Nemo with a smile toward Patton.

"Do you know where the library was?" said Patton.

"Somewhere in eastern Europe I think," said Alex. "It was all very hazy rumors traded late at night on the dark web. But wherever it came from, someone offered it for sale. I tried to make an offer, but I was too late. The seller told me it went to a private buyer in Germany named Ingrid Weiss."

"Never heard of her," said Patton.

"She has a special interest in books stolen by Nazis. Runs some charity called Columbia House that tries to return books to the families they were stolen from."

"I've heard of doing that with paintings and sculptures," said Patton, "but books? Didn't the Nazis burn books?"

"Not all of them," said Alex. "Weiss has emailed me a number of times asking me to donate books in my collection that might have been stolen."

"And did you?" said Patton.

"The day she presents me with documentary evidence that I own stolen books and that she has tracked down their legal owners, I'll certainly hand them over."

"But she doesn't know what books are in your collection, does she?" said Nemo.

"That is her disadvantage," said Alex with a smile.

"Do you still have the emails from Ingrid Weiss?" said Patton.

"Let me see," said Alex. He opened a file drawer behind his desk and flipped through the folders, pulling one out and opening it. "Here we are. I have six emails from her, though they're practically identical, except for the date. Her wording is a little old-fashioned—like she learned English at a Swiss finishing school. Here's one. 'Dear Mr. Lansdowne, I write to entreat you again to consider assisting my efforts to recover books stolen by the German Third Reich. The pleasure of a reply is requested and I shall await your response with anticipation. Yours Sincerely, Ingrid Weiss.'"

Patton happened to be watching Nemo's face during this recitation and noticed his eyes widen and his cheeks go pale. "May I see that?" he asked in a weak voice.

"Certainly," said Alex, passing him the page.

"What's the matter?" said Patton after Nemo had had time to read the message over several times.

"Do you have secure Internet access?" said Nemo to Alex.

"As secure as they come," said Alex, indicating the laptop on his desk.

"Do you mind if I check my email server?" said Nemo. A moment later he was tapping away on Alex's computer as the others looked on.

"Does this little exercise have a point?" said Ruthie. "Because I'd rather like to take my car and go home."

"In my experience," said Patton, "brief though it is, he doesn't like to explain what he's doing until after he's done it."

"And as I told you before," said Nemo, still typing, "you can't take your car and go home. You are in this neck deep, and considerably deeper should you choose to leave us. Printer connected?"

"Yes," said Alex.

In another moment, Nemo had printed out a single page which Alex passed to him. Nemo shut the laptop and turned to face Patton and Ruthie.

"This is the message I received on my secure server which led to my getting hired to handle Fleming."

"You mean he's killed other people?" said Ruthie, the panic edging back into her voice as she took a step toward Patton and away from Nemo.

"What do you mean, *other* people?" said Alex.

"Nemo's murderous tendencies are not the point," said Patton. "Is that something you'd like to read to us?"

"Read yours once more," said Nemo, turning to Alex. "The email you received from Ingrid Weiss."

"Very well," said Alex, picking up the paper again. "'Dear Mr. Lansdowne, I write to entreat you again to consider assisting my efforts to recover books stolen by the German Third Reich. The pleasure of a reply is requested and I shall await your response with anticipation. Yours Sincerely, Ingrid Weiss.'"

"And here is mine," said Nemo. "Dear Sir, I wish to engage your services for an elimination project. Price and terms are negotiable. The pleasure of a reply is requested and I shall await your response with anticipation."

"That last sentence is exactly the same," said Ruthie.

"Like a fingerprint," said Patton.

"It's Weiss," said Alex.

"Do you mean to tell me," said Patton, "that Ingrid Weiss, the person who has the catalog we're looking for, is the person who hired you?"

"It looks that way," said Nemo.

"But she doesn't have the decrypted message," said Patton, "so she might have no idea the catalog is important."

"Do you have an address for this Ingrid Weiss?" said Nemo to Alex.

"As a matter of fact," said Alex, "I do. Ever been to Munich?"

"Is that our next move?" said Patton. "Going to Munich?"

"Don't look at me," said Alex. "My next move is breakfast."

"We have to find that catalog," said Nemo.

"Do we?" said Ruthie. "Couldn't we just burn the message and the decrypt and go home and forget about this whole thing?"

"Weiss won't stop until she finds the message," said Nemo.

"Yes, but if we destroy it . . ." said Ruthie.

"We can't destroy it," said Nemo. "It's in my head and yours."

"And mine," said Patton.

"And mine," said Alex.

"You and I might hold up to, what did you call it, to 'enhanced interrogation,'" said Nemo to Patton, "but I'm not sure Alex or Ruthie would keep quiet for long."

"What's 'enhanced interrogation'?" said Ruthie.

"What he did to Fritz," said Patton. Ruthie shivered.

"I can tell you right now, I wouldn't keep my mouth closed," said Alex.

"We could kill him," said Patton, deadpan but with a glance to Nemo that said she was just having some fun.

"I'd rather you didn't," said Alex. "The mess, you know. And I just cleaned the house."

"I've no intention of killing anyone, Mr. Lansdowne," said Nemo. "Nonetheless I think endangering a loved one might keep you . . . cooperative."

"I don't have any loved ones," said Alex.

"You have your collection," said Nemo.

"Are you saying—" said Alex.

"I'm saying," interrupted Nemo, "that I am a man with resources. And if anything happens to me or any of my companions, this whole place and all its disgusting contents will burn to the ground—and I doubt the authorities will much care."

"But if something goes wrong it's not necessarily my fault."

"True. So you'd better hope nothing goes wrong."

For the first time since they had arrived at his house, Alex looked nervous. Beads of sweat appeared on his forehead. "You wouldn't . . ."

"Trust me," said Nemo, taking a threatening step toward Alex, "you don't want to know what I would and wouldn't do. So keep your fucking mouth shut and your door locked and maybe, if you're extremely lucky, you'll never see me again."

"So your plan," said Patton, in a voice clearly meant to ease the tension, "is to march into the office of the very person who has been hunting us across two continents and ask her to hand over something she might well consider her most valuable possession."

"Well," said Nemo, "when you put it like that . . ."

"I'm not saying it's a bad plan," said Patton. "I just wanted to get it clear in my head."

"In what way could it possibly *not* be considered a bad plan?" said Ruthie.

"It's just not a complete plan," said Patton.

"It's not an office," said Alex. "I looked it up when she kept emailing me, and the address for Columbia House is literally just a house in suburban Munich. She actually lives on a street once named for Hermann Göring."

"Of course she does," said Patton.

"Aren't we forgetting another possibility?" said Ruthie.

"What's that?" said Patton.

"We send this Ingrid Weiss the decrypted message and go our separate ways."

The room fell silent for a moment before Alex spoke. "But she's the bad guy. Even I can tell that."

"So," said Nemo, "we just have to figure out a way to convince this bad guy and anybody else in her house to come out and leave the place unguarded, break in, find a book that we might not even recognize if we saw it, get out before anyone sees us, and not leave a trail when we go." Nemo said this not in a tone of despair, but in one of excitement, as if he had already put together a plan.

Patton stepped toward Ruthie and took her hand. "It'll be fine," she said. "You won't have to do anything but lie low for a few days. And all Nemo and I need is a way to send Weiss misleading information, someone who's an expert on military-level surveillance, a few thousand euros in cash, a description of this catalog, and some serious chutzpah."

"And, unless I'm mistaken," said Nemo, "we have all of that right in this room. Now, Alex is right about one thing."

"What's that?" said Alex.

"Breakfast."

After Alex had fried up some eggs and bacon and toasted a few slices of stale bread, they all stood around the kitchen eating off china from Carinhall, Hermann Göring's castle-like home northeast of Berlin. Alex had offered to let them dine at a table once used by Hitler, but Patton demurred, wishing they could eat their overcooked eggs off paper plates. Ruthie kept near Patton during the meal, and Patton wondered how Ruthie would react when the time came for them to part. They needed to keep Ruthie in their camp not just intellectually but emotionally, so Patton supposed a goodbye kiss of some magnitude was in order. She found herself excited by this prospect.

After breakfast, they adjourned to the room in which Ruthie had used the Enigma machine. The machine still sat on the table and as Nemo spread out a map of Munich and the surrounding area that Alex had given him, the collector returned Enigma to its glass case.

"You know this table was once used for—" began Alex, but Patton cut him off.

"Don't tell us. Seriously. We'd rather not know."

"What did you mean earlier," said Ruthie to Nemo, "when you said we have everything we need right in this room?"

"Well," said Nemo. "Patton did not deny it when I accused her of being retired from army intelligence nor did she deny being an intelligence systems analyst. And as I'm sure you know if you have tiptoed around the American military at certain points in your career as I have, one of the jobs of an intelligence systems analyst is the placing, monitoring, and retrieving of surveillance equipment."

"I thought you were a librarian," said Ruthie.

"Surprise," said Patton with a shrug.

"And I'm guessing Alex knows what this catalog looks like," said Nemo, "since he tried to buy it."

"I have a written description and a photograph from when it was on the black market," said Alex. "It's a ledger about fourteen inches tall bound in red leather with the word 'Accounts' on the spine in gold. Probably Himmler used a standard account book. Oh, and there's a swastika on the front cover."

"Lovely," said Patton.

"And as far as the cash and the chutzpah," said Nemo, "you don't get far in my line of work without a good supply of both."

"But that still leaves the problem of sending Weiss misleading information that will make her abandon her headquarters," said Ruthie.

Nemo smiled across the table at Patton. "You want to field this one?" he said.

"While some of us were losing our heads over the car accident last night—"

"What car accident?" said Alex.

"Long story, I'll tell you later," said Patton. "Anyway, while some of us were in a state of shock or panic, Nemo kept his cool and removed two small black bags from the back seat of the car."

"You noticed that, did you?" said Nemo.

"Now, if I had to guess about the contents of those bags," said Patton, "I'd say that one of them at least has a cell phone that our late friends used to communicate with Weiss. We will use that phone to convince Weiss it's worth her while to leave home."

"I never would have thought of that," said Alex.

"This is not my first time sending misinformation to the enemy," said Patton.

"They did it during World War II all the time," said Ruthie.

"If we are really up against a group of Aryan supremacists who have a chance at obtaining massive wealth using Nazi secrets," said Nemo, "this still is World War II. Now, we have no idea what this message means until we find that catalog, but we have to convince Weiss that we do know and that wherever we're headed is the site of . . . of whatever she's looking for."

"The secret to manufacturing gold?" said Ruthie doubtfully.

"Something like that," said Nemo, leaning over the map. "So we need someplace that's close enough to Munich to tempt her to come after us herself, and also believable as a place the Nazis would keep a hidden secret."

"There," said Alex, pointing to a spot on the map southeast of Munich and right on the Austrian border. "Berchtesgaden."

———

When Jean Simpson landed in Vienna, she would have to decide whether to go first to Munich or Prague. She had already reached a librarian at the National Library of the Czech Republic who was willing to meet with her but had had no such luck at the Bavarian State Library in Munich. Still, Ingrid Weiss lived in Munich, and more than anything, Jean wanted to confront the owner of Columbia House and ask her just what she meant by sending people stolen library books and passing them off as Nazi loot.

And Jean had another reason for going to Munich. In all her travels around Europe, she had never visited the site of her grandparents' death, and Dachau lay just fifteen miles or so north of central Munich. She had seen pictures online of the memorial site—the reconstructed barracks where her grandparents had been imprisoned, the guard towers and the postwar memorials. But she had never felt the need to stand there and pay her own tribute. Now, after the way Ingrid Weiss had abused the memory of her grandfather, she felt drawn to the site, as if she could somehow defend the honor of the grandfather she never knew by standing on the spot where he had been silenced by the Nazi Reich. She thought of the words of one of the memorials at Dachau, inscribed in Hebrew, French, English, German, and Russian: "Never again." There was certainly no comparison between Ingrid Weiss's little ruse and the genocide of the Nazis, but nonetheless, Jean wanted to put a stop to whatever was going on at Columbia House. She wanted to look Ingrid Weiss in the eye and say, "Never again."

Jean managed to sleep a few hours on the overnight flight to Vienna.

The conference organizers had booked a block of rooms at a cheap hotel outside the Ringstrasse, but Jean had decided to treat herself to two nights at the Hotel Sacher across the street from the opera house. Her room wasn't ready when she arrived at the hotel at nine, so she drank two cups of *Franziskaner*—strong Viennese espresso topped with frothy, rich, steamed milk and made magical with a lump of cream—in the café, then presented herself to the concierge and asked if he could book her a train to Munich. If she resisted the temptation to get off the train in Salzburg, he informed her, she could be in Munich by early afternoon.

When he handed her the ticket, the concierge slipped her a carefully wrapped slice of Sacher torte. "In case you get hungry," he said.

As the train pulled out of Vienna in the morning light, Jean switched on her phone long enough to check her messages. Other than a "Bon voyage and be careful," from Peter Byerly there was nothing worth reading. She switched off the phone and settled back in her seat, watching the foreign landscape slide by the window.

———

Ingrid awoke to the warmth of the morning sun pouring through her bedroom window. With a lull in the activities in the basement, she had come upstairs to sleep for a few hours, and now felt much refreshed. She lay in bed for a moment, though, staring at the cracks in the ceiling and remembering nursing her grandfather in this very room during his final days. Eva had called him a deluded old man, but Ingrid had never known anyone with a sharper mind and a keener memory than her grandfather Helmut. True, he did not breathe a word to her of his relationship with Himmler until his final weeks, when it was clear the cancer would soon complete its work. But then he had spoken with pride of his friendship with the Reichsführer and of their mutual pursuit of a project that could ensure the future of the Reich and its ideals even in the face of the unstoppable forces of the Allied armies. He spoke of his time with Himmler in great detail—he remembered the menus of meals they had shared, the brand of cigars they smoked, even the punch lines of Himmler's favorite jokes. But when it came to the project that they worked on together, Grandfather Helmut had only spoken in the most general terms until a few hours before his death. Then he had sent the nurse away, summoned Ingrid into his room, and told her she must listen carefully to what he had to say.

"The future of the Reich depends on it," said Helmut, and at first Ingrid thought what her associate Eva would think five years later—that her grandfather, in his dying hours, was no longer aware of the world around him and was back in 1944, waiting for his friend Heinrich Himmler to walk through the door. But as he spoke, Ingrid realized that, if Projekt Alchemie was real, then there truly could be a future for the Reich, or at least for its ideals of Aryan supremacy. Because Ingrid understood, as she heard her grandfather repeat the words of Heinrich Himmler, that the Reichsführer had been right—someday all it would take to change the world would be money. Looking at the world around her, she knew that day had come.

Her grandfather told her about a message encoded on an Enigma machine. "They took it," he said in a weak voice. "The filthy Americans who came to Dachau took it from my brother, from Albert. You have to find it, Ingrid. Himmler's final message about Projekt Alchemie, the message with the secret of vast wealth to be used for the return of the Reich. You must be the one to find it."

He had died a few hours later and Ingrid had dedicated the last five years of her life to tracking down that message. She had recruited like-minded associates and they had confirmed the Weiss family story that Ingrid's uncle had been found shot in the head in the woods just outside Dachau. They had traced the names of every American soldier at Dachau that day, including soldiers never prosecuted for the war crimes they committed at the camp—lining up the few remaining German officers and executing them without trial.

Most of those Americans had died by the time Ingrid went looking for the message, and she feared she might be too late, but then, posing as a researcher working on an oral history project, Ingrid heard a story about a soldier named Jasper Fleming who had disappeared into the woods outside the camp and returned a few minutes later looking pale and sick. "A lot of us got sick that day," said the man she was interviewing. But not a lot of them went off into the woods toward the very spot where her uncle Albert was murdered, Ingrid thought.

Jasper Fleming had proven hard to track down, but they finally found him through his subscription to a newsletter for veterans of the Forty-Fifth Infantry Division. When Columbia House placed an advertisement in the newsletter for plans to build your own Enigma machine, Jasper Fleming had been the only person to place an order. Ingrid knew she had her man. It took months to lay the plan and to raise the money to hire a professional hit man who would leave a clean path to Fleming's house for Karl and Erich. They had left nothing to chance. And then everything had gone wrong and now they were hunting their own contract killer and some woman across the English countryside.

———

"OK," said Nemo, "Ruthie and Alex will stay here while Patton and I take care of business in Munich."

"Sounds good to me," said Alex.

"I'm going with you," said Ruthie, looking at Patton with the same pleading eyes she had used at the bar on Harvard Square when Ruthie didn't want Patton to go home early and, more important, didn't want her to go home alone.

"Look," said Nemo. "Patton is ex-military. I've seen how she acts under fire and I trust her not to fuck things up. You work at a museum doing math." Though she knew he hadn't intended it, Nemo's words cut Patton deeply. Yes, when she had been under fire in Alta Vista that morning she had kept her cool, but that hadn't always been the case. There had been times when the sound of a car backfiring had sent her diving to the sidewalk, her breath shallow and her pulse racing. She had spent two days in bed shivering after a helicopter had flown over her house. Even certain images on television could send her into a panic or a depression or something that felt like both. Even though Veterans'

Affairs called it post-traumatic stress disorder, Patton preferred the World War I term—shell shock. And she never knew when that shock would hit, what would trigger it. Ever since she left Alta Vista with Nemo she had been waiting for it to kick in and she feared it would attack at the worst possible moment. So maybe it wouldn't be such a bad thing to have another member of the team. Someone whose touch—and Patton, in her independence, hated to admit this even to herself—could calm her. Patton had discovered that after they killed Erich. She had reached for Ruthie's hand to soothe her and found, when that almost forgotten skin touched hers, that a peace seemed to radiate from it. Nemo would be next to useless if Patton suffered an attack of shell shock, but Ruthie might just bring her out of it and, in doing so, save them all.

"Maybe she's right," said Patton, crossing to Ruthie and standing shoulder to shoulder with her. "Maybe she'd be safer with us."

"I don't really care about her safety," said Nemo.

"OK," said Patton, "maybe *we'd* be safer."

"What do you mean?"

"I mean if we leave her behind, this Ingrid Weiss character is bound to send out another Fritz and Franz duo. They know we need an Enigma machine and they know about Alex and his collection. If they find her here they'll put two and two together. And how long do you think she'll hold out against enhanced interrogation?"

"Not long," said Ruthie.

"But if she's with us we can, you know, keep an eye on her."

"Plus," said Alex, "if she's *not* here, I can deny knowing anything about all of this."

Patton and Ruthie looked at Nemo, and Patton felt like a schoolgirl for a moment, asking permission to bring her new friend home.

"I also speak German," said Ruthie. "Or at least enough to help out when we get there."

"Enough to help me write some text messages?" said Nemo.

"I think I could manage."

"Fine," he said at last. "Can you shoot?"

"No," said Ruthie.

"Well there's no time to teach you," said Nemo. "We'll just give you a pistol and hope for the best."

"Where do you plan on getting a pistol?" said Patton.

"Are you kidding?" said Nemo. "We're sitting on an arsenal here."

"We're sitting in a museum," said Patton. "What makes you think any of this stuff works?"

"Of course it works," said Alex. "I've spent years restoring everything here, including weapons. But I'm afraid they're not for sale."

"Nobody said anything about a sale," said Nemo. "It's more of a loan that I had in mind."

"I told you," said Alex, "I don't pick sides, I just collect things. And I don't let anything off the premises, especially weapons."

"Well how about this," said Nemo, crossing to Alex in a flash, grabbing his neck, and pushing him back against the wall, lifting him so that his toes barely touched the ground. "You loan us some weapons and some ammunition and I won't break your neck and leave you to rot on the floor as the last exhibit in this house of horrors."

"That seems reasonable," squeaked Alex.

Nemo lowered him to the floor, let go of his neck, and patted him on the shoulders. "I thought you might find that a fair arrangement," he said. "Now, if we're all done with negotiations, let's get what we need and get to London."

"Why are we going to London?" said Ruthie.

Nemo shook his head as if he were frustrated by the inane questions of a toddler and said simply, "Supplies."

TZUSO MPTMB IWDMG SHSLS

SECTION THREE: MUNICH

VIII

"Did the rest of you get any sleep?" said Ingrid as she descended into the basement with a pot of coffee and a basket of puddingbrezels delivered by the local bakery.

"We took turns on your couch," said Gottfried, taking a pastry. "Until things started to happen this morning."

"Bring me up to speed," said Ingrid, sliding into a chair and cradling a mug of coffee to her chest.

"Do you remember that woman who called wanting to talk to you about a book Columbia House sent her?"

"She left a number, right?" said Ingrid.

"Right," said Gottfried. "Well I've been keeping an eye on that number and this morning it came online for a few minutes and you'll never guess where it is."

"Surprise me," said Ingrid.

"On a train leaving Vienna and headed in our direction."

"I thought she was American," said Ingrid.

"She is," said Dietrich. "And not only American, she's from North Carolina."

"This means nothing to me," said Ingrid, taking a bite out of a puddingbrezel. "I don't know American geography."

"You don't have to know American geography," said Eva. "It's the same state where Jasper Fleming lived. The same state where Karl and Erich followed your assassin and his newfound sidekick."

"Wait," said Ingrid, sitting up, "are you telling me you're tracking another person from the same place in America?"

"Not the same place," said Gottfried, "but nearby."

"That can't be a coincidence," said Ingrid.

"Tell her the best part," said Dietrich.

"The best part," said Gottfried, "is that Karl and Erich came back online, too."

"Where are they?" said Ingrid.

"In London, and listen to this." Gottfried tapped a few buttons and a message appeared on one of his computer screens. "Nemo dead. Girl has paper and ticket to Munich. Details below. Buy us ticket on same train and we will watch her."

"Karl must have typed this," said Eva, squinting at the phone. "He can't even spell properly."

"Do you have any way to confirm this?" said Ingrid.

"The woman did buy a train ticket," said Gottfried. "She used a computer at a library in West London and her own credit card."

"She's run out of cash," said Ingrid. "Without Nemo, she has no idea how to play this game."

"I booked the train for Erich and Karl," said Gottfried. "It doesn't leave until late this afternoon and it arrives in Munich early tomorrow morning. I can try to get back in touch with them if you want them to move in earlier."

"No," said Ingrid. "Why cause a scene in London with CCTV and police on every street corner when she's coming right to us."

"Two Americans are coming right to us," said Eva.

"And Jean Simpson could be in Munich this afternoon," said Gottfried.

"She can't possibly know about the message," said Ingrid.

"Unless this Patton Harcourt told her," said Eva.

"When does her train get in?" said Ingrid.

"If she really is coming to Munich and not just going to be a tourist in Salzburg, ten past one," said Gottfried.

"Do you have a picture of her?" said Ingrid.

"Of course," said Gottfried. "I keep a dossier on everyone you send a book to. It's all printed out and waiting for you." He handed Ingrid a slim file folder.

"Dietrich, when the time comes get down to the station and watch for her. If you see her, just follow. It might be nothing, but I'd very much like to know what Jean Simpson is doing in Munich."

"I'll take Eva with me," said Dietrich. "You know, in case this woman goes into the toilet or something."

Ingrid rolled her eyes.

———

Patton looked out the window at the Netherlands slipping by below them. It was a clear day, and she could see a patchwork of colors as they flew ten thousand feet over the tulip fields. They had stowed the fruits of an excursion into London behind the seats of the six-passenger Beechcraft. Along with the cache of Wehrmacht weapons and ammunition from Alex Lansdowne was a black duffel bulging with cameras, microphones, and a tablet—everything Patton needed to run a surveillance operation, all purchased at a store in West London. Nemo had also retrieved €50,000 and a pistol from a safe deposit box in Kensington. Ten thousand of those euros paid for this bumpy flight to a field outside Munich. The noise of the engine made conversation difficult, and the tiny cabin threatened to bring on a bout of her claustrophobia. She would have gladly given up the view of the tulip fields in exchange for a different mode of travel.

Their campaign of disinformation had begun as soon as they arrived in London and Nemo insisted that Patton use her credit card to buy a train ticket.

"I thought you said they would be tracing my credit card," said Patton.

"That's the whole point. If you buy one ticket to Munich they'll think I'm out of the picture. You book a train for early this afternoon and they won't expect you in Munich until tomorrow. Meanwhile, we take a private plane from an airfield outside London and we've got the whole night to set up our surveillance net." "Private plane" had sounded nice when Nemo first said it. The reality, thought Patton, as the plane hit another patch of turbulence, was anything but luxurious.

At a public computer terminal in the Paddington Library, Patton had used her credit card to book a ticket on the Eurostar to Paris and a connecting train to Munich, arriving about nine o'clock the next morning. "I hope they can hack that," she said.

"We'll give them a little help," said Nemo. He pulled a cell phone out of his pocket and switched it on.

"I thought we weren't allowed to use those," said Ruthie.

"This isn't mine," he said.

"The cell phone of Fritz and Franz?" said Patton.

"Got it on the first guess," said Nemo. "And Erich gave me the code to unlock it. I tried it while you were buying your tickets."

"Erich didn't give us any code," said Patton. "All he said was something about . . ."

"About the Fourteen Words," said Nemo. He held out the phone and let Patton and Ruthie watch as he keyed in the numbers 1-4-1-4 and the screen sprung to life. "And here," he said, "is a strand of text messages to 'I. Weiss.'"

"We could probably find out all sorts of things on that phone," said Ruthie.

"Yes, and we could also make it easy for them to follow us," said Nemo. "But if we send them a quick message and then turn it off again . . ."

"Then they'll think Fritz and Franz are following me on a train to Munich," said Patton.

"Exactly," said Nemo. He told Ruthie what to type and she did her best to render his message in German, then turned off the phone. "That should keep them busy," he said.

Ruthie sat next to Patton and, as they had crossed over the English coast, she had slipped her hand into Patton's. Patton had not resisted, nor had she let go. She didn't know if what she felt for Ruthie was latent affection or simply a desperate need for human connection in a time of crisis. Either way, Ruthie's soft, cool hand calmed her nerves and swept a little wave of fondness over her.

She felt a twinge of guilt about how she had manipulated Ruthie back in Bletchley. She had seen right away that Ruthie still carried, if not a torch, certainly a candle for her, and she had had no qualms about using that fact to her own advantage. But she did have pleasant memories of that summer in Boston. Patton had joined the army a few months later, and while Ruthie was not the last woman she had slept with, she was the last woman she had spent night after night with, the last woman she had lain awake next to all night in the cool summer air. She had no illusions about pursuing a relationship with Ruthie when this was all over, but she allowed herself, as the plane bounced her up and down, to indulge in a fantasy that—once they had solved the mystery of Projekt Alchemie and Nemo had disappeared back into the ether—she and Ruthie might spend a few days together at some remote hotel in the Alps, rediscovering what had made that summer in Boston so special.

Nemo did not sleep, though he suspected the others thought he was dozing. He closed his eyes and slowed his breath and tried to think about only what he needed to think about. Why did he suddenly care so much about something? Since the day he had walked away leaving a dead body in the kitchen and Jack in the bedroom, he had cared about nothing but himself. A career that required him to be invisible also required him to insulate himself from the rest of humankind, to disconnect from anything that might awaken feelings of compassion or concern. But now those feelings had been awakened, and he feared they might be his undoing. He should be concentrating on the most basic task at hand—find and eliminate Ingrid Weiss to send a message that no one double-crossed Nemo. Yet again and again he found that thought slipping away, replaced by a desire to protect Patton—Ruthie, too, but especially Patton.

Not since Jack had he felt protective of another human being. And Jack, too, kept rearing up in Nemo's mind. Where was he now? A Black man in his thirties in America who had grown up with no family, no permanent home—life was probably not great for Jack, but if Ingrid Weiss and her ilk got their way it would be even worse. As he felt the plane beginning its descent, he tried to push thoughts of Jack out of his head and focus on the task at hand. Even if Projekt Alchemie was nothing but a conspiracy theory put forth by the obsessed acquaintances of people like Alex Lansdowne, that did not change his desire to put an end to Ingrid Weiss and her plans.

Ruthie squeezed Patton's hand as the plane bounced against the grass landing strip. She had been waiting so long and now she would finally have a chance to show Patton what she was made of. Now everything would be different.

————

JUNE 1944

Helmut Werner pored over a pile of papers on his desk, checking to be sure everything was in order before he tossed them into the fire. He had been working on Projekt Alchemie in secret now for six years. Helmut had a small office in Wewelsburg Castle where, as far as anyone else knew, he toiled away at the monotonous task of processing the paperwork with which the Nazis were so obsessed. Reports in envelopes marked "Top Secret" arrived at Helmut's office every day. No one seemed to notice that none of those reports ever left the room in which Helmut toiled alone. He had retained the rank of section leader because, Himmler had said, promotion might cause suspicion. But Himmler rewarded Helmut well with fine food, fine cigars, fine brandy, and, above all, a close personal relationship with the Reichsführer—something no money or rank could buy.

Helmut pushed back his chair, picked up the stack of papers on his desk, the contents of which he had reduced to a few carefully memorized facts, and tossed them onto the fire, where the flames jumped up eagerly to consume the secrets of Projekt Alchemie. Just when the fire was at its most intense, the door behind him opened and Helmut turned to see Reichsführer Himmler striding across the room.

"Heil Hitler!" said Helmut vigorously.

Himmler returned the greeting but without enthusiasm. He looked exhausted, with dark circles around his eyes and his skin almost sallow.

"What's wrong, my friend?" said Helmut. "Are you not well?"

"The Allied invasion has begun," said Himmler. "At Normandy. We will repel them, but many men will be lost. Many have been lost. And the Eastern Front grinds on."

Helmut swallowed hard. Everyone knew an Allied invasion from England was inevitable—still the thought that the Americans and the English, doubtless some of them even Jews, now prowled the roads of northern France, territory belonging to the Third Reich, turned his stomach.

"I at least have good news," said Helmut, trying to sound upbeat. "The numbers I have received are very promising."

Himmler slid into one of two chairs by the fire. "Have a cigar with me, old friend. We have not had a chat in far too long."

"We have both been busy," said Helmut. He took two cigars out of a box on his desk and handed one, along with a silver lighter, to the Reichsführer. The lighter had been a gift to Himmler from Hermann Göring, and the Reichsführer had passed it along to Helmut. Helmut took a seat in the other chair and leaned forward as Himmler lit his cigar.

"I begin to wonder," said Himmler, returning the lighter to Helmut and leaning back in his chair, "if we should act now. The Reich could use the resources of Projekt Alchemie."

"True," said Helmut. "But I do not doubt the wisdom of your original plan. If we crush the Allied invasion, nothing is lost. But if, God forbid, the Americans and the filthy Bolsheviks close in from either side—surely, as you have said, Projekt Alchemie is the Reich's insurance policy."

"I truly thought that Projekt Alchemie would save the Reich," said Himmler with a sigh.

"It *will* save the Reich," said Helmut. "Perhaps not today, if things go poorly perhaps not even this year or this century, but it will save the Reich. You taught me that in this very room."

"Did I?"

"Yes," said Helmut. He could recall Himmler's words as if they had been spoken moments ago. One of the reasons Helmut had been so suited to his job, and had lasted so long in it, was his near perfect memory, and now he repeated what Himmler had told him when they embarked on Projekt Alchemie together.

"You said that today, in order to rid the world of Jews and Gypsies and all the lesser races it takes political will and ingenuity and above all superior military might. But someday, you said, all it will take will be money. Someday, money will choose the leaders and write the laws; money will protect those who work outside the law and hide the true power brokers. Money will allow all that we were never able to accomplish to finally come to pass. And when that day comes, you said, our 'silly little experiment with alchemy,' as some have called it, will be waiting, ready to provide all that money and transform the world."

"I said that?" said Himmler.

"You did," said Helmut with pride that he had been present at such an insightful proclamation.

"You always did know how to make me feel better," said Himmler, taking a deep pull on his cigar.

"The words were yours, Reichsführer," said Helmut. "All yours."

———

Jean stepped out of the Munich train station unaware that Dietrich Mueller and Eva Klein were watching her. She loved traveling alone, and especially the excitement of unplanned excursions. She had eaten a bratwurst on the train, washed it down with a good German beer, and now, standing in the center of a bustling European metropolis, she felt she could not be any farther from her life in Ridgefield if she were walking on the far side of the moon. She was, for the next few hours, at no one's beck and call. No conference schedule, no students, no department chair or administrators. Jean Simpson was a free woman, and she nearly laughed as she reached the front of the taxi queue. Only when the dispatcher asked, in German, for her destination, did her mood sober somewhat as she replied, in English, "Dachau concentration camp."

Eva had slipped into the line behind Jean and had no trouble overhearing and understanding her directions to the driver. As the cab pulled away, she pulled out her phone and called Ingrid, stepping back toward where Dietrich waited on the sidewalk.

"Her grandparents died there according to Gottfried's dossier," Eva explained.

"I remember," said Ingrid.

"So do we follow her or do we forget about it?"

The line went silent for a moment and then Ingrid said, "Let her go. She's on some sort of personal pilgrimage. Probably got interested in family history when we sent her that book. Come back so we can be ready when the others get to Munich."

"She says to come back," said Eva to Dietrich, but he only smiled broadly at her.

"What?" she said.

"We have to eat some lunch," he said. "And then we'll probably get caught in traffic. It could be two hours before we get back."

"And I'll bet I know what you'd like to spend two hours doing," said Eva.

"There are three hotels right across the street," said Dietrich, taking Eva's hand. "Someone will have a room."

Jean felt a pang of guilt as soon as she stepped out of the taxi and walked toward the main gate of Dachau. She was a historian (albeit an art historian) yet she had paid little attention to her own family history. Her Jewish grandparents had died in this camp, but to her they had always been more myth than reality. She had never met them, only seen one picture of them, and never heard any stories about them—her mother had been three when she parted from her parents and came to America. Nor had Jean ever felt particularly Jewish. Her great-aunt Marta, who had raised Jean's mother, had married an American and quickly changed from Marta Hochberg to Martha Kelly. So far as Jean knew, Martha had never set foot in a temple in America. At Christmas and Easter, Jean's mother had told her, the family went to the Presbyterian church. That scant connection to religion had carried into Jean's own life, though her father had convinced her mother to move from the Presbyterian to the Episcopal church. Neither of them ever talked about Jean's Jewish heritage.

Now she walked through a pair of wrought iron gates bearing the sickeningly ironic slogan, "*Arbeit Macht Frei*" or "Work Will Make You Free." Jean hadn't even known that those words, made so famous on the gates of Auschwitz, had also mocked her grandparents when they arrived at Dachau. Jean realized, as she entered the camp, that she didn't even know exactly when her grandparents had arrived there or when they died. Her grandfather had lost his job at the university because of anti-Semitic laws passed in 1933, and he and his wife had died in Dachau sometime between then and the end of the war. Why had Jean never tried to find out more? Her guilt turned to shame as she read the placards on the few remaining buildings of the camp describing how the prisoners had been used as forced labor at a munitions factory, and how Nazis executed four thousand Soviet prisoners of war at a nearby firing range. She read of how Nazis stripped new arrivals of their clothes and forced them to give up their few remaining possessions—wedding rings, watches, everything. She shivered when she saw a photograph of Heinrich Himmler inspecting the camp in 1936. Had her grandfather been there? Or did he and his wife become prisoners after *Kristallnacht* in 1938? It suddenly burned in her gut that she did not know.

She had tried not to look at the memorial opposite the main gate when she first entered. Instead she walked quickly through the historical exhibitions and out into the main part of the camp, where some of the prisoner barracks had been reconstructed. Her mind swirled with emotions. She wanted to stay as long as possible and to leave immediately. She wanted to forget about the conference in Vienna and spend the next week in the Dachau archives searching for information about her grandparents, and she wanted to forget that anyone connected to her was ever imprisoned in such a place. In the end she spent an hour or so wandering from one part of the camp to another before finally standing in front of the memorial she could no longer ignore.

On one side of the wall were the words "May the example of those who were exterminated here between 1933–1945 because they resisted Nazism help to unite the living for the defense of peace and freedom and in respect for their fellow men." Jean stood looking at those words, inscribed in several languages, for a long time. In the light of that sentiment, the activities of Ingrid Weiss and Columbia House seemed a slap in the face. For whatever reason, Ingrid pretended to honor those words, while actually belittling them by stealing books and "returning" them to those who had lost family members in places like this.

Jean felt ready to return to Munich and confront Ingrid Weiss; she felt ready to do what she could to "unite the living for the defense of peace and freedom;" and she knew, as she looked at those words, that someday she would return and delve into the archives to learn more about her family's past. But for now, she walked to the other side of the memorial and stood by an entombed urn of the ashes of an unidentified prisoner to see the words that would serve as her mantra as she sat in the taxi bound for Columbia House: "Never Again."

———

The pilot had radioed ahead for a car to be waiting for them and the driver was happy to take cash to drive them to a nearby rental office where "Domingo Suarez" of Barcelona would rent a black minivan with tinted windows. The driver was even happier when Nemo offered him €1,000 to run an errand later that night.

"Ethnic ambiguity comes in handy," said Nemo as they pulled out of the parking lot, their gear secure in the back. He had spoken with a thick Spanish accent to the rental clerk as Ruthie and Patton waited outside with the bags. Now he drove toward Munich as Patton showed Ruthie how to use a Luger in the back seat.

"I really have no interest in firing a gun," said Ruthie, her hand shaking as she gripped the pistol.

"Good," said Nemo. "All you need to do is learn how to hold the damn thing still and look like you're planning to shoot. The last thing we want is for someone inexperienced to start firing."

"And I suppose Patton has plenty of experience after her career as . . . What was it?" said Ruthie.

"Intelligence systems analyst," said Patton. "I joined a few months after Boston, and yes, I have some experience with firearms."

"Why didn't you tell me?" said Ruthie. "Why didn't you write or call or anything?"

"It was the army," said Patton "The United States Army. I don't know what it's like in England but this was during the days of 'Don't ask, don't tell,' so I wasn't about to reach out to a former lover."

"You thought if you sent me a postcard the army would find out you were a lesbian?"

"Tell her why you're not in the army anymore," said Nemo.

"Wouldn't you like to know?" said Patton.

"Yeah, I would, actually. If I'm going into a firefight with somebody, I'd like to know why they left the military. I need to know I can trust you not to . . . to lose it."

"You think I got crippling PTSD and they booted me out?" said Patton.

"I just want to know I can count on you under pressure," said Nemo.

"I would think that after the sniper fire in Alta Vista you'd be able to answer that question," said Patton.

"OK, OK, don't tell us," said Nemo. He turned his head just long enough to catch Ruthie's eye in the back seat. "She's a secret keeper, this one," he said.

"I'd noticed," said Ruthie.

"Look," said Patton, "are we going to play-psychoanalyze Patton

Harcourt, or are we going to put an end to Ingrid Weiss's quest for Aryan supremacy?"

"Fine, we'll change the subject," said Nemo. "So you two were lovers?"

"Oh, just drive the car," said Patton.

They had a few hours until dark and a few more until the occupants of Columbia House could be counted upon to depart, so Nemo decided that rest and food were in order. He stopped at a grocery and stocked up on cheese, salami, fruit, bread, and bottled water, then drove into Munich and parked in a parking garage. With the tinted windows, no one would know that they spent the next few hours in the van, eating, dozing, and, in Patton's case, trying not to remember that day in Kandahar. Dark, enclosed spaces tended to trigger flashbacks.

There had been three of them and two of the enemy in that dim room. They had come across the two Taliban so suddenly that none of the five had moved for a split second, but then Bailey had one of the enemy in a choke hold and Thomas had the other against the wall with a gun to his forehead. The enemy weapons sat useless on the other side of the room. These guys, Patton thought, had not expected company. Patton took care of the zip ties and shoved the restrained men to the floor. Then the three Americans stepped back for a moment, wondering what to do next. They could still hear shouts and gunfire outside. They knew they might be here for a while.

Patton tried to calm the surge of adrenaline that had come with the sudden confrontation—she did not need adrenaline right now, she told herself. Better save it for later. She could see in the eyes of Thomas and Bailey that they were doing the same thing. After a minute or two of the five of them staring at each other, more in curiosity than in contempt, Bailey spoke up.

"Maybe they know something."

"You speak some Arabic," said Thomas to Patton.

"A fair amount," said Patton, already afraid where this conversation might lead.

"Look," said Bailey, "we're not going to find that weapons cache sitting in here in the dark, unless . . ."

Patton had been disturbed by how naturally Bailey took to this work. They did not teach you this in intelligence training. None of this was regulation. But the one time Patton mentioned that fact, Bailey shot her a look of contempt and said, "You want to try to save those guys out there, or do you want this scum to be comfortable?"

And so Patton had served as interrogator, asking the older of the two soldiers the same few questions over and over as Bailey first pummeled his face a few times and gradually worked his way up to a knife twisting into his kneecap. Patton knew the real object here was not to get the older soldier being tortured to talk—they could all tell he would never break—but to scare the younger one, who looked about fifteen, so badly he would say something. That was precisely what happened. His voice trembling, he gave up the name of the village where weapons were stored and from which reinforcements were being sent down to the firefight raging outside. Patton wrote everything down and then took out her map to determine coordinates.

"Maybe this kid has even more to tell us," said Bailey, stepping toward the youngster quivering in the corner. Bailey lifted him up by his jacket but the buttons popped off and the jacket came open, slipping off one arm as the boy fell back to the floor.

"Fuck," said Thomas as Bailey stepped away.

"You son of a bitch," shouted Bailey, staggering backward across the room and stepping on Patton's map.

"You guys want to calm the fuck down," said Patton. "It's kind of important what I'm doing here."

But Thomas just said, "Fuck" again, this time fear creeping into his voice.

"What the hell?" said Patton, looking up from the map at Thomas and Bailey plastered against the wall as far away from the boy as they could get. The man with the knife in his knee had passed out and the room was quiet for a moment during a lull in the fighting outside. Thomas and Bailey had gone pale, and Patton followed their gazes across the room to the boy whose jacket now hung loosely from one arm. You didn't have to be Army intelligence to see that he wore a suicide vest.

———

Jean had gone through a gamut of emotions on the ride back into Munich. She had felt anger as she left the memorial behind, the tears on her cheeks no great surprise to the driver. Then, as the camp disappeared behind them, she calmed into a deep sadness. As they eased back into the crowded streets on the north side of Munich she could not subdue a genuine curiosity. What game was Ingrid Weiss playing? Why had she disrespected Jean's grandfather and the grandparents of others who had received books from Columbia House? When the taxi pulled up in front of an unassuming house, mostly hidden behind a wall on the quiet residential Döbereinerstrasse, she wanted, more than anything, not to punish Ingrid Weiss but just to extract an explanation.

"Here you are," said the driver in perfect English.

Jean had not paid much attention to their surroundings as they drove through the Obermenzing district, but now she felt something must be wrong. "But this is a house," she said.

"Yes," said the driver. "There is the number, and there is the street sign."

There was no doubt that the sign on the corner read *Döbereinerstrasse* and that the house number matched that on the Columbia House letterhead.

"When you are ready to go back to the central station," said the driver, "there is an S-Bahn station right around the corner where you can get a train."

Jean paid him with a credit card, then watched as he drove away, leaving her on a cobblestone walkway on the edge of a narrow street. She stood for a moment, comparing once again the street name and house number to the address on the letter from Ingrid Weiss. She had expected an office building, some lifeless modern glass monstrosity filled with faceless corporations. Instead she stood among an explosion of life—trees hung over garden walls, carefully tended shrubbery spilled out to the edge of the single lane street, flowers bloomed in profusion and the few sounds she heard were distinctly domestic—a crying baby, a vacuum cleaner, a pair of garden shears clipping rhythmically. Another taxi moved slowly down the street toward her, and she thought there might not be room for it to pass, so, to make space in the street more than because she felt brave, she pressed the button by Ingrid Weiss's gate and waited.

And waited. And waited. The taxi stopped several houses away. The vacuum cleaner shut off and the baby quieted. The garden shears continued their steady clip, clip, clip. After several minutes and two more pressings of the button, Jean turned to go. It was nearly six o'clock and if she wanted to get back to Vienna tonight, she should catch a train soon. She felt a wave of disappointment—to have come all this way only to be met by a locked gate and an unanswered doorbell. Maybe she should spend the night in Munich and try again first thing in the morning. Or at least come back later in the evening. Maybe Ingrid Weiss would be home in an hour. She turned to go, took a step away from the gate, then heard a fuzzy voice coming through a speaker on the wall.

"*Ja? Wer ist es?* Who is it?" The voice sounded tired and annoyed.

Jean jumped back to the gate and stood on her toes to speak. "Miss Weiss? My name is Jean Simpson. I came to . . ." Jean hadn't thought what she would say to convince Ingrid Weiss to open the door. If she said she had come to confront her about the fraud she was perpetrating, the gate would certainly remain locked. "To thank you for a book you sent me. A book that belonged to my grandfather."

"Ah, Miss Simpson," said the voice, suddenly syrupy. "How nice of you to come all this way. Do come in." A buzzer sounded, the gate clicked unlocked, and Jean pushed her way into a lovely front garden. She walked the four steps that separated the gate from the front door and before she could knock she heard the sound of latches being undone on the other side. In another second the door swung open and there stood a woman who could not have been more than a few years older than Jean. She had blond hair fading to gray, square shoulders, and kind blue eyes. She smiled broadly at Jean—the smile of a sister or a long-lost cousin.

"What a lovely surprise," she said, and Jean found that, for the moment at least, she could not be angry. Even her curiosity had ebbed. Ingrid Weiss had a presence that did more than put Jean at ease—it made her feel a comfort and safety akin to what she felt curled up on the couch in her childhood home reading a good book while her mother made soup in the kitchen. She could not resist smiling but could find no words to say.

Ingrid reached out and took Jean's hand, pulling her gently toward the door. "Won't you come in and have a cup of tea?"

Since they had spotted her standing in front of Ingrid's house ringing the bell, Dietrich and Eva decided they had better pretend they had changed their minds and followed Jean Simpson all day. Ingrid might not like the story, but it would be better than, *We spent the afternoon at the Hotel Amba and just happened to notice Miss Simpson standing on your doorstep as our taxi pulled up.*

"That is her, right?" said Eva as Dietrich paid for the taxi.

"Absolutely," said Dietrich. "Unless there's another American woman in that outfit wandering around Munich."

"You don't think she came all the way here just to say thank you to Ingrid?"

"Not a chance," said Dietrich. "We'd better go in the back way."

They had stayed in the taxi until Jean had disappeared through the front gate; now they circled around behind the house, tapped the code into the security pad on the garden gate, and slipped into the house through the back door just in time to hear Ingrid asking Jean Simpson if she took her tea with honey and lemon. The back door opened directly into the kitchen and Ingrid made a not altogether pleasant face when she entered the room and found Dietrich and Eva sheepishly lurking out of sight of the sitting room where she had left Jean Simpson. Ingrid managed to convey, in a single glance, *Where the hell have you been, some sleazy hotel by the looks of it, go downstairs and tell Gottfried what's going on, and I'll deal with your little transgression later,* but all she said was "Lemon and honey coming right up."

"I guess I don't have to ask where you two have been," said Gottfried when Dietrich and Eva descended into the basement. "You might at least take a comb with you so it's not quite so obvious."

Eva blushed deeply but said nothing.

"We have a visitor," said Dietrich, trying to change the subject.

"You know you could keep your hands off each other for a few days while we're in the weeds here," said Gottfried.

"I said we have a visitor," said Dietrich.

"I mean really, you're like a couple of students constantly sneaking off for a little—"

"He said we have a visitor," said Eva sternly. Her blush was gone and she seemed ready to take charge.

"I know we have a fucking visitor," said Gottfried, whispering through clenched teeth. "Unlike some people, I was here when the bell rang. And if you don't talk more quietly, our visitor will know that Ingrid is not alone."

No one spoke for a moment, and then the tension in the room seemed to ease of its own accord. "Any idea who it is?" said Gottfried.

"It's our old friend Jean Simpson," said Eva.

"I thought she went to Dachau," said Gottfried.

"She came back," said Dietrich, "and now she's upstairs drinking tea with honey and lemon."

"Do you think Ingrid will send her away?" said Gottfried.

"My guess," said Eva, "is that she didn't come here to say thank you. She knows or she thinks she knows. And if she confronts Ingrid . . ."

"Then we implement Operation Waistcoat," said Gottfried with a smile.

Dietrich nodded, but Eva said, "You don't think that's a bit of an overreaction?"

"It's perfect timing," said Gottfried. "In a few hours Karl and Erich will have the decrypted message and the secret of Projekt Alchemie. Thanks to crowdfunding, we now have enough money to outfit the Fox's Den. We don't need this place anymore, and what could gain greater sympathy for Columbia House than Operation Waistcoat?"

"What do you mean sympathy?" said Dietrich.

"People see the results," said Gottfried, "they jump to the obvious conclusion, and the donations start pouring in."

"Maybe she really did come to say thank you," said Eva. Just then a red light began blinking on the center of one of Gottfried's computer screens.

Gottfried nodded toward the screen, stood up from his chair, and took a pistol out of a desk drawer. "Then again," he said, "maybe not."

IX

Ted Grosswald, Bob Macmillan, and Franklin Rendell had traveled from their homes across the United States to Alta Vista and then from Alta Vista to London where the trail of Patton Harcourt had gone cold. Now, they sat in a pub on a spring afternoon drinking beer and wondering if this was all really worth it.

"I want to look her in the face before I do it," said Bob, who had always been the one to egg the other two on. Even when they had been in basic training together it had been clear he would be the leader, and when difficult jobs arose, he would step up and do them.

"You know murder is a crime over here, too," said Ted.

"You getting cold feet?" said Bob.

"Not cold feet exactly," said Ted. "I just think we ought to be careful. I don't want to spend the rest of my life in some English prison."

"Nobody's going to prison," said Bob. "Look, she's on the lam, for some reason or other. Maybe she got wind we were on the move, I don't know, but whatever the reason, it works to our advantage."

"How do you figure that?" said Franklin. He had sat silently sipping his beer most of the evening, but Ted and Bob knew him well enough to know that behind that silence his mind worked a mile a minute. If Bob could be trusted to dive headfirst into a problem Franklin would carefully weigh all available information to come up with the best solution.

"Nobody knows where she is, right?" said Bob. "So if we find her and take care of business, no one will know where to look for her."

"But *we* don't know where she is," said Ted.

"True," said Bob.

"What I don't understand is this," said Franklin. "The going theory in Alta Vista was that something in her past caught up to her so she went into hiding. But *we're* the thing in her past. So who put those bullet holes in her house? Who is she running from? Figure that out and maybe we'll know where she's going."

"Maybe we're not the only people who have a score to settle," said Ted.

"All I know is this," said Franklin, draining his glass. "If something doesn't change by this time tomorrow, I'm going home."

"We're on the brink," said Bob. "After all that time of her hiding out up in those mountains, we're on the brink. I can feel it."

"I think that's three pints of beer and jet lag you feel," said Franklin, pushing back his chair and standing up. "I'm going to go take in a few sights. I'll see you soldiers in the morning."

―――――

Whether she called it PTSD or shell shock or anything else didn't matter. Whatever term you used or didn't use it meant that you would freak the fuck out on occasion because the army put you in a situation no human being should ever have to face. Kandahar, the knife in the knee, the suicide vest in the windowless room—that had been the situation for Patton. The moment she flashed back, her mind turned dark and her pulse rushed and her mouth got so dry she couldn't swallow. Ironic, she thought, that she could be completely calm under gunfire in her own kitchen, but sitting in the back seat of a parked van brought on the churning stomach and the double vision. Small, dark spaces, the shrink had said. The first thing you can do is avoid small, dark spaces. Easy for her to say. What if you're forced to spend a few hours with a needy old flame and a friendly assassin hiding in a Munich parking garage? Then how do you avoid small, dark spaces?

"I need to go for a walk," said Patton, after gritting her teeth for two hours.

"A walk?" said Ruthie. "We're supposed to be hiding out, aren't we? And you need to go for a walk?"

"Yes," said Patton sharply as she opened the door, "I need to go for a walk. Is there part of that sentence you don't understand?"

"I just . . ." Ruthie recoiled from Patton's venom, looking chastised and confused.

"Let her go," said Nemo quietly. Patton didn't understand how a man who had spent so little time in the company of other people could so quickly comprehend her feelings. It had taken him one glance at her face in the murky light that came in through the open door to flash her a look of complete understanding. "Just keep your cap pulled down, don't look up at any CCTV cameras, and be back by dusk."

"And you're going to just leave me here with him?" said Ruthie.

"You'll sleep better without me," said Patton, and then, already feeling the terror starting to ebb away just from the simple act of deciding to leave, she added, with a wink, "You never did get much sleep with me around, anyway."

Following Nemo's advice, Patton kept her hat pulled as low as it would go and hung her head so that no one, and no CCTV camera, would get a good look at her. This meant her impression of Munich was mostly of sidewalks and shoes. She wandered the streets for a couple of hours, noting her path carefully so she would be able to return to the van. She eventually emerged onto a wide grassy square and could not resist a quick glance up.

On the two sides stood the neo-classical behemoths of a pair of museums—the Staatliche Antikensammlungen and the Glyptothek and in front of her stood the grand city gate, or Propyläen. She had arrived at the Königsplatz, one of the great plazas of Munich. Here, Patton shouldn't have felt the sense of doom that descended upon her in the dark confines of the van lifting. She was surrounded by a wide-open space and huge, beautiful buildings; the sky behind the Propyläen blazed with reds and oranges as the sun set over Munich, and only a few other pedestrians shared this vast, stunning space.

But her mood only darkened, and the fiery sunset did nothing to help. As soon as she saw the sky against the Propyläen her memory began to play a film on which she enhanced the original black and white with the colors before her, the colors of flame and fire. She had watched that film for the first time in middle school and several times thereafter, including in a class on military history that she took after joining the Army. It had been taken in Berlin on May 10, 1933, but the same thing had happened that night in cities across Germany, including in Munich here in the Königsplatz—university students and Nazi officials burning tens of thousands of books. Patton almost thought she could feel the heat of those flames that had tried to, in the words of the oath that the students took, "destroy and combat subversive and un-German literature."

Patton had loved books since her second-grade teacher had read the class *From the Mixed-Up Files of Mrs. Basil E. Frankweiler.* She had taken classes in the library school as an undergraduate and, if there had been such a thing as a minor in library science, she would have added it to her math degree. She knew as much about the topic as most people with a master's degree in the subject.

The Holocaust, when she first encountered its history in middle school, revolted her, made her sick to her stomach. Yet those crimes against humanity had not, Patton thought, been crimes against *her.* She was, after all, as lily white as they came. Not until later did she discover the extent to which Nazis had murdered homosexuals. But the book burnings she took personally. And now she stood on the site of one such burning and could not clear her mind of those images in the newsreel of German students delighting in the destruction not just of books but of ideas. She was sure that, if it had been written before 1933, her beloved childhood favorite would have been tossed into those flames. After all the author, E. L. Konigsburg, was Jewish.

Patton turned on her heels and walked out of the plaza as fast as she could without breaking into a run. Twenty minutes later, back in the van, despite the growing darkness and the confined space, she actually felt safe. She did not say anything to Ruthie or Nemo about where she had gone, but she leaned against Ruthie and held her hand and cried for a few minutes. Then she drew a deep breath, sat up, and said, "Let's go get the motherfuckers."

———

"We do make every effort to ensure that we have properly traced the provenance of the books we return," said Ingrid. "I'm very sorry if we made a mistake in your case. As you can imagine, it can be very difficult to prove ownership of a book after eighty years."

"Yes, but it's not only *my* book that was returned incorrectly. I spoke with several other people who received books from Columbia House with the same inconsistencies, the same forged inscriptions, even the same handwriting in those inscriptions."

"That certainly is a mystery," said Ingrid.

Jean found this conversation frustrating. Whatever she said Ingrid simply nodded sympathetically and responded in meaningless platitudes. It was like trying to pin down an American politician in the midst of a scandal. But she wasn't about to give up this quickly after having come so far.

"I don't believe it *is* a mystery," she said. "I believe that you forged those inscriptions knowing full well those books did not belong to the people you sent them to."

"That's a bold accusation to make to a philanthropic woman in her own kitchen," said Ingrid. "Do you have any proof?"

"I have images of four different books," said Jean, "all stolen from libraries, all with forged inscriptions, and all given away by you. I wonder how many of these books are stolen." She pointed to the bookcase that covered one wall of the sitting room.

"You think I would steal books?"

"All the Columbia House books I traced had been stolen from libraries here and in Prague." Jean could see in a flash that she had struck a nerve. Though the look of panic that crossed Ingrid's face lasted only an instant before being replaced with her previous implacable calm,

Jean had confronted enough students about plagiarism to know when she had shaken her opponent.

"Would you pardon me for just a moment," said Ingrid, pulling her phone out of her slacks pocket. "This infernal thing keeps vibrating and I need to turn it off." She tapped twice on the screen, then set the phone down on the table. "Now, where were we?"

"You were about to explain why you have been giving away stolen library books in an effort to convince me not to call the police."

"The police? I don't think that will be necessary."

"It certainly won't," said a voice from behind Jean.

"Jean Simpson, this is my associate Gottfried Bergman."

Jean had never come face-to-face with the barrel of a gun and her first thought when she turned to see Gottfried leveling a pistol at her was that the opening reminded her of a train tunnel. Then she pictured a train speeding out of it and exploding into her forehead and she thought for a moment she might lose control of her bowels.

"I wonder if you might come with me, Miss Simpson," said Gottfried with a sweetness that belied the threat of his weapon.

"I . . . I . . ." Jean tried to stand, found that her legs had turned to jelly, and fell back into the chair.

"Oh, for God's sake," said Ingrid impatiently. "Do I have to do everything around here?" She shoved her chair back from the table, stood, and grabbed Jean by the arm, yanking her upright. Jean stumbled forward as Ingrid pulled her toward the door to the basement, Gottfried keeping the gun trained on her the whole time. "Down!" shouted Ingrid as Jean teetered on the brink of the steep wooden staircase.

Jean steadied herself with the bannister and managed to make it to the bottom of the steps. She emerged in a large square room, lit with the glow of several computer screens and three bare lightbulbs hanging from the ceiling. In the far corner a man brushed a few strands of hair out of a woman's face.

"Can you two keep your hands off each other for five minutes?" snapped Ingrid.

Dietrich stepped away from Eva and walked up to Jean, standing uncomfortably close and staring at her face. "So this is our volunteer for Operation Waistcoat."

"I'm not a volunteer for anything," said Jean, who had started to regain her nerve.

"Have a seat," said Ingrid, ignoring Jean's comment. She nodded toward an uncomfortable-looking ladder-back chair in the corner opposite the computers.

"No, thank you," said Jean.

"I said have a seat!" shouted Ingrid, spitting at Jean. In another instant, the two lovers had each grabbed one of Jean's arms and forced her into the chair. Gottfried stepped toward her, the gun still trained on her face. She should have listened to Peter, thought Jean. She should have called the police first. But who knew that someone who stole library books would be a . . . a what? What was Ingrid Weiss? A kidnapper? A terrorist? Jean had no idea, and that, more than anything else, even more than the gun in her face, frightened her. If she didn't know Ingrid's game, she couldn't play.

"What do you want?" said Jean as calmly as she could manage.

"She just came to us?" said Gottfried, switching to German and ignoring Jean.

"We followed her here," said Eva, stepping forward. "She went to Dachau first and then she came here."

"I rather doubt you followed her the whole time," said Ingrid. "But that is not our concern at the moment. The question is, what do we do with her?"

"She's perfect for Operation Waistcoat," said Dietrich. "She came here of her own accord, the surveillance footage is already uploaded to the external server, and according to Gottfried, we have enough money now to relocate to the Fox's Den. Operation Waistcoat turns a problem into an advantage."

"And the money will pour in," said Gottfried.

"Soon money will not be a problem anyway," said Ingrid.

"Yes," said Dietrich, "but until then it could come in handy."

"Very well," said Ingrid. "Will it fit her?"

Dietrich smiled what Jean could only think of as an evil grin as he said, "It's adjustable."

"Excellent," said Ingrid. "Now we just need to wait to hear from Karl and Erich."

Jean did not speak enough German to follow the whole conversation, but she caught bits and pieces—enough to be both puzzled and concerned.

The message came quicker than they expected but what they did not know, what they could not know, was that the message had been sent not by Karl and Erich but by an English-speaking cab driver whom Nemo had paid €1,000 to drive to Odelzhausen, just northwest of Munich, turn on Karl and Erich's phone, and send a message to Weiss that translated roughly, "They got off the train in Stuttgart. Now in a car heading to final destination—Berchtesgaden. Meet us there for intercept and completion of Projekt Alchemie. HH." The cabbie would type the message in German, and deliver the phone to Berchtesgaden, the small town on the German-Austrian border where Adolf Hitler had built his Eagle's Nest retreat. There he would type one more message and then he would go about his business, €1,000 for the better. It was the easiest money he had ever made.

"I always thought it would be Berchtesgaden," said Ingrid.

"We can be there in less than two hours," said Dietrich.

"But we've been there a dozen times looking," said Eva. "What makes you think this time will be any different?"

"Because this time we will know where to look," said Ingrid, smiling. "In a few hours Projekt Alchemie will succeed. I only wish the great Reichsführer Himmler could be here to see his dream realized. Now we will prove him right and the Aryan will be supreme once more."

"What do we take with us?" said Gottfried.

"We take weapons, explosives, and your hard drive," said Ingrid. "Plus our bags. There's no time for anything else."

"But what about the books and the—"

"It needs to look like we weren't here," said Ingrid, "not like we packed up. Besides, once the money starts rolling in, it won't make a difference."

"You're sure this will work?" said Eva.

"Operation Waistcoat will absolutely work," said Dietrich. "Projekt Alchemie is more a leap of faith."

"It's time to leap," said Ingrid.

Five minutes later they had filled the trunk of Ingrid's BMW with every piece of weaponry in the house along with the four bags they always kept packed for this possibility. Gottfried had removed one laptop and an external hard drive that kept all their files, then set in motion the program that would wipe the memory of everything he left behind. Dietrich had used a can of black spray paint to leave some evidence on the garden wall.

"Are you sure we're not forgetting anything?" said Eva as Ingrid started the car and backed toward the street.

"Anything we've forgotten we can buy," said Ingrid. "Nothing is irreplaceable."

It wasn't until they were halfway to Berchtesgaden that she realized those words were not exactly true. She had left behind one irreplaceable item. She had purchased it as a way to feel closer to Heinrich Himmler, the man for whom her grandfather had worked, and who had begun Projekt Alchemie. Late at night, when sleep would not come, Ingrid would leaf through the pages of the ledger—a list of all the books in Himmler's secret library of the occult. She had, of course, obtained copies of nearly every book on that list that mentioned alchemy and read them all carefully, but they had shed no light on Himmler's secret project. And naturally she had made a digital copy of the ledger. Still, she loved the physical feel of the book, a book that Himmler himself had held and used again and again. She liked to run her finger down those columns and imagine that library and the great man himself pulling a book off the shelf and sitting by the fire as he read. Now the ledger sat on her bedside table fifty miles away. She would miss that means of communing with Himmler, but now was no time for sentimentality. The Reichsführer himself had set them on the road to Berchtesgaden and soon they would realize his dream and Projekt Alchemie would change the world.

———

Nemo, Ruthie, and Patton had parked at the end of the street and saw the lights go out at Ingrid Weiss's house. A few moments later, a black BMW pulled out from behind the house and disappeared in the opposite direction.

"They took the bait," said Nemo.

"It can't be that easy," said Ruthie.

"It's not," said Patton. "But give me a half hour and I can make it a lot easier."

They had assumed that Weiss did not work alone and would not leave her lair unguarded. But Patton would set up a surveillance system that would give them infrared eyes inside the house, allowing them to pinpoint anyone left behind and monitor their movements. As uncomfortable as she had been earlier in the stuffy back seat of the car, she now felt almost exhilarated. She was in her element, doing what she had trained to do and doing it well.

Her first priority was to remain hidden from whomever was inside. They did not want to sacrifice the element of surprise when the time came to breach the house. But Patton was a master at spotting security cameras (of which there were three outside the house) and staying out of their line of vision. They might have to come into view of one camera when they entered the house, but that would give anyone monitoring only a split-second warning. She hadn't done this in years and she loved it—climbing walls and slinking through shrubbery to place her equipment as close to the house as she could. At the back she found a small window to the basement that had been painted over on the inside—the perfect place for an infrared detector to spot anyone hiding down there. She placed two more detectors in the garden, one of them in a tree to get a good scan of the top floor. She also placed several microphones at strategic points. She might not be able to hear every word spoken inside the house, but she would hear enough. Thirty minutes later, back in the van, she pulled up the feeds from her equipment on an iPad. She did not see what she expected.

"That's weird," she said.

"What is?" said Nemo.

"It looks like we have just one person still in the house."

"Good news for us," said Nemo. "Should be pretty easy to neutralize one person. Where is he?"

"He or *she*," said Patton pointedly, "is in the basement. But they're not moving."

"So sitting at a desk or something?" said Ruthie.

"In a chair, I'd guess from the position," said Patton, "but not typing or writing or talking on the phone, or even reading."

"How can you tell?" said Nemo.

"Look," said Patton, pointing to a glowing red shape on the screen. "No movement at all. I've been watching for five minutes now and nothing."

"Asleep?" said Ruthie.

"It's an awfully strange position to sleep in," said Patton.

"So somebody is passed out in a chair," said Nemo. "Who cares? We go in, we neutralize someone who is already basically neutralized, we find the book, and we get out. It's an easy job."

"That's what worries me," said Patton, "and it should worry you. You know as well as I do that no job should be this easy. Somebody wants us to *think* this is a simple job."

"Maybe it's not a person," said Ruthie.

"It's hard to reproduce a human heat signature," said Patton. "It just concerns me."

"OK," said Nemo, "your concern is noted. I'm concerned, too, but I'm not calling off the operation just because I'm concerned. Clearly they are up to something, but so are we, and we've been one step ahead of them the whole time. So we go in cautiously, we look out for trip wires and booby traps, and as long as that heat signature in the basement doesn't move, we take our time."

"Look," said Ruthie, pointing to the iPad. "It's moving." The head and shoulders of the glowing red figure on the screen shifted slightly from side to side. "Maybe they woke up."

"Let's go," said Nemo. "Before they come upstairs."

Nemo eased the van into the drive from which the BMW had emerged and they armed themselves with the antique weapons Alex Lansdowne had provided. Patton climbed the wall again, but this time pressed the button on the inside that opened the back gate. Nemo had brought a set of lock picks from his apparently bottomless black bag of goodies, but they proved unnecessary. The back door was unlocked.

"Not a good sign," said Patton, as they stepped into the kitchen.

"You start looking around for that book," said Nemo to Ruthie. "Patton and I will go downstairs and take care of that heat signature."

The house was pitch dark, with blinds and curtains keeping even the dim lights of Döbereinerstrasse from penetrating its rooms. Nemo had given Ruthie a flashlight and she stepped into the sitting room to find two large cases of books. It might take some time to locate the ledger, she thought, and she began scanning the shelves.

It took only a minute for Nemo and Patton to discover the door to the basement stairs. Weapons drawn, they decided to risk flipping on the light switch. Whoever was down there had been sitting in the dark for quite a while, so maybe the light would blind them long enough for the two of them to get downstairs. As soon as the stairs flooded with light, they heard a weak voice.

"Oh my God, who's there? Help me, please help me."

"Doesn't sound too threatening," said Nemo as they descended the stairs, guns drawn.

"Why is she speaking English?" hissed Patton.

Nemo leaped around the corner at the foot of the stairs, ready to fire if necessary, then lowered his gun when he saw a disheveled woman zip-tied to a wooden chair and looking at him with a desperate expression.

"Not exactly the SS," said Nemo, almost laughing as Patton entered the basement behind him. "Who the hell are you?"

"My name is Jean Simpson," she said. "They all left. They left me here. I don't know how much time I have. You have to help me."

"What do you mean you don't know how much time you have?" said Nemo, casually looking around the room. "If ever a place looked like a super villain's secret lair, this is it."

"Help me, please," said the woman, beginning to cry.

"It's OK," said Patton, crossing slowly toward the woman. She still thought this whole thing might be a trap, and she certainly wasn't going to trust this woman, but the zip ties were pulled tight, so it seemed safe to at least pretend to offer her consolation. "We can help you." She laid a hand on the woman's shoulder and felt her trembling. This was no cold-blooded killer, she thought.

"I'm not sure you can," said Jean. "And I'm not sure how much time you have."

"Why do you keep saying that?" said Nemo, turning from his examination of the room.

"Open this jacket," said Jean, "and you'll see why."

Patton immediately stepped away. Now it sounded like a trap.

"Open it, please," said Jean, and Patton thought she sounded both honest and genuinely panicked.

"Oh for God's sake," said Nemo. "Open the fucking jacket." He walked across the room and pulled open the windbreaker the woman was wearing.

"Fuck," said Patton, the blood draining from her face as she fell backward into a chair by the computer table.

"What's that?" said Nemo. "What the hell is that?"

Jean didn't respond, only wept more openly. Patton merely repeated, in a soft voice, "Fuck."

Ruthie could find nothing resembling the ledger in the bookcases in the sitting room or anywhere else downstairs. A large desk and a filing cabinet both had locked drawers, and she supposed she might get some help from Nemo in opening them, but for the time being she would search the rest of the house. She climbed the stairs, all the while hearing Patton's voice in her head saying, *No job should be this easy.*

The upstairs consisted of two monastic bedrooms and a shared bath. One of the rooms looked like it hadn't been used in a long time; the other was clearly where Ingrid Weiss slept. The bedcovers were rumpled; a paperback book lay open, spine up, on the dresser; a robe hung on the back of the door; and a pair of slippers sat on the floor by the bed. And there, on the bedside table, lay a worn, clothbound ledger with a faded gold swastika on the cover. *No job should be this easy,* but this one was. Just because Patton had been in the military and Nemo was some sort of killer didn't mean their paranoia always translated into reality, thought Ruthie as she picked up the book. She opened the ledger and saw immediately that this was what they had come for. Page after page contained one column with the titles of books—even in German, she recognized enough words to identify them as titles—and another column of numbers. And at the top of the first page, centered above the initial entries, read the words "*Heinrich Himmler Bibliothek.*" The Library of Heinrich Himmler. Ruthie whisked up the volume and raced down the stairs and back to the kitchen where the door to the basement stood open.

"I've got it," she shouted. "I've got it. Let's get out of here." When no one answered she started down the basement stairs, a little more cautiously than she had rushed down from the bedroom. *No job should be this easy.* Maybe Patton had been right. Maybe something had gone wrong. Maybe the others were gone or dead. But when she reached the bottom step and turned the corner, shakily holding the pistol she had withdrawn from her pocket on the way down, she saw Nemo standing in the middle of the room and Patton sitting in a chair—both apparently perfectly healthy. And then Patton said, "Fuck."

———

Alta Vista had proved a great place to avoid flashbacks to that room in Kandahar. Patton had had no trouble staying out of windowless rooms and other dark or close spaces. And she certainly didn't encounter any explosive vests in the rural North Carolina mountains. It could have stayed that way, she thought, if Nemo hadn't dragged her into all this. Now she struggled to breathe and felt her heart racing. Her vision blurred and a sound that no one else heard pounded in her head—the sound of gunfire and shouting and fear and death.

The man with the knife in his knee did not stir, but the younger one, the one in the suicide vest, smiled at the three Americans. They had no idea how the vest was triggered. True, they had zip-tied his hands, but there could be a timer or a remote trigger.

"Patton, get out of here," said Bailey.

"I'm not leaving just because I'm a woman," said Patton.

"It's not because you're a woman, for fuck's sake," said Bailey. "It's because you understand the intel. Get out of here and stay alive and radio in those coordinates."

"But can't we all—" said Patton.

"Go!" shouted Bailey, who had his rifle trained on the boy in the vest.

Feeling violently ill, Patton did not stay to argue. Clearly Bailey had a plan and if the vest hadn't detonated in the past hour, maybe he had time to execute it. The light had begun to fade outside, which worked to her advantage as she crawled out of the house, looking for any sort of cover. A hundred feet away, a Humvee lay on its side, smoldering—probably the victim of an IED. She saw no one else in the street, though she suspected snipers were watching. Most of the gunfire seemed to come from the next street over. Gripping her rifle in one hand and her radio in the other, she made a dash for it, skidding into the shelter of the vehicle as bullets exploded into the dirt behind her. Two dead Americans lay next to the Humvee, but she had no time for mourning. Safe for perhaps a minute or two, she felt her adrenaline kick in and she radioed the coordinates of the village that the man in the suicide vest had given up.

The strike would come soon, she thought. In the meantime, she watched for Bailey and Thomas to emerge from the house. Though it seemed like hours since she left them, it had only been about ninety seconds. She risked a peek out from behind the Humvee and was suddenly thrown backward by a shock wave. The house exploded in all directions, sending a shower of rubble over Patton. A ball of fire rolled out into the street and the air filled with dust so thick she could see only a few feet. She fell back behind the Humvee, cowering from the bricks and stones that fell around her. Then, silence. All gunfire ceased and Patton heard only a high-pitched ringing in her ears. The dust began to settle and again she looked out from her hiding place. In the middle of the street lay Bailey. He, at least, had made it out. She put down her gun and crawled toward him. He was a big man, but Patton was strong— she could drag him to the relative safety of the Humvee. But when she arrived at Bailey's side, she saw what she had not seen in the distance in the fading light and dusty air. Only the top of Bailey's body had escaped the house. The explosion had torn him neatly in half. Then everything went black.

When Patton woke up, she was in a hospital in Germany and they still hadn't told her the worst part.

———

"We just leave her, right?" said Nemo, sounding uncertain for the first time since Patton had met him.

"Don't leave me," said Jean. "Please, God, don't leave me."

"What's going on?" said Ruthie.

"You want to field that one?" said Nemo, but Patton could not form words at the moment and only breathed rapidly, feeling the room start to spin.

"No?" said Nemo. "Well, Patton here is having some sort of severe panic attack which, if I'm not mistaken, has something to do with PTSD."

"What makes you say that?" said Ruthie, rushing to Patton's side and taking her hand.

"Because I have the same problem," said Nemo. "Only I have a different trigger. Patton's trigger is apparently explosive suicide vests."

"Why would she be triggered by a—"

"Yeah, the second part of what's going on is that Miss Jean Simpson here is wearing a vest that could reduce this whole house to dust and splinters at any moment. I think that gets you caught up."

"Well . . . well shouldn't we do something?" said Ruthie, pulling away from Patton and edging back toward the stairs.

"You got any suggestions?" said Nemo.

"I don't know," said Ruthie. "Diffuse it or something."

"OK, I'll just use my extensive expertise from years on a bomb squad to diffuse it. Why didn't I think of that before?"

"You were on a bomb squad?" said Ruthie.

"No, I wasn't on a fucking bomb squad!" said Nemo. "Jesus, don't they have sarcasm in England?"

"What do we do?" said Ruthie.

"You leave," said Patton. She had used her focusing exercise to think about the waterfall near her house in Alta Vista—the sound of the water splashing against the rocks, the way the sun sifting through the trees sparkled in the droplets and the birds sang overhead. She stood up slowly, still feeling unsteady, and took a step forward. "Do you have the ledger?"

"Yes," said Ruthie, holding up the book. "I have it."

"Then take it and go. Both of you," said Patton. "We can't leave her here alone, so I'll stay with her."

"Like hell we can't leave her alone," said Nemo. "Besides, you're the librarian. You're the one who knows about books. This is a search for a rare book now and you're the expert."

"We can't leave her," said Patton, making eye contact with Jean Simpson who pleaded with her silently.

"Maybe the thing doesn't even work," said Ruthie.

"Maybe," said Nemo darkly. "But Ingrid Weiss doesn't strike me as someone who would make that kind of mistake."

"Go," said Patton. "While you still can."

"No," said Nemo, pulling out his gun and pointing it at Patton. "You go. I'll stay here with her."

"Oh, now you're going to be noble?" said Patton.

"Go," said Nemo calmly. "Go now or I'll blow your fucking head off." He reached into his pocket and pulled out the keys to the van, toss- ing them to Ruthie. "Get out of here."

"Is there anything you can do?" said Jean between sobs.

"Go," said Nemo. "I've got this."

Ruthie grabbed Patton by the hand and yanked her toward the stairs. Patton gave one last look at Nemo, then followed Ruthie up and out of the house. As soon as the cool night air hit her face, Patton felt steadier. The attack hadn't passed, not by a long shot, but she could at least function in the short term.

"Give me the keys," she said.

"Are you sure you're OK to drive?" said Ruthie.

"Give me the goddamn keys," said Patton. She needed to feel some modicum of control, even if it was only driving the van.

"Fine, fine," said Ruthie, handing over the keys to the van. In an- other minute, Patton was pulling out into the street and easing the van to the end of the block and around a corner. There she turned off the engine and tried to regulate her breathing, her hands still on the wheel.

"What are we doing?" said Ruthie.

"We're waiting," said Patton.

"But he said . . ."

"We're waiting," Patton repeated. "Give him ten minutes. You can time it if you like. Ten minutes and then we go."

But they didn't have to wait ten minutes. Three minutes later a great boom shook the van and a flash of light lit up the street. A second later, a fireball rent the night air where Ingrid Weiss's house had been a moment before. Patton felt immobility overtaking her, but she forced it away, bat- tling with everything that she had to start the engine as bits of glass and splinters of wood rained down on the van. It was Kandahar all over again.

———

"Did it work?" said Ingrid, as she navigated the car toward Berchtesgaden.

"Give me a minute," said Gottfried. "I just detonated a few sec- onds ago."

"If it didn't work, it's not my fault," said Dietrich. "Everything was rigged properly."

"If it didn't work, we're going to have a very unhappy woman in the basement when we return," said Eva.

"If we return," said Ingrid.

"We'll have to return," said Eva. "We can't have her spouting off to the police, and they're bound to find her sooner or later."

"All I know is I rigged the explosives correctly," said Dietrich. "If Gottfried screwed up the communications, that's not my fault."

"Why do you just assume Gottfried screwed up the communication?" said Ingrid.

"I don't," said Dietrich, "I'm just saying . . ."

"It worked," said Gottfried with a hint of triumph in his voice.

"Are you sure?" said Ingrid.

"I planted a seismic detector in the bushes across the street in case we ever did this," said Gottfried. "Ran it off the neighbors' Wi-Fi. The second I hit 'detonate' that thing went off the charts."

"Brilliant!" said Ingrid. "No more Jean Simpson and no evidence of the true nature of Columbia House."

"Plus," said Eva, "you are now the sympathetic victim of a terror attack. Your house blown to bits just because you were trying to help out the descendants of Holocaust victims."

"How long do we wait before we send the message to the police?" said Gottfried.

"I think we should wait a couple of hours at least," said Ingrid.

"Why?" said Eva. "An explosion like that, the police will be on the scene in minutes and the press won't be far behind. The last thing we want is for them to find their own evidence instead of using ours."

"She's right," said Dietrich. "We tell them where to look, and that's where they'll look."

"OK, send it now," said Ingrid.

"You sure it won't seem suspicious?" said Gottfried. "Coming so soon."

"How long has it been?" said Ingrid.

"Six minutes," said Gottfried.

"And you're sure you can send it so they can't trace our location?"

"Absolutely," said Gottfried.

"Give it ten minutes," said Ingrid. "Then do it."

———

Patton sat behind the wheel of the van shaking as the pages of books, some of them in flames, fluttered down around them. She could feel blackness closing in on her and Ruthie's screaming in the back seat didn't help. Lights flicked on in the houses nearby and doors opened. She could dimly hear shouts over the ringing in her ears and Ruthie's ruckus.

"Stop it," said Patton as calmly as she could muster, but Ruthie seemed not to hear.

"Oh God, oh God, that woman," she shouted. "What do we do? What do we do?"

"You stop it," said Patton, more forcefully this time. In a situation where she had no control, trying to control Ruthie might yank her out of the fog and back to reality. Nothing would remove the blackness, but maybe she could unfreeze herself if she could just get Ruthie to shut up. When the hysterics continued, she picked up her Luger off the seat, turned around, and pointed it squarely at Ruthie.

"If you don't shut the fuck up," she said, "I swear to God I will waste you." She meant it, too. At that moment, she needed something or someone to shoot, and Ruthie made a convenient target. But Ruthie must have seen the earnestness in Patton's eyes. Instantly her screams stopped, and while she continued to breathe like some sort of panting dog, Patton could deal with that a bit more easily. In the midst of her panic and darkness and the eruption of her horrific past into her bizarre present, Patton barely detected something else bubbling up in her psyche. It took her a moment to isolate with all the psychological background noise, but once Ruthie had quieted down she realized something surprising—she felt sad that Nemo was dead. Not just sad, but almost brokenhearted.

How had she become emotionally attached to a man hired to kill her friend, who had more blood on his hands than some of the terrorists she had hunted, who had committed cold-blooded murder right in front of her? It wasn't love, this thing she felt for Nemo, but it might be affection, or perhaps attachment was a better word. In spite of his ruthlessness, he had treated her well; he had protected her when he could have easily left her behind to protect himself. With him gone, she wasn't sure what happened next. Did she and Ruthie continue the search for Projekt Alchemie? Did they try to find item AL1533 in Himmler's library and keep working to outfox Ingrid Weiss? Or did she drive to the nearest airport and fly home and forget this entire mess, including the mess of her feelings for Ruthie, which, she realized as she lowered the gun, were far more complicated than she had suspected.

The renewed banging on the van made it hard to think. How was debris still falling several minutes after the explosion, thought Patton. And why wouldn't it stop so she could think. But the banging didn't stop, and then Ruthie started back up again.

"Jesus Christ, aren't you going to open the door?"

"What do you mean?" said Patton.

"The door! He's banging on the door."

"Who's banging . . ." And then Patton looked up and saw Nemo's face, twisted in the most beautiful fury, pressed against the window of the front passenger door as his fist pounded against the van. The flood of joy crashing into the darkness that had enveloped her was almost more than she could take and for a few seconds, she couldn't move. Then, as she reached for the door handle to let him in, another realization crashed over her. He had not been noble or selfless, he had left that poor woman to be blown apart.

She paused for a moment, but when Ruthie shouted, "For God's sake let him in," Patton reluctantly opened the door.

"Help me," said Nemo, as soon as the door opened.

"Oh just get in," said Patton. "Honestly I can't even look at you right now after you let that woman . . ."

"Look," said Nemo, "can we save whatever bullshit you're upset about for later and get this lady in the van."

"Get the lady?" Patton did not comprehend at first. Her overloaded brain couldn't keep up with the sudden shifts in reality. But then she saw that Nemo had Jean Simpson draped over his left side. Conscious, alive, Jean Simpson, who looked unable to walk by herself, but otherwise quite unexploded.

Before Patton could move, Ruthie jumped out of the van and helped Jean into the back. In another moment, the doors slammed and Nemo collapsed into the passenger seat. "Are you OK to drive?" he said.

Patton couldn't answer the question. She couldn't speak. For a few seconds the only sound in the van was the gradually slowing breathing of Nemo, Jean, and Ruthie. Then Patton realized she had been holding her breath, gulped in some air, and felt her vision clearing.

"I said are you OK to drive?" said Nemo, more gently this time.

"I think so," said Patton.

"Then get us the hell out of here."

Patton drove. She had no idea where, but she drove. No one spoke for several minutes until finally Ruthie asked, "What happened back there?"

"I just cut the damn vest off her and hoped for the best," said Nemo. "I guess whoever wired her up wasn't expecting a rescue party."

"Jesus," said Ruthie. "That was . . . daring."

"Thank you," said Jean softly. "Thank you."

"Ah, it was nothing," said Nemo. "All in a day's work."

"Good for you," said Patton, allowing relief and something approaching respect for Nemo to creep into her. She smiled and turned to him briefly. "Fucking good for you."

"Who are you people?" said Jean, in a slightly stronger voice.

"We just drive around and look for people who need rescuing," said Nemo.

"No, seriously," said Jean.

"Do you have the ledger?" said Nemo.

"Yes," said Ruthie. "I've got it right here."

"So what does it say? What is item AL1533?"

"I haven't looked yet," said Ruthie. "Let me see if I can find it." Ruthie began to flip through the ledger, squinting to read the entries in the light of the streetlamps.

"What is that?" said Jean.

"Just a list of old books," said Ruthie.

"You scared the hell out of me back there," said Patton to Nemo, speaking for the first time since she started driving. Her pulse had almost returned to normal, and although she still felt a hint of dark terror in her gut, she felt more like a functional human being than she had since they first saw the vest on Jean.

"Not upsetting you wasn't exactly my first priority," said Nemo. "And you managed to make the van almost impossible to find. God only knows how many neighbors saw me lugging Jean around looking for you."

"You're the one who told us to go."

"Out of the house, I told you to go, not out of the damn neighborhood."

"You might want to be a little more specific next time. Besides, we were barely a block away," said Patton, and then, most unexpectedly, she laughed.

"What the hell is so funny?" said Nemo. But Patton made no attempt to explain. How could she? She had no intention of admitting that arguing with Nemo made her happier than she thought possible so soon after a traumatic episode. She wished they could keep sparring for hours, but Ruthie interrupted the discussion.

"Here it is," said Ruthie. "Number AL1533. My German isn't perfect, but I think it says, 'Medieval alchemical scroll after George Ripley, circa 1550.'"

"What does that mean, 'medieval alchemical scroll'?" said Nemo.

"That part I understand," said Patton. "But who is George Ripley? And what does he have to do with Himmler?"

"What is that book?" said Jean, who seemed to be recovering her strength. "What are you looking at and why are you talking about a Ripley Scroll?"

"Wait a second," said Nemo, turning toward Jean. "You know about this Ripley guy?"

"I'm an art historian," said Jean, "so certainly I know about Ripley Scrolls."

"Who did you say you were again?" said Nemo.

The van was stopped at a red light, and Jean suddenly found three faces staring into hers. She wanted nothing more than to be in a deliciously comfortable bed at the Hotel Sacher in Vienna, rather than in the back of a van driving through the empty streets of Munich in the dead of night. Ingrid Weiss had wanted her dead; these strangers had saved her—was that reason enough to trust them and to become involved in whatever they were doing?

"I wonder if you could just drop me at the train station," said Jean. "I'm supposed to be in Vienna tomorrow for a conference."

"Afraid we can't do that," said Nemo. "Ruthie here will tell you— once you see our faces, you pretty much have to come along with us."

"It's true," said Ruthie.

"Listen," said Patton. "We look after our own and you are one of our own now. If you don't trust Nemo after he risked his life to save you, you must not trust anyone."

"Your name is Nemo?" said Jean.

"As far as you know," said Nemo.

"As far as anyone knows," said Patton.

The light turned green and Patton drove forward, her attention still on the stranger in the back seat. "I've seen medieval scrolls," she said. "In some classes in library science, rare books, that sort of thing. But I've never heard of George Ripley."

"Have you ever heard of Peter Byerly?" said Jean.

"Sure," said Patton. "He's a legend in rare books. Discovered that Shakespeare manuscript, right?"

"OK, so you *do* know something about books," said Jean, sounding satisfied. "Fine. George Ripley was an English alchemist. Lived in the fifteenth century, I think. I don't really know much about him, but there are these scrolls called Ripley Scrolls—mostly made in the sixteenth and seventeenth centuries and supposedly copied from the same original, although they show a lot of variation. I was always sort of vague on the exact connection to Ripley himself, because for me the point was the artwork. Each scroll is, I don't know maybe fifteen feet long when you completely unroll it. And they're full of these amazing color illustrations showing things like how to make gold out of lead and how to make the Philosopher's Stone. The secret to eternal life. All that sort of thing. Of course the science is bunk, but the art is exquisite."

"Is that all we're chasing?" said Nemo. "Some medieval crackpot's idea of how to live forever?"

"There has to be more to it than that," said Patton.

"Where can we find these scrolls?" said Nemo.

"Most of them are in the British Library in London or the Bodleian in Oxford. There are a few in other rare book libraries in the US. I read something about one that went missing before the war, but I don't think there are any in private collections."

"But didn't you say they're all different?" said Ruthie.

"There are variations, yes," said Jean.

"So we don't just need to see *some* Ripley Scroll, we need to see *this* one," said Ruthie, tapping her finger on the ledger.

"The one that went missing before the war," said Nemo with a smile.

"How exactly are you going to find it if it's gone missing?" said Jean.

"We know who the last owner was," said Patton. "If that's any help."

"Who was it?" said Jean.

"Reichsführer Heinrich Himmler," said Patton.

"In that case," said Jean, sitting up and looking fully alert for the first time since she escaped Ingrid Weiss's house, "I know where it is. We need to go to Prague."

———

To: Bavarian State Police
From: Ingrid Weiss, Columbia House, Munich

When the recent terrorist attack on my house and the headquarters of the charitable organization Columbia House was carried out, I was lucky enough not to be at home. My associates and I are now in hiding and in fear for our lives. However, I am able to provide the authorities with some information about the attack.

Several days ago I received a threatening phone call from a woman calling herself Jean Simpson of Ridgefield, North Carolina, USA, who seemed to want to interfere with the charitable work of Columbia House. It is not unusual for us to receive such calls from anti-Semitic or white supremacist groups, and I did not give the matter any thought. Like all such calls, we logged it carefully and added a photograph, taken from social media, to the record. We believe that Simpson was the bomber responsible for the attack on Columbia House. Our security system took a photograph of her on our doorstep a few hours ago. This photograph was automatically uploaded to our secure off-site server and is attached to this message. When we investigated Jean Simpson after her phone call, we discovered she had been traveling in Europe with a woman named Patton Harcourt, an American wanted for questioning in the murder of Art Handy. The attached photo of Patton Harcourt is from her military file several years ago. We will forward any more information we uncover in our own investigation through our secure email server.

"Isn't Simpson dead?" said Eva.

"Yes," said Ingrid, "and they'll figure that out quickly enough. They'll assume she was the bomber and be that much more inclined to believe the rest of the message."

"And they'll go off hunting for Harcourt," said Dietrich.

"Even if she had nothing to do with Simpson," said Eva.

"Exactly," said Ingrid. "And with the police hunting her all across Europe, we can be free to execute Projekt Alchemie."

"Karl's phone has stopped moving," said Gottfried, who was in the back seat lit by the glow of his laptop.

"Are they at the Eagle's Nest?" said Ingrid. Hitler's mountaintop retreat had been turned into a restaurant, but rumors about a vast network of tunnels in the mountain below had persisted for years. Surely, she thought, the decrypted message would help them find their way into the mountain and to the secrets it hid.

"No," said Gottfried, sounding puzzled. "They're at a place called the Hotel Edelweiss. He said the woman and the assassin checked in and he and Erich are going to get a room and grab some sleep. He says to watch the front of the hotel and meet them in the morning."

Ingrid smiled. "How much farther to Berchtesgaden?" she said.

"About twenty miles," said Dietrich.

"Park across the street from the hotel," said Ingrid. "We can take turns sleeping. In a few hours Projekt Alchemie will be complete."

———

At a modest hotel near Paddington Station, Ted was the first one of the three downstairs for breakfast when the story ran on the TV in the corner of the breakfast room. Because he hadn't had his coffee yet, he didn't pay much attention. A terrorist bombing in Munich, anti-Semitism a suspected motive. He thought nothing of it as he loaded his plate with eggs and sausage at the buffet. The news went on to yesterday's decline in the FTSE precipitated by the failure of trade talks between someone and someone else. Ted didn't care. He just wanted food and caffeine. He had finished two cups of coffee and most of his eggs when Bob and Franklin came skidding into the room, looking like they had raced each other down the stairs instead of waiting for the world's slowest elevator.

"Did you see the news?" said Bob, taking a chair, picking up one of Ted's sausages with his fingers, and chomping a bite off the end.

"That's my breakfast," said Ted.

"No time for breakfast," said Bob. "We're going to Munich."

"Why the hell would we go to Munich?" said Ted.

"He didn't see the news," said Franklin. "You should watch the news."

"Here, here it is," said Bob, pointing to the television. And there, in the center of the screen, against the background of the smoldering remains of a house, was a photograph of Patton Harcourt wearing her army dress uniform. Below her on the screen, under the banner

"Breaking News" read the words: "American Patton Harcourt Wanted in Munich Bombing."

"Holy shit," said Ted. "Is that . . ."

"That's her," said Bob.

"Why the hell would she blow up a house in Munich?"

"I have no idea," said Bob. "But she finally made a mistake. We've got forty minutes to get to the airport."

ZSQWE FEQCR ZONJL KJGK

SECTION FOUR:
PRAGUE

X

Jean had a vague idea, from maps she had looked at earlier in the week, that Prague was northeast of Munich and so, since Nemo insisted they stay off the grid as long as possible, Patton took the first highway she could find marked *Norden* and hoped for the best. Jean had explained her investigations into Columbia House and how she had discovered that Ingrid Weiss had been giving away books she had stolen from libraries, fobbing them off as Nazi loot being returned to its rightful owners.

"I knew she was bad news from the minute I got that book in the mail," she said. "And when I found out some of the books she had stolen, including the one she sent me, came from the National Library of the Czech Republic in Prague, I started reading up on it, and I came across an article about how Himmler's occult library had been discovered there a few years ago."

"Seems like something Alex Lansdowne would have known," said Patton. "Strange he didn't mention it."

"I don't trust him," said Nemo. "All that business about not choosing sides."

"He did give us the guns," said Patton.

"Because he knew I'd break his neck if he didn't. I've seen his kind before—people who only care about their own hides, who would never take a risk for anyone else."

"Doesn't that pretty much describe you?" said Patton.

"Not always," said Nemo, thinking of Jack. "I rescued you, didn't I?"

"And me," said Jean.

"Fair enough," said Patton.

"Listen," said Jean, "I told you everything I know about Ingrid Weiss, so do you want to tell me how you ended up in her basement just in time to save me?"

"I'll tell you this," said Nemo. "You're right about Weiss being bad news."

"We think she is running some sort of Aryan organization," said Patton. "Something tied to the sick ideals of Heinrich Himmler and a racist manifesto called the Fourteen Words."

"And apparently Himmler discovered the secret to alchemy," said Nemo, "so if Weiss finds that, she'll have limitless money to promote her agenda."

"But we're still one step ahead of her," said Patton.

"OK, I was with you until the part about alchemy," said Jean. "Do you seriously believe . . ."

"We don't know what to believe," said Patton, "but Weiss obviously believes, and does so strongly enough to kill to get what she wants. You of all people should realize that."

"So where is Ingrid Weiss now?" said Jean.

"If all has gone to plan," said Nemo, "she's waiting outside a hotel in the German Alps south of Munich."

Ruthie dozed in the back seat and soon enough Jean fell asleep as well. Patton followed roads north and east and eventually began to see signs reading *Praha.*

"Are you sure you don't want me to drive for a while?" said Nemo when they had been on the road for a couple of hours, but Patton insisted that being in control made her feel better after what had happened in Munich, and he didn't press the subject. He understood flashbacks and traumatic episodes. Even if he had never been to a doctor, never had anyone tell him that he suffered from PTSD, he thought he understood what Patton had felt in that basement when they discovered the suicide vest. The same thing he felt every time he saw a ten-year-old boy who reminded him of Jack. He would not ask her about it now, but the time might come, he thought, when they could talk.

––––––

Ingrid Weiss also slept in her car, across the street from the Hotel Edelweiss in Berchtesgaden. But Gottfried stayed awake, listening to the news on the radio and following the updates online. First came reports of an explosion in Obermenzing, followed by speculation that there had been a gas leak. It didn't take long, though, for police to confirm that this had been no accident. Then, just before dawn, came the news that police had received a mysterious message from the owner of the house implicating two women in a terrorist attack. Apparently no one had been killed in the attack. Both of the women had escaped—a detail Ingrid Weiss would find none too pleasing, thought Gottfried. Within an hour the press had put together that information with what they had learned about the charitable work of Columbia House and concluded that the explosion had been an anti-Semitic attack by a white supremacy group. When a cameraman crossed the police line behind the house and took a photograph of a swastika spray-painted on the remains of the back garden wall, the case for anti-Semitism became even stronger. By the time the dawn light painted the sky around the Alps, every media outlet had warned all of Europe to look out for two terrorists—Patton Harcourt and Jean Simpson. Photographs of both had been broadcast and posted online. The four associates of Columbia House had just enlisted the help of every law enforcement officer in Europe. Gottfried closed his computer and turned off the radio. Even if Simpson had somehow escaped, everything had gone to plan. He leaned back in his seat and allowed himself to sleep for an hour, a smile on his face.

––––––

Patton was the only one awake as she steered the van through the streets of Prague in the early morning light. The library would not open for several hours, and she couldn't bear the thought of spending that time cooped up in the van, hidden away in some parking garage, so when she saw a seedy-looking hotel just off Wenceslas Square with a sign in English that said *Park Behind*, she steered the van through a low stone arch and into a tiny, mostly deserted car park.

"Where are we?" said Nemo, his eyes still not open.

"The Hotel Charles III," said Patton.

"I thought Charles IV was the famous monarch from Prague," said Jean.

"He was," said Patton.

"It's five in the morning," said Nemo. "Do you really think they'll have any rooms?"

"Trust me," said Patton. "They'll have rooms. But you're the one with all the false identities, so you go book them."

And so, Mr. John DeWitt of Providence, Rhode Island, booked the last two double rooms at the Hotel Charles III, and within fifteen minutes all four of them were asleep in beds that were only marginally more comfortable than the van seats in which all but Patton had dozed for the past three hours. Jean did not even complain about sharing a room with Nemo. Ruthie and Patton both feigned nonchalance about bunking together.

Ruthie awoke just after eight and took what passed for a shower, though the plumbing delivered water at a rate more like that of an IV drip. Still, after two days on the run it felt good to clean up. She only wished she had clean clothes to change into. Jean had said the library opened at nine, so Ruthie had just decided that she'd better wake up Patton when a knock came at the door. Nemo and Jean stood in the hallway, barefoot and rumpled. Clearly neither had partaken of the limited pleasure that was the Hotel Charles III showers.

"Have you seen the news?" said Nemo, forcing himself past Ruthie and into the room.

"Our TV doesn't work," said Ruthie.

Nemo turned the knob on the TV that was old enough to have a knob on it, but nothing happened.

"What's going on?" said Patton groggily as Jean sat on the end of her bed, looking shaken.

"The news," she said in a quiet voice.

"What news?" said Patton, sitting up slowly and clutching the sheet to her chest. She had slept in her bra and panties and had no intention of giving Nemo a show.

"Get dressed," said Nemo sharply. "And then come into our room, but don't let anyone see you."

"Why shouldn't I let . . ."

"Just do it," said Nemo, turning for the door.

"Hey," said Ruthie, "there's no need to . . ." but Nemo had already left the room before she could reprimand him.

"Don't worry," said Patton. "He gets that way. And he usually has a good reason."

"It's a good reason," said Jean as Patton pulled on her pants and grabbed her sweatshirt from the windowsill where she had hung it to air out.

Two minutes later, they all sat on the ends of the twin beds in Nemo's room, watching the news coverage of the explosion in Munich. Patton, still not fully awake, did not register the words on the bottom of the screen, but when the image of the remains of Ingrid Weiss's house was replaced with two faces, she took a sharp breath. Patton's last military ID photograph and a grainy but unmistakable image of Jean filled the screen.

"Shit," said Patton.

"Shit is right," said Nemo.

"How the hell did they get this?" said Patton.

"Apparently poor Ingrid Weiss, who is now a victim of anti-Semitism, sent the police a message implicating you two."

"But Ingrid Weiss thinks Jean blew up in the house," said Patton.

"Yes, but the police know she didn't," said Nemo.

"How does she even know about me?" said Patton.

"Must have been Fritz and Franz," said Nemo. "Luckily you don't look anything like your photograph, thanks to the magic trick we pulled back at Heathrow."

"Yes, but I do," said Jean. "Maybe I should stay here while you all go to the library."

"No," said Patton. "You have to go. You're the one who knows about these Ripley Scrolls. You're the art historian."

"You're the librarian," said Jean.

"Yes," said Patton, "but didn't you say you already had a contact at the library?"

"Well, I can't very well walk in there now and say, 'I'm Jean Simpson.'"

"Knock it off, you two," said Nemo. "Patton is right. Jean needs to be there. So we just need to do some work."

"What do you mean by work?" said Jean.

"Well, I didn't always look like this," said Patton.

———

Gottfried awoke with a start as Ingrid slammed the car door. It took him a moment to realize she had gone for coffee and pastries and that he had slept much longer than he intended. The midmorning sun glittered off the snow-covered peaks of the Bavarian Alps that rose over the roofline of the hotel, and the street outside bustled with traffic.

"Thought you might sleep all day," said Ingrid. "I had to get Dietrich to monitor Karl's cell phone."

"No movement," said Dietrich.

"Why are they sleeping so late?" said Eva. "It's nine thirty."

"Maybe they're not sleeping," said Gottfried. "Let me have that laptop."

"If they don't move by the time we finish breakfast," said Ingrid, "we're going in. Or at least I'm going in. And if they've fucked this up, well, I won't shoot them in a public place, but let's just say Karl will miss his kneecaps."

"Damn," said Gottfried.

"What is it?" said Eva.

"The signal is getting weaker."

"What does that mean?" said Ingrid.

"It means that idiot Karl forgot to charge his phone and the battery is dying. Once it goes out, we've got no way to follow them."

"That's it," said Ingrid, handing her coffee to Gottfried. "I'm going in. If you see the woman, don't wait for me. Follow her."

Ingrid Weiss had the sort of face and bearing that allowed her to project the aura of a cultured, upper class, powerful German woman even when she had spent the night in the front seat of a car. She strode across the lobby of the Hotel Edelweiss to the main desk where the clerk immediately snapped to attention.

"Good morning," Ingrid said sweetly. "I'm so pleased to be here. Your hotel is as lovely as the agent said."

"Thank you, *gnädige Frau*," said the clerk. "And how may I assist you?"

"I believe the rest of my party has already checked in," said Ingrid. "Herr Karl Gruning and Herr Erich Koepler."

The man looked down at his computer screen for a moment and then replied. "I'm afraid we have no one by those names registered at the hotel."

"They often register under false names," said Ingrid, tossing her hair. "They have some misguided notion that their fame is substantial enough they need to travel incognito." She pulled out her phone and opened a photograph of Karl and Erich, showing it to the clerk. "I believe they checked in last night."

"I was on duty until eight," said the clerk, "and I certainly didn't see them. We only had two parties check in after that and they were all women."

Ingrid knew she had only a few seconds to think. She couldn't show a picture of Patton Harcourt or ask for her by name, because, thanks to Columbia House, all of Europe was looking for Patton. Could Karl and Erich have hidden somewhere in the hotel without checking in? She couldn't very well ask to search the hotel, so perhaps her best move was to check in. It might look odd that she had no reservation, but she could act incensed that they had lost it. She smiled at the clerk and was just about to take out her credit card when Gottfried dashed into the lobby.

"Frau Weiss!" he called out. "Frau Weiss, may I speak with you a moment?"

Ingrid glared at him but crossed quickly to where he stood staring at his cell phone screen. "What is it?" she hissed.

"They're moving," he said and then, looking confused, he added, "or at least the phone is moving." He took a few steps across the lobby to where a custodian carried a trash bin toward a service door.

"Excuse me, sir," said Gottfried to the man, surreptitiously slipping his phone into his pocket. "I think I may have . . . dropped my phone into one of the trash bins in the lobby. Do you mind if I take a look?"

The custodian looked nonplussed and shot a glance at the desk clerk who shrugged. Ingrid felt bile rising in her throat. Thirty seconds later, Gottfried pulled a cell phone out of the trash bin.

"Thank you, sir," he said in a weak voice, and he and Ingrid power-walked out of the lobby and back to the car in silence. Ingrid took the driver's seat and as soon as Gottfried was in, she screeched away from the curb, drove a short distance down Maximilianstrasse, and pulled into a parking spot at Franziskanerplatz. For a moment no one said anything, then Ingrid began banging her hands against the steering wheel.

"Fuck, fuck, fuck!" she said. "I'll fucking murder them, I swear to God. I'll murder all of you incompetents if I have to."

"What is it?" said Eva. "What happened?"

"The bitch duped us," said Gottfried. "She dumped Karl's phone in the lobby trash bin."

"You mean . . ." said Eva.

"Karl and Erich were never here," said Gottfried. "And if the woman was here, she's long gone. God knows if any of those messages were even from Karl. If she had the phone . . ."

"Then the assassin could still be with her," said Eva.

"How could you fucking let this happen," shouted Ingrid at no one in particular.

"Calm down," said Gottfried. "The police are still looking for the woman. She's bound to turn up sooner or later."

"Yes," said Ingrid, "and if she has the message it gets taken into evidence. We need to find the woman *first*, get the message, and then hand her over to the police."

"So what now?" said Eva. "We've blown up your house, we're further from finding the message than ever."

"Now we're fucked," said Ingrid, dropping her head against the steering wheel.

"Not necessarily," said Dietrich, looking at his phone.

————

Alex Lansdowne watched the images on his television and shook his head. His visitors of the previous night had apparently gotten themselves into some significant trouble. They never should have poked their nose into Ingrid Weiss's business, he thought. He had assumed that when they got to Munich, Weiss would put on a performance and convince them they had got the wrong end of the stick. He never thought she would blow up her own house and he certainly didn't think Ruthie Drinkwater and her friends would blow up anything. Perhaps he never should have told them about Ingrid. Perhaps he should have mentioned that he had a digital copy of Himmler's library catalog, obtained when the book was on the market a few years ago. But Alex had done what he always did with intruders: just enough to get rid of them. And he had been honest with them, telling them that he did not choose sides. He had given them no reason to trust him; he had merely sent them packing so he could get on with his day. It had occurred to him that he might be able to use them to add some interesting Nazi artifacts to his collection, and he had taken the necessary steps to preserve that possibility. But now, with a European-wide police investigation underway, he feared he might end up more deeply involved in this whole affair than he had previously hoped. He switched off the television and picked up his phone.

————

It took longer than Nemo would have liked, but by ten fifteen Jean's long, curly, blond hair was short, dark, and straight. She sported a new pair of glasses, olive-colored skin, a highly visible tattoo of a dragon on her forearm, and a nose ring. She looked almost nothing like the woman in the photograph on television. Nemo had even gone out and found her some new clothes—a pair of jeans and a pale green V-neck T-shirt.

"These are going to be too small," said Jean when he presented her with his purchases.

"That's the point," said Nemo. "And wear this." He handed her a lace brassiere that she held as if it were a dead animal.

"This is much too big," she said. "I told you it was a bad idea for a man to go shopping for a woman."

"That's what this is for," said Nemo, pulling several rolls of gauze out of his bag.

"Are you asking me to stuff my bra?" said Jean in disbelief.

"Trust me," said Nemo.

When Jean emerged from the bathroom, she felt ridiculous. The T-shirt pulled tight over her fake breasts and she couldn't imagine anyone would fall for the illusion.

"Perfect," said Nemo.

"You've got to be kidding," said Jean.

"Believe me," said Nemo, "no man is going to spend much time looking at your face."

"You're a pig," said Jean, crossing her arms over her chest.

"You do look kind of hot," said Patton. "Doesn't she, Ruthie?"

"I don't think it's only men who will be distracted," said Ruthie.

"Honestly, you look good," said Patton. "You don't look anything like yourself."

"I think I should be insulted," said Jean, "but I'm too mortified."

"Patton's right," said Nemo. "Now when we get there, it's all about confidence. Jean Simpson is being hunted all across Europe and she knows it. So you march right in and make no effort to hide who you are and no one will suspect a thing. By the time Interpol runs their security footage through facial recognition software, we'll be long gone."

"How do you know?" said Jean.

"It's my job to know," said Nemo.

"And what exactly is your job?" said Jean.

"Don't ask," said Patton. "You don't want to know."

Because Jean could not present herself by name at the National Library of the Czech Republic, and because they had no credentials that would get them any farther than the main public rooms, they had planned for Nemo to identify himself as Peter Byerly, a man just famous enough in rare book circles for his name to be known, but not famous enough for his face to be recognized, or so Jean had claimed.

It was just before eleven when Jean and Nemo stepped out of the hotel, leaving Patton and Ruthie alone in their room.

"You could go out," said Patton. "Nobody's looking for you. You could take a walk, see a little of the city. We've got a couple of hours at least."

"I'd rather stay in," said Ruthie, sitting next to Patton on her sagging bed. She took Patton's hand in hers and squeezed it. "I like staying in . . . with you."

Patton hadn't felt an embrace, hadn't felt lips on hers, hadn't slipped in between sheets with the luxurious feel of bare skin on bare skin in a long, long time. She didn't even want to think how long, because if she figured it out, it would probably make her cry. Over the past two days, her feelings about seeing Ruthie again had evolved. At first, she had just used an old flame to get what she needed—access to the Bombe. But it felt like something more now. Maybe not love, not quite yet, but certainly fondness and attraction and the memory that, in bed at least, they had been damn good together. Patton had heard of people who used sex to battle PTSD, hoping that the oxytocin that flooded the brain would wash away some of the darkness. She had never taken that approach herself, but then she had never had much opportunity to try. Now she had a couple of hours in a hotel room with someone who knew every inch of her body and whose hand was reaching up ever so tentatively to brush the side of her breast.

With enthusiasm she turned and pulled Ruthie into her arms.

———

The false Peter Byerly received a hero's welcome at the National Library of the Czech Republic. To Jean's relief, no one questioned the identity of his somewhat trashy-looking wife. As she had predicted, the staff knew his name but not his face. A librarian who insisted on being called Andrea ("My last name is inelegant for Americans to pronounce," she claimed) met them at the main entrance and listened as Nemo explained that he was doing research on occult writings and needed to examine some materials.

"Would you like to see the Baroque Library before we go to the reading room?" said Andrea.

"That would be lovely," said Jean and as Andrea led them back outside, Nemo glared at her.

"We don't have time for sightseeing," he hissed.

"Trust me," said Jean. "Peter Byerly would want to see this library. It's one of the most beautiful rooms of books in the world. We turn down an invitation for a private viewing and she'll know we're not the real Byerlys. She's probably already suspicious of this ridiculous getup."

The National Library of the Czech Republic is housed in the old town of Prague in a huge complex called the Klementium. Most of the buildings once belonged to a monastery, and Jean could imagine robed monks crossing the same courtyard through which Andrea now led them. They entered another building, then climbed a seemingly endless metal spiral staircase before emerging into a series of plain rooms displaying reproductions of some of the Klementium's treasures. Andrea ushered them through a door on the side of the third room, flicked a light switch, and even Nemo found his breath taken away.

They stood at one end of the Baroque Library, an eighteenth-century Jesuit library housed in a room so beautiful that Jean struggled not to weep as they walked its length.

"The tourists are only allowed to look in from the end," said Andrea, "but special guests can walk all the way in."

Down the center of the marble floor stood a variety of huge globes, overhead glowed frescoes dedicated to the arts and sciences, and in between, on two levels of elaborately decorated shelves, stood thousands of ancient volumes.

"I love to visit this room," said Andrea, "it feeds my soul."

Jean tried to imagine the joy of walking into this room—though "room" seemed too prosaic a word to describe this glorious space—on a regular basis and came even closer to weeping.

"We can stay for a few minutes, if you have the time," said Andrea.

"Of course," said Nemo in a voice that Jean could swear was choked with emotion.

They stood in silence for what seemed like hours and seconds—time didn't seem to exist in this space. Jean tried to memorize the designs in the woodwork, the intricacy of the globes, and especially the frescoes overhead. Then Andrea led them back down through the now pedestrian-seeming courtyard, back to the main part of the library, and into what she described as a "private reading room," a space far less elegant than the Baroque Library, but still possessing a series of columned bookcases that contained volumes from the eighteenth and nineteenth centuries. Down the center of the room stood a long table, lined with cushioned chairs on either side.

They had decided that if they asked for several items, if Weiss somehow followed them, she wouldn't know which one contained a clue. Jean thought that if one of the "books" they looked at was a Ripley Scroll, it would be the most likely to hold secrets about alchemy, but they had found several other treatises on the subject listed in Himmler's catalog and gave Andrea a list of nine items they wished to see. She left them alone in the reading room and went to retrieve the books.

"How long do you think this will take?" said Nemo.

"I don't know what we're looking for," said Jean. "I've seen several Ripley Scrolls over the years and I honestly can't imagine one that includes the actual secret to alchemy. All I can really do is look and tell you if I see anything unusual."

"I don't like this place," said Nemo, pacing. "No quick exit."

"Are you expecting trouble?" said Jean.

"I always expect trouble," said Nemo.

They waited in awkward silence for almost twenty minutes and

Jean was on the verge of asking Nemo about his career again—to break both the awkwardness and the silence—when Andrea returned with an armload of books.

"Not all of them yet," she said, "but a good start I hope." She set the stack of books, some of them the size of family Bibles, on the table. Jean noted a polished wooden box at the bottom of the pile.

"Is that the Ripley Scroll?" she said, pointing to the box.

"Yes, it's quite a treasure," said Andrea. "We actually just discovered it a few years ago and there has been a lot of talk about trying to determine its provenance."

"Why is that?" said Nemo.

"Don't you know?" said Andrea. "All these books you called up are from the occult library of Heinrich Himmler. You know, the Nazi leader."

"Are they really?" said Nemo. "How interesting."

"He almost certainly stole them from various libraries and collectors around Europe," said Andrea, "and there is some question about whether we should try to find where they came from and return them—especially with items as valuable as the Ripley Scroll."

"I think I'd like to start with that," said Nemo.

"I thought you might," said Andrea, extracting the box from the stack of books. "There has been a lot of interest in this since we discovered it. My colleague downstairs said he spoke to a woman on the phone about it a few minutes ago."

Jean saw Nemo's face harden and she knew exactly what he was thinking. Had Ingrid Weiss called about the Ripley Scroll? And if so, how the hell had she found out about it? Was she headed to Prague? How much time did they have before she got here? All this flashed across Nemo's face in an instant, but Andrea noticed nothing. She was busy unrolling a medieval scroll elaborately decorated with color illustrations and the entire length of the massive library table.

At the top of the scroll a bearded man in a green cloak held a massive glass flask inside of which a series of circular vignettes showed various alchemical experiments. Below the flask was a stylized tree filled with strange creatures. Near the bottom of the scroll, a bizarre green dragon held some sort of creature in his mouth. In the center of it all, a bird with the crowned head of a queen stood on a circle of water. Above the bird, in a yellow circle, a man in purple robes wearing a golden crown held aloft a casket of gold. Nemo leaned over the scroll, trying to make out some of the words that flowed from the mouths of the creatures or lined the tops and bottoms of the pictures. As Peter Byerly, he was supposed to be an expert, so he couldn't very well ask what all this meant. Yes, he could see it might record the work of some crackpot medieval alchemist, but it certainly did not look like an actual recipe for creating gold.

Jean made a pretense of looking at the scroll from top to bottom, though she had already spotted the irregularity.

"Have you seen many of these before?" she asked Andrea.

"I haven't," said the librarian. "It's something I know needs further investigation, but it's a bit out of my field. Someone in the manuscript department will get to it sooner or later, I imagine. You know we have over six million items in the collection, so even important pieces like this often get overlooked." As Andrea secured the far end of the scroll with two book weights to prevent it from rolling up on itself, Jean scribbled in her notebook and then passed it to Nemo.

"I wonder, Andrea," he said, having glanced at the note, "if the library has a copy of Romano's book on representations of the Magi?"

"I could certainly check for you, Mr. Byerly."

"Please," said Nemo as Andrea strode toward the door, "call me Peter."

As soon as Andrea had left the room, Jean pulled Nemo by the arm to the center of the scroll. "Do you see that," she said, pointing to the man in purple holding the golden casket.

"Is that the gold that the alchemist has created?" said Nemo.

"He doesn't belong there," said Jean. "That yellow circle is supposed to be the sun. Someone has added this figure at a much later date. You see the style—it was done by a different artist than whoever created the scroll originally."

Nemo leaned close to the figure. While the alchemist at the top of the scroll looked almost like a caricature, this man, though much smaller, had eyes that glowed with life and exquisite detailing in his garments. On the back of his robe, Nemo could just make out, stitched in gold, the letter *M*.

"Who is he?" said Nemo.

"His purple robes are the color of royalty," said Jean, "and he wears a crown inscribed with Persian letters." Nemo squinted at the crown and saw something that looked like modern Arabic. "He has an 'M' on his robes and he's carrying a gift of gold."

"How do you know it's a gift?" said Nemo.

"He's Melchior, the King of Persia—one of the three wise men, the magi who brought gifts to Jesus after he was born. According to tradition, Melchior brought the gift of gold."

"If he's an ancient figure associated with gold, it doesn't seem so strange to find him in an alchemical scroll," said Nemo.

"Well it is unusual," said Jean. "I've never seen him in a Ripley Scroll and, as I said, he was clearly added later on. If this scroll has some sort of clue about Himmler's secret, Melchior is that clue."

"So why did you have me ask for that book about the magi if you already knew who he was—just to get Andrea out of the room?"

"No," said Jean. "Because there's something else odd about this Melchior. I could swear I've seen him before."

———

Ted, Bob, and Franklin stood just behind the police barrier on Döbereinerstrasse, close enough to see the blackened ruins of Ingrid Weiss's house. Many of the nearby homes already had plywood covering windows that had shattered in last night's blast.

"Let me try to understand this," said Ted. "We couldn't sit together on the plane and you said we couldn't talk in the taxi, so please explain to me now. If every cop in Europe is looking for her, how exactly are *we* supposed to find her?"

"Look," said Bob, "twelve hours ago we didn't know that we would track her to Munich. So let's give it some time. We've been here twenty minutes."

"My daughter graduates from high school in three weeks," said Ted.

"Right," said Bob, "in *three* weeks. We have time."

"What do you think, Franklin?" said Ted.

"I think there's no way in hell she's guilty," said Franklin. "And I doubt they have any real evidence against her, which means even if they find her, they won't hold her for long."

"If she's not guilty then why would this Ingrid Weiss person set her up?" said Bob.

"An excellent question," said Franklin. "Makes you wonder if this Weiss character might kill Patton Harcourt before we can."

———

"What do you mean you've seen him before?" said Nemo.

"There's something familiar about those robes and the awkward way he's holding the casket of gold. See the elbow—it doesn't bend quite right, like the artist either used a model who had broken his arm at some point or else just . . . wasn't good at elbows."

"You can recognize him because of a funny elbow?"

"I'm an art historian," said Jean. "It goes with the territory—having a good visual memory. Plus I took a class on artistic anatomy a few years back and we did this whole track on paintings in which the artist had misrepresented human anatomy. I could swear I saw this Melchior. I just don't remember where he's from."

"And you're sure he's the only thing . . . strange about this scroll?" said Nemo. "What about all this writing? Couldn't that be a clue?"

"It all looks pretty standard," said Jean.

"So you're telling me I dragged my ass halfway across Europe to discover the secret of alchemy and all we've found is a wise man with a funny elbow?"

"There is no secret to alchemy," said Jean calmly.

"Well there's some damn secret," hissed Nemo. "Something that's worth murdering people on two continents to discover."

"And what makes you think this wise man isn't keeping a secret," said Jean, running a finger across the purple-robed figure almost as if he were a pet.

"Here we go," said Andrea, bursting back into the room with an oversized art book in her hand. "Ernesto Romano's *Immagini dei Magi*."

"I've always loved that Burne-Jones painting of the Adoration," said Jean, admiring the front cover of the book.

"My wife is an art historian," said Nemo, remembering he was supposed to be Peter Byerly, the great rare book scholar.

Jean slipped into a chair and began flipping through the book. Nemo glimpsed color reproductions of paintings that all had one thing in common—they all depicted the Adoration of the Magi, three wise men bringing gold, frankincense, and myrrh to the infant Jesus. With Andrea simply standing there, he suddenly felt out of character. How could she not see that he was not a scholar or a man with even an iota of knowledge about old books? How could she mistake him for Peter Byerly, whoever that was (Jean had tried to explain to him on the walk to the library, but Nemo had been watching for tails and had not paid much attention). He felt he should be making some sort of comment about books or manuscripts but he had no idea what to say or where to begin. And, though he knew it could only have been a minute or two since she sat down, Jean seemed to be taking forever with that damn book. He supposed he should sit down and look at some of the other books from Himmler's library that Andrea had brought—make some small attempt to have it appear that they had not come with any single-minded purpose vis-à-vis the Ripley Scroll, but as soon as he thought this he feared he would somehow betray his ignorance about books by mishandling one of these treasures. Finally, he decided to take advantage of the fact that Andrea seemed unwilling to leave them alone and address her directly.

"Strange that someone else called about the Ripley Scroll on the same day we did."

"Not particularly," said Andrea. "Even with six million items, that sort of coincidence happens all the time."

But Nemo feared it had been no coincidence. He felt certain that Ingrid Weiss had somehow found out what they already knew. "I wonder if it was someone I know," he said, feigning absentmindedness.

"If you'd like to wait," said Andrea, "maybe I can find out. My colleague said she was driving in from Germany later today."

"Oh goodness," said Jean, suddenly pushing back her chair and leaping up. "I've completely lost track of the time. We have that luncheon engagement, remember, dear?" She took Nemo's arm and, being sure that Andrea couldn't see, squeezed it hard. Nemo got the message.

"Oh, you're right," he said. "I'm so sorry we have to run, Andrea. Perhaps we can stop by later this afternoon or tomorrow to look at the other books?"

"I'll keep them set aside for you," said Andrea. "Would you like me to show you out?"

"I'm sure we can find the way," said Jean, pulling Nemo toward the door. Neither of them spoke until they were back in the warm sunshine of Prague and had pushed their way through the crowds into the open space of Old Town Square. There, just past the ancient astronomical clock, Jean finally turned to Nemo.

"I knew I had seen that Melchior before," she said as the sea of tourists seethed around them. "And I knew it would be in Romano's book. He's from an Adoration of the Magi by Antonio Pegronini."

"Never heard of him," said Nemo.

"Most people haven't," said Jean. "He wasn't particularly good. To make it as an Italian Renaissance artist, you had to know your anatomy, and like I said Pegronini didn't."

"So what good does it do us to know that somebody altered Himmler's alchemy scroll with a copy of a bad painting?"

"A *detail* from a bad painting," said Jean. "It might not do us any good at all. But it might also be worth a trip to Brenner."

"Where's that?"

"In the north of Italy on the Austrian border," said Jean. "About as close as you can get to Germany and be on Italian soil."

"And why do we want to go there?"

"Because in the hills above the village is the Chapel of the Magi and in that chapel is a fresco by Antonio Pegronini."

"Let me guess," said Nemo, "The Adoration of the Magi."

"Exactly."

XI

FEBRUARY 1945

"Rossini?" said Himmler. "Like the composer?"

"*Si*, Herr Himmler, but no relation."

"And you are Italian?"

"*Si*, Italian. But I do work for Herr Göring. He recommends me, I believe."

"He does," said Himmler. He considered the diminutive Italian man before him—his olive skin and dark hair, combined with what he lacked in stature, proved his inferior race. And yet, Göring had praised his peculiar talent. Himmler could clearly see the paint under the man's fingernails. A sign of uncleanliness or of passion for his work, he wondered. It hardly mattered. Himmler needed an artist and Signor Rossini was the only one at hand.

"You know this scene?" said Himmler, sliding a color photograph across his desk.

Signor Rossini picked up the photo and held it close to his face. "*Si, si,*" he said. "*Adorazione dei Magi.* The Adoration of the Magi."

"And you can paint this, just as it is in the photograph?"

"*Si,*" said Rossini. "I can paint this."

"How long?"

"Three weeks. Maybe four."

"You have three," said Himmler. "I will arrange for your transport tonight. The supplies will be waiting for you there."

"It is difficult to do such work without an assistant," said Rossini.

"We are in a war Signor Rossini," said Himmler. "We all have our difficulties."

Helmut entered Himmler's office as the small Italian man left, escorted by an SS storm trooper. "Who is that?" said Helmut, with a hint of disdain in his voice.

"He is none of your concern," said Himmler. "Not yet."

Three weeks later the Italian, clutching his hat, stood once more in Himmler's cavernous office at Wewelsburg Castle.

"And this photograph is *after* you did your work?" said Himmler, when Rossini had pulled a snapshot out of his pocket.

"Yes, Herr Himmler, after."

"This is excellent work," said Himmler.

"Yes, it is," said Rossini. "Fresco painting is not easy. I admit, I am quite proud of it."

"Pride is a dangerous thing," said Himmler with a slight threat in his voice. "We should take pride in the Reich, not in our own accomplishments in its service."

"Yes, Herr Himmler."

"You may call me Reichsführer Himmler."

"Yes, Reichsführer Himmler."

"Now," said Himmler, stepping out from behind his desk and crossing to the long table. "Come look at this." He indicated a scroll unfurled on the table, covered with bizarre colored illustrations.

"A lovely piece," said Rossini. "As a collector, you must be . . ."

"Proud?" said Himmler.

"Pleased," said Rossini.

"You see this spot," said Himmler. "Can you paint this same figure here?" He indicated a figure on the photograph Rossini had brought him.

"The same figure from the fresco in that spot on the scroll?" said Rossini.

"Exactly," said Himmler.

"It can be done," said the man. "But why?"

"Yours is not to question why," snapped Himmler.

"I beg your pardon, Reichsführer. How soon do you need this?"

"Soon," said Himmler. "Yesterday would be ideal. My secretary will get you whatever materials you require. You will work here."

"I prefer to work in my—"

"You will work here," said Himmler, ending the discussion. As Rossini left the room in the care of his secretary, Himmler wondered if he had waited too long, or if the clues he was leaving were too subtle. With the Reich in disarray and the Allies closing in, he now wanted only one thing—for Projekt Alchemie to be the means by which, when the time was right, the Reich and all it stood for would rise once more.

A moment later Helmut Werner entered the room. "Another visit from your Italian friend?" he said.

"His final visit," said Himmler. "He shall work here for a day or two and then I should like for you to escort him . . . out."

"Certainly, Reichsführer."

Two days later, Helmut walked with Signor Rossini along the banks of the Alme just below the castle. The Italian had been silent since they left Wewelsburg and Helmut knew better than to try to find out what the little man had been doing for Himmler.

"You are right," said Rossini, when they reached an isolated stretch of the river. "This would be a beautiful place to paint. Perhaps I should return with my easel."

"I don't think that will be necessary," said Helmut. He drew his Luger and shot Rossini twice in the chest, watching emotionless as the man fell backward into the stream and floated away, disappearing around the bend.

———

Patton lay on her back looking up at the ceiling, the cool air wafting through the gap in the drapes and caressing her bare skin almost as effectively as Ruthie had. She remembered this, though it had been a long time, this almost out-of-body experience she had after sex, looking down on her contented self and not quite able to simply revel in the luxury of the moment, always somewhat bemusedly wondering, *How the hell did you get here, Patton Harcourt?* Ruthie had demanded nothing of Patton—no explanations about her behavior in the van back in Munich, no apologies for fifteen years of silence. And Patton had remembered Ruthie's body, had admired how it had ripened, had delighted in the way it still responded to her touch.

As she mentally floated in the air, looking down on two naked, satisfied women, Patton couldn't help wondering if, in another version of her life, things might have been different, or if, perhaps, it wasn't too late for this version. She tried to imagine mixing choux pastry on a Sunday morning with Ruthie. It was a beautiful vision of marital domesticity that Patton could almost see herself embracing. One thing was for sure—she could certainly see herself embracing Ruthie far beyond this lovely morning.

"I'm sorry about, you know, back in Munich, after the explosion," said Patton, reaching for Ruthie's hand without looking at her.

"You mean when you threatened to waste me?" said Ruthie, giving Patton's hand a squeeze.

"It wasn't one of my finer moments."

"You were upset."

"No, it was more than that. The vest, and that basement, and the explosion—they brought back some shit that happened in Afghanistan."

"PTSD?" said Ruthie.

"God, I detest that term," said Patton. "It's so clinical. Let's just say that what happened over there fucked with my head and you were in the wrong place when it came crashing back. Anyway, I'm sorry."

"I'd say what you just did to me was a rather thorough apology."

"We should probably get dressed. They could be back anytime."

"Or we could just put on those lovely complimentary bathrobes they have in the wardrobe," said Ruthie, poking Patton in the side.

"You mean the ones with all the glamour of a hospital gown," said Patton.

"And half the coverage," said Ruthie, jumping up and bouncing across the room under Patton's admiring eyes. A moment later, they were wrapped in the skimpy bathrobes sitting on the side of the bed.

"Are you hungry?" said Patton.

"Do you mean for food or . . ."

"For food," said Patton. "Not that I'm opposed to . . ."

"We'd probably better stay here until they get back. I can go get us something then."

"Maybe we should go across the hall and see if we can get any news updates on the TV," said Patton.

"You mean see if they've caught us yet?" said Ruthie.

"It would be nice to know if there is a ring of Czech police around this hotel."

"If there are I can't see them," said Ruthie peeking through the drapes out the window.

"Anyway, I'm going to check the headlines, just in case anything's changed."

"Are you going to put on some proper clothes?" said Ruthie, pulling the curtains shut and leaning against the wall, allowing her bathrobe to fall open.

"Do you want me to put on some proper clothes?" said Patton, loosening the tie of her own robe.

"I think you know the answer," said Ruthie.

"Come on, we can scoot over there in these luxurious robes. Just let me grab my gun."

"A pistol. How romantic," said Ruthie.

"Can't be too careful," said Patton.

Ruthie giggled and followed Patton into the hall where they fumbled with the key Nemo had left them, hoping that no one got off the rickety elevator or came out of one of the other rooms. But the second-floor corridor of the Hotel Charles III remained quiet in the early afternoon, and soon enough Ruthie was pulling the shoulder of Patton's robe down while Patton flicked on the TV in time for the news headlines.

The explosion in Munich was the third story and at first nothing seemed different from a few hours ago. Patton could feel Ruthie's lips fluttering against her shoulder and was just about to protest, weakly, that they couldn't possibly, not here in Nemo's bedroom, when the feed switched to a reporter in front of the remnants of Ingrid Weiss's house. In the background, a small crowd had gathered at the police barrier.

"Shit," said Patton, sitting up so suddenly she was afraid for a moment she might have given Ruthie a split lip. She pulled her robe back up and leaned forward until she was just inches away from the screen. "Shit," she said again.

"What is it?" said Ruthie.

"Lucky they're standing so close. Otherwise I never would have seen them."

"Seen who?" said Ruthie.

"Those three guys there," said Patton, pointing to three men who stood stolidly at the police barrier staring toward the site of the explosion.

"Who are they?" said Ruthie, now sitting forward on the edge of the bed with Patton.

"They may have been promoted since I last met them, but I knew them as Sergeant Bob Macmillan, Private First Class Ted Grosswald, and Private First Class Franklin Rendell."

"And why are you so concerned to see them?" said Ruthie.

"No reason really," said Patton. "It's just that they want to kill me."

———

Ingrid had spent ten minutes on the phone with Alexandr, her source at the National Library of the Czech Republic. She had visited the library several times to examine books from Himmler's library and gotten to know Alexandr well enough that he recognized her voice as soon as she called. She had never told him that she owned Himmler's library catalog and she never let him see her refer to the digital copy of the register she kept on her iPad. She came to the library, she said, to try to understand the scope of Himmler's collecting and to trace where some of his books had come from. She had no intention, she said, of forcing the library to return books that had been stolen, but if she could trace the provenance of some of Himmler's books, she would certainly share that information with Alexandr. Then, when his back was turned, she would steal one or two old volumes to be "returned" to their "rightful owners" by Columbia House.

She had long suspected that the secret to Projekt Alchemie was buried somewhere in Himmler's collection of occult books, but with eleven thousand volumes to examine and no idea what to look for, she had no chance of discovering anything useful without the message her grandfather had told her about. Still, it came as no surprise when Dietrich suggested that their next destination should be Prague. What did come as a surprise was his specificity.

"We need to find something called a Ripley Scroll at the library in Prague," he said.

"How do you know that?"

"A source," said Dietrich.

"Trustworthy?" said Ingrid.

"Absolutely," said Dietrich.

And so, when the library in Prague opened, Ingrid had called Alexandr to confirm that there was something called the Ripley Scroll in the Himmler collection. An hour later, Alexandr had rung back to say that not only did the collection contain such a scroll, but that a man and a woman had come to examine it. So Ingrid had turned the car toward Prague.

———

By the time Nemo and Jean got back, Patton and Ruthie had dressed and Patton had returned her attention to the television and the coverage of the Munich bombing.

"Couldn't find anything to do in your own room?" said Nemo as he sat down on the end of the bed.

"We've got a problem," said Patton.

"I'll say we've got a problem," said Nemo. "Somebody else has been asking about the Ripley Scroll and I'll bet you a thousand bucks it's Ingrid fucking Weiss."

"This is a different problem," said Ruthie, nodding toward the television screen. "Three ex-soldiers are hunting Patton."

Nemo picked up the remote and snapped off the television. "What do you mean they're hunting her?"

"They want to kill me, OK," said Patton. "And they've tracked me as far as Munich."

"This is why you weren't surprised when Franz started taking pot-shots at your kitchen back home," said Nemo. "You expected it."

"Sooner or later," said Patton.

"At least we know where to go next," said Jean timidly.

"What do you mean?" said Ruthie.

"Turns out it's a good thing Ingrid Weiss provided us with an art historian," said Nemo. "Jean figured it all out."

"So where do we go?" said Ruthie.

"We'll tell them on the way," said Nemo. "Let's get packed fast and get out of here. As it is we probably won't make it before dark."

"Can we please get something to eat first?" said Patton. As soon as Nemo had shut off the TV, the hunger she had been ignoring had crested over her like a wave.

"Let me go," said Ruthie. "My picture's not on the news."

"Fine," said Nemo, "but make it fast. And once we're on the road, I'd like Patton to explain about this bounty squad that's chasing her."

"I must say," said Jean after Ruthie had left, "I don't miss my conference in Vienna one little bit. I haven't felt this alive in years."

VTNLP TBKRJ GVSCQ AHHXX

SECTION FIVE: BRENNER

XII

Nemo insisted on driving and the first twenty minutes or so of their journey was taken up with consuming the sandwiches Ruthie had bought at a café around the corner from the hotel. Nemo had finally agreed to use the van's navigation system—after all he had rented it with a false name. Patton pointed out that Ingrid Weiss and her gang would discover soon enough where they were headed so they were essentially racing at this point. They had left Prague and were heading back toward Germany on the E50 when Nemo said what they had all been thinking.

"You want to explain to me why three people are trying to kill you? Because I've been wondering ever since we met why you seemed to expect that sniper."

"What sniper?" said Jean.

"Just let her tell the story," said Nemo. "We've got a long drive ahead, so she has plenty of time."

And so Patton told them. She told them about Kandahar and the man with the knife in his knee and the explosive vest and how the upper half of Bailey's body had flown out of the house with the explosion. And then she told them the rest.

She hadn't learned the rest herself until much later. The explosion had spooked the enemy and the firefight ended. Patton had passed out after

seeing Bailey, and though technically conscious when the medic evacu-
ated her, she didn't remember anything until three days later, when she
awoke in a hospital bed in Germany. She had a minor gunshot wound to
her left arm and a few broken ribs from the force of the explosion. Not
enough, she thought, to warrant being sent all the way back to Landstuhl.

"Why am I here?" she asked of everyone who came into her room,
but they only responded by taking her blood pressure or temperature.
Not until the third day did a member of the JAG Corps appear in her
room to say that, while there would certainly be an investigation, he
didn't think a court-martial was likely under the circumstances.

"What circumstances?" said Patton. And then he told her.

Her radio message of the coordinates of the village that the man in
the explosive vest had given them triggered an air strike. Patton Jackson
Harcourt, whose family members had died in friendly fire incidents in
three different wars, had called in an air strike that had killed all but
three members of an American squad—nine soldiers. When the JAG
officer told her, she had cried so long and so hard that the nurse had
to reconnect her saline drip to keep her from dehydrating. She had
spent three months in psychological care in Germany, and eventually, as the officer had predicted, there had been an investigation and
a hearing, though not, ultimately, a court-martial. The hearing had
made no final determination about what had happened. Had Patton
or Bailey or Thomas (neither of whom survived to testify) gotten the
name of the village wrong or had the man in the vest lied to them? Or
had Patton radioed the wrong coordinates? Had she misread the map
or reversed two numbers when she made the call under duress? She
had sat in that hearing room and listened to every sickening possibility,
and the whole time she had stared into the eyes of the three surviving
members of the squad—Bob Macmillan, Ted Grosswald, and Franklin
Rendell. She had memorized their faces, mentally recorded the sounds
of their voices when they testified, and absorbed their hatred. Though
they never made any specific threats against her, she knew that one day
they would retire from the military and would have a score to settle
with her. She assumed, as a matter of course, that they would one day

track her down and kill her, and she didn't even fear that day. She deserved it, so why not expect it?

Then the hearing had ended and the three men whose comrades had gone home in flag-draped coffins were recalled to duty and Patton had received a medical discharge and had hidden in the mountains of North Carolina. Her legal address, as far as the US Army was concerned, remained her parents' home in Illinois, but she never went there. She never knew how, exactly, her parents found out that she had visited the curse of friendly fire on the family once again, but they must have known. She could only guess how disappointed in her they must be. But she had made no attempt to contact them either while she was in Germany or when she returned stateside. She had changed her email and shut down all her social media accounts, and disappeared into the hills.

"So when I came under fire the morning we met," said Patton to Nemo, "I assumed it was those three, finally discharged and clever enough to track me down."

"But it wasn't," said Nemo.

"Yes, but that doesn't really matter now, does it?" said Patton. "They are on my trail which means they are on your trail. At this point you'd be better off leaving me behind."

"We couldn't do that," said Ruthie. "We won't do that. Will we?"

"Of course we won't leave her behind," said Nemo. "She knows too much."

But Nemo knew in that moment there was another reason. A reason that had not entered his life for a long, long time. He had actually come to care for Patton Harcourt. There were elements of this empathy that scared him—it bore too much resemblance to the protective feeling he had had toward Jack. But he decided to forget about his fear and embrace his first actual human connection in decades. After all those years alone, Patton felt like a friend, and he was not going to give that up just because some soldiers were hunting her.

"What makes you so certain these men want to kill you?" said Jean. "I mean, I understand that they're upset, but they'd be risking their own freedom."

"I saw it in their eyes," said Patton. "I could just tell."

"But it wasn't your fault," said Jean. "The inquiry said you weren't to blame."

"An inquiry needs things like evidence; these are guys who lost nine of their best friends. No, more than friends; your unit is your family."

"But it was years ago," said Jean. "Don't you think they'd be more reasonable now?"

"If they're reasonable, why are they coming after me? And besides, who says killing me is not reasonable? In the end it was my fault. One death in exchange for nine—that seems a small price to pay."

"Can we talk about something else," said Ruthie, with a slight edge of panic in her voice. "Like where exactly we're going?" While Patton seemed resigned to her own murder and Jean was determined it wouldn't happen, Ruthie sounded plain scared. They had escaped the two Germans in England and they had escaped the explosion in Munich. Patton imagined that Ruthie didn't fancy having to do any more escaping.

"Why don't we talk about what Patton and Ruthie got up to while Nemo and I were at the library," said Jean.

"What do you mean?" said Nemo.

"How did you know?" said Patton.

"I work on a college campus," said Jean, "and besides, I'm not blind."

"Apparently I am," said Nemo.

"These two are having a little fling," said Jean with a smile.

"Or," said Ruthie tentatively, "it might be more than a fling." She reached out a trembling hand and laid it on Patton's shoulder.

"Yes, it might be," said Patton, putting her hand on top of Ruthie's and feeling her heart give a little leap. Did Ruthie feel the same way she did?

"Well," said Nemo after an awkward moment of silence, "suppose Jean tells us about this place we're going."

"It's a tiny village the South Tyrolean Alps called Brenner," said Jean. "The population is something like five hundred people."

"I've heard of the Brenner Pass," said Patton.

"That's the place," said Jean.

"Sounds peaceful," said Ruthie.

"Not exactly," said Jean. "I went through there one time on an art tour of northern Italy. The Brenner Pass is one of the major routes through the Alps and has a four-lane highway and a railroad. The pass is so narrow that the village is basically smack up against the railway with the highway just on the other side. But the valley beyond is beautiful—green meadows spreading out from the village and the mountains springing up on every side, first the tree-covered hills and then the higher, rocky, snowcapped peaks." Jean sounded almost wistful as she recalled her previous visit to Brenner.

"And have you seen this chapel?" said Nemo.

"No," said Jean. "We didn't even stop. It was a bus trip from Innsbruck to Venice. We left after breakfast and had lunch on the Grand Canal."

"Tell me again how some tiny chapel in the Alps is going to give us the secret to alchemy?" said Ruthie.

"We don't know," said Nemo. "We just know we need to get there before Ingrid Weiss."

"So drive faster," said Ruthie, and Nemo did.

By the time they reached Innsbruck and began the twenty-five-mile climb toward Brenner, the sky was aflame with the Alpine sunset. They had stopped once for gas and food, and to take turns in a single-hole restroom. In Brenner, the sky was still light, but the streetlights had come on and lights twinkled in the houses across the valley.

"Now where?" said Nemo.

Jean had bought a map of South Tyrol at the gas station and she now spread it out on her lap. "The only thing that Romano's book says," she said, "is that the Chapel of the Magi is in the mountains to the west of Brenner, just steps from the Austrian border. There's only one road that leads to any place that fits that description, so it shouldn't be too hard to find."

At Brenner they exited the highway and drove through the village, then Jean directed Nemo onto a narrow, unmarked road about a mile south of town. The road quickly turned to a gravel track that took them high above the valley through a series of hairpin turns. Enough light remained in the sky that, when they emerged from the forest into a less steep Alpine meadow, they could just see the silhouettes of the peaks in the distance and the utter lack of buildings ahead. Nemo drove slowly over a road that had not been built for rental vans, bouncing the passengers as they crept toward Austria. After a couple of miles and a few more switchbacks, the road, if one could call it that, turned left and followed the line of a ridge south along relatively level terrain.

"According to the map," said Jean, who had been following each curve of the road, "that's Austria about fifty feet over there." Nemo slowed to a crawl and they all squinted through the gloaming, trying to catch sight of any sort of structure.

"Did they have any hotels back in Brenner?" said Ruthie. "I'd rather not spend the night out here. It's so . . . empty."

"What's that," said Patton, pointing to a barely discernible shape down the hill to the left. Nemo stopped the van and they all looked, but no one could say for sure if what Patton had seen was a building or a rock. Nemo managed to maneuver the van so that the headlights pointed toward the shape and they all exhaled disappointed breaths.

"Rock," said Ruthie.

"Maybe Ruthie's right," said Jean. "Maybe we should come back in the morning when we can see better."

"No," said Nemo and Patton in unison.

"Whatever is hidden out here," said Nemo, "we have to find it before Weiss catches up with us. She called the library while we were there. We spent about forty-five minutes there and it took us another forty-five to leave Prague. Assuming she drove from Berchtesgaden to Prague after she called the library and then spent an hour or so there figuring out the clue in the scroll, we've got about a four-hour lead on her. I'm not about to waste one minute of that."

Nemo eased the van back onto the road and continued forward as the darkness deepened. Over the next mile or so they spotted two more shapes that, when illuminated by the headlights, proved to be rocks. Then the road turned to the left and headed downhill.

"We're moving away from the border now," said Jean. "I think we must have passed it. It has to be on that stretch before we turned down-hill." Nemo turned the van around and they drove the mile-long stretch of the Austrian border again with no luck. When he turned around again the darkness had deepened to the point that they had no hope of spotting any structures more than a few feet off the road.

"It's pointless," said Ruthie. "We'll never find it in the dark."

"Too bad we can't drive the van sideways so we can use the head-lights," said Jean.

"It's only a mile-long stretch of road," said Nemo. "I'll park the van in the middle and we'll split up into two teams, one walking each way. I've got a pretty powerful flashlight in my bag; the other team will just have to use phones." Minutes later they all emerged from the van into the cool Alpine night. Patton took a deep breath of the fresh air and realized that, unlike Ruthie, she would be happy to spend the night out here.

"Patton, you come with me," said Nemo. "We'll go forward, you two go back the way we just came." It took only a few minutes for the bouncing lights of Ruthie's and Jean's phones to disappear into the night.

"Should I be worried about this thing between you and Ruthie?" said Nemo to Patton.

She thought for a moment before answering. "No. I mean, Ruthie might be taking it seriously, but I'm not. Still, it's useful for . . . being sure she's loyal." It was the first time she had really lied to Nemo.

"And what about your PTSD," said Nemo. "Should I be worried about that?"

"Not out here," said Patton. "There's a reason I retired to the moun-tains back home. Being on top of a hill like this makes me feel safe."

"You know I have it, too," said Nemo. "PTSD. I mean, no one ever called it that, but I read things."

"Do you want to talk about it?" said Patton.

"Not now," said Nemo. "But maybe if we get out of this. I never talked to anyone about it before. It might be nice."

Throughout their conversation Nemo had been playing the flashlight beam across the landscape, but it died away mere yards from the road. "We're going to have to get off this road and go down the hill a little bit," he said, and just then they heard Jean's cry.

Minutes later, Nemo and Patton arrived breathless where Jean and Ruthie stood on the road.

"It was Ruthie's idea," said Jean, grinning in the glow of her phone.

"I realized, we don't have to look for the chapel," said Ruthie. "We just need to look for a path that leads to the chapel."

"And we found it," said Jean, training the light of her phone onto the ground where a path worn into the grass wound down the hill.

"Have you tried it?" said Patton.

"Not yet," said Ruthie. "We wanted to wait for you, in case . . ."

"Well come on," said Nemo, forging ahead down the path. Patton grabbed Ruthie's hand and they followed with Jean close behind. Within a few steps the road disappeared in the darkness behind them and they all kept their lights trained on the path so as not to lose the way or trip on a rock. They had gone no more than a hundred yards when Nemo stopped and looked up, pointing his flashlight ahead. "Is that a building down there?" he said, but no one answered. Instead, all three women rushed past Nemo and in another moment they all stood in front of a small stucco structure about the size, Patton imagined, of a one-room schoolhouse. It had two arched windows on each side and a thick wooden door on the side that faced away from the road. A notice on the door read: *Cappella dei Magi Chiuso al Pubblico.*

"What does that mean?" said Nemo.

"Closed to the public," said Jean.

"Perfect," said Patton. "We won't be disturbed by any tour buses."

"Yes, but the door is locked," said Jean.

"So how do we get in?" said Ruthie.

"Window," said Nemo.

"I don't think they open," said Jean.

"No," said Nemo, shining his flashlight at the window to the left of the door. "But they break."

"We can't do that," said Jean. "That's against the law. It's breaking and entering, destruction of property."

Nemo burst into a hearty laugh. "I'm sorry," he said. "Did someone give you the misconception that we are on a law-abiding excursion? Do you know what I do for a living? Do you know what we've already done to get this far?"

"No," said Jean, shrinking from Nemo. "I don't know either of those things."

"Let's just say it's a lot worse than breaking windows," said Patton, searching the ground for a nice-sized stone.

"Not that way," said Nemo when he saw Ruthie pick up a rock. "We don't want to damage anything inside if we can avoid it."

"You're such a conservationist," said Jean.

"Hey, I conserved your ass," snapped Nemo.

Patton had ignored this exchange, instead searching for something with which to break the window. A few pine trees stood nearby, and she managed to break off a dead limb from one and hand it to Nemo.

"Better," he said. The windows were set deep into a thick wall, and Nemo hoisted himself up until he stood in the window frame. "Look," he said to Jean in a conciliatory voice, "it's not even stained glass. Just an ordinary leaded glass window." With that, he stabbed through the window with the branch and the sound of breaking glass rent the peaceful night. It took him a minute or two to clear all the glass out of the window frame with the branch, then he hopped through the open archway and disappeared into the darkness. In another moment, the thick wooden door swung open.

"Nothing but a latch on this side," said Nemo as the others entered the pitch-black chapel.

Nemo played his flashlight beam around the room. The nave held three pews on each side of a narrow aisle. In front of them, a wide step led up to the altar and to one side of the nave a door stood ajar.

"The sacristy," said Jean. "Maybe there are candles."

Five minutes later, with candles and matches they had found in the tiny, windowless sacristy, they had illuminated the small space with warm light. Candles stood in the brass candlesticks on the altar, in brackets at the end of each pew, and in the votive rack on the opposite side of the nave from the sacristy. The whitewashed walls of the chapel reflected the light, and the space felt as brightly lit as if it had been outfitted with electric lights. All this light spilled onto the point of focus of the entire building—the space behind the altar. There, filling the entire wall from the stone floor to the arched ceiling, was a brightly colored fresco showing the three wise men presenting their gifts to the infant Jesus. In the middle of the trio stood a figure Nemo recognized from the Ripley Scroll—the purple-robed Melchior with his casket of gold.

APRIL 1945

Helmut had many regrets about that day—regrets that reached back months before those final few hours at Dachau. Chiefly, he regretted allowing his younger brother, Albert, to join the SS. Early in the war, that would not have even been a possibility. His brother, though obviously of the same pure blood as Helmut, had a meager physical build. With his scrawny legs and arms and his sunken cheeks Helmut found it hard to believe that Albert came from the same stock he did. But just because Albert had a weak body did not mean he couldn't talk his older brother into foolish things.

"I'm old enough to serve," Albert had said five months ago when Helmut had stopped by the family home for a few hours. "I want to join the SS."

"You're fourteen," said Helmut.

"The Wehrmacht wouldn't turn me away," said Albert. "Plenty of boys my age have enlisted."

"The SS is not the Wehrmacht," said Helmut with pride.

"Which is why I need your help," said Albert. "I cannot stand to live here one more day with Mother and Gretel and be treated like a child. I'm ready to be like you. I'm ready to be a man."

"Are you?" said Helmut. Albert was hardly SS material, but then again, beggars could not be choosers. With the losses that all the armed forces had suffered of late, even scrawny teenagers had been sent to the front lines. Albert, he knew, wouldn't last ten minutes in battle, but Helmut could use an assistant, and if he took Albert under his wing the boy could get his wish to join the SS and maybe Helmut could protect his brother.

"You could make a call," said Albert in a pleading voice. "I know you could."

And so Helmut had made the call, and worse, he had taken his brother, Albert, on that final journey to Dachau. Himmler had radioed from the north of Germany, where he was fleeing from German forces, having been denounced by Hitler for attempting to negotiate peace with the Allies a few days earlier. "Go to Dachau," he said. "Await my message. If I must, I will tell you the final secret of Projekt Alchemie."

As they made their way south, Helmut explained to his brother that Himmler had a special place in his heart for Dachau. It was where his quest after alchemy began, and even though the first "alchemists" he met there turned out to be frauds, it was where he hit upon the idea that made Projekt Alchemie a reality. With the Allied troops closing in fast, Helmut and his brother would close up the last branch of Projekt Alchemie that operated in the laboratory there.

When they arrived, most of the guards and staff had left. Helmut led Albert into the main building and found it empty. In the laboratory they found a small amount of gold, which Helmut pocketed, then the two men destroyed everything that might give a hint of the true purpose of that room.

"Do you hear shouting?" said Albert as they left the laboratory behind. Helmut could hear the fear in his brother's voice. They could still escape the Allies, he thought. He could get Albert safely to Switzerland. But not yet.

"You stay here," said Helmut, leaving Albert in an empty corridor while he went to the radio room. Using Himmler's private settings he enciphered a message on the Enigma machine and sent it out. "Dachau laboratory secured. Allies nearby. I await your instructions." Helmut knew that he could keep the secret of Projekt Alchemie safe. Even if he failed to evade the Allies, at worst he might spend a little time in prison. Himmler, however, had no delusions about his fate. If he did not share the secret, soon enough it would be lost forever.

By the time Himmler's reply came a few minutes later, the shouting Albert had heard had come closer and Helmut heard gunshots. He had already loaded a piece of letterhead in the typewriter and he typed the letters as he listened to the Morse code. He had just finished the message when Albert burst into the room looking pale and shaken.

"They're here!" he shouted. "We have to go. They're here!"

"Just a few more minutes," said Helmut, pulling the Enigma message from the typewriter. "I just have to decrypt this message." Helmut reset the Enigma machine and began to type in letters from Himmler's message, copying out the letters that lit up on the machine. He had written as much as "Projekt Alchemie," when Albert yanked the paper away from him.

"There's no time," he shouted. "We have to go or they'll find us."

Before Helmut had a chance to react, Albert ran from the room. Helmut dashed after his brother but when he emerged from the building, Albert was nowhere in sight. Helmut turned right and ran out the main entrance of the camp. Judging from the sounds he heard, the Allies would be in sight any moment. He ran across the railroad tracks and only then did he realize that Albert must have turned left toward the camp enclosure. Helmut had not told his brother about the camps. If Albert rounded the corner of the brick building and saw the inner enclosure, he would have quite a shock.

He could now see the Americans on the railway line near the main gate. Helmut had no choice but to dive deeper into the woods, hoping to avoid detection. He feared for his brother's life, feared the retribution he would face from his mother if he had to tell her Albert had died at the very end, but much more he feared the loss of Himmler's message. As much as he loved his brother, the boy was simply one more soldier in the service of the Reich; in the Reichsführer's message lay the only hope for the future of that Reich.

Three hours later, creeping through the woods after the shooting had abated, Helmut found his brother's body. Albert had been shot in the head without ever having drawn his weapon. Some cowardly American had murdered his little brother. Before he sat down to weep, Helmut searched his brother's body, turning out his pockets and canvassing the area nearby—but the message, and all that it could accomplish, was gone.

———

"So here we are," said Jean. "Does someone want to explain to me how an empty chapel holds the secret to turning base materials into gold?"

"What can you tell me about that painting?" said Nemo.

"Not much," said Jean. "It's a fresco—painted on wet plaster directly on the wall. Pegronini was an extremely minor late Renaissance painter, flourishing around 1550. It's possible he didn't even paint this. According to Romano's book, the attribution came much later. Other than that, there's not much to say. It's a fairly standard image of the Adoration of the Magi with typical iconography—the three Magi representing both the three ages of man and the three races descended from Noah. Here is Balthazar, with his myrrh—Pegronini portrays him as a dark-skinned African or Indian, which is typical of the time period. Mary is dressed in her traditional blue, though I have to say both her gown and Melchior's purple robe are not quite the right shade. I couldn't see that in the photograph in Romano's book, but whoever did the restoration was no expert in Renaissance colors."

"What do you mean 'whoever did the restoration'?" said Patton.

"According to Romano," said Jean, "the fresco was damaged by leaks in the wall. By the early twentieth century, it was in pretty bad shape. Romano says it was restored in the 1940s."

"During the war?" said Patton.

"He didn't say," said Jean.

"But if so, wouldn't that be strange? To undertake a restoration project in the middle of a world war?" said Patton

"I suppose," said Jean.

"Are you thinking what I'm thinking?" said Nemo.

"If you had something you wanted to get out of German territory late in the war," said Patton, "the Brenner Pass was an obvious way out."

"And this is one of the first places you get once you leave Austria," said Nemo.

"Which was German territory at the time," said Patton. "Maybe it's not the secret of alchemy hiding in this chapel."

"Maybe it's the actual gold," said Nemo with a smile.

"There's no place here to store any significant amount of gold," said Jean. "There's no crypt. Where else could it be?"

"Let's just say for the sake of argument that the fresco was restored toward the end of the war. The wall behind it would have to be rebuilt to prevent leaking, right?"

"I suppose," said Jean.

"So what if that wall is built out of gold?" said Nemo.

"That's preposterous," said Jean.

"I don't know," said Ruthie. "It seems like a reasonable hypothesis to me."

"But there's no way to test it," said Jean.

"Sure there is," said Nemo. "We scrape the painting off the wall."

"You can't, you can't possibly do that," said Jean. "You can't just destroy a fresco because of some cockamamie theory. That's a priceless work of Renaissance art."

"A minute ago, you said the artist was extremely minor," said Nemo. "Now suddenly it's priceless?"

"Besides," said Patton. "It's not really Renaissance art. You said yourself it was practically destroyed by moisture. This is really a mediocre fresco from the 1940s."

"You still can't destroy it," said Jean.

"Your objection is noted," said Nemo.

"What if it were a Michelangelo or a Raphael?" said Jean.

"But it's not," said Patton.

"But if it were. Would you still be so intent in peeling it off the wall?"

"Look," said Nemo, "there are two ways this plays out. Either we chip away at that fresco to see what's behind it or Ingrid Weiss and her gang do it. If there really is a cache of gold back there, is having this painting survive another couple of hours worth the price of putting all that money into the hands of a bunch of Aryan supremacists?"

"I cannot be a part of this," said Jean, slumping down into the front pew.

"Fine," said Patton. "You're not a part of it. If anyone catches us, we'll say you did everything you could to stop us."

Jean thought of all the times she had made donations to projects to save or preserve or restore Italian frescoes. She knew she could do nothing physically to stop Nemo and any attempt she made to keep him from the fresco would probably end up with her injured or worse and would do nothing to save this artwork. To her, it did not matter that it was of no great significance. An artist, actually two artists in two different centuries, had poured their souls into this fresco. And now she would have to watch its destruction. Jean leaned back in the pew and wept.

Nemo and Patton left Ruthie with Jean while they returned to the van to fetch the tire iron—the only thing any of them could think of that might be helpful in chipping plaster off the wall.

"You're right," said Ruthie, sitting next to Jean and putting an arm around her shoulders, "Pegronini wasn't a very good artist. Even I can see the perspective is all wrong. And besides, who would come all the way up here to see a not-very-good painting?"

"That's not the point," said Jean, her sobs subsiding. "You just don't destroy art."

"I understand how you feel," said Ruthie, "but this is bigger than all of us. And it's certainly bigger than a forgotten old painting."

"You don't think there's any way to stop them?" said Jean.

"I don't think so," said Ruthie, squeezing Jean's shoulders. "Now you sit here and enjoy that painting and I'm going to see if there is anything else useful in that closet."

"Sacristy," corrected Jean.

"Right."

Ruthie took a candle and rooted around in the sacristy, but didn't find much—a few flower vases, an old missal, a small glass bowl she supposed must be for holy water, but nothing that would be of use to them in their current situation. When she returned to the nave, Jean had calmed down and now simply sat staring at the fresco, as if she wanted to memorize it, preserve it in her mind as a way of compensating for its destruction.

"All right," said Nemo, striding back into the chapel with Patton in his wake, "let's do this before Weiss shows up."

"We've got at least a few hours," said Ruthie.

"And we might need them," said Nemo, approaching the fresco with the tire iron. He hesitated for a moment, pressing his hand against the cool plaster. "Where to start?"

"Melchior's golden casket," said Jean softly. She had left her seat and joined the others standing by the altar.

"Fine," said Nemo.

He approached the painting with reverence, almost as if he were approaching Christ himself, though instead of gold, frankincense, or myrrh, he brought the gift of a tire iron. Despite the chilly night, his hands sweated against the cold metal. Nemo had spent plenty of time in churches. If you wanted to disappear in a big city, the back of a church wasn't a bad place to do it. He liked Catholic churches especially—not just because of the paintings and mosaics and the ornate woodwork and tiling and all the rest of it, works of art you could look at all day for free. He liked confessionals. He never confessed his actual sins, or at least not the worst ones, the ones that made up his career. But he liked sitting in the dark and talking to someone who could not see him. His only real therapy had come in churches.

He looked at the three kings before him—life-sized figures in a scene he seemed about to step into. The artist had portrayed them as a dark-skinned African, an Arab, and a dark-haired Caucasian who was certainly *not* Aryan. The inferior races, Himmler had called them. And if the supremacists saw them as inferior, how much more so would they view Nemo, a man of unknown but well-mixed racial origins? A mongrel, as people had called him. Well, this was one mongrel who would stand up to the likes of Ingrid Weiss and her cronies. He hadn't done much good with his life, but now he had a chance. Certainly the Magi would understand that. Certainly the Christ child would understand. Almost reflexively, though he rarely did it even in the confines of a church, Nemo muttered a short prayer under his breath. Then so the others could hear, he said, "Lord, forgive me," and struck.

At first the picture looked no different, even as flakes of colored plaster fell to the floor and the ringing of the tire iron hitting the wall echoed in the chapel. The other three stepped back as Nemo swung the iron three times. Five times. Ten times. Then stopped.

Where Melchior's casket had been, glittering in golden paint, a ragged hole an inch or two deep still glittered, reflecting the same golden light of the candles.

"Is that—" said Patton, stepping forward and reaching up to feel the interior of the wall. Her fingers touched not rough stone or brick, but smooth, cold metal.

"Gold," said Nemo.

"How much?" said Ruthie.

"Can't tell," said Nemo. "I hate to say it, Miss Simpson, but it might all have to go."

And in the end it all did. Once Nemo got a good start, they could pull chunks of plaster off the wall with their hands.

"Clearly gold doesn't make a good surface for a fresco," commented Jean, resigned to the fate of the artwork.

The more plaster they cleared, the more gold they revealed. By the time Pegronini's fresco lay in a heap around them they had uncovered a wall of gold ingots eight feet high and twelve feet wide gleaming bright despite the residue of plaster.

There before them stood Reichsführer Heinrich Himmler's insurance policy for the future of the Reich.

"Where did all this come from?" said Patton, basking in the glow of the wall of gold.

Jean, whose grandparents had died in the Dachau camp, did not answer but wept silent tears, because she knew in an instant the answer to the question. It came from wedding rings cherished long after a spouse had passed, signs of a bond that neither separation nor death could break. It came from brooches handed down from grandmothers, bestowed on their favorite granddaughters, the ones who took the time to visit and to write. It came from watch covers and watch chains and watch fobs no longer needed as time no longer mattered to those who had carefully polished those covers and chains and fobs, week in and week out, year after year. It came from necklaces and bracelets and earrings worn for the reassurance of the weight on the neck or wrist or earlobe, a weight that meant safety if anything went wrong, a reassurance that had proved specious. It came from teeth carefully, or sometimes not so carefully, removed—usually, but not always, postmortem. It came from the rims of eyeglasses and from the collar studs and cuff links and money clips of those who would never again need to attach collars or link cuffs or clip money. A coin here, a bauble there, multiplied by eleven million. Yes, Himmler had found a way to turn what were, in his warped mind, "base materials" into gold.

"It came from people like my grandparents," said Jean in answer to Patton's question. "Eleven million people like my grandparents." They all stood reverently for a moment looking at the gold and letting this grim proclamation about its provenance sink in.

Nemo stood on the altar to reach the top of the golden wall and remove one of the ingots. He knew gold would be heavy, but he hadn't expected it to be quite this heavy, and the bar slipped from his hand and thudded to the floor. The four of them stood for a moment looking at the bar and its markings. Clearly stamped in the gold were two symbols. The first read *25 KG.* The second was a swastika.

"Nazi gold," said Nemo. "That son of a bitch Himmler wasn't lying when he said Projekt Alchemie was a success."

"Twenty-five kilograms," said Patton, counting, "and this wall is . . . thirty-two ingots high and eighteen across. That's just over . . . fourteen thousand kilos."

"Anybody know the price of gold at the moment?" said Nemo.

"Around fifteen hundred dollars an ounce," said Ruthie.

"Which makes the value of this wall . . ."

"Something north of seven hundred million dollars," said Patton.

"We're going to need a bigger van," said Ruthie.

"We're going to need more than a van," said Nemo.

"And if Weiss and company are headed our way, we're going to have to work fast," said Patton.

"So we're just going to steal seven hundred million dollars in gold?" said Jean. "Doesn't this belong to someone?"

"It belongs to Heinrich fucking Himmler," said Nemo. "You want to return it to him?"

"It doesn't belong to him," said Patton, laying a hand on Jean's shoulder. "It belongs to all the people he stole it from, and for them, yes, we're going to keep it away from Ingrid Weiss."

"I still don't understand," said Jean. "What would Ingrid Weiss do with all that money anyway?"

"Are you kidding me?" said Nemo. "You want to know what an Aryan supremacist who walks in the footsteps of Heinrich Himmler and lives by the Fourteen Words can do with seven hundred million dollars? If the whole point of her project is to 'secure the existence of our people and a future for white children,' what won't she do? Do you know how little it costs these days to hire Russian hackers to rig an election? How a small investment can turn whole populations against immigrants, against religious and ethnic minorities, against each other? You want to know how little it costs to hire an assassin to remove any opposition you might face, because I can tell you and it's nowhere near seven hundred million dollars. Hate is cheap, and seven hundred million dollars will buy an awful lot of it."

"But if Weiss is on her way here, how are we going to move all this before she arrives?" said Ruthie.

"I saw a dump truck parked at a building site just before where we turned off the main road," said Nemo. "It's not even midnight yet, and no one will miss it until morning. I'll go steal it and take Jean with me to drive the van back up here. Patton, you and Ruthie can start taking this wall apart. That path isn't too steep. I might be able to back the truck up close to the chapel to load it."

"But then what do we do?" said Jean. "Drive a stolen truck and all this stolen gold . . . where?"

"Zurich," said Nemo. "I have an account with a bank there and I can arrange for them to have a vault ready for us, no questions asked. It's not even a four-hour drive."

"So we just drive a stolen truck from Italy to Austria to Switzerland?"

"No one checks license plates," said Nemo. "Now let's get going. We should still have a few hours before Weiss finds this place."

"You should," came a voice from the back of the chapel. "But you don't."

Jean had already met Ingrid Weiss, and none of the others needed to be told the identity of the woman standing in the doorway and pointing a rifle at them. She was flanked by two men and a woman, all holding pistols.

"It probably wasn't a good idea to leave your weapons in the van," said Ingrid.

XIII

For a moment, nobody spoke, then Ruthie strode down the aisle toward the newcomers. Patton was stunned by Ruthie's bravery. Of the four of them, Ruthie was the last one Patton expected to confront gun-wielding criminals. But then, she thought, Ruthie always was full of surprises.

"Sorry it took so long to call," said Ruthie to Dietrich. "I had to wait until we made a rest stop."

Patton felt as if she had been struck in the chest. She could not breathe as she tried to process what was happening. Ruthie embraced Ingrid and her companions in turn with kisses on the cheek. Patton tried to wrap her mind around the fact of this betrayal. There would be no domestic bliss, no long nights under the covers together, no revival of the long dormant relationship. And Patton had not manipulated Ruthie; on the contrary, Ruthie had manipulated her.

"You?" said Nemo, apparently as confused as Patton.

"And yes, I told them about Prague, too," said Ruthie with sudden vitriol in her voice. "You should keep a better eye on me. Not such a big shot now, are you?"

"But how?" said Patton.

"Dietrich recruited me ages ago," said Ruthie. "Long before you got involved in all this. He knew if they ever found the message they might need someone at Bletchley."

"But why . . ." said Patton.

"One percent," said Ruthie. "And one percent of seven hundred million dollars is a tidy sum. The money I inherited from my great-aunt is pretty thin on the ground these days, and one has to keep the lights on, you know. Getting my revenge on you for dropping me all those years ago, well that was an unexpected coincidence and a lovely bonus."

"Did you get the truck?" Ruthie addressed this last question to Dietrich.

"How did they know they would need a—" said Nemo.

"You all were busy tearing down a wall," said Ruthie. "Easy enough for me to send a text message."

"It should be here in about ten minutes," said Dietrich. "Along with a two-man crew. If we back it up to the other side of that wall and knock a hole through, we should be able to get it loaded in a couple of hours."

"As long as it's before dawn," said Ingrid.

"And what about . . ." said Jean, not sure how to finish the question.

"What about you?" said Ingrid with a smile. "I'm afraid the three of you have finished your job. You've done well, but this time it won't be so easy to escape the explosion. Is there someplace we can lock them up?"

"That room over there," said Ruthie, pointing to the sacristy. Although the heavy wooden door stood open, there was a key in the lock and in another moment Patton felt the barrel of Ingrid's rifle urging her forward into yet another small, dark space.

The door of the sacristy was thick enough to prevent their having any hope of breaking it down, but not so thick that they couldn't hear the approach of the truck, the thudding of sledgehammers against the outer wall, and the grunts as the crew loaded one twenty-five-kilogram bar after another. The process seemed to last forever.

"Are you all right, Patton?" said Nemo.

"Weirdly, yes, I am," said Patton. "For the moment at least." She had expected to plunge into a full-blown panic attack when locked up in the pitch-dark sacristy, but her mind was apparently still so busy trying to process Ruthie's treachery that it didn't grasp the fact that this situation would normally trigger her PTSD. And the mere fact that Nemo had asked if she was OK, had acknowledged her condition, comforted her in a small way. She knew she might not be OK at any minute, and that, even if she remained perfectly calm, they still faced a dire situation, but she did everything she could to focus on the sounds coming from outside that locked door, to glean any information she could that might help them. If only she spoke German.

Jean did speak German, or enough to catch bits of conversation. She managed to gather that, once they had loaded the truck, Ingrid and her cohorts would be driving to someplace called the Fox's Den. They had mentioned the same place back in the basement in Munich. She didn't suppose knowing their code word for a secret hiding place would do much good but listening helped distract her from the helplessness of their situation and she found herself surprisingly calm, especially given the way she had panicked back in Munich faced with similar circumstances. But a lot had happened since Munich.

"Do you really think they're going to blow us up?" said Jean, when the conversation outside the door had stopped.

"Well, there's no vest this time," said Nemo. "But we know they like explosives and it would certainly help them out if the people they tried to pin the Munich bombing on died in another explosion. Covers up the fact that they pulled the wall of the chapel apart, kills us, makes it look like we were hiding out here and something went wrong. It ties up a lot of loose ends."

"I'm not sure I like being a loose end," said Jean.

"So what's your plan?" said Patton, after they had sat quietly for what seemed like hours, listening to the clink of gold bars hitting one another as they slid into the truck.

"I haven't got one," said Nemo.

"I thought you always had a plan, that you always prepared for every possibility."

"I did," said Nemo, "until now. But then, as you know, I've broken every rule on this job—first and foremost by bringing you along."

"I'm glad you did," said Patton.

"At least now you won't have to worry about those soldiers coming after you," said Nemo.

"But we have to try something," said Jean. "We can't just sit here and die; and worse than that we can't just sit here and let Ingrid fucking Weiss walk away with seven hundred million dollars."

"Salty language for a college professor," said Nemo. "But I'm afraid that's all we *can* do. We have no weapons, not even any sharp objects. We emptied every candle and match out of this place and Weiss's stooges emptied out everything else before they put us in here. Our assets are the clothes on our backs and, as I recall, a prayer book sitting on the counter."

"And our brilliant minds," said Patton.

"Yeah," said Nemo, "those, too."

At that moment they heard a sound they had all been dreading. The building rumbled as someone cranked the engine of the truck outside. The sound grew louder for a few seconds as the engine revved, then they heard the grinding of gears and the gradual fading of the sound as the truck pulled away.

"Timer?" said Patton.

"Probably," said Nemo. "Cell service around here is not reliable enough to use a remote detonator. But they'll want to be well off the mountain before it goes. I'd say we have a half hour or so."

"My grandparents died in Dachau," Jean said softly. "I had never been there until two days ago. Before I went to confront Ingrid Weiss, I went to the memorial at the camp, and they have a monument there that says, in five languages it says, 'Never Again.' I guess maybe five languages isn't enough."

"She won't win," said Patton. "She can't win."

At that moment they heard a click from outside the door.

"Sounds like something just activated," said Patton.

"Given my career choice," said Nemo, "this is not something I thought I would ever have the opportunity to say, but, ladies, it's been an honor serving with you."

———

APRIL 1945

The night of his brother's murder, Helmut Werner traded his SS uniform for civilian clothing he found in an abandoned house a few miles away. Keeping off the roads, he spent two weeks escaping on foot to Switzerland. Only when he arrived did he hear of the final capitulation of Germany to the Allies and the death of Adolf Hitler. Changing his name and passing himself off as a German civilian refugee, he lived in Switzerland for six years before returning to his homeland, marrying, and raising a family while working as a civil servant in what was now called West Germany. Himmler had prepared Helmut well for life after the war. When he left Dachau, Helmut had nearly 50,000 Swiss francs sewn into the lining of his coat. He transferred these to the pockets of his new clothes and was staying at a small hotel near St. Gallen when he heard on the radio that Himmler had committed suicide while in custody. He climbed up to his room and wept.

Lying awake in bed that night, Helmut recalled the day that Himmler had shared with him the true nature of Projekt Alchemie.

"So it's not alchemy at all," said Helmut with a smile.

"I wouldn't say that," said Himmler. "We take something base and worthless and we turn it into something of value. The vermin arrive in the camps and they become mine. Their gold fillings and their jewelry and their watches become mine. The things they have left behind in their stinking hovels become mine. They serve the Reich with their labor, and they serve the Reich with their ill-gotten gold, and then they serve the Reich by dying to cleanse it of their filth and make way for a master race."

Over the years, Helmut had helped collect tons of gold from the camps and from branches of the SS. Helmut oversaw the melting of that gold into twenty-five-kilogram ingots. He transported those ingots wherever Himmler told him to—never to the same place twice. For while Himmler said he trusted Helmut, no one other than the Reichs-führer himself knew where and how the gold was being hidden. And in those final days, Himmler had finally given Helmut the greatest gift—the gift of trusting him with the future of the Reich, of giving him the location of the gold and allowing him to decide when the time came to use it. But Helmut had lost that gift before it had been fully bestowed, and the Reichsführer's gold, ready to finance the return of his ideals of Aryan supremacy, had disappeared.

———

Ingrid had insisted that Gottfried drive the dump truck. They had spot-ted it at a construction site and paid the crew €10,000 apiece for a few hours' work and to look the other way when they stole the truck, but she didn't trust them not to drive off with a few hundred million euros' worth of gold, and she certainly had no intention of leading them to the Fox's Den. Dietrich and Eva rode in the car with Ingrid, and the hired hands drove Ruthie in a rental car that Gottfried had picked up in Innsbruck. They had instructions to drop her at the train station there, then go home and forget everything they had seen.

"I thought you'd be happier," said Dietrich as Ingrid accelerated onto the highway. "You seem . . . reserved."

"We're a long way from the end," said Ingrid. "And even when Pro-jekt Alchemie is complete, our work is just begun."

"Yes," said Dietrich, "but did you ever believe we'd make it this far? Eva figures that haul is worth six hundred million euros at least. Can you imagine what we can do with six hundred million euros?"

"I've been imagining that ever since my grandfather lay on his death-bed," said Ingrid. "Ever since he told me about Himmler and his vision for a better world. Maybe that's why I don't feel elated at the moment—the reality doesn't seem that different from the way I've imagined it."

"You don't talk much about your grandfather," said Dietrich.

"He was a great man," said Ingrid. "He was willing to die in the service of Projekt Alchemie, in the service of the Reich."

Dietrich glanced at Eva, sleeping peacefully in the back seat. "So am I," he said.

———

Patton wrapped an arm around Jean's shoulders, trying to offer her some comfort, not because she herself felt any strong desire for human contact at the end. The fear of death, Patton discovered, was much worse than death itself. Now that the fear had passed and she had resigned herself to the end that we all must eventually face, she felt serene. It would be over in a flash, she thought. Not such a bad way to go.

Jean wept, silently not hysterically, and leaned into Patton's embrace. Only Nemo seemed about to panic here at the end.

"Fuck," he said. "I really wanted to find Jack." Patton had never heard him mention anyone named Jack, but there was no time now for explanations, so she just listened as Nemo said, "I'm so sorry, Jack. I'm so sorry."

They heard another click, and Patton felt Jean's body tense, then came the searing light and . . . nothing else. Not an explosion, not the fleeting sensation of a body tearing apart, just a voice, cutting through the sunlight that poured into the sacristy.

"Stupid idiots left the key sitting on the altar."

"Who are you?" said Jean, extricating herself from Patton's arm and walking toward the voice, unable to see in the blinding light. "Are you God?"

"Christ, no," said the voice. "I'm Alex Lansdowne. Who are you?"

"No time for chitchat," said Nemo, stumbling into the light. "We've got to get out of here."

Patton followed Nemo out of the sacristy and they all made for the door. As the fresh air hit her face and filled her lungs, Patton didn't know if the surge of adrenaline that propelled her up the hill toward the van would plunge her into another traumatic episode or fill her with the elation of survival. For now, it made no difference, as long as she got away from that chapel before it exploded.

Two minutes later, they stood panting next to their van and Alex Lansdowne's rental car. The sky was pink with the last tinges of sunrise and the cold Alpine air stung Patton's lungs as she felt herself torn between laughter and tears. She managed to stave off both long enough to turn to Alex and say, "What are you doing here?"

"I came after you," said Alex.

"But how?"

"I figured you might find some good Nazi memorabilia, so I put a tracking device in the stock of one of the guns I lent you," said Alex. "I didn't think much about it until yesterday when I happened to turn on the news—something I don't do very often—and heard about the explosion in Munich. I knew Weiss was trouble and at that point you were all driving south through Germany, so I flew to Munich and followed your signal here."

"I thought you said you were apolitical, that you were just a preserver of artifacts," said Patton.

"Well Nemo did threaten to burn down my place if anything happened to you, so my interest is not totally unselfish," said Alex. "But I did decide to pick a side and make a stand."

"We appreciate the rescue," said Nemo, leaning against the side of the van, "but as far as making a stand against Ingrid Weiss, I'm afraid you're too late. She left with three quarters of a billion dollars in Nazi gold about a half hour ago and we have no idea where she's headed."

Alex gave a low whistle. "I'd always heard rumors of a secret stash of Nazi gold," he said. "I've got a whole notebook devoted to the various theories about where it came from and where it went, but I never thought Ingrid Weiss would be the person to find it."

"We found it," said Patton. "Weiss stole it."

"Just how much do you know about Ingrid Weiss?" said Jean, who had finally caught her breath after the dash to escape the chapel.

"What I *know* is not a lot more than you know," said Alex. "She's some sort of businesswoman who runs a charity that returns stolen Nazi items, mostly books, to their families of origin. That's what I know. But the folks who trade conspiracy theories late at night in the darkest recesses of the Internet claim that her grandfather was some sort of influential Nazi—Himmler's secret right-hand man or something like that—and that all her charitable work is an attempt to expiate the guilt she feels about her family's past."

"I can believe the grandfather bit," said Patton, "but I doubt that woman feels the slightest twinge of guilt. We think she wants to use the gold to promote the ideals of the Third Reich."

"Especially Himmler's rubbish about Aryan supremacy," said Jean. "That woman's tried to kill me twice now, but what really makes my skin crawl is hearing the way she talks about Himmler—like he was some kind of god or something. And now she's got . . . all that money. All that money to promote her sick agenda."

"She stole it from you; why don't we steal it back from her?" said Alex. "I wouldn't mind adding an ingot of Nazi gold to my collection."

"Is that all you care about?" spat Patton, suddenly angry. "Your goddamn collection? What about justice, what about civil rights, what about racial equality?"

"Yeah, sure, I care about all that stuff, too," said Alex. "I came here to help you, didn't I? I got noble, didn't I?"

"OK, let's just take it down a notch," said Nemo. "We're all on the same side here. Of course we want to steal the gold back from Weiss, if you can call it stealing when Weiss stole it from us and Himmler probably stole it from half the population of Europe. The problem is, she's got a solid head start, and we don't know where she's going."

"I thought you said you overheard them talking," said Alex.

"Well they didn't exactly say, 'We're going ninety miles north to hide the loot in the barn with the red swastika on the side,'" said Patton.

"They said *Fuchsbau*," said Jean softly.

"What was that?" said Alex.

"They said they were going to someplace called the *Fuchsbau*. It means the Fox's Den."

"The Fox's Den?" said Alex with a wide grin. "Well, why didn't you say so? We can be there in a couple of hours."

"You mean you know where it is?" said Patton.

"Of course I know where it is," said Alex. "What kind of Nazi historian and keeper of conspiracy theories would I be if I didn't know where the Fox's Den is?"

"Well, whatever it is, let's go," said Patton.

"Does one of you want to ride with me?" said Alex.

But before anyone could answer, an unfamiliar voice said, "You're not going anywhere."

Nemo, Patton, Jean, and Alex stepped in front of the van and came face-to-face with three men, whom only Patton knew to be Ted Grosswald, Bob Macmillan, and Franklin Rendell. They each stood in a shooting stance and each held a Beretta M9, just like the one Patton had been forced to leave behind in North Carolina.

"Hello, gentlemen," said Patton. "It's been a long time."

———

Ingrid Weiss finally laughed. She couldn't believe she had accomplished the mission her grandfather had laid upon her shoulders. True, she now lived in what amounted to a damp cave with little in the way of modern amenities, but the hundreds of millions of euros in gold sitting in a dump truck in an adjacent chamber would soon put that to right.

"What's so funny?" said Gottfried. "Because if you're laughing at the fact that the only place that Dietrich and Eva can sneak off to now is a dank cavern then I am prepared to laugh along with you."

"You're forgetting the ever so comfortable cab of that dump truck," said Ingrid. "But I'm laughing because I'm happy. Happy that we can finally begin the real work of Columbia House."

"You don't actually think we're safe here?" said Gottfried.

"For the time being," said Ingrid. "We'll let the authorities jump to the conclusion that the terrorists blew themselves up in Brenner, lay low for a while, then take the gold to Switzerland."

"Somebody in Munich has been poking their nose in our business," said Gottfried, hunched over his laptop. He had rigged the Fox's Den with a satellite receiver aboveground and they had cleaned one of the rooms and outfitted it with lights powered by a generator that sat in a niche on the side of the entrance tunnel. On their last trip to the Fox's Den they had detoured to the IKEA outside Munich and purchased a few chairs and the table where Gottfried now worked.

"I don't know if it's the press or the police," he said, "but neither is good news. I did my best to obfuscate our ownership of this place, but sooner or later they'll figure out we're here."

"And by then we'll be long gone," said Weiss. "Soon enough we'll hear news reports that the terrorists have been killed. We can wait that long."

"We nearly got lost in here," said Dietrich, entering the room holding a flashlight in one hand and Eva's hand in the other. "Every time we come I find more tunnels and chambers. I wonder why Himmler didn't just hide the gold here?"

"Too many people knew about it," said Ingrid. "And your job was not to explore the Fox's Den. I asked you to check the perimeter."

"We did check the perimeter," said Eva. "There's nothing out there."

"Fine," said Ingrid. "I want one of you to walk that perimeter every two hours. It's nine o'clock. I'm going to get some sleep. Wake me at noon, unless something happens."

"Why is she always the one who gets to sleep?" said Dietrich.

———

"Are you Ruthie Drinkwater?" said Bob Macmillan, pointing to Jean with his gun.

"No," said Jean, "why do you ask?"

"We just wanted to thank her for getting in touch with us on Twitter, letting us know where Patton here was headed."

"Jesus," said Nemo, "is there anyone that snake didn't call?"

"That was my fault," said Patton. "I saw these fine fellows on TV and I told Ruthie their names."

"Look," said Bob, "there doesn't need to be any trouble with the three of you. You're free to go. We just want Patton."

"Pretty convenient for you," said Nemo. "The woman you're hunting is wanted on terrorism charges and now you can shoot her in the middle of nowhere and let the authorities think it was some sort of double cross."

"Who says we're hunting her?" said Bob.

"It doesn't look like you came to play checkers," said Jean.

"If you want Patton," said Nemo, "you'll have to go through us."

"That's not really a problem," said Bob.

"Speak for yourself," said Alex. "I might be newly noble, but I'm not *that* noble."

"Look," said Bob, "we can do this the easy way, or we can do it the hard way."

"Listen," said Nemo, "you only want one body to deal with, so let me help you out. Give me five minutes. Just five minutes to tell you some things and then if you still want to kill Patton, we won't stop you."

"We won't?" said Jean.

"Fine," said Bob. "Five minutes."

"There's a few things you should know about Patton," said Nemo. "Do you want to know what her life has been like since Kandahar? Ten years of nightmares and insomnia. Constant flashbacks. Migraine headaches. Four suicide attempts. Patton suffers every day because of what happened in Kandahar, and I don't mean, *Ooh, she's so sad about the bad thing she did*. I mean serious suffering. You kill her now, and you're doing her a favor. You really want to punish Patton Harcourt? Make sure she stays alive."

Patton hadn't spoken to Nemo about how the guilt of Kandahar weighed on her. Yes, she had occasional flashbacks and nightmares, but she never had migraines, and she certainly hadn't attempted suicide. She just walked through every day oppressed by the burden of responsibility and guilt she would feel for the rest of her life. Nonetheless, she understood Nemo's strategy, and she did her best to look sickly and miserable. She had expected to embrace the punishment meted out by the surviving members of the unit she had decimated, had expected to face the death she deserved calmly and with resignation. But she had just escaped from a death she was facing calmly and with resignation, and suddenly she had no interest in dying. So if Nemo could talk her way out of this, she wasn't about to contradict him.

"That's it," said Bob. "That's your big pitch? Patton will suffer more if she stays alive?"

"That's half of it," said Nemo. "The other half is this: You may be retired, but in your hearts—hell, in your souls—you are United States soldiers, aren't you?"

"Damn right we are," said Franklin.

"Right, so as American soldiers, you need to ask yourself this: Do you want to get revenge on a fellow soldier for a mistake that tortures her every day of her life, or do you want to help win the last battle of World War II?"

"What the hell are you talking about?" said Bob. "World War II has been over for seventy years."

"Yeah, that's what I thought," said Nemo.

"Me too," said Jean. "I thought that until the past few days."

"You keep out of this," said Bob. "You want to explain what the hell you're talking about?" he said to Nemo.

"OK," said Nemo, "but this part might take more than five minutes."

"I'll give you six," said Bob, never lowering his gun a millimeter.

But though Bob did not lower his gun, Ted and Franklin lowered theirs as Nemo reached the end of his story.

"Seven hundred million dollars?" said Franklin. "Are you serious? Do you know what a terror organization could do with that kind of money?"

"Look, why should we care about any of this?" said Bob. "We came here for Patton—I say let's do what we have to do and get out of here."

"Are you fucking crazy?" said Nemo, stepping fearlessly toward Bob's outstretched gun. "Why should you care? *Why should you care?* Other than the fact that you took an oath to support and defend the United States against all enemies, foreign and domestic, how about the fact that the three of you standing there are Jewish, Black, and, I'm taking a guess here, queer? How do you think your civil rights will fare in a world run by people put in power by Ingrid Weiss?"

"What do you mean queer?" said Ted. "I mean yes, I'm Jewish and of course Franklin . . ."

"Oh, you always were blind to the obvious," said Bob. "You didn't ask and I didn't tell."

"Franklin, did you know . . ."

"Of course I knew," said Franklin. "But aren't we straying a little off the subject here? Why should we believe anything this guy says?"

He could not have timed his question any better, for at that moment, as his words hung in the air like a cartoon balloon, the chapel exploded. The sound of the blast rent the crisp morning air and sent all seven of them diving for the cover of the vehicles as, seconds later, debris began to rain down on them. Most of what fell this far away from the explosion was pebbles and bits of plaster, but it took them all a moment or two to realize they were not in any real danger. In that time, Patton saw that Ted had dropped his Beretta and it lay right in front of her. As the others stood up and dusted themselves off, she picked up the gun by the barrel and held it out to Ted.

"This is yours, I think," she said as Ted, looking mystified, took the gun back. "Look, I'm not going to try to escape you. I'll stay unarmed; I'll stay with at least one of you all the time; and when this is over, I'll surrender to you and you can do whatever you want. But Nemo's right. This is important. This *is* the last battle of World War II and we are the only soldiers available to fight it."

"She did give my gun back," said Ted.

Everyone looked to Bob who stared hard at Patton for a long minute.

"What happens to the gold?" he said.

"I beg your pardon," said Nemo.

"I said, what happens to the damn gold? If we help you and get it away from these Aryans, what do we do with it?"

"Why are you asking?" said Patton warily.

"Because," said Bob, "it occurs to me that a few million dollars in the bank accounts of the families of the soldiers you killed might settle your debt without any . . . unpleasantness."

"No," said Patton. "Absolutely not. Every penny of that gold goes to fight people like Ingrid Weiss. It goes to civil rights organizations and people fighting anti-Semitism and groups campaigning for LGBT rights. It goes to do everything Himmler would hate."

No one contradicted Patton. No one spoke as Bob looked at Patton, looked at his gun, and then looked at her again.

"Fine," he said at last. "I don't like it, but fine. You don't leave my sight and you ride in our car."

"Done," said Patton.

"Ride where?" said Franklin.

"Good question," said Bob. "You've told us this is the last battle of World War II, but do you have a battle plan? Do you even know where the battlefield is?"

"Weiss and her gang are going to the Fox's Den," said Alex, stepping forward with his hands raised. "And if you'd put that gun down for a minute, I can explain to you where that is and why it's not going to be easy to fight them there."

Bob glanced at Ted and Franklin who nodded. He lowered his weapon. The seven of them now stood in a circle perhaps twenty yards across and for a moment no one spoke. Finally, Alex said, "Well, don't just stand there. Jean, get the road atlas out of my car and the rest of you come over here where I can talk to you without shouting."

"So you're in charge now?" said Bob.

"Yeah," said Alex. "For the next ten minutes. When my field of expertise runs out, someone else can be in charge. Does that suit you?"

"It suits me," said Nemo, crossing over to Alex. Jean walked to Alex's rental car and retrieved a road atlas from the passenger seat, doing her best to keep an eye on the soldiers the whole time. Maybe it was because someone had twice tried to blow her up, but she didn't trust them not to start shooting at the slightest provocation.

Alex took the atlas from Jean as the others gathered round. "You've heard of the Wolf's Lair?" said Alex.

"Hitler's underground headquarters on the Eastern Front," said Franklin. "They do teach us military history, you know."

"Well if, like me, you had dwelled in the recesses of the Internet late at night, you would have heard the theory that Heinrich Himmler had an underground hideaway, too. A place called the Fox's Den. It was just a rumor until recently, when an acquaintance of mine—a fellow collector, if you will, was doing some field research."

"What do you mean by 'field research'?" said Franklin.

"Even seventy years after the end of the war, there are still relics sitting in fields and forests all over Europe. Most of them aren't worth much—uniform buttons, shell casings, that sort of thing. But we search, nonetheless. I've found firearms, medals, and once an Enigma rotor—all with a good map, a thorough knowledge of the war, and a metal detector."

"So what did this friend of yours find?" said Nemo.

"I wouldn't call him a friend," said Alex. "But he believed Himmler's underground complex still existed. He thought Himmler hadn't hidden there at the end of the war because it was filled with treasure he wanted to hide from the Allies. The Fox's Den was supposedly in the foothills of the Bavarian Alps south of Munich—a big underground complex with a single entrance—easy to guard. This collector liked to brag about all the things he found on his research trips. I could never quite tell whom he was trying to impress—other collectors, or historians, or Aryan supremacist groups, or all three. One night I was talking with him online and he let slip that he had discovered the Fox's Den outside the town of Oberammergau. Said someone had hired him to find it and financed the whole excursion quite generously. I was off to Germany the next day, and it wasn't too hard to find the spot, since I knew what I was looking for. But there was a nice shiny new security fence around the whole site. Whoever had bought it didn't want anyone like me nosing around."

"Can you lead us there?" said Patton.

"Oh, I can lead you there," said Alex. "But then what will you do? Even if you could make it through the modern security the new owners have installed, you'd still have to contend with an underground complex with a single long tunnel as its entrance. They could pick us off one by one before we were fifty feet into the mountain."

"So there's no way we can get in?" said Bob.

"Not that I can see," said Alex.

"Well," said Patton, "we'll just have to get them to come out."

"And the gold?" said Nemo.

"If what I have in mind works," said Patton, "they'll bring it with them. What do you know about Operation Fortitude?"

"I know it won World War II," said Franklin.

"What's Operation Fortitude?" said Nemo.

"It was the great Allied fake out," said Franklin. "Fake armies, false intelligence, even General Patton traveling to eastern England to rally troops that weren't there. All to fool the Germans into thinking the invasion of the mainland was coming at Calais instead of Normandy."

"Exactly," said Patton. "And it worked. Even a month after D-Day the Germans were still bracing for an invasion at Calais, keeping divisions away from the Allied advances."

"So what's your idea?" said Bob. "We build a fake army?"

"Something like that," said Patton. "Operation Fortitude worked because the Germans believed the false intelligence fed them by double agents and because Allied intelligence on the Germans was accurate— thanks largely to the codebreakers at Bletchley. We need to do two things—get intelligence on Ingrid Weiss and her cronies, and feed them false intelligence about what's going on outside the Fox's Den."

"And," said Bob, "since you were in army intelligence . . ."

"I know how to do both of those things. How long will it take us to get to the Fox's Den?" said Patton, turning to Alex.

"Maybe an hour and a half," said Alex.

"And is there someplace we can stop for supplies? A hardware store or something?"

"There might be someplace in Innsbruck," said Alex.

"Great," said Patton. "I'll ride with Bob and Ted so they can guard me; Jean, you ride with Alex, and Franklin can ride in the van with

Nemo. Now let's get the hell out of here before someone shows up trying to find out why the Chapel of the Magi just exploded."

No one questioned Patton's commands. If Alex knew navigation, Patton knew intelligence, and the three American soldiers seemed willing to let their quarry be their commander for the moment.

In the soldiers' rental car, Ted drove, while Bob sat in the back with Patton, his hand on his gun and his eyes never leaving her. After they crossed into Austria, Patton broke the silence. "I'm surprised it took you so long to find me."

"We agreed to wait until we were all out of the army," said Ted. "Bob stayed in for another seven years. By then you'd disappeared."

"But then we saw that news story from Alta Vista about how someone had taken a shot at you," said Bob.

"And we figured maybe you'd pissed off some other unit," said Ted.

"No, that was Weiss's men," said Patton.

"Jesus," said Bob. "She had guys in Alta Vista? What the hell for?"

"She thought I had information that would lead her to the gold," said Patton. "As it turns out, I did."

They rode in silence for a few minutes before Ted said, "If Weiss is sending snipers to remote corners of the US, then Nemo is right."

"How so?" said Bob.

"He said we took an oath to protect and defend the United States. The way I see it, if she sends murderers or assassins or terrorists or whatever you want to call them, to operate on American soil, then protecting the United States is exactly what we're doing by going after her."

"I hadn't thought of it that way until Nemo pointed that out," said Patton.

"What do you know about this Nemo guy?" said Ted. "Who is he?"

"Do either of you speak German?" said Patton, ignoring Ted's question.

"Mine's pretty good," said Bob. "I was stationed there for four years and I . . . met a lot of Germans."

"We need to monitor the news," said Patton. "Do you think you could follow a radio broadcast?"

"Just find the damn BBC World Service," said Bob. "We've got satellite radio on this car."

Ted flipped on the radio and fiddled with the dial until a smooth British voice flowed through the speakers.

"We need to know what the police know about the explosion in Munich," said Patton.

As a feature story about English agriculture played, Patton closed her eyes and thought of Ruthie. During her training for intelligence work, Patton had learned the warning signs of a potential double agent, yet Ruthie had fooled her completely. A double agent right there in Bletchley Park—imagine the catastrophe, thought Patton, if one had been there during the war. Whoever such an agent had duped might have been responsible for the deaths of millions and the loss of the war. Now Ruthie had duped Patton, the one among them who should have known better, should have seen right through her. And, if this last-ditch effort didn't work, Patton would certainly deserve whatever punishment Bob Macmillan and his cohorts meted out.

They had stopped at Ortner und Stanger in Innsbruck for supplies and were winding their way through the Alps just past the town of Mittenwald when the top of the hour rolled around and Ted turned up the volume on the radio.

"From the BBC World Service this is the news at eight o'clock GMT. Police in Munich continue to sift through the remains of a house destroyed in an explosion last night. The house was the headquarters of a charity called Columbia House which repatriated artifacts stolen by the Nazis to their rightful owners. Detective Christian Ulrich has confirmed that the attack was an act of terrorism but will not comment on whether it may have been motivated by anti-Semitism. In the meantime, donations are pouring in from all quarters to help Columbia House rebuild and to further their mission. Detective Ulrich has announced he will hold a press conference this afternoon."

"So the cops don't know the real purpose of Columbia House," said Ted.

"Or they're not saying," said Patton. "God, it makes me sick that people are giving money to that Nazi bitch."

"Probably part of their plan," said Ted. "It's a pretty good idea for a fundraiser. Blow up the person who's about to rat you out and get tons of money in return. Still, that story didn't tell us much."

"It told us enough," said Patton with a smile. For the first time in the drive, she looked out the window with awe at the view of the surrounding Alpine landscape. "How much farther?"

"We should be there in about thirty minutes," said Ted.

"Excellent," said Patton. Turning to Bob, she added, "It's beautiful up here, isn't it?"

Bob did not reply.

KLHQB EZVXP CEEXF NIKVB OXIS

SECTION SIX: OBERAMMERGAU

XIV

Christian Ulrich hated press briefings. He had never liked standing in front of people—not when he gave reports as a schoolboy in front of the class, not when local civic groups asked him to speak, and certainly not when he had to stand before the press and admit he had no answers to most of their questions. Or at least no answers he was willing to give at the moment. But with the new message from Ingrid Weiss and the explosion in Italy, he felt he had to make some sort of official comment. He had spent the past hour working on his statement and considering what he knew.

He knew, after talking with some of her associates in the United States, that Jean Simpson was no terrorist. He knew there was something fishy about Columbia House—apparently some of the books they had "returned" had forged inscriptions and invented provenances. He knew the finances of Columbia House were a tangled mess—probably intentionally tangled—and that the charity was €2 million in debt to two German banks. And he knew there was something very odd about the "victim" of a terrorist attack sending the police what amounted to a press release and then disappearing into the wind. More than anything, he knew he wanted to have a chat with Ingrid Weiss. But he wouldn't talk about any of that this afternoon, he thought, as he stepped in front of a confrontational bristle of microphones and read from his paper.

"I have a short update on the bombing that took place in Döberein-erstrasse. We continue to search for Jean Simpson and Patton Harcourt to question them about the attack. With regard to the explosion in northern Italy early this morning, we do believe the two incidents may be related, but how remains uncertain. The Bavarian State Police are working to-gether with the Italian Polizia di Stato to coordinate investigations."

"Are the bodies of the terrorists at the Italian site?" shouted one re-porter. Ulrich knew that the tabloids were already speculating that the Italian chapel had been a hideout for Simpson and Harcourt. The rumor mill had the two suspects dying in an accidental explosion.

"I won't confirm that at this time," said Ulrich, reflecting that this statement was technically true.

"Where is Ingrid Weiss?" shouted another reporter, but Christian pushed his way through the crowd and back into the security of the police headquarters. He hadn't lied to the reporters, but he had left out a lot. His top priority was finding Ingrid Weiss, and if he needed to use the press to help him do that, he was happy to do so. So he had not mentioned that Jean Simpson was no longer a suspect, he had not said that Ingrid Weiss was certainly guilty of fraud and possibly of much more, and he hadn't passed along the information that the Italian Poli-zia had agreed to keep quiet for at least a few hours—the fact that there had been no bodies at the Italian blast site.

Christian still didn't understand Ingrid Weiss's game, but he knew it was more than giving away stolen library books. If he could convince Weiss the explosions had been pinned on two terrorists who were now dead, she might show herself and he could bring her in for questioning. So no, he hadn't told any lies to the press, not yet. But if that was what it took to flush out Ingrid Weiss, he wasn't above manipulating those reporters in any way that served the cause of justice.

———

By eight o'clock that night, Ingrid's elation that they had secured the gold and would be able to use it to promote Himmler's racial ideals had been tempered with boredom. Eva and Dietrich had gone on patrol every two hours and seen nothing. The news from Munich simply repeated the same information. The cave was cold and damp and ill lit, and lying low, it turned out, was tedious business. She had been thrilled several months ago when Gottfried had secured two bank loans, hired some amateur Nazi historian to find the Fox's Den, and purchased this property through a hidden subsidiary of Columbia House. But the excitement of hiding out in a facility constructed by Himmler faded quickly. True, they seemed safe here, but she looked forward to the time when she could take a hot shower and sleep in a proper bed. They just needed to hear that the police had recovered the bodies in Italy and blamed the explosion in Munich on Jean Simpson and Patton Harcourt. Then she could emerge from hiding, the relieved victim, cash an insurance check, humbly acknowledge an outpouring of donations, and quietly begin the true work of Columbia House.

Shortly after ten o'clock, as Ingrid lay awake on the IKEA mattress that passed for a bed, Gottfried called out to her.

"What is it?" she said, striding into the space where Gottfried had set up his computer. "And where the hell are the others?"

"On patrol," said Gottfried. "Or more likely shagging in the woods. But it's the latest news you should worry about. Christian Ulrich has released another statement."

"Christian Ulrich?"

"The man in charge of the Munich investigation. It just posted on *Süddeutsche Zeitung*. Listen to this. 'The search for Ingrid Weiss, owner of the home destroyed in this week's blast in Munich, is over. Bavarian State Police authorities have located Weiss near Oberammergau and plan to take her into protective custody later this evening. In a statement, Christian Ulrich of the Bavarian State Police said that while he understands Weiss's desire to remain hidden while her safety is compromised, he believes the police are better suited to provide her security than her current location. Ulrich promised another briefing tomorrow following his interrogation of Weiss.'"

"How the hell did they find out where we are?" said Ingrid, anger and bile rising in her like a geyser.

"How did who find out?" said Dietrich, just entering the room hand in hand with Eva.

"The police," said Gottfried. "They're on the way here."

"If this is your fault," spat Ingrid, turning on Dietrich and Eva, "I will never forgive you. You were supposed to be on patrol."

"We *were* on patrol," protested Eva.

"Looks like you were patrolling one another," said Gottfried.

"Which one of you betrayed us?" said Ingrid, pulling her Luger out of her belt.

"Ingrid, calm down," said Eva. "None of us betrayed anyone."

"She's right," said Dietrich. "How could we have? We haven't seen anyone. We don't even have phones. Only Gottfried can communicate outside this place."

"Don't look at me," said Gottfried. "If I wanted the police to come here, would I tell you they were on the way?"

"Then how the fuck did they find out?" shouted Ingrid, her voice echoing through the cavern.

"Listen," said Eva. "It doesn't matter how they found out. What matters is what we do. If the police are on their way here, we've got to get out."

"She's right," said Gottfried.

Ingrid stood staring at the damp ceiling for a moment, then let out a wail of frustration and anger, firing three rounds into the dimness overhead.

"Feel better?" said Eva.

"No, I do not fucking feel better," said Ingrid. "But you're right," she added in a calmer voice. "We need to go. We'll move up the transfer. Gottfried, call the bank in Zurich, then pack everything that can be traced to us into the car. I'll drive the truck."

"You can't drive the truck," said Gottfried.

"Why not?" said Ingrid, turning on him, her gun still drawn.

"You're the one they're looking for. If they put up roadblocks and see you driving a dump truck, the game is up."

"He's right," said Eva. "Gottfried and Dietrich should drive the truck. You and I can go in the car. You should ride in the trunk until we're out of the country."

"Lovely," said Ingrid in a bitter tone.

"Remember," said Gottfried, "this is for Himmler."

"I know, I know," said Ingrid. "Won't make it any more comfortable. But let's get going. We leave in ten minutes."

Gottfried used the satellite link to call the bank in Zurich, then passed the phone to Ingrid. Because of the voice recognition software, she would need to give the account number and the instructions. Ingrid explained that a dump truck would arrive between 2:00 a.m. and 4:00 a.m. She gave the license number and instructed that the contents be placed in her private vault. At a Swiss bank, it went without saying that absolute discretion was required. Ten minutes later, Eva drove a black car out of the entrance to the Fox's Den, Ingrid Weiss folded into the trunk. Behind them, Gottfried drove the truck, Dietrich sitting in the passenger seat. They had, of course, changed the plates on Ingrid's car. But that precaution, and Ingrid's miserable ride in the trunk, proved unnecessary. Eva encountered no roadblocks or checkpoints between Oberammergau and Vaduz. Just inside Liechtenstein, she pulled over and let Ingrid out of the trunk. By 2:00 a.m. they had checked into the hotel in Vaduz, but even with a hot shower and a luxurious bed, Ingrid could not sleep. She waited up to hear from Gottfried and Dietrich.

Gottfried took a more northerly route than Eva—the farther apart the truck and Ingrid's car, he reckoned, the better. When he had only driven for a few minutes, they had a problem. Just after turning onto the main road, he had hit a deep pothole and apparently it had damaged the fuel tank. Gottfried noticed the fuel gauge sinking rapidly and had to make a quick decision—return to Oberammergau or press on to the next service station in Saulgrub a few kilometers away. He elected to go on to Saulgrub and by a stroke of good fortune, the service station manager was still there. Patching the leak in the tank took a half hour or so and with a fresh tank of fuel, Gottfried and Dietrich drove the rest of the way to Zurich. Dietrich made up for lost time by speeding the whole way, nearly running one car off the road. Despite another short delay in Zurich, just after 3:00 a.m., well within the window Ingrid had given the bank manager, they turned from Ferkelstrasse, into the garage entrance of the Central Bank of Zurich.

"Call Weiss and tell her we've arrived," said Gottfried.

Though stiff and a bit bruised from her ride in the trunk, Ingrid finally felt in a celebratory mood when Dietrich called. She insisted on opening a bottle of champagne, and she and Eva toasted their success, toasted Himmler, and toasted the Reich. Ingrid felt a great relief. She still had to deal with the German police, but with the gold safe, however that situation turned out—even if the police proved she had blown up her own house—it didn't matter. In prison or out, Ingrid could now begin the work her grandfather had set her to do.

XV

SEVENTEEN HOURS EARLIER

10:00 A.M.

The entire plan rested on the fact that Alex had seen a dump truck slowly descending the road from Brenner to Innsbruck as he drove up the opposite side. At that early hour of the morning, it had been one of the few other vehicles on the road and Alex, ever the admirer of German engineering, had seen the familiar medallion on the front grille and taken just enough notice that he was later able to identify it as a Mercedes 4144 K. "The cab was painted fire engine red," he told the others when they had found a picture of the right truck on Franklin's phone.

"And you're sure it was the 4144 K?" said Nemo.

"Pretty sure," said Alex.

"Pretty sure lands us all dead in a ditch and hands Ingrid Weiss a fortune in gold," said Nemo stepping toward Alex. "Fuck pretty sure. I need you to be sure."

"OK, OK," said Alex. "Let's just take it down a notch. I'm sure."

"He's not sure," said Nemo, turning away.

Patton had never seen Nemo look this worried. "Look," she said, "right now his intel is the best intel we've got. So we move forward. We proceed with caution but we move forward because it's the only thing we can do."

The seven of them sat squeezed into one room at the Hotel Wittelsbach in Oberammergau. They had used Bob's credit card to book three rooms, but only one was ready this early so they plotted in a wood-paneled bedroom with windows looking out at the Alps. Because the three soldiers were not on the radar of either the police or Ingrid Weiss and her cronies, they suddenly had three cell phones they deemed safe to use. Since their arrival in Oberammergau an hour earlier, they had put those phones to good use.

"What was the investigator's name again?" said Jean.

"Christian Ulrich," said Ted, pointedly adding, "and yes, I'm sure," when he saw Nemo turn toward him.

"Christian Ulrich," repeated Jean. *"Hallo, kann ich bitte mit Christian Ulrich sprechen?"*

"He's a lead investigator for the Bavarian State Police," said Franklin, as his thumbs flew across his phone.

"OK," said Bob, "I found a truck. Just this side of Munich, about an hour away. Four years old, forty-five thousand euros, and it even has the red cab."

"Where the hell are we going to get forty-five thousand euros?" said Alex.

"At least there's one thing that's not a problem," said Nemo. "I can take care of that."

"You have forty-five thousand euros burning a hole in your pocket?" said Bob.

"I have savings," said Nemo.

"Great," said Patton. "Bob, you and Nemo go get the truck and I'll go . . ."

"You're forgetting our agreement," said Bob.

"Fine," said Patton, "Franklin and Nemo go get the truck. Ted, you and Jean keep monitoring the news, and Bob can come with me and Alex to do reconnaissance on the Fox's Den."

"Are you sure you need me out there?" said Alex. "It's just that word, 'reconnaissance'—it sounds dangerous."

"Considering that you're the person who actually knows where the Fox's Den is," said Patton, "yes, it might be somewhat helpful to have you with us. Now come on."

"Are you sure this plan will work?" whispered Nemo to Patton as she stepped toward the door.

"Not in the slightest," said Patton. "Now go get us a truck."

An hour later, Alex had led Patton and Bob deep into the woods, skirting widely around the security fence that marked the edge of the Fox's Den property. They found a spot that gave them a view of a hundred or so meters of the fence line and of the forest behind it. There, they pulled out the high-powered binoculars Franklin had bought in Innsbruck and settled in behind some bushes to watch. Alex, whose only job had been to lead them there, quickly dropped off to sleep, leaning against a tree, and Patton and Bob passed the binoculars back and forth every thirty minutes or so, taking turns with the watch.

After an hour, Patton felt more relaxed than she had since the bullets had started flying in Alta Vista. This was military surveillance, and she understood military surveillance. Working together with another soldier, communicating only by gesture, patiently watching and listening—to Patton this was like meditation, a mental discipline that focused and relaxed her mind as the training took over and she didn't need to make decisions or plan actions or even think. She only had to watch and listen.

At ten past one, with the sun high in the sky, two people, a man and a woman, walked along the inside of the fence. Patton had the binoculars and she motioned to Bob, who could see the pair easily with the naked eye. They came to a stop about fifty meters away and spoke in hushed tones for a moment. Then, they did the last thing Bob or Patton expected from a patrol. They looped their arms around one another and began to kiss. Not perfunctory dry kisses, but deep, long, passionate kisses. Practiced kisses. The sort of kisses that seriously contemplated progressing to something much more than kissing.

"That's the patrol we've got to outfox?" Bob whispered, smiling.

Just as Patton was beginning to think Ingrid Weiss's posse might not be so hard to outsmart she heard a loud groan behind her. She looked back in horror to see Alex Lansdowne, standing up, stretching, and letting out a prodigious yawn. She glared daggers at him, but he did not seem to notice. Before she could move, Bob grabbed Alex's ankle and pulled him to the ground, covering the idiot's mouth with his hand. Patton could just hear Bob whisper, "Shut the fuck up."

When Patton looked back toward the fence, she could see that the two paramours had disentangled themselves and were looking right at her. She plastered herself to the ground and held her breath. She did not speak much German, but she could easily guess from the tone of their voices what they were saying. *Did you hear something? Maybe it was just an animal? Should we report it? Should we go looking for whatever it was?*

The man pulled a pistol out of his pocket and walked up to the fence, scanning the woods. *"Wer is da?"* he shouted. Who is there? Patton ran through scenarios in her mind. What if they came outside the fence? Could she and the other two pretend to be hikers lost in the woods? Or would it be better to make a run for it so they could live to fight another day. She and Bob might be able to do that, but Weiss's guards looked young and fit. Rotund, middle-aged Alex Lansdowne would never outrun them. She looked toward Bob, catching his eye and silently communicating, *What should we do?* Bob wore an expression that said simply, *Hope for the best.* Patton started imagining what lost hikers would say and decided she would tell the patrol they were bird-watching—hence the high-powered binoculars.

"Wer is da?" said the man again, but this time the woman tugged on his sleeve and shook her head. The man lowered his pistol, turned to the woman, and gave her another long, lingering kiss. Then they walked on, disappearing around a curve in the fence line. Five minutes later, when they had not heard another sound, Patton sat up.

"For somebody with a house full of Nazi shit, you know dick about warfare," said Bob before carefully lifting his hand from Alex's mouth.

Alex pulled himself into a sitting position and rubbed his lower back. "Did you have to yank me down like that? That fucking hurt," he said softly.

"It didn't hurt enough, if you ask me," said Bob. "You pull another stunt like that and not only will you blow the whole operation, you could get us killed. And if they don't kill you, I will."

"It's OK," said Patton. "It's OK. They didn't see us. Lesson learned on Alex's part, I'm sure."

"Damn right," said Alex.

"You hope they didn't see us," said Bob. "Who knows what they're going to report."

"They're not going to report anything," said Patton with a smile. "Because no one wants to report, 'We think there was someone out there, but we're not sure because we were busy sucking each other's faces off.'" Bob gave a light chuckle and the tension in the air seemed to waft away.

"What time did they arrive?" said Patton.

"One eleven," said Bob.

"OK, I'll mark it," said Patton, taking out a notebook and pencil. She wrote: *Patrol A: 1:11 p.m.* and then slipped the notebook back in her pocket. This time Alex stayed awake, alert, and hidden as they all lapsed back into quiet, waiting for the next patrol.

To some, it would have seemed a tedious afternoon, sitting on hard ground and watching as nothing happened, the only sounds the breeze in the trees and an occasional burst of birdsong. But Patton loved it. She even came to feel companionable toward Bob as they passed the binoculars back and forth. She did not blame him for wanting to kill her, and as far as she could tell, he was a good soldier. He had patience, a much-underrated quality in the military, thought Patton. At 3:12 p.m. the same two people appeared again, walking ten meters or so on the other side of the fence line. They held hands, but this time they did not stop for a snog. More important, they did not stop to look for the source of the mysterious noise they had heard the last time. Patton recorded the time in her notebook, and they waited for a third data point. At four o'clock, Alex asked if there was anything to eat. Bob hissed at him to be quiet and Patton felt a sense of satisfaction that she and the man who had come to kill her were in perfect sync about how to operate. At seven minutes past five, the patrol returned. The man drank something from a can, though whether it was soda or beer the observers couldn't tell.

"Every two hours like clockwork," whispered Patton when the patrol had passed. "That gives us plenty of time. Alex, you stay on watch and text us if you see anything."

"And don't make any fucking noise," said Bob.

Patton grabbed the small day pack that held her equipment, nodded to Bob, and they set off toward the fence, treading on the softest, quietest parts of the forest floor.

With wire cutters purchased in Innsbruck, they easily cut a row of links on the fence and pulled back a flap big enough to wriggle through. They chose a spot hidden by a clump of young trees and bent the fence back into place before heading into the Fox's Den property, walking side by side, alert to any sounds other than their own footsteps and breathing. Bob kept his gun drawn, but now he did not train it on Patton.

"It will be on the highest spot on the property, above the tree line," whispered Patton, nodding to the right where the land sloped up toward the edge of the forest.

"I don't like the idea of going out in the open," said Bob.

"You won't," said Patton. "You'll stay in the edge of the forest and cover me. It's not like I can run away."

"I'm not worried about—"

"Stop," said Patton, grabbing Bob by the arm. This time she did not whisper but spoke in a sharp tone that Bob could not ignore. He stopped and looked at her, nonplussed.

"I thought you wanted to stay quiet," he whispered.

"I do," said Patton in a nearly inaudible voice. "But look." She nodded toward a few twigs lying on the ground just in front of Bob.

"What?" said Bob. "What are you talking about? It's just . . . holy shit."

"You see it?"

"Is that?"

"That is an S-mine. Himmler must have mined his perimeter."

"Do you think . . ." said Bob.

"Do I think it's still live? I certainly don't want to be the one to find out. You know as well as I do that there are still live explosives from World War II all over Europe."

Patton still had her hand on Bob's arm, and she could feel him trembling. She guided him to the left, steering far clear of the tiny metal rod with the three wires protruding from the top.

They slowed their pace now, examining the ground in front of them before each step. In another hundred meters they reached the edge of the forest and Patton saw what they had come for at the top of a slight rise, tucked among a group of boulders. They sat down in the cover of the forest as Patton double-checked her equipment.

"I never would have seen that mine," said Bob, turning to look at Patton for the first time since they avoided the explosive. He still sounded shaken as he added, "You saved my life."

"Maybe," said Patton. "Probably the thing doesn't even work any-more."

"Yes, but one more step and I could have blown sky-high."

"Look, you're a soldier. You know that saving lives during battle is just doing your job. So let's forget about it and get on with the job, OK. Besides, there are a thousand things that could go wrong in the next few hours and we just avoided number three. Now keep an eye out for that patrol."

Patton was just about to dash across the fifty meters or so of rocky open space between her and the top of the hill, when she spotted some-thing that made her sigh, "Oh crap," and sink back down next to Bob.

"What's wrong," said Bob.

"Looks like that paranoid bitch has a surveillance camera up there," said Patton. She pulled out the binoculars to confirm what she already knew. Fifty meters away stood the very thing they had come to find, a small satellite dish that provided Ingrid Weiss with her sole method of communicating with the outside world from her underground bunker where no cell signal would reach. The dish was mounted on a pole shoved into the rocky soil, and just below it, on the same pole, was a video camera.

"Maybe you can get around behind it," said Bob. Before he had finished his sentence, Patton watched as the camera pivoted clockwise a quarter turn.

"If it turns like that, I can't get behind it," said Patton with a smile.

"But I might be able to stay ahead of it. Set a timer on my mark." She watched through the binoculars until the camera pivoted again and said, "Mark." On the next pivot she said, "Mark" again, and so on until the camera had made two full revolutions.

"Thirty seconds between each mark," said Bob.

"If it's a wide angle," said Patton, "there's only one position where it won't see me coming."

"Think you can get up that hill carrying a pack of equipment in under thirty seconds?" said Bob.

"We're about to find out," said Patton. She slung the pack over her shoulder, took several deep breaths, and waited. Ninety seconds later, the camera moved to the position pointing directly away from her and Patton ran. The loose stones slipped under her feet and she immediately realized she should have stretched before she did this. She had been sitting still most of the day and her muscles were tight. She tried to keep a count going in her head and when she reached fifteen, she was barely halfway there. The hill seemed twice as steep as it had from below. She gasped for breath in the thin mountain air and did her best to put on a burst of speed, thinking she just might make it when her foot slipped again and she came down hard among the stones. The fall knocked the breath out of her, but there was no time to worry about that. She had maybe eight seconds left and if there was one thing basic training had taught her it was how to crawl across the ground. She shimmied toward the pole, covering the last few feet almost like a snake and pulling herself into the shadow of the satellite dish just as she heard the camera start to move. She pivoted around, staying behind the camera as it turned, then did her best to breathe. After two minutes of scooting around the pole every time the camera moved, she finally felt able to function. She gave Bob a thumbs-up and got to work.

Luckily, the motor on the camera made a slight noise a second or so before each turn, so Patton was able to anticipate those movements and match them to her own. Tapping into a communications system while having to move every thirty seconds was not exactly easy, but she finished the job, took a breath, and got ready to sprint down the hill.

When the camera was pointed away from the clump of trees where she knew Bob was hiding, she took off. She had not realized how dizzy moving around behind the camera had made her feel until she started running. Now, with every step she took the view in front of her seemed to shift. The trees kept moving to the left it seemed, but when she adjusted her direction, they were back to her right. Finally, Patton closed her eyes and just ran with the slope of the hill. After a count of fifteen, she felt her foot catch on something and opened her eyes just in time to watch the forest floor rushing up to meet her. She put her right hand out just in time to scrape a layer of skin off the heel of her palm and do nothing to lessen the impact of the hard ground on her ribcage a split second later. Patton knew that a battle-hardened soldier shouldn't mind a little fall like this, but damn, it hurt. She wanted nothing more than to scream in pain, but before she could take a breath, Bob was at her side, pressing his hand over her mouth.

Patton took a few deep breaths through her nose and steadied herself, allowing a small adrenaline surge to deaden the feeling in her body from sharp pain to dull ache. In those seconds she also saw that she had made it far enough down the hill to be below the angle of the camera. She nodded to Bob and he lifted his hand.

"Sorry about that," he said. "I couldn't let you scream. Just in case someone is out and about."

"Thanks," said Patton, pulling herself up into a sitting position. "Not sure I could have stopped myself without you."

"That was quite the balletic maneuver," said Bob, unsuccessfully trying to stifle a laugh.

"Very fucking funny," said Patton. "I'll be lucky if I didn't break a rib."

"So do we have ears?" said Bob.

"If I did my job right," said Patton, "and I assure you I did, we should be able to hear every phone call and read every text and email. Incoming and outgoing."

"Good," said Bob. "Now let's get the hell out of here before Alex does something stupid."

Ten minutes later, Patton and Bob had rejoined Alex on the other side of the fence, having used a pair of pliers to close up the cuts in the fence links. A careful patrol would notice the fence had been cut; they had no concern that the patrol they witnessed would notice anything. The entire excursion onto the Fox's Den property had taken less than thirty minutes. By the time Dietrich and Eva passed by on the seven o'clock patrol, Alex, Bob, and Patton were back at the hotel.

8:00 P.M.

"Shit," said Patton.

"What is it?" said Franklin.

"Dammit," said Patton. "I don't understand what's wrong."

"What's wrong?" said Nemo, who had just stepped into the room.

"I just said I don't know," said Patton. She said at the desk in the corner of the room, wearing a pair of headphones and poking away at a laptop. "It's not working," she said.

"What do you mean it's not working?" said Nemo.

"What do you think I mean?" said Patton, yanking off the headphones and throwing them down on the desk. "The feed that I smashed my damn rib cage to get is not working."

"Won't that . . ." began Jean.

"It'll fuck up the whole plan," said Patton. "Without that feed there is no plan."

"Can you fix it?" said Nemo. "I mean, without going back."

"I don't know," said Patton. "It was working fine an hour ago, but now . . ."

"Have you tried turning it off and back on again?" said Alex. "That usually works for me."

"I really don't think . . ." said Patton.

"Just try it," said Franklin.

So Patton tried it, powering down the laptop and booting it back up. Two minutes later, with the headphones back on, she smiled. "It's working," she said.

"Told you," said Alex.

"OK, fine," said Nemo. "You've made a small contribution to the effort. Your technical expertise is noted."

"Hey, without me you wouldn't even know where Weiss is hiding," said Alex.

The room fell silent and Nemo pulled up a chair next to Patton and stared at the computer screen. When she took the headphones off a minute later he whispered, "So you didn't even try rebooting. You're some technical genius." He smiled and squeezed Patton's arm, then said, in a loud voice, "Anything worth listening to?"

"No calls yet," said Patton. "We expected that. But I can also monitor the websites they look at, and they're following the news on *Süddeutsche Zeitung*. It's the website for the main Munich newspaper."

"Good," said Nemo. "It'll be dark soon. Then we'll make the call."

They had booked the two additional rooms in order to take turns grabbing a bit of sleep, but now they all sat in the suite they had designated as "headquarters." The remains of a tray of sandwiches sat on the coffee table, Ted and Franklin sprawled on the couch. Bob and Jean hunched over a desk, working on Jean's script in German. Alex ate. Nemo paced.

"I'm just curious," said Franklin. "I mean, as long as we have a little time to kill here, how can you just stroll into a truck dealership and give them an account number and the next thing you know you're driving away in a Mercedes dump truck? No offense, but you don't seem like the type to have a Swiss bank account."

"The whole point of having a Swiss bank account," said Nemo, "is not seeming like the type who would have one."

"He's not going to tell you anything," said Ted. "You might as well have another sandwich."

"Did you secure the load?" said Patton, taking off her headphones.

"Found the perfect thing," said Nemo.

"If we're going to start in an hour, we should get into position," said Patton. "Bob and I scouted out a spot for the sniper, so we'll go there."

"Franklin's a better shot than I am," said Bob. "He should go with you. I know German so I'll go with Alex to the service station."

"I thought you wanted to guard me at all times," said Patton.

"I trust you," said Bob. "Besides, what the hell does Alex know about truck repair?"

"I've restored six Panzer tanks not to mention motorcycles, trucks, armored vehicles—"

"OK," said Bob, "we get the point. Let's go before the damn place closes. What time will Jean make the call?"

"Nine thirty," said Patton. "They should leave no more than an hour later. Nemo, are you good to drive the truck alone?"

"Before I met you I did everything alone," said Nemo. "I think I can handle driving a truck for a few hours."

9:00 P.M.

Patton and Franklin had parked the rental van on the outskirts of Oberammergau just past where the gravel track that led into the forest toward the Fox's Den met the main road out of town to the north. In the deepening dusk, she led him up to the crest of a hill that provided both cover, in the form of a cluster of trees, and a view of the spot where any vehicle turning onto the road would pass through a pool of light cast by a street lamp.

"You'll have a clear shot from here," said Patton, "but you'll only get one shot."

"Not a problem," said Franklin.

"It has to be low."

"Trust me," said Franklin.

Bob and Alex arrived at the service station five miles to the north just as the manager was about to flip the sign to *Closed*.

"You can have a fill-up," he said in German, "but if you need anything else it will have to wait until morning."

"You speak English?" said Alex.

"English? Yes," said the man. "With all the tourists here, of course I speak English."

"How would you like to make ten thousand euros in the next two hours?" said Bob.

"Ten thousand euros?" said the man, his eyes lighting up as Bob pulled out a stack of cash from the black bag he carried. He had no idea why Nemo carried around that kind of cash, but it certainly had the desired effect on the manager.

"What do you want for your ten thousand euros?" said the man.

"We want to rent your service station for a couple of hours and buy one large tank of diesel."

"And borrow a couple of pairs of coveralls if you have them," added Alex.

"That's all?" said the man.

"That's all," said Bob.

"You can stay here and keep an eye on us," said Alex. "Just let us take care of any customers."

"There won't be any customers," said the man. "Everyone in Saulgrub knows I close at nine and the tourists don't drive after dark—not on these roads."

Ten minutes later, with the manager happily counting his windfall in his office, Bob and Alex pulled oil-stained coveralls over their clothes.

"Won't they be expecting us to speak German?" said Alex.

"I know enough," said Bob. "I thought with that collection of yours, you'd know German, too."

"I mostly know military terms," said Alex, as they settled onto a bench outside the garage door and watched the road.

For the next hour Alex talked about his collection and Bob listened, never quite sure whether to be impressed or horrified.

9:30 P.M.

"The pacing is getting on my nerves," said Jean, but her words had no effect on Nemo. He had not felt like this for a long time. Usually, on the verge of a job, he entered a state of serene calm, his hyper-focus on the work at hand pushing everything else out of his mind. Nemo was a relaxed killer. But tonight's exercise was not a normal job. In a normal job the only thing at risk was Nemo's own life, something on which he had never placed a particularly high value. In a normal job, he had no notion of the ultimate goal of those who pulled the strings. "Never know the client's endgame" had been one of his rules, after all. But tonight was different. Tonight, he had an intimate understanding of the stakes, of what might be accomplished in the case of success and what would certainly be lost in the case of failure. Yet it wasn't just the fear of the evil that Ingrid Weiss could do with $700 million or the knowledge of the good someone like Patton could do with that same resource. Nemo had, in the past few days, found himself in the uncomfortable position of having friends. Patton especially, but even Jean and Alex—hell, even those American soldiers. He had never worked with anyone else, and he had felt a fondness growing within himself as they had laid their plans. But friends could be taken away, friends could die, you could lose friends like he had lost Jack. So a knot in the pit of his stomach and a darkness settling into the back of his mind, Nemo paced. And even though he thought of Jean as a friend, and even though his pacing drove her crazy, he couldn't stop.

"It's time," said Ted. "Are you sure you're good to make the call?"

"I'm good," said Jean. "Bob and I worked out the script."

"Just make the damn call," snapped Nemo.

"OK, OK, don't get your panties in a wad," said Jean. "I'll make the call."

It took her nearly ten minutes to finally get put through personally to Christian Ulrich and then she was glad, despite her knowledge of German, that they had written out a script. She hadn't felt the least bit nervous as her call was handed around to various underlings at the Bavarian State Police, but as soon as she heard Christian Ulrich's personal cell phone ringing, her mouth went dry and her mind went blank. All at once, her insides realized this was no longer just a casual investigation into some missing library books. She remembered what Nemo had said back in Brenner—this was the final battle of World War II. For the first time, she felt like one of the soldiers.

"Mr. Ulrich, my name is Ingrid Weiss. I understand that you'd like to talk to me."

"Frau Weiss," said the surprised voice on the end of the line. Jean felt sure she heard the clatter of a fork being dropped onto a plate. She had interrupted Ulrich's dinner. "How surprising to hear from you."

"I will tell you everything you want to know," said Jean, sticking to the script, "but first I need you to do something for me."

"What could I do for you?" said Ulrich.

"If you do this, then tomorrow morning I will ring you and give you my location. You can send officers to bring me and my associates into protective custody and we will answer all your questions."

Ulrich responded with a rush of German, the words coming far too fast for Jean to translate. This was where he was supposed to say, slowly and calmly, "Yes, of course, I will do whatever you like." But he had spoken much longer than that sentence required and Jean had no idea what he had said. Did he already know where Weiss was? Had he detected an American accent behind her stilted German? Jean froze. The script in front of her became a blur and she felt the silence on the line stretching out far too long for comfort.

Her face must have telegraphed her panic because Nemo hissed at her, "Say something."

Finally Jean managed to stutter, in German, "I did not hear."

Ulrich seemed unfazed, speaking much more slowly this time. "I only said that I think we could keep you much safer than you are now, given the circumstances."

Jean breathed an inward sigh of relief. The conversation was back on track. She noticed that Ulrich did not define the "circumstances." She suspected he knew much more about both of the explosions than he had said in his press conference, and that he was withholding information in order to lure Weiss from hiding. Of course telling the press a blatant lie was a little different from not telling the whole truth, but she suspected Ulrich would cooperate.

"I need you to issue a statement as soon as we conclude this call. Say that the Bavarian State Police have located Ingrid Weiss near Oberammergau and that they will be taking her into protective custody this evening. And I need that statement to appear on the website of *Süddeutsche Zeitung* within the hour."

"What makes you think I can guarantee that?" said Ulrich.

"I'm sure you have influence. I look forward to meeting you tomorrow," said Jean and hung up.

Christian did have influence. He could easily get a statement on the *Süddeutsche Zeitung* website. But then what? Should he send a team to Oberammergau? Certainly Weiss wouldn't give away her position—that must be a ruse, an attempt to put him off the trail. Christian didn't know Weiss's motives, and he certainly didn't plan to humor her for long, but he would play along for now. If he didn't have Weiss in custody by midday tomorrow, he would name her as the chief suspect in both bombings and have every police officer in Europe searching for her. Ten minutes later, a breaking news alert popped up on the *Süddeutsche Zeitung* website.

10:15 P.M.

Patton had explained to Nemo how to listen in on Ingrid Weiss's phone conversations, so he knew exactly what to do when the laptop she had left on the desk began ringing. He clicked on "Listen," and he and Ted stood still and silent. Jean had a pad of paper perched on her lap, ready to take notes and translate as needed. The laptop would also record the conversation. This call was the pinch point of the entire operation. If Weiss did not make the move they expected in the way that they expected, all was lost. But Nemo, who had stopped pacing, knew a thing or two about the behavior of intelligent criminals and he also knew a thing or two about Swiss banking.

The call began with a recorded woman's voice speaking German: "Welcome to the Central Bank of Zurich. Please state your name and account number."

Then came the voice of the woman who had been trying to kill them: "This is Ingrid Weiss, account number 4572-8965-9086." Jean's pen moved rapidly, recording the numbers.

The line clicked a few times and then a man's voice came on. "Frau Weiss, how nice to hear from you. How may I serve you this evening?"

"I wish to deposit some items in my private vault," said Ingrid. "The items will be delivered between two and four a.m. by my associates in a truck with the Austrian registration plate I–27174T. Please transfer the entire contents of the cargo area to my vault A268. The code word is Columbia."

"Thank you very much Frau Weiss. We will be happy to take care of that for you. Can you please repeat the account number one more time for our voice recognition software?"

"Yes, it's 4572-8965-9086."

"Thank you."

The red light on the laptop switched off as the line went dead.

"Perfect," said Jean, looking up from her notes.

"Was it what we wanted?" said Nemo, who did not understand German.

"Exactly what we wanted," said Ted with a smile.

Nemo loved that Swiss banks made themselves available twenty-four hours a day for their best customers. This was not the first time that had come in handy. The manager of the Central Bank of Zurich was happy to establish an account for Oliver Moores, as Nemo identified himself. He had all the necessary identification on file at his current bank, and by transferring €1 million to his new account, he qualified for a reduced price on the rental of a large personal vault. Within fifteen minutes, the newest customer of the Central Bank of Zurich had arranged to transfer a truckload of unidentified cargo, to arrive between 3:00 and 5:00 a.m. into that vault. "The truck has a German registration," said Nemo, "license number M–KL 7214."

"Thank you for your patronage," said the manager before ringing off.

"Why the later time?" said Ted. "Weiss said between two and four."

"It's going to look suspicious enough having two identical trucks making deliveries in the same night. Giving them the exact same times would just raise more red flags. I think we can make sure that their deposit doesn't happen before three."

Five minutes later, Jean and Ted had driven Alex's rental car past the gravel track that led to the Fox's Den and pulled over to the side of the road. Nemo was driving north toward Saulgrub in the truck they had bought in Munich, the cargo rattling in the back.

10:30 P.M.

"Jean says Weiss made the call," said Patton, putting down Franklin's phone. "They could come out any minute."

Franklin lay prone on the ground, the Karabiner 98K German infantry rifle he had borrowed from Alex propped on a rock. He had taken a few test shots in the woods earlier, to be sure the aim was true and to practice loading the cartridges. The rifle didn't have a stripper clip, so he had to load cartridges one at a time. This didn't particularly worry him—he would only need one shot. He'd never handled a rifle of this vintage, but it took him only a couple of shots to get the feel of it.

Patton watched the gravel road with a pair of night-vision binoculars, and as expected, five minutes later, she saw the shape of the truck moving between the trees. "She has her lights off," said Patton, "but she'll have to flick them on when they get to the main road." The truck slowed to turn onto the paved road and Patton noticed a second vehicle, a black sedan, also with its lights off, in front of it. Just then, the phone vibrated in the grass next to her.

"Patton, this is Jean, Ted and I are in place."

"Good," whispered Patton. "There's a black sedan turning your way."

"We'll follow," said Jean.

The sedan flicked on its lights as it turned right down the road toward Austria while the truck turned left and slowly started north. It couldn't have been moving more than about ten miles an hour when it passed under the streetlight and Franklin took his shot. Just as Patton flinched from the percussion of the gunshot echoing off the mountains, she saw the truck make a sudden lurch down and then back up. Through the binoculars she saw what she had not noticed before—a large pothole in the northbound lane of the road. Simultaneous with the realization came a whisper from Franklin.

"Missed." It wasn't an expression of anger or exasperation, merely a calm statement of fact. The truck began accelerating and the next few seconds seem to move in slow motion. Patton never took her eyes from the truck, but she heard Franklin throwing back the bolt, loading a second cartridge, and snapping the bolt in place. He moved so fast it was a single continuous sound, followed without pause by his second shot. When the echo of that shot had faded away, neither of them said anything for several seconds. The truck disappeared around a curve.

"That was some serious Lee Harvey Oswald reloading you did there," said Patton. "Do you think you got it?"

"I got it," said Franklin.

"How can you be sure?" said Patton.

"I'm a sniper," said Franklin. "I know."

Patton had encountered this insistence on knowing exactly where the shot had gone in other snipers. She had also never known a properly trained sniper to be wrong. If Franklin said he made his shot, she believed him.

"And by the way," said Franklin, as he stood up. "Alex was right. That truck was a 4144 K."

10:45 P.M.

When Patton and Franklin passed the service station in Saulgrub, Weiss's truck had just pulled in. Nemo, she knew, had parked their truck around the corner so he could leave without being seen. Patton smiled as she saw Bob and Alex sitting on the bench out front in greasy coveralls.

Franklin drove, not because he didn't trust Patton, but because her job was surveillance and intelligence and she couldn't do much of either behind the wheel. They had followed a trail of diesel fuel on the road all the way from Oberammergau; it certainly made things easier that the truck had made it to Saulgrub without completely running out of fuel. Franklin pulled the car into Römerweg, a residential street a short way down the main road from the entrance to the service station. They couldn't quite see the station from where they parked, but that meant no one at the station could see them waiting.

"Looks like you've got a fuel leak," said Bob striding up to the truck where Gottfried and Dietrich sat in the cab.

"We hit a pothole south of Oberammergau," said Gottfried. Bob did not know the German word for "pothole" but he plowed on.

"Probably threw up a rock and punctured the tank. I can fix that for you if you like."

"Thanks," said Gottfried. "We can pay cash."

"That's good," replied Bob. "Otto and I will fix your tank." He nodded at Alex, who hopped up and began an inspection of the truck.

Alex had already removed the license plates from Nemo's truck. All he needed to do was switch them for the plates on Wiess's truck without being seen from the cab. It had seemed simple enough when they talked about it in a cozy hotel room. Now, with the cool night air making his fingers numb, he lay on the ground in front of the cab trying to twist off a rusted nut that held the license plate in place. The damn thing wouldn't budge.

"Is the store open?" said Gottfried to Bob, who had been squatting by the fuel tank examining the leak. The last of the diesel fuel was still dripping out onto the forecourt and he figured he'd better let that stop before he started patching. Besides, there was no hurry. He was just about to stand when he saw Alex's head peek around the front right tire.

"Wrench," hissed Alex. "I need a wrench."

Bob had taken everything he needed to patch the tank from a rack in the garage. He assumed there would be a wrench in there someplace, but how could he disappear into the building to retrieve it and keep these two Germans in the cab at the same time?

"I don't have one," he whispered to Alex. Then, standing, he told Gottfried, "Sorry. The store's closed."

"I'm sure you could get us a bottle of soda," said Gottfried. "Maybe some pretzels?" Bob did not quite understand everything Gottfried had said, but it made no difference. The beefy German was now opening the door to the cab and climbing down. "I'll be right back," he said to his companion. Now Bob had to somehow keep this guy from walking around to the front of the truck and seeing what Alex was up to. That damn collector better hurry up, he thought.

Alex heard the door to the truck open and saw Gottfried's feet as the German stepped onto the forecourt. Alex's thumb and finger were bleeding where they had slipped against the stubborn nut. What kind of idiot was he not to bring a wrench? But the nuts on Nemo's truck had come off like they'd been sprayed with WD-40 on a daily basis, so Alex just hadn't thought about it. Now not thinking was about to get him into big trouble. He heard Bob babbling in German and then saw feet moving toward the front of the truck. Who cared about his bleeding fingers, he thought, this was war. He gripped as hard as he could and turned, feeling the sharp edges of the nut digging deep into his flesh, but also feeling it turning. He twisted the nut off, slipped off the plate, and held it behind his back with his bloody hand just as Gottfried appeared around the front of the truck.

"What are you doing?" said Gottfried when he saw Alex kneeling in front of the truck.

Alex had no idea what the man had said, so responded with the one German phrase Bob had taught him in case of an emergency. "Checking for damage," he said. Gottfried stood looking at Alex for several seconds as Alex tried to decide whether to stand up. At the moment, he was partially shielding the spot where the license plate ought to be and he was afraid if he moved, the driver would be sure to see that the plate was missing. Or worse, he might see the plate Alex had taken off Nemo's truck lying on the pavement just under the truck's bumper. So he knelt there, smiling like a schoolboy, hoping the German didn't notice anything amiss.

After an agonizing few seconds, the German strode past him, trailing Bob in his wake and saying words Alex did not understand.

"You must have some Coca-Cola in there," said Gottfried.

Bob followed Gottfried into the store, hoping that the other German would stay where he was. He managed to distract Gottfried with the search for Coke long enough for Alex to get Nemo's license plate onto the front of the truck. When they came back out, Alex was smiling and wiping his hands on his coveralls. Alex hoped the German didn't notice the streaks of blood this left behind.

"Aren't you supposed to be fixing my truck?" said the German.

"*Ja, ja,*" said Alex, having no idea to what he was responding and hoping that "yes" was the correct answer.

After that things went more smoothly. The driver climbed back into the cab and passed a Coke to the other German. Alex went to the garage to find a wrench with which to remove the rear license plate, and Bob got to work on repairing the bullet hole in the fuel tank. Once Alex found a wrench he thought would work he slipped Nemo's rear plate into his coveralls and rejoined Bob at the fuel tank. He wasn't sure what the Germans could see in their rearview mirrors, so he shimmied underneath the truck to reach the spot where the rear plate was mounted. The wrench made the job considerably easier and he had just swapped out the plates and was about to put the nuts back on when he heard the passenger side door open and saw the feet of the second German heading toward the back of the truck.

Alex grabbed the license plate he had just removed off the pavement, and pulled himself back under the truck, trying to squeeze his body behind the rear wheels on the passenger side. The German crossed behind the truck and shouted a question at Bob. For several seconds he stood where he might easily have spotted Alex or noticed that the wrong license plate was on the back of the truck and its nuts were missing. Alex held his breath.

Bob answered the German but the man didn't move for a moment. He asked something else and seemed to be pointing to the back of the truck. Alex was on the verge of feeling both foolish and terrified—on the verge of doubting that there was $700 million worth of gold in this truck, but ready to believe that this German had memorized his license number and would start shooting under the truck at any moment. Then the feet turned, walked past the back of the truck, and disappeared into the store. Thirty seconds later, Alex had screwed the nuts back on and crawled under the truck reemerging where Bob was working.

"What the hell did that one want?" he whispered.

"Just the bathroom," said Bob. "Nothing to worry about."

Alex, who felt like he had been facing imminent death and the failure of the operation seconds earlier, seriously considered slapping Bob across the face for saying there was nothing to worry about, but he knew better than to pick a fight with a former soldier, so he stood up, brushed himself off, and headed back to the garage. When he was sure no one was watching, he walked around the back and down the side street to Nemo's truck. In five minutes, he had attached Weiss's license plates and Nemo was on his way.

11:00 P.M.

Jean and Ted had followed the black car out of Oberammergau and then west through a narrow Alpine valley eventually crossing over into Austria and hugging the shores of Lake Plansee. Had the moon been full or had they been driving by day, it would have been a spectacular journey.

"Are you really going to kill Patton?" said Jean. She couldn't believe her life had taken such a severe turn that this question was even possible, but she had grown fond of Patton and of fighting for justice, and if the soldiers intended to murder Patton, she would do her best to stop them. Not that she could imagine any way to stop them, but then again, she couldn't imagine being party to the destruction of a medieval fresco, or barely escaping her own murder twice in as many days, or stealing a truckload of Nazi gold.

"It's up to Bob, I suppose," said Ted. "He's the ranking officer. But, honestly, I've kind of lost my taste for it. I mean, if we really want revenge, it seems like revenge against Patton for accidentally killing nine guys pales in comparison with revenge against Heinrich Himmler for murdering six million Jews."

"Did you lose anybody in your family?" said Jean.

"I don't know," said Ted. "Isn't that awful? I don't even know. My grandfather fought in the Pacific, but never talked about it. Our family excelled at not talking about things. And we weren't exactly observant Jews, either. I never went to Hebrew school and we only went to temple on high holy days. By the time I was a teenager, we didn't even do that. I found out about the Holocaust from a television documentary."

"Jesus, that must have been . . . I don't know, a blow."

"I was eight and I couldn't sleep so I went downstairs and turned on the TV and just held my breath, it seemed like. I never did sleep that night—I was too afraid of nightmares, not that they could have been any worse than the reality I had seen on TV. I just lay in bed and cried the rest of the night. When I asked my parents about the Holocaust the next morning they said it was an awful thing and we shouldn't talk about it. It was a long time before I discovered that wasn't the attitude of every Jew."

"My grandparents died in Dachau," said Jean. "We talked about it some, but not a lot."

"I'm sorry," said Ted. "I mean, sorry that your grandparents died in a camp, not that you talked about it."

"I don't know which would be worse," said Jean. "Being constantly reminded of that horror or pretending it never happened."

"Trust me," said Ted, "denial was worse."

"They're turning onto the highway," said Jean. "Looks like they're heading north."

11:30 P.M.

Franklin and Patton heard Ingrid's truck start up and pull back into the road. Their job was simple—slow down the truck as much as possible. Nemo had a thirty-minute head start and the cargo in his truck shouldn't take much longer than that to unload. Still, they wanted to avoid any awkward meetings of the two vehicles, and of course the Germans needed to arrive after 3:00 a.m. The first forty miles of the drive to Zurich was on a two-lane highway and Franklin planned to drive at a snail's pace in front of the truck, speeding up and weaving erratically when the road straightened and provided a possible passing zone. By the time they were a mile outside of Saulgrub the truck had caught up and within another mile the driver had begun to show his impatience, flashing his high beams and blaring his horn as Franklin crept along at twenty-five miles an hour. If all went well, by the time they reached the four-lane highway, they would have bought Nemo another twenty or thirty minutes and insured that Weiss's truck did not arrive at the bank too soon.

All did not go well.

At the first stretch of straight road, just a few miles into the drive, the truck engine roared behind them and, even though Franklin was driving the van astride the center line, the Mercedes came bearing down on them, one wheel throwing up dirt and gravel from the road-side. It happened too quickly for Franklin to react, and besides, he didn't want to cause an accident. They wanted this truck to get to Zurich, not to turn over in a ditch and dump its load where the next passing police officer would see it. So Franklin swerved back into his lane, and watched as the taillights of the truck faded into the darkness ahead of them.

"Should I try to pass them and get back in front?" said Franklin.

"It would look pretty suspicious," said Patton. "The whole idea is they need to not know anything funny is going on. I'll call Nemo and warn him and we'll just hope he got enough of a head start."

"Tell him this guy drives like a maniac," said Franklin, feeling a drop of sweat slip down his forehead. "Nemo better speed."

12:45 A.M.

Bob and Alex had been a quarter mile behind the truck when it passed Franklin and Patton. They had passed the van and fallen in behind the truck but, like Patton, had concluded that any attempt to pass the speeding truck and then slow down would arouse suspicion. So they followed at a respectful distance.

"I wonder if we should warn Nemo?" said Alex.

"Patton probably already did," said Bob, "but why don't you try just in case."

"Patton told me," said Nemo when Alex called. "I'm driving this damn thing as fast as I can."

"He's still got thirty minutes on them," said Alex after hanging up. "That should be enough, right?"

"Maybe," said Bob. "But Weiss's goons better not get there before three." Neither of the men said anything else until they reached the four-lane highway and saw a sign for Zurich.

"So how did you start collecting all this Nazi stuff?" said Bob.

"I grew up in London," said Alex, "and they were building a new gymnasium at my school when they dug up an unexploded German bomb from World War II. It had been right underneath our playground. I found that fascinating, that something like that could still exist. As a teenager I started going to antiques markets like Portobello Road and Camden Passage and buying anything I could find from the war. I noticed pretty quickly that there were a lot fewer German artifacts for sale than British ones, so I decided to collect those. I liked the challenge. It started out with things like uniform buttons and medals and eventually led to . . . everything."

"You ever serve in the military?" said Bob.

"No," said Alex.

"I did nineteen years," said Bob. "I loved most of it, made closer friends than I ever would have doing anything else. Brothers. And sisters, too. But I never understood why anyone would want to collect all those reminders of death and violence. Especially from the enemy. Maybe our worst enemy ever."

"It's hard to explain," said Alex. "It does fascinate me—the way the minutiae of history can be revealed through ordinary objects. But when I look back on it, what really motivated me was trying to win the game.

Trying to have a bigger collection than the other guys. It's almost a co-incidence I ended up collecting Nazi memorabilia. I think I would have had the same attitude whatever I collected."

"I can't imagine living with all that stuff," said Bob. "It would . . . weigh on me, I think."

"It does," said Alex. "But then again, it got me involved in all this. It helped Patton and Nemo find the gold. Still, when this is over . . ."

"Gonna sell it all?"

"I don't know," said Alex. "Being away from it has been . . . liberating. It might be nice to escape it once and for all."

"I can understand wanting to escape something that's taken over your life," said Bob.

"You mean something like wanting to kill the person who killed your friends?"

"Yeah."

"So what are you going to do?"

"I don't know," said Bob, shaking his head. "I don't know."

1:45 A.M.

Jean flicked off the headlights and eased to the side of the road a hundred meters or so behind where the black sedan had pulled over. Few cars passed in either direction, and when the road looked empty, the driver got out of the car and opened the trunk.

"What is he getting out of there?" said Jean.

"I think it's a she," said Ted. "And it looks like . . ."

"That's another person," said Jean.

"Another woman from the looks of it. I wonder why she was riding in the trunk?"

"Maybe because she's wanted by the police," said Jean.

"You think . . ."

"I think that's Ingrid Weiss," said Jean. "It's hard to tell from this distance and with so little light, but if I had to guess."

The two women got back into the black sedan and pulled back

onto the road. Twenty minutes later, Jean and Ted watched from across the street as they left their car with a valet and entered a resort hotel on the outskirts of Vaduz, Liechtenstein. This time Jean got a good look.

"That's Weiss," she said. "And the other woman was in that basement when they tied me up."

2:00 A.M.

Bob and Alex continued following the truck to Zurich while Patton and Franklin considered whether to divert toward Vaduz. When they received the call from Jean, they had just rounded the end of Lake Constance near Bregenz. Vaduz was barely a half hour away. Even though they had no idea if Nemo would be done at the bank before the Germans showed up, their part in the operation had officially ended. The prospect of checking into a luxury hotel in Vaduz was appealing, but Patton kept imagining the scene when Ingrid Weiss's truck showed up while Nemo's was still being unloaded. Even if the bank held the one truck outside while the other was being unloaded, Nemo would have to drive by the Germans in an identical truck, and that was sure to arouse suspicion. If the Germans started asking the bank manager questions, who knows what might happen, even given the famous discretion of Swiss bankers. She felt sure that, if the two trucks met, there would be trouble. Plus, if Weiss's truck kept on driving as fast as it had been when it passed them, it would certainly make it to the bank before 3:00 a.m. Even if Nemo managed to get out before that, the truck arriving before the appointed time could lead to awkward questions.

"I think we should follow them to Zurich," she said. "In case we can come up with any way to slow them down."

"If that's what you think, that's what we'll do," said Franklin. They drove on in silence for a few minutes, keeping Alex's car and the truck in sight. Then Patton took a deep breath and began to say what she had wanted to say for years.

"I really am sorry about what happened in Kandahar. And even though I've never attempted suicide, Nemo was right about the nightmares and the guilt and the . . ."

"PTSD," said Franklin.

"Oh, yeah," said Patton.

"Me, too," said Franklin.

"Sorry."

"Look, about Kandahar," said Franklin. "I know you didn't mean to do anything wrong. Hell, maybe it wasn't even your fault. It's just that we lost . . ."

"Family," said Patton.

"Yeah," said Franklin.

"I lost family that day, too."

"And then we had all these years since when we relived it in nightmares and flashbacks and failed therapy. So I guess we thought by killing you we might finally leave Kandahar behind."

"I get that," said Patton.

"I don't know about Bob and Ted, but for me . . . well, now that I've met you, now that I know you, that seems a pretty stupid solution to the problem. I'm not saying I'm going to stop the others from doing what they want to do, or what they think they have to do; and I'm not saying that I forgive you and I'm totally OK with you. I'm just saying, I'm not really interested in killing you anymore."

"I don't have any interest in stopping the others, either," said Patton. "I've got no desire for running or being hunted or playing games. When this is over, my life is in their hands, and honestly, I'll be fine with whatever they decide. Even though I haven't tried suicide, if I thought it would balance my guilt, I would have done it a long time ago."

"So you're OK if they decide to kill you?"

"Yeah," said Patton. "But I'm also OK if they decide we should all work together against people like Ingrid Weiss or if they decide to cut me out of that work altogether or if they decide I should spend the rest of my days scrubbing floors and mowing lawns for the families of your unit. I fucked up, and whether I could have avoided what happened, we'll never know, but my fault or not, it happened *because* of me, so it's about time I face whatever music the survivors think I deserve."

"Damn," said Franklin, "this is not the conversation I thought we'd be having when I was thinking about hunting you down all those years."

"Yeah, well I never expected to team up with a guy like Nemo to steal three quarters of a billion dollars from a bunch of racists, so, you know, life is some weird shit."

"What's the deal with Nemo, anyway?" said Franklin.

"Trust me," said Patton. "You don't want to know."

Nemo arrived at the Central Bank of Zurich at 2:23 a.m. After pulling into the spotless garage, he rolled down the window to hand the attendant a slip of paper with Ingrid Weiss's account number on it along with a sealed envelope. Then he pulled his cap down and picked up a newspaper, hiding behind it as the bank manager checked the registration plate on the truck and gave instructions to his employees. Nemo continued to "read" the paper as he heard the cargo being unloaded and transferred to Ingrid Weiss's vault. At 2:49 a.m. his phone rang.

"They're about five minutes out," said Alex. "That German son of a bitch drives like a crazy man."

"Hold on a second," said Nemo. He rolled the window down just enough so his voice could be heard in the garage. "How much longer?" he shouted in English, hoping someone would understand.

From behind the truck he heard a conversation in German and then a voice replied. "Twenty minutes."

"There's a thousand euros in it for you if you can make it ten," shouted Nemo. Again he heard voices behind the truck and then a man appeared outside his window.

"A thousand for me and a thousand for my assistants?" he said quietly.

"Done," said Nemo, pulling out the cash and passing it through the window.

"OK, ten minutes," said the man.

Nemo rolled the window back up and returned to the phone. "You've got to buy a little more time. Six minutes at least, to get us past three a.m. Ten would be better to be sure I'm out of here."

"He needs ten more minutes," said Alex. "If they get there before three o'clock not only will they see the other truck, but they'll be early for their time slot and the bankers will ask questions."

"How the hell are we supposed to give him ten more minutes?" said Bob. They were driving on a four-lane road in central Zurich. The truck came to a stop at a red light and Bob pulled into the left lane, stopping beside the Germans. "At least I can get in front of them," he said.

"Which is fine if they keep following the same route we do," said Alex, "but it still won't slow them down until we're on a side street and that might not be until we're a block away."

"Thank you so much for telling me what I already know," said Bob. "That's tremendously helpful." The light turned green and Bob accelerated quickly enough to get in front of the truck by a few car lengths.

"I just don't understand how . . ." began Alex, but he never finished his sentence. At that instant a van darted out from a side street, through a red light and rammed into the front corner of Alex's car. Alex felt the seat belt lock him in place, but neither car had been going very fast so he thought, as the car spun around, he might escape any real injury. Then he heard a screeching noise and saw the headlights of the dump truck heading right for him. It flashed across his mind that it might be a good idea to pray when the screeching stopped and he looked to see the grille of the truck a few feet outside his window.

Alex could not open his door, but he heard much of what transpired in the street over the next few minutes. A woman jumped out of the van and approached the dump truck. She seemed to be weaving erratically as if she had been drinking for the past several hours. Then, as she passed into the glow of the headlights, Alex realized it was Patton.

Patton had been truly impressed with Franklin's driving. When he saw the truck stopped at the light, he had managed to go around the block and come out of the side street just in time. Then he had managed to hit Alex's car in such a way that it spun around and blocked most of the road but neither it nor the van Franklin was driving sustained enough damage to make it undrivable. And, he had managed to stop the van where it blocked the one part of the road the truck might have gotten through. In an instant, Patton was up and weaving toward the dump truck, banging on the window and shouting "*Bitte*" in a loud voice with a thick American accent.

"Can you tell us how to get to the Matterhorn!" Patton shouted. "Ma-ter-horn," she repeated slowly, over enunciating each syllable. "It's a mountain. A big old mountain. This is Switzerland, right?"

Patton climbed onto the step leading to the driver's side of the cab and continued to bang on the window. She didn't think the Germans would drive away with her on the truck, especially given the secrecy of their mission.

"Do you all live here? Do you live in Switzerland? We're not still in Germany, are we?"

Franklin had stayed in the van, but now Bob emerged from his vehicle and strode over to the truck.

"Hey, lady, what do you think you're doing?" he said. He made as if he were trying to pull her off the truck. "Leave those guys alone. They probably have someplace to go." Bob had seen Franklin's car coming at them a split second before impact and he'd never been happier to be in a car accident—though perhaps "accident" wasn't quite the right word. He had waited ninety seconds before getting out of the car. Nemo said he needed at least six minutes. They were already a quarter of the way there.

After Bob and Patton had "struggled" for another minute or so, Patton still clinging to the side of the truck, the window rolled down slightly and the driver said, *"Aus, aus!"* waving toward Patton.

"Don't you *Aus* me, mister," said Patton. "I'm just asking if this is Switzerland."

"Ja," said the man, and then, switching to English he added. "Yes, this is Switzerland. Get off my truck."

"Then where is the goddamn Matterhorn?" said Patton, grabbing the driver's shirt sleeve. Bob glanced over at Franklin and saw him hold up four fingers. Just another couple of minutes.

"I'm sorry, sir. I'll take care of her. You be on your way. I'll deal with the police."

"Get her off my truck," said the driver, sounding more exasperated than angry.

"Maybe I should take her to the Matterhorn, *ja*," said Bob with a wink at the driver, but this did not elicit a chuckle or even a smile. After another thirty seconds or so of Bob pulling on Patton's arm, she finally stepped off the truck.

"Fine," she said, "I'll just find the Matterhorn by myself." She staggered off up the road away from the accident and, of course, directly behind the truck. The German cranked his engine and honked at her, but by the time she got out of his way and he had backed up and turned onto the side street a block behind, another two minutes had gone by.

As soon as the truck disappeared, Patton and Bob ran back to their respective cars. Franklin took small side streets and wound their way back toward the highway that would take them to Vaduz; Bob drove to the rendezvous point a few blocks from the bank.

At 3:02 a.m., a man banged on the side of Nemo's truck and shouted, "All done, thanks for the tip." Thirty seconds later, Nemo was out of the garage and back on the street. As he turned the corner at the end of the block, he saw the headlights of a Mercedes dump truck swing onto the street he was just leaving. Five minutes later, he met Alex and Bob on a quiet street corner.

"Did it work?" said Bob. "Did you make it out in time?"

"I think so," said Nemo. "Another thirty seconds and they would have seen me for sure. But I don't think they did."

"So what's that mean?" said Alex. "Did we do it?"

"I think maybe we did," said Nemo, a broad smile blooming across his face.

Alex and Bob took the truck to Vaduz, on the assumption that Weiss's delivery crew would rejoin her. Nemo drove Bob's car back to the bank and followed Weiss's truck, just in case it headed somewhere else.

It did not.

5:00 A.M.

Nemo had followed the truck all the way from Zurich to Vaduz and into the car park behind the hotel. Hardly inconspicuous, he thought, but of course Weiss and her associates believed they had finished the job, that they had hundreds of millions of euros in gold sitting safely in a vault at a Swiss bank. Bob and Alex had parked the other truck on the outskirts of town, but once the drivers of Weiss's truck disappeared into the hotel, Nemo phoned them and by 6:00 a.m. they had switched the registration plates back and all seven of them sat once again in a luxurious hotel suite.

"If we leave now we can be back in Brenner by nine o'clock," said Patton. "We find a nice wooded area near the chapel, you shoot me with one of Alex's German guns, and they'll pin it on Ingrid Weiss and her cohorts. You won't have to worry about a thing."

"I'm not fond of that idea," said Nemo.

"Did I just hear the word 'fond' escape your mouth?" said Patton.

"What about the police?" said Franklin. "They're bound to be prowling around investigating the explosion."

"So we go nearby but not too nearby," said Patton. "And you use a silencer."

"Honestly," said Ted, "I'm not all that fond of the idea either. What exactly do we accomplish by killing Patton?"

Everyone looked to Bob, and Patton felt perfectly content. She honestly didn't care what he said. They had taken the gold away from Ingrid Weiss and Patton believed that these six people would use it well. She trusted Nemo with much more than her life, and she knew he would have no qualms about eliminating anyone who got out of line. If her time had come, fine. If the three soldiers could kill her and pin it on Ingrid Weiss, so much the better.

"When will you call Ulrich?" said Bob.

"As soon as you decide what to do about Patton," said Jean.

"I think what I'd like to do with Patton," said Bob, "is introduce her to some widows."

"Honestly," said Patton, "facing them would be a lot harder than facing the muzzle of Alex's gun."

"I know," said Bob, with a wry smile. "I also know that you saved my life, and that has to be worth something."

"She saved your life?" said Franklin.

"Maybe," said Patton.

"So let's just put a pin in the whole revenge thing for now," said Bob. "I'm not saying there isn't still a part of me that's dying to put a bullet in you, but I can ignore that voice for the time being."

"Good," said Nemo. "Ignore it. Because we've got work to do."

"True," said Patton, "and we have seven hundred million dollars to do it with."

———

The Criminal Investigation Division of the Liechtenstein National Police has a total of sixteen officers. Eight of them arrived at the Park Hotel Sonnenhof shortly after 11:00 a.m. to arrest Ingrid Weiss and her three associates on a variety of charges filed by the Bavarian State Police and the Italian Polizia di Stato.

Christian Ulrich had received a call from Jean Simpson thirty minutes earlier, explaining exactly what had happened at the house in Munich and at the chapel in Brenner. She had, of course, said nothing about the gold. Simpson expressed a willingness to come to Munich and swear an affidavit. Simpson's desire to remain anonymous would be only a slight stumbling block in pursuing his case, because everything she said fit the evidence now coming in from forensic teams in Germany and Italy. Weiss and her associates would be extradited to Germany later that day and would ultimately be convicted of fraud, terrorist activity, and attempted murder. In Italy, they were convicted in abstentia for destruction of a cultural artifact.

No law enforcement agency or government brought charges against Ruthie Drinkwater, who disappeared with the help of an advance payment she had received from Dietrich. After the trials ended, Ruthie received a message from Ingrid in prison and traveled to Switzerland where, with a phone call and voice print from Ingrid and a password and account number, she gained access to Weiss's vault at the Central Bank of Zurich. There she stood slack-jawed before a stack of steel and aluminum blocks purchased from a building supply store in Innsbruck. On top of the pile she found an envelope containing a slip of paper reading simply, "Looks like the Allies win again."

ARRT
CODA

When the British police discovered that the two bodies they found in Buckinghamshire belonged to men wanted for murder in the United States, they informed the Alta Vista authorities of the discovery. One of the men had died in a car accident, the other was an apparent suicide. Everyone agreed there was no need to investigate further and cases on both sides of the Atlantic were closed.

Jean Simpson phoned the Hotel Sacher and paid her bill with a credit card. The hotel manager agreed to ship the bag she had left with the valet back to the United States. A week later she ran into Peter Byerly at the Ridgefield library.

"How was your trip?" said Peter.

"Eventful," said Jean.

"You do know that the German police interviewed me about you. They thought you were a terrorist."

"Yes, I saw on the news," said Jean. "Apparently a case of mistaken identity."

"Of course it was," said Peter with a wry smile. "And did you manage to find out anything else about that woman who sent you the book?"

"Didn't have the time," said Jean.

A few months later when Peter showed her an article about the conviction of Ingrid Weiss, Jean responded, "Well, what do you know about that."

Patton discovered, on returning to Alta Vista, that she had inherited Jasper Fleming's house on Lone Pine Road. Nemo said it would do very nicely for him, thank you very much. When Patton asked if it was safe for a retired assassin to live someplace other than Argentina, Nemo explained that he checked after every job to be sure no investigation remained open.

"I was good at what I did," said Nemo. "They always ruled it accidental death, or natural causes, or suicide."

"So I just have to live next door to a killer?" said Patton.

"A retired killer," said Nemo.

"I feel so much better."

Patton and Nemo talked often about their PTSD. Patton had never liked group therapy but talking to Nemo always made her feel better. Nemo often disappeared for days at a time. The third time this happened, Patton asked where he had gone, and Nemo finally told her the story of how he became an assassin and lost a brother.

"So now I'm looking for Jack," he said.

Patton offered to help him with the search. "After all, I am an intelligence analyst," she said.

"It's nice having a friend," said Nemo, "but some things I need to do alone."

On some days, on his dark days, Bob still wanted to kill Patton; and as she told him, on her dark days she wanted him to kill her. But with help from professionals, with good medication, and with a deepening respect for and friendship with one another, those dark days came less often. Bob came to Alta Vista about once a month, sometimes just checking in, sometimes taking Patton away for a few days to introduce her to one of the families who had lost loved ones that day in Kandahar. Both Patton and Bob found those introductions exhausting and tearful and, in a strange way, exhilarating. Only two of the families she met still harbored deep anger toward Patton. She didn't blame them. She had also seen how forgiveness had brought a measure of peace to the others, so she stayed in touch and available even to those who still hated her, hoping that the connection might do them all some good.

Franklin and Ted had wives, families, and careers far from Alta Vista and while they stayed in touch by phone and text, they visited far less often than Bob, who was still a bachelor, still suffering the effects of "Don't ask, don't tell" which, as he and Patton had discussed, made it easy to have a one-night stand and virtually impossible to have a committed relationship.

Franklin and Ted did, however, come to Alta Vista for a quiet evening at Patton's house celebrating the establishment of the Jasper Fleming Fund for International Civil Rights. Jasper, after all, had protected the key to discovering Himmler's cache of gold, and had made all this possible. Jean Simpson was there, and Art Handy's widow, Renée, had accepted an invitation to join their group. The only board member who did not attend the dinner was Alex Lansdowne, who had, it seemed, retreated back into the sanctuary, or perhaps the prison, of his collection. Patton and the others rarely heard from him.

For dessert that night, Patton served chocolate ganache–filled profiteroles. She had finally mastered the choux pastry. It turned out the trick was to make it without coming under sniper fire.

CSHN GKN
THE END

Note: For those who have an Enigma machine the starting settings to decode the Enigma message and the sections headings of this novel are:

Plugboard: AT CL EK HI JO MY PR

Rotors: III, I, II

Rotor Setting: R, H, H

Ring Settings: A, U, G

Reflector Umkehrwalze A

AUTHOR'S NOTE

Henrich Himmler is, of course, a real historical figure, and the words he speaks in Chapter I are taken from the transcript of a speech he delivered in January 1937. Many of his other actions and words in this novel are my own invention. Other historical characters act more or less in keeping with the historical record including Alan Turing, Dilly Knox, Gordon Welchman, Mavis Batey, Heinz Kurschildgen, and Karl Malchus (the last two of whom really did try to convince Himmler that they had mastered alchemy). The workings of the Enigma machine and the breaking of the code using the Bombe, the checking machine, and some first-class deduction and mathematics have been simplified somewhat but are essentially the same in this novel as the heroic work conducted at Bletchley Park during World War II.

ACKNOWLEDGMENTS

This book really began when I met Mavis Batey (née Lever) in 1997. At the time I had no idea that she had been a key figure in the breaking of the Enigma Code. On one occasion I got her to talk a little about her experience working at Bletchley, but it wasn't until after her death that I discovered just how intimately involved she had been in the codebreaking. I thank Mavis for her friendship and her heroism. I had another acquaintance who worked at Bletchley—the mother of my dear friend Chris Stockwell. Betty Stockwell (née Swan) worked at Bletchley (and other locales) as a technician for the Bombe and other equipment. I didn't know this about Betty until after her death, and this is one of the remarkable things about the thousands who worked at Bletchley—they did work that was as important, if not more important, as any done in the war, then quietly returned to their lives where they didn't breathe a word about Bletchley for decades.

Mark and Catherine Richards organized the first trip that my wife, Janice, and I made to Bletchley Park—before it had been saved from ruin by lottery money and turned into a proper museum. We have been back twice and highly recommend it to anyone interested in World War II, computers, codebreaking, or this novel. Watching the reconstructed Bombe Phoenix at work is a remarkable experience.

Janice has a passion for Bletchley and the work that went on there which has inspired my own interest. She also listened patiently as I read this novel aloud on our back porch during the early days of COVID. Janice's suggestions, both large and small, led to many improvements in the manuscript.

Anna Worrall is a patient, wise, encouraging agent who helped shape the manuscript, always pushing me in fruitful directions. Madeline Hopkins provided thoughtful and careful editing that eliminated many inconsistencies in a complicated story. And to all the rest of the staff at both the Gernert Company and Blackstone Publishing, I am grateful for their faith in me and their commitment to the world of books and reading. It is a commitment they share with another group to whom I am indebted—the booksellers of the world (and particularly those at Bookmarks in Winston-Salem), who have dedicated their lives to keeping reading alive.

I thank my children, Jordan and Jimmy, and their wisely chosen spouses, Jim and Conor, for more than can possibly be expressed here, but especially for their unwavering support and enthusiasm for my work.

We live in a world in which we enjoy a wide range of freedoms and those freedoms have been preserved by both the monumental efforts of entire nations and moments of bravery and genius on the part of individuals. The lack of either of these could tip the scales the other way. May we always remember that and be grateful for those efforts, both widely heralded and forever secret, that have come before our own.